THE
PRESIDENT'S
DOSSIER

ALSO BY JAMES A. SCOTT

The Iran Contradictions

THE PRESIDENT'S DOSSIER

A THRILLER

JAMES A. SCOTT

OCEANVIEW PUBLISHING

SARASOTA, FLORIDA

ISBN 978-1-60809-466-0

Published in the United States of America by Oceanview Publishing

Sarasota, Florida

www.oceanviewpub.com

10 9 8 7 6 5 4 3 2

PRINTED IN THE UNITED STATES OF AMERICA

Time will tell, but Silence is
The Code of the Village Triflers

THE
PRESIDENT'S
DOSSIER

CHAPTER 1

Fall 2017
Lenny's Place, Washington, D.C.

AT THREE THIRTY in the afternoon on a Wednesday, I sat alone at the bar, nursing a scotch, and wondering how my career, my love life, and my country could have been ruined by just one man—the President of the United States.

Lenny's was quiet at that time of day. The three-martini lunch crowd had gone and the three-martini-after-work crowd wouldn't arrive for ninety minutes. I needed the peace and semi-darkness of a familiar refuge to figure out what the hell was happening to my life and how to deal with it.

My immediate problem was getting a job. After ten years at the CIA, in positions of increasing responsibility, potential employers should have been in a bidding war for my services. Yet, after three weeks of interviews, I hadn't gotten so much as a nibble. Maybe the rumor that the Agency might revoke my top-secret clearance was the reason.

As I mulled over solutions, a guy came in. His expensive suit and cowboy boots told me he didn't belong. He stopped at the door to let his eyes adjust to Lenny's tasteful gloom. The sun was behind him, casting his long shadow across the floor. As he scanned the room, I could hear the uh-oh theme from a bad spaghetti western playing in my head. My gaze dropped to the black attaché case in his left hand. I was hoping it didn't contain an Uzi. Call me paranoid, but I had been working some very sensitive issues at the Agency. I could think of lots of people who would be relieved if I and what I knew died in a pool of blood on Lenny's floor.

"Velma." I called to the barmaid, Lenny's wife. She tends bar during business lulls to save on personnel costs. Velma is forty-something and a looker. She sauntered down to my spot.

"Refill me and leave the bottle on the bar. I may need a weapon." I cut my eyes to the suit, who was coming my way.

Velma followed my gaze. She poured, left the bottle, and moved down the bar.

The suit eased his six-feet-plus, 260 pounds onto a stool one place removed to my left and parked the attaché case on the stool to his left. If he made a fast move for it, his head was going to have a traumatic meeting with the scotch bottle. He pointed to it and told Velma, "I'll have the same, a double."

Velma poured his drink and set the bottle down next to my right hand.

I was in a foul mood and decided to mess with him. "Hi, sailor. Come here often?"

"First time," and he was not amused. "I'm more of a Mayflower Hotel bar guy."

"You're here on business, then."

"Yes. My business is with you, Max Geller. I'm a lawyer, Bill Bowen." He put his card on the bar next to my left elbow.

"What's in the attaché case?"

"A lot of money." He said it in a low voice, glancing down the bar at Velma.

"Show me . . . and keep your right hand on the bar."

He was confused momentarily. Then, he got it. "I'm not a threat, Mr. Geller."

"Every lawyer is a threat." I was thinking of my current live-in.

Bowen leaned toward the stool on his left, popped the locks, and opened the case. I saw four bulging manila envelopes inside.

"Can we talk in private?" asked Bowen.

"About what?"

"About something private." He was a touch irritated. So was I until he added, "I have a job offer for you."

With an okay from Velma, Bowen and I went to the lone table in Lenny's small, private dining room. Bowen downed his drink in one gulp and placed the attaché case between us on the table. "Would you be interested in earning ten million dollars?" he asked.

"Who do I have to kill?"

"No one. We want you to find some people and interview them."

"They must be pretty important people. Who are they?"

"You're aware of the dossier that's being circulated concerning the president's alleged activities in Russia and his collusion with the Russians; we want you to track down the *original* sources and verify the allegations."

"Or refute them?"

"If those are your findings, yes . . . but we believe the allegations to be true."

"Who are *we*?"

"I should've said *they*. I'm just a messenger for *they*." He gave me a humorless smile.

"Okay, who are *they*?"

"A group of people who, like you, are not fans of the president. Like you, *they* think the president is a traitor and a serious threat to this country."

"I don't work for people I don't know."

"I believe you know Ben."

"Ben who?"

"Ben Franklin." Bowen took a large manila envelope from his attaché case and shoved it across the table.

I looked inside. It was stuffed with neatly bound stacks of hundred-dollar bills.

"Part of your retainer," said Bowen. "I have three more envelopes in this case . . . for expenses. I can provide additional funds as your investigation progresses."

"There are already four investigations in progress to verify the dossier," I reminded him, "one by the special prosecutor at the DOJ, two in Congress, and one at the CIA. Why not let them handle this?"

Bowen assumed a professorial tone. "As you know, the CIA director is the president's political ally. The congressional investigations are slow and only one of them is serious. If history is any indicator, the special prosecutor's investigations could drag on for years. Furthermore, we"—*there goes that word again*—"have reason to believe steps are being taken to cover the president's tracks, steps that will confound those investigations and keep them out of the Oval Office."

"Who believes this, *we* or *they*?"

"Please don't be tedious, Mr. Geller. I was told you're a serious person."

"Yeah, well, I seriously don't want to get trampled by the herd of government investigators already working this case. Why did you come to me anyway? Why not go to a private spy outfit?"

Bowen sighed heavily to let me know I was testing his patience. "We discussed that option. We settled on you because you are under the private spy outfit radar, and you have the contacts and a skill set best suited for this endeavor."

"And those skills and contacts would be . . . ?"

"You're resourceful, you worked for the CIA in Russia, you have Russian contacts, you speak the language. Also, I believe you know

Jeffrey Ironside, the MI6 agent who assembled the dossier on the president."

"And how am I supposed to earn the ten million dollars, go to Jeffrey Ironside and convince him to name his sources for the dossier dirt?"

"I'm afraid that wouldn't work. To date, Mr. Ironside has refused to reveal his sources. I doubt he would simply give them to you. As I said, we—my employers—selected you because you have a reputation for being resourceful. How you identify Mr. Ironside's sources would be a product of that resourcefulness."

I gave him a skeptical look and let the silence build until Bowen added, "There is another reason why we selected you. You have a reputation for . . . ah . . . beneficial disregard for legal obstacles to mission accomplishment."

And how did he know that? "So, you don't care if I break laws to verify the dossier?"

The humorless smile again. "We don't *want* you to break any laws, but . . ."

"That's asking a lot."

"Yes, it is, ten million dollars' worth."

Bowen took two documents from his attaché case and slid them across the table. "We don't want to rush you. Here's your contract. Review it and let me know if it's satisfactory."

"When do you want to know?"

Bowen checked his Rolex. "In five minutes. I'll wait." Another phony smile.

The contract bound me to a corporation in Panama. I read and signed it, a copy for him and one for me. Bowen reached for his copy, but I pinned it to the table with a forefinger. "It says that one million dollars will be deposited in my bank account before I begin work. Don't you want my account number?"

"Is your account in the States?"

"Yes."

"I'm afraid that won't do. We've established an account for you, in Switzerland. Here's the number." Bowen handed me a slip of paper and a printed form. "This is the authorization form required by the bank. It's a joint account that requires your signature and mine to release funds."

"*They* were very sure of themselves."

"*They* do their homework." That smile, again. "I assume you would prefer to handle your own personnel and logistics. However, now that you're with us, I'm authorized to tell you that I'm your quartermaster." He handed me a card. "Call this number day or night, if you need people, equipment, or money. Someone will answer. Leave a number. I'll return your call within twelve hours. If you need a faster response, tell the person who answers the phone."

Bowen snapped the attaché case shut and pushed it across the table. He stood to leave and added, "I assume you'll be traveling. If you need passports, I'll need photographs and some lead time. Good hunting."

When Bowen had gone, I went to the bar. "Velma, is your security camera working?"

"Twenty-four-seven."

"Can you print a head-and-shoulders photo of the guy I was just talking to?"

"No, but I can make you a copy of the disc. Will that do?"

It would. She did. I put the disc copy into my new attaché case full of new hundred-dollar bills.

The kitchen staff had arrived. I decided to have a soft drink and do some mission planning for my new job, while I waited for the dining room to open.

By the time I was halfway through my steak dinner, I had received a half dozen cell phone calls from Claudia and ignored them. She was

my love life—maybe my former love life—that presidential interven-
tion had ruined. I just didn't have anything positive to say to her. I was
considering the dessert menu when my cell phone rang again. This
time, it was Rodney, my former CIA boss, the one who fired me. He
wanted to meet me in Georgetown right away. For a guy who had
spent weeks as a leper, I was suddenly very popular. Why?

CHAPTER 2

RODNEY WANTED TO meet me at his Georgetown home. Rodney was not his real name; it was his *nom de guerre*, as he would inform you in fluent French. His real name was Prescott Hamilton. At the Agency, we speculated that he chose "Rodney" from a classic he read at his New England prep school or his Ivy League alma mater. Rodney was well bred and old money. He loved to show off both. Hence, the meeting in his home for selected colleagues, but I was no longer a colleague. What was going on?

When we were seated in his study, I started the conversation. "Did you ask me here to give me my job back?"

"No." Rodney was usually blunt and sometimes truthful.

"What about my appeal to being fired?"

"Dead in the water. You knew that when you submitted it."

"I didn't write that stuff about Walldrum. My girlfriend wrote it. I'm not Claudia!"

"The two of you communicated using your official email account and what you wrote characterized the president in a way that reflected bias. Both of you should have known better, given the current political environment."

I didn't hide my anger and Rodney changed the subject. "You had a visitor earlier today at Lenny's. What did he want?"

"How did you know I had a visitor?"

Rodney gave me a look that asked, "Are you serious?"

"He offered me a contract to find and authenticate the sources for the allegations against the president in the Ironside Dossier. You probably know that, too."

Rodney explained, "After you left the Agency, we got word that Bowen was looking for a skilled operator with Russian experience to vet the sources of those allegations. We didn't know he would pick you, but we made sure he got your name . . . along with some lesser qualified people."

"How did you do that?"

"That's above your pay grade."

"I'm no longer employed by the Agency. I don't have a pay grade."

"Exactly. Your pay grade is zero."

"Is this an Agency operation?"

"No . . . and yes."

"What the hell does that mean?"

"You know that certain intelligence activities have become politicized since the election. As a result, some operations don't make it to the Seventh Floor for approval."

"Are you telling me I'm involved in an off-the-books operation?"

"No. I'm telling you that nobody knows what's going on between the Seventh Floor and the White House. So, we professionals are not divulging operations that could impact the political processes . . . or be impacted by it."

"Who is Bowen working for?"

"We don't know."

"So, you got me a job. What do you want in return?"

"The same thing Bowen wants, the names of the sources who gave Jeffrey Ironside the information in his dossier, if the dossier allegations are facts, and if his sources were in positions to know those facts."

I told Rodney, "Bowen is paying me eight figures. What do I get from you?"

"The thanks of a grateful nation."

I laughed and got up to leave.

"What do you want?" Rodney asked.

"I want my job back."

"That's not going to happen. Besides, if you pull this off, you can start your own intelligence agency. What's number two on your wish list?"

I hadn't thought past number one, but, at that moment, the next best thing to working for the CIA was having the CIA working for me. "I might need Agency help to pull this off."

"What did you have in mind?"

"Bowen gave me an around-the-clock support number."

"I'll match that and throw in a secure satellite phone. One caveat: you deal only with me. You're to have no contact with other Agency assets anywhere in the world."

"If I get the information, who will see it?"

"Why do you care?"

"Exposing Russian sources could get them killed."

Rodney uttered a derisive grunt. "I don't give a damn if some Russians get a bullet in the head, Max. Putin is trying to steal our country. President Walldrum is helping him. I want the White House cleaned out and some real patriots in there. So, get on with your part of it."

CHAPTER 3

IT WAS LATE when I got home. I entered the front door and looked into the dining room to my right. Claudia was sitting at the table, eating and reading a legal brief. There was no place setting for me and the Cabernet had taken a serious hit.

Claudia announced, "Rodney called. He wanted a meeting. I tried to reach you. Are you still not taking my calls?"

"Rodney found me."

"Where were you?"

"Interviewing."

"What were you interviewing, a scotch bottle? I called Lenny's. Velma said you were sitting at her bar all afternoon."

Jesus, this is already like being married, I thought, as I headed for the stairs.

"Did Rodney give you back your job?"

"No." I went up to our bedroom, found a suitcase, and started packing. Claudia didn't come up. I was glad. When I was packed, I called a cab and took my suitcase downstairs. Claudia hadn't moved. The Cabernet bottle was almost empty.

"I'm sorry they fired you." That was her first apology in three weeks.

"Me, too."

She added, "I shouldn't have taunted you in that email. I was angry after our fight . . . and you wouldn't answer your phone. You shouldn't have written what you did in your reply. That temper is what got you fired."

Apology rescinded? "What got me fired," I told her, "was that you exposed my attitude about the president in *your* email. My answer didn't matter. I knew I was in trouble when I opened your message. That's why I exploded. Don't you understand? There are people at the Agency who monitor everything I do, say, write. We agreed that politics stays in this house!"

I knew her legal brain agreed with me, but her gut wouldn't let it go. "We'd never have had an argument if you weren't so bullheaded and illogical. You said you believe a man is innocent until proven guilty. You can't abandon that standard when it comes to the president, just because you don't like him or his politics. Everyone should be held to the same standard."

I wasn't taking the bait. Calmly, I said, "That standard is fine, if the suspect is some dirtbag K Street lobbyist. If he's threatened by an investigation, he'll hire a lawyer and go on buying congressmen until the FBI gets the goods on him.

"The president should be held to a different standard because he's unique. If he gets desperate, he could say, 'To hell with it,' and start a nuclear war." I took my Burberry coat from the hall closet and pulled it on.

"Uh-oh, the dreaded trench coat. Heavy action going down in spytown." She glanced at my bag. "What's with the suitcase?"

"I got a job today. It requires some travel. Will you be here when I get back?"

"When are you coming back?"

"I don't know."

"Well, then, I don't know if I'll be here."

There was silence while we digested that exchange.

Claudia took another sip of wine and said, "You're Mr. Superspy. If you're so convinced the president is guilty, why don't *you* go get the goods on him?"

"Will you marry me if I do?"

"You can't afford me."

"I never could. You knew that when you moved in." Claudia was a six-figure lawyer on a partnership track with her firm.

She wasn't surprised by my question. "Was that your usual proposal?"

"Number five. How many times do I have to ask?"

"As many as it takes." That was the Cabernet talking.

My marriage proposal wasn't sincere. Claudia knew it. In times of stress, it had become my perverse way of reminding her that I understood the terms of our relationship. Her eighteen-hours-a-day-and-weekends work schedule didn't leave time for a husband and Claudia didn't want one. What she did want was that partnership at her law firm. I was a rest stop and sexual filling station on her way to a corner office.

Outside, my cab honked. I picked up my suitcase and grabbed the doorknob.

Her voice softened. "Did you pack warm socks . . . and your silencer?"

"It's not a silencer, it's a sound *suppressor*. Too bad it doesn't work in this house." That was my scotch talking.

I took the cab to the Ritz-Carlton at the Pentagon City mall and made a public telephone call to Sherri Layton. She had the chops I needed for this mission: CIA experience, fluent Russian, and connections to a competent talent pool of brains and muscle. Sherri was a single mother when we started out together at the Agency. We dated briefly, until the father of her child reentered her life, crippled her financially, and disappeared, again. Just when Sherri's career was taking off, her income needs caused her to leave the Agency and enter the lucrative world of security contracting. Over the years since she left, I had steered Agency jobs to her company, and we had worked together in the field on a few. Our romantic relationship was dead, but mutual trust and respect were alive.

"Layton Security Services. Can I help you?" asked the male voice.

"This is Max Geller. I have a job offer for Sherri."

"I'll connect you, sir."

Sherri Layton answered, a smile in her voice. "Max! I thought you'd forgotten me."

"No chance of that. Is your passport current?"

"Always."

"I need a month of your time in Europe and east, starting Monday. What'll it cost?"

"I'm obligated for a few days during that period. I'd have to cancel. Let's say five thousand a day and expenses."

"Deal. Find me two computer hackers, a couple of speed readers, and a four-man heavy metal band. I want everybody in London by Monday evening. The band has to bring its own instruments. No local procurement. Copy?" I didn't want Sherri's guys running around London trying to buy guns.

"That'll require a chartered aircraft."

"That's okay for the band. The rest of the team goes commercial. If the band gets jammed up in customs, the show has to go on. Book separate hotels near the Savoy. You take a suite big enough for a team meeting. Text me when everyone is in place."

"And Sherri, get people who might not have a file in the U.K."

"Is this a company op or ... ?"

"Or. I was fired three weeks ago."

"Oh. Sorry."

I had one more piece of vital business with Ms. Layton. "Sherri, when I get to the airport, I'm going to mail you a surveillance video disc. About 3:30 p.m., a suit wearing cowboy boots comes into Lenny's. Claims to be a lawyer named Bill Bowen and he's connected to a corporation in Panama. I'll send you the address. I need the book on Mr. Bowen and his employer."

"When do you want it?"

"I need accuracy, not speed. Get it right. See you in London."

My second call was to Tommy Leeds in London. Tommy was an intelligence freelancer and professional colleague. We had worked together when I was in Europe and had our own code. I had used Tommy when we couldn't have CIA involvement.

When Tommy answered, I said, "This is Dolby." That was the name he knew me by. "I'd like to arrange baggage service." Baggage service was code for a black bag job, a surreptitious break-in to plant a bug or steal something. In this case, the something was the names of the sources for the allegations against the president in the Ironside Dossier.

"Baggage service is possible. What's the origin and destination for the bag?"

"The origin is London, destination is Washington." The break-in would be in London. A destination was bogus, to throw off eavesdroppers.

"I'd like to have expedited service. I'll call with details on Thursday." Tommy knew I wouldn't call. I was telling him to expect a fax with the encrypted address for the break-in. He was to use our Thursday Code to decrypt it.

I added, "The bag will be large and heavy. I suggest you send a man around before the pickup to be sure you send adequate staff to manage it on shipping day." Translation: *You'll need detailed surveillance ahead of the break-in. The target may have lots of security devices.*

I went to the hotel's business center, wrote out the coded address, and faxed it to Tommy.

On the way to Dulles Airport, I called Bowen to let him know I was on the clock and told him where I'd be staying. My first mistake.

CHAPTER 4

THE FLIGHT TO London was long, but eleven hours after talking to Sherri and Bowen, I checked into the Savoy. A message was waiting for me at the desk: *News from Bowen. Call me when you settle in.* No name. The phone number was for a room in the Savoy.

Besides me, there were now three people who knew I was in London, where I was staying, and the purpose of my visit. That was way too many. In two weeks or less, a lot of people would be trying to find me or someone with my profile. At that point, the fewer people who knew me and my address, the better my chances of staying out of prison and collecting that ten million dollars. Rodney had an incentive not to tell anyone about me, but Bowen was another story. I had to verify that the anonymous note came from his rep and stop him from telling anyone else about me. I dialed Bowen's number from memory. Disconnected. That was a bad sign.

I stood in the hall outside of the room mentioned in my anonymous message and dialed the occupant on my cell. I pressed my ear to the door and heard the phone ring. A faint female voice said, "Yes?"

I answered, "Got your note. Meet me at the bar in five minutes."

I broke the connection and kept my ear to the door, trying to hear if she made a call. She did, but all I heard was her muffled voice. I waited. A minute later, she opened the door. I shoved her back into the room and checked to make sure she was alone.

She was angry. "What the hell are you doing!" Then, she recognized me.

"You wanted to meet me. I'm here." I snatched her purse and found her wallet.

"Let's see who you are. Jillian Rucker," I read from her driver's license. I rummaged through her purse and compared her passport to the license.

"Okay, Jill Rucker, why are you here and why is my direct line to Bowen dead?"

"Bowen sent me to be your paymaster and quartermaster. I don't know why your line is dead. Maybe Bowen and his client want to distance themselves from this operation in case it goes wrong. I'm the cutout between them and you. Any problem with that?"

I had a big problem with that. One, the moving parts were multiplying. Two, if Bowen wanted deniability, why involve Jill Rucker. She was one more person who could connect him to my operation and corroborate my story, should I ever have to tell it.

I replaced the documents and handed Ms. Rucker her purse. "What do you bring to this party besides money and a cell phone?"

With sarcasm and innuendo, she said, "I'm sure I can be useful. I speak Russian, I can shoot"—she looked me up and down—"and I can kick your ass in a fair fight."

"Those are the *minimum* qualifications for my team," I informed her. "I'll start you as an intern and see how you perform. You should know that I speak Russian, too. I don't plan to shoot anyone and I don't fight fair in an ass-kicking contest."

Before she could reply, I asked, "Do you know why I'm in London?"

"Conducting research, according to Bowen."

Good answer, but was that what Bowen told her or did she make it up to put me at ease? If she wanted to put me at ease, why tell me about her shooting and hand-to-hand combat skills? CIA work gives you an ear for inconsistencies and a gut full of paranoia.

"How can I help you?" she asked.

"Give me your cell phone."

She tossed it over. I pulled up her number, memorized it, and tossed the phone back.

"Keep your phone handy. I'll call if I need you. Otherwise, don't contact me and stay out of my way." I left her and went to my room to get some sleep.

The alarm woke me at 2 a.m. I went to the lobby and gave the desk man two one-hundred-pound notes—the Savoy is upscale and requires upscale bribes. In return, he gave me the outside number Jill Rucker called from her room phone while I had been standing at her door the previous day. I dialed it.

"Yes?" answered the guy on the other end.

I used my tough voice. "I want to call Bowen tomorrow. What's the best time?"

"Who's calling?"

"If you need to know, Bowen will tell you after I talk to him."

Hesitation on his end followed by rustling pages. "Call between ten and noon."

I hung up. *Mr. Bowen, you have been reacquired.* I had no intention of calling him any time soon, but, now, I could contact him directly without going through Jill Rucker.

CHAPTER 5

EXCEPT FOR THE meeting with Jill Rucker, I spent my arrival day in London resting. The next day was my first workday. I called Tommy Leeds and arranged a morning meeting with him at his flat. Tommy had already taken a preliminary look at the target building. He was not happy.

In his South London Cockney accent, he yelled, "Do you know who lives in that bloody building, Jeffrey bloody Ironside!" Tommy gave me a disgusted look. "Sure, you do. Ironside is retired MI6 and everybody wants to know where he got the information for that damned dossier. If he's on his game, he'll be expecting something like this."

"That's why I picked you. You're the best thieving villain I know, and I know a lot of thieving villains."

I added, "Look on the bright side," as if there was one. "Since his office, apartment, and garage are in the same building, you only have to execute one entry."

"That's the bloody bright side for you. You don't have to get by his security."

"Tommy, just name a price that will get you and your team inside that building."

That got his attention. "Whatever it takes?"

"Blank check," I said.

"Exactly what do you want, once we're inside?"

"Everything. Photograph the contents of his safe, his file cabinets, right down to his desk calendar, if he has one. I'm particularly interested in travel documents, credit card receipts, and phone bills."

"Not much in file cabinets these days, mate. You want us to copy his hard drive?"

"Of course."

"It'll be encrypted."

"Let me worry about that. And get his emails, too, if you can."

"How much time do we have to perform this little miracle?"

"You'll have plenty of time. Ironside will be vacationing in Ibiza for ten days." That's what Rodney told me. I assured Tommy, "He's being watched. If he checks out of his hotel early or changes his plane reservation, my sources will notify me. I'll warn you."

"Your sources in Ibiza, do they know what my team will be doing in London?"

"No. They don't know there is a London operation." That was true. Rodney's people in Ibiza didn't know about London.

"When do we go?"

"Ironside leaves for Ibiza tomorrow."

CHAPTER 6

Fourteen Months Earlier, Headquarters,
British Secret Intelligence Service (MI6), London

JOCK MCALLISTER HAD warned Sydney that this day might come. He was feeling vindication and dread as he knocked on his supervisor's open door.

Sydney Swope-Soames frowned up from her reading. "What is it, Jock?"

"Heard the latest news from the Colonies?"

"No. Have our American cousins started another revolution?"

"Of sorts, yes. While we were sleeping, Ted Walldrum won the presidential nomination for the Republican Party."

"God, no! Who saw that coming?"

"No one, apparently, but now it's happened, what do we do about the material Novak gave us on Walldrum?"

"Well, if the file was sensitive when Walldrum was one of many possibilities, it's radioactive now that he has a chance at the presidency. We'll need a decision from the minister. Prepare a packet. I'll make the calls and set up a meeting for us."

"Right." Jock was leaving, but turned back when Sydney called his name.

"Jock. For what it's worth, I recorded in the file your recommendation to read the Americans in on the Novak material months ago.

That was the correct call. Too bad our betters didn't listen. In any case, full marks for you."

Full marks, thought Jock, sarcastically. "Thank you, Sydney, but it's extraordinary."

"What is?"

"How often we get full marks . . . and fail."

Sydney's expression and voice hardened. "Our job is to feed our customers good intelligence. There are no guarantees they will consume it or share it with friends."

"Well, this time, those at the feast are going to choke on it."

* * *

Later, London, MI6 Headquarters

Jock entered Sydney's office anticipating that Novak was the issue, once again. "You wanted to see me?"

"Close the door and sit down." Sydney's tone was part anger, part frustration. "The Novak material has boomeranged its way back to us."

"They didn't show it to the Americans?"

"No. Our betters have determined that simply giving it to the Americans at this late date would be tantamount to interfering directly in the U.S. presidential election, or so it might appear to voters and political parties in the States."

Jock took up the thread. "And, of course, the Americans would be peeved that we had not brought the dossier to their attention earlier."

"Why, Jock, what a suspicious mind you have."

"So, we simply sit on the dossier?"

"We should be so lucky. No, direction from on high is that we must devise a way to get the compromising material on Candidate

Walldrum to the Americans in such a way that our fingerprints—and by *our fingerprints* I mean those of MI6, our minister, and certainly those of the prime minister—do not appear thereon."

"And this is what the prime minister wants?" asked Jock.

"It's none of our business what the P.M. wants. It is not for us to know if the P.M. has even seen the material. Our business is to convey Novak's allegations to the Americans in such a way that it cannot be traced back to the British government."

Jock smiled. "So that, if, by chance, Candidate Walldrum is elected president, he will not hold a grudge against said British government."

"Precisely," agreed Sydney. "Now that you have clarified the issue for yourself, how do we get the job done?"

"Well," mused Jock, "we can't very well stand in Trafalgar Square and shout, 'Who wants to tell the Americans that one of their presidential candidates has been compromised by the Russians,' can we?"

"No, we cannot. We need a cutout who is not in our intelligence services—or the government, for that matter—and who would logically have access to the Novak material. That's the sticky wicket, because, as far as we know, no one outside of government has seen that material."

"Novak has seen it," Jock reminded her. "We're protecting him and paying his bloody resettlement pension. Maybe he could help us."

"Novak isn't coming out of the shadows," Sydney assured him. "He's afraid he'll end up like Litvinenko, with a lethal dose of Russian polonium in his afternoon tea."

"What about Jeffrey Ironside? He debriefed Novak and he's retired."

"Yes. Jeffrey might do," agreed Sydney. "He's worked in Moscow and Russia Section here at headquarters. What's he doing these days?"

"He's a contract investigator for corporate headhunters."

"Well, then, he sounds like our man. He has the perfect credentials. If the Americans raise questions about the source of the allegations, they should stop at Jeffrey Ironside's doorstep, and we will have plausible denial. Good."

Jock cleared his throat. "Having Ironside volunteer the allegations is simply another version of the Trafalgar Square scenario. We need someone from the American side to employ Ironside to investigate Candidate Walldrum's activities in Russia."

A thoughtful Sydney said, "Yes . . . yes, of course. I believe I know someone who can cause such a request to be channeled to Ironside. However, Ironside can't simply give the Americans our entire Novak debriefing file. We'll have to create a dossier on Walldrum that looks like an authentic investigative work product that Ironside would normally compile for his clients. Would you prepare the document?"

"I'll get right to it. Do we have a deadline?"

"Yesterday . . . and, Jock, this project must be 'eyes only,' for just us. No typists, no copies, no computer files. Also, I suggest we drop Novak's name from the material and call it the Ironside Dossier. We don't want outsiders asking about Novak."

CHAPTER 7

Fall 2017, Night, Battersea, London,
Across the Street from Ironside's House

THE MAN PEERING through his telescope at Ironside's house cursed and dialed the Russian Embassy in London.

"Kostya," answered the embassy man. His real name—which he never used—was Konstantine Zabluda.

"There is a problem at Ironside's house."

"What kind of problem?"

"I think MI6 is also watching the house. I was ready to send in my team. I sent Lenoid out to walk the dog and check the block before we went in. He saw a car stop behind a house directly across the street from Ironside's. Two men got out and entered the rear of the house. Lenoid was suspicious. He hid in the bushes to observe.

"Minutes later, two other men came out of the house. Lenoid heard one of them say in English, 'How long do we have to stay on this bloody graveyard watch?' The other man answered, 'Until Ironside returns from vacation.' They got into the same car and left. I think MI6 is watching the house in shifts."

"Neutralize them now and get into that house. Moscow wants to know his sources."

"That is another problem. While the MI6 men were changing shifts, a British Gas van arrived at Ironside's house. Four workmen got out and put up gas leak inspection signs. They are in the house now."

"Are they a legitimate utility crew?"

"No. They're searching the house. I'm using laser equipment to overhear them. I hear Irish, British, and American accents. What do you want me to do?"

There was a pause at the embassy end before Kostya said, "Irish, British, and American. They're freelance, working for themselves or someone else, but not MI6. MI6 will either take them down or alert Ironside. If MI6 takes the gas crew down, wait until they leave. Then, take out the MI6 watchers and search Ironside's house."

"What if MI6 doesn't take away the gas crew?"

"Split your team. Have one section follow the gas crew. Let them lead you to the sources, if they locate them. Have the other section search Ironside's home. Maybe they can find something the gas team didn't."

"What about the MI6 watchers that Lenoid spotted?"

"I'll send you some men to deal with them. Make it clean. We want the *damage* to be blamed on accomplices of the gas crew."

CHAPTER 8

A Warehouse on London's Outskirts

THE FOLLOWING MORNING, Tommy was briefing me on the items taken from Jeffrey Ironside's office, home, and garage. In turn, Tommy pointed to long tables containing computers and stacks of documents. "On the first table you have photographs of the items in his safe and copies of the documents we found there. Ironside did have documents in a file cabinet. Copies are on the second table . . ." Tommy gave me a tour of the remaining tables. The last one contained three laptop computers. Tommy said, "His hard drive is on the first computer. My man cracked his encryption for you—no extra charge." He smiled. "Ironside's password was 'Churchill1940.'

"His emails are loaded on the second computer. Hard copies are in the box next to it.

"The third computer contains digital copies of all the files and hard copies in this room. That's in the event you have to decamp from this location in a hurry." Tommy gave me a knowing smile. "We also created an index of hard copies, by table." He made a sweeping gesture toward the tables. "You didn't request it, but given the volume of documents, and the fact that you're racing against time—and the competition—I thought you could use one. That *will* cost you extra, old boy. Say, twenty thousand to my account, if you're successful?"

"I can manage that. Well done. You *are* a proper thieving villain."
We shook hands.

Tommy held on and gave me an intense stare. "If you're doing what
I think you are, you'll have competition and some *serious* villains in
your path. Should your operation go sideways, this can't come back to
me or my crew."

"What's bothering you, Tommy?"

"Is Ironside still in Ibiza?"

"Yes. He has several more vacation days. Why do you ask?"

"His place was wired like BBC headquarters. It took my team hours
to locate and disable his surveillance cameras, alarms, and booby
traps. I can't guarantee that we found them all. If Ironside hasn't
bolted for home, that's a good sign our intrusion didn't alert him. In
any event, I suggest you get cracking and find what you're looking for
before he returns to London."

* * *

To keep the operation compartmented, I brought my crew in after
Tommy, my thieving villain, departed. The eight of them arrived in a
sedan and Mercedes van. I assigned them to the various tables and
gave them their mission briefing.

"Focus on the period between June 2015, when Walldrum began
his run for the presidency, and January 2017, when the dossier on his
alleged Russian activities was reported in the news media. During
that period, Jeffrey Ironside developed the dossier. Your job is to identify his sources for the allegations in that dossier. I want a
twenty-four-hour log of his travels and everyone he communicated
with by any means—in person, by phone, email, snail mail, or smoke
signal. I don't care if it was his maid or his pizza delivery boy. I want

his bank and credit card statements, utility bills—anything that happened in his life during that period. I want to own Ironside's history.

"When you find anything in the hard copies or computer files related to that period, give it to Sherri. She'll maintain the master events log."

Sherri wore jeans, boots, and a fleece-lined jacket. She removed the jacket and dropped into a chair.

Just in case they had been on another planet for the past year, I told them, "Ironside was a Russian expert for MI6. He is also a meticulous record keeper. So, we have his daily calendars.

"Benny here—" I turned to a thin thirty-year-old in glasses, a green cardigan, and tan corduroy pants—"is going to check those calendars for anything related to Sherri's master events log.

"If you find documents in Russian or about Russia and Russians, give them to me or Sherri. We speak and read Russian.

"Okay. If there are no questions . . . let's get to work."

Over the next eight hours, Sherri collated documents from the crew and built the master events log. Suddenly, she said, "Max, I think we've got something. Look here."

I scanned the wall projection of the log spreadsheet while Sherri guided my attention with a laser pointer. "During the twenty-month window you gave us, we can't find anything remotely related to Russia or Russians.

"Ironside took only two foreign trips, both on direct, round-trip flights to the United States. Based on his credit card and bank account statements, he was reimbursed for both trips by Synthesis-PSG, the firm that hired him to investigate then-candidate Walldrum. I'm guessing the first trip in the summer of last year was a hiring interview. The second trip was in December. Again, I'm guessing, but that trip was probably to deliver the dirt dossier to Synthesis-PSG."

I asked, "Did you check our copies of his passport?"

"He has two. One under an alias, but no Russian stamps or visas in either."

"Either he had a third passport," I speculated, "or Ironside didn't go to Russia to collect the dirt on Walldrum. Where did he go? Did he buy train tickets, bus tickets?"

"We found no records of those," replied Sherri.

One of the computer operators piped up. "He used his credit card to buy petrol—gasoline—outside of London after his first trip to the States."

I said, "Put it up."

The receipt appeared on the wall screen. Ironside bought gas on July 28th.

I turned to Sherri. "Let's see the events log for that week."

Ironside's calendar for the month of July appeared on the screen next to the petrol receipt. Sherri announced, "On the 25th, he printed a *D* beneath the date. On the 27th there's an *L*, and on the 28th, he's inked in *R*. He bought gas on the 28th. Maybe *R* means he returned home on that date. *D* could mean the day he departed for his trip."

I chimed in, "And *L* could be a source."

I told one of our hackers, "Ironside drives a 2016 Audi Q5 SUV. Pull up the specs and get me the gas tank capacity and average fuel consumption—in gallons and miles, none of that liters and kilometers crap."

Sherri said to her crew, "Somebody, get me a map of Great Britain up here."

A staffer produced the map and taped it to the wall beside the screen.

Seconds later, the hacker announced, "The Q5's tank capacity is 19.8 gallons; average miles per gallon is 18 in the city and 26 on the motorway."

"Ironside bought gas on the 28th?"

"Yes," confirmed the staffer.

I said, "Assume that he topped off his tank. How much gas did he buy and where?"

Sherri had the answer. "Seventeen gallons at Penruith station on the M6 motorway."

"If he was visiting a source—let's call him Source Lima, for the *L* on Ironside's calendar—it would have been bad tradecraft to gas up in the same town. So, he drove, maybe, fifty miles back toward London and still had about three gallons in his tank before filling up at Penruith."

Working her calculator, Sherri announced, "He burned about fifteen gallons to get to his source. That would put the source about three hundred fifty miles north of London, somewhere in a search fan east or west of the M6 motorway."

"What's out there?" I asked.

"Not much," replied Sherri. She had drawn the search fan on the map.

One of our hackers announced, "Ironside has a news article on a Russian colonel named Vasili Bogdanovich in his computer." Sherri and I went over to read it.

I noted, "The colonel died in a plane crash near Cape Town in 1998."

Sherri read down the article. "It says none of the bodies were recovered."

I said, "Put up Ironside's address book and go to the *L*s." There were no *L* entries. "Check the *K*s and *M*s. Look for addresses outside of London."

"Wait." Sherri snapped her fingers at the man on the third computer. "Check the black bag team's index for his garage. Did they download the GPS from his SUV?"

"Sorry, no."

A solution occurred to me. "You've got the vehicle identification number for the SUV. Can you hack into his GPS?"

"Sure."

"Okay. Download his directory and give me all addresses between two-fifty and three-hundred-and-fifty miles north of London near the M6 motorway." Sherri and I watched over his shoulder as the hacker worked his digital mischief.

Minutes later, he told us, "There's only one address in his GPS that fits your criteria. It's in the town of Dumfries." He printed the address and gave it to me.

Sherri went to the map and stuck a pin in the town's name.

I went to the office and called Rodney on the satellite phone. When he answered, I said, "It's me. I may have located a source." I read the address in Dumfries. "I need a history on who lives there and everything you have on a Russian colonel named Vasili Bogdanovich. Email the info to me ASAP."

Rodney hesitated. "I'll see what I can do." He added, "I was about to call you. Your friend just left Ibiza prematurely and didn't check out of his hotel. He's traveling on a yacht owned by a company affiliated with his former employer."

"Can you have local assets block calls to the Dumfries address for the next eight hours?"

"I'll try, but they'll be hanging out in a brisk British wind. You'd better bring bacon."

As I ended the call, Sherri came in. "What's up? You look stressed."

"Ironside just snuck out of Ibiza on a MI6 yacht. He—they—may know about us or Tommy's team. We need to speed things up. We're taking the security team to Dumfries. Let's go see if Source Lima checks out."

*   *   *

Two hours later, with most of my crew back at their hotels, Sherri and I were in the sedan, speeding north on the M6 motorway toward Dumfries. I was behind the wheel. She was riding shotgun with my computer on her lap. Our four-man security team followed in a van with DHL delivery service markings.

Sherri read from the email Rodney sent us. "Source Lima's name is probably Lucas Novak. He was born in Czechoslovakia and became a naturalized British citizen in 1999. He's a retired construction engineer. His last job before retirement was with a British construction firm in Dubai. The firm went out of business in 2000, the same year Novak retired and purchased the Dumfries house."

"The *L* on Ironside's calendar is for Lucas," I guessed. "What did we get on Colonel Bogdanovich?"

Sherri read more from the email. "Vasili Bogdanovich started his professional life in the KGB. He was an up-and-coming young major in 1991 when Yeltsin did away with the KGB. Bogdanovich survived subsequent reorganizations of the spy and security services, which evolved into the Federal Security Service—FSB. His survival is attributed to his father-in-law, General Grishin. The general and Bogdanovich worked in the FSB directorate responsible for subverting tourists and businessmen visiting Russia.

"In 1998, Putin took over and reorganized the FSB. He purged the top leadership. Bogdanovich was on his way to South Africa when his plane crashed into the sea. All aboard went missing and were presumed dead."

I tried to fit the pieces together. "And one year later, Lucas Novak becomes a citizen. Two years later, he buys a house in Scotland."

"Are you thinking what I think you're thinking?" asked Sherri.

"I'm thinking it took a year in a safe house for MI6 to wring Colonel Bogdanovich dry from his dip in the Atlantic, along with everything he knows about Russian spying. Then, Bogdanovich—alias Lucas Novak—was off to a quiet retirement in Dumfries and a pension, courtesy of the British taxpayer."

"That's what I thought you were thinking."

*   *   *

An hour later, Sherri and the security team squeezed into the sedan. I switched over to the van with the phony delivery service logo. We continued to Dumfries. The security team set up a discreet perimeter around Novak's home. With a dummy package in hand, I walked to his front door and rang the bell.

From the speaker above the bell, a Russian-accented voice asked, "What do you want?"

In my best British accent, I said, "DHL. Package for Lucas Novak."

"Leave it at the door."

"You have to sign for it, mate."

Long pause. "The door is open. Come in. I'm upstairs bathing my dog."

I entered a narrow hallway, wall to my left, living room to the right. I took a few steps forward and fell over the tripwire, landing facedown on the floor.

Novak bounded out of the living room, gun in hand, and jammed his foot into my back. "Move and I'll kill you." He searched me quickly and found no weapons.

"Who are you?" he demanded.

"I'm not a threat. I just want to ask you some questions about the Ironside Dossier."

"What happened to your British accent?"

"I'm an American."

Novak grunted. "What makes you think I know anything about that dossier?"

"You're the only person Jeffrey Ironside visited after he was hired to get Russian dirt on Walldrum. He didn't go to Russia; he came to you . . . Colonel Bogdanovich."

"Are you CIA?"

"No. I used to be. I'm freelance now. I'm being paid to verify the contents of the Ironside Dossier. I believe you were Ironside's source. That's why I'm here."

"Who's paying you?"

"An American citizen has offered a reward to anyone who can verify the dossier. You help me and I'll pay you a hundred thousand pounds."

"Besides you, who knows about me?"

"I don't know, but I'd bet a lot of people are looking for you. If you don't help me, they'll keep coming."

"Maybe I'll shoot you as a warning to them."

"You would be committing suicide if you did," warned Sherri.

Novak looked up to see her standing in his hallway, pointing her pistol at him. She had entered through the back door.

"Drop the gun," Sherri ordered.

While Novak was considering his next move, I rolled over and twisted the gun from his hand. Getting up from the floor, I assured him, "We didn't come here to harm you. We just want information." I gestured Novak to a chair in the living room. "Tell us about Jeffrey Ironside and the dossier he compiled on Walldrum."

Novak ignored me and glared at Sherri, who remained standing, casually holding her gun at her side. He shifted his hostile gaze to me. "Why should I help you? If Moscow discovers that I'm alive, I'll be dead in a month. Your money will be of no use to me."

I said—and I meant—"I didn't want to do this, but we're pressed for time." I tapped a number into my cell phone, but didn't dial. I showed the display to Novak. "Recognize this number?"

"No."

"It's the Russian embassy in London. If you don't talk to us, I'll call it right now and give them your real name and this address."

"That won't get you the information you seek. Why would you feed me to Moscow?"

"Because you're standing between me and ten million dollars. If you won't talk to me, I'll make damn sure you don't talk to anybody."

"You are a ruthless man, Mr. Who-Ever-You-Are."

"Believe it. So, who will you talk to, me or Moscow?"

Novak studied his shoes before saying, "It's going to be a long night. There is a bottle of vodka and glasses in the cabinet over the kitchen sink."

Sherri got the vodka and a glass for Novak and bottles of water for herself and me.

Novak downed a shot of vodka and began his story. "Russia in the 1990s was like the Wild West. Okay, the Wild East. The Berlin Wall was gone, along with the Soviet Union. The new government in Moscow was privatizing oil leases, minerals, everything. It was a buyers' market for oligarchs and the mafia. They—and the government officials helping them—were stealing more money than you can imagine. They couldn't buy enough caviar, dachas, and Mercedes to soak up all of it.

"While they were raping Mother Russia, they worried that one day the people would realize what was happening and the orgy would come to an end. There might be riots in the streets, revenge killings. There is one lesson of history that Russians know well: when the masses get fed up, you don't have enough guns to stop them.

"To prepare for that day, corrupt government officials, the oligarchs, and the criminal gangs needed . . . an exit strategy. That strategy involved moving lots of money out of Russia and into countries where they could enjoy the good life if Russia went up in the flames of revolution or drowned in debt. The best place for the good life was the United States. The problem was how to move all those millions—maybe billions—into the States without alerting your tax authorities—and without the Russian people finding out that you're robbing them blind."

"And the solution was . . . ?" I asked.

"They needed money laundering businesses that were cash-intensive, like real estate development. Over time, the mafia and the oligarchs established such companies in various countries, including the States, but they could launder only a fraction of the money that had to be moved.

"Along comes Ted Walldrum, New York real estate developer extraordinaire, all ego, all penis, drowning in debt, and no money. His businesses had gone belly-up. The banks were into him, up to his small intestines." Novak hunched his shoulders as he flashed a weak smile of apology to Sherri. "Banks wouldn't loan him another dime." Novak chuckled. "He owed them so much money, they couldn't even foreclose.

"At the time, I was working for what eventually became the FSB. My section was responsible for identifying and recruiting—or compromising—foreign business people who might be of use to Russia then or at some time in the future.

"We had a developer in the States approach Walldrum. Our man said, 'Ted, you are a great real estate visionary. You're just going through a bad period right now. It happens to all visionaries. The bank bureaucrats always run at the first sign of trouble, but we believe in your vision. Let us lend you some cash at a reasonable interest rate. We'll even defer the interest. Pay us back when you're on your feet.'

"He bit like a hungry dog. We connected him to a German banker who ran a wealth management fund for some oligarchs. The fund loaned Walldrum money through the bank to conceal its Russian origin.

"We let him get used to the money. Then, while he was still struggling financially, our guy took him aside, bought him something nonalcoholic, and said, 'Ted, the people lending you money from their wealth fund could use your help. They need to move some money out of Russia and into the United States. Your businesses would be ideal for that. Can we count on you?'"

Novak uttered a little laugh at his memory of the kill. "He had no choice. He was hooked on the oligarchs' loans and the lifestyle they supported. Once he laundered the first dollar, we owned him . . . from the 1990s on."

"You keep saying *we* and *ours*," I noted. "It sounds like the FSB was working for the oligarchs."

Novak grunted. "Everyone was working for the oligarchs or the mafia, and they worked for Putin. They were—and are—one organism, inseparable."

"Were you responsible for building the dossier on Walldrum?"

"Yes."

"How did you do that?"

"I ran agents who encouraged and recorded on film his vices, sexual and so forth. And, of course, I recorded compromising conversations about his money laundering activities. We built a dossier on him that would choke a Siberian tiger."

Novak poured himself another vodka as I asked, "Did you keep records of bank accounts and money transfers?"

Novak laughed. "I was an *apparatchik*, a low-level officer. No one was going to trust me with oligarchs' bank account numbers. If anyone in the FSB kept details of the money transfers—which I doubt— it would have been General Grishin, my director."

Sherri asked, "Without bank account numbers, what was the compromising information on money laundering?"

"The *kompromat* was the process. We recorded discussions of how much money would be moved and when, approximately. How the money would be laundered. Which real estate projects were involved. And, of course, how the thieves in Russia would gain access to the money after it was laundered. Specifics like dates, accounts, and access codes were left to bankers. The operation was compartmented by design." He laughed. "With account numbers and access codes, a lot of FSB officers would have made themselves instant millionaires."

"And instant targets," I added.

Novak observed, "You, yourself, are a target in return for millions. Is it worthwhile?"

"I see your point."

Sherri focused on essentials. "How did you and the dossier get to London?"

"Yeltsin established the FSB in 1995. My duties didn't change. I continued to build dossiers on prominent businessmen, including Walldrum. But in 1998, everything changed. Putin became our director. He reorganized the FSB and replaced key officers with his own people. That included General Grishin, my superior and father-in-law. Putin's people had an intense interest in the dossiers compiled by my section. They came to our secure reading room to study the dossiers and question us about the contents. Although they attempted to conceal it, they had a special interest in the Walldrum dossier.

"After Putin was elected president, there were changes in management of *kompromat* dossiers. The most developed dossiers in my section were removed and taken to Putin's office—the Presidential Administration—where they were stored and maintained.

"Officers working overseas, who had detailed knowledge of the oligarchs' financial dealings, were recalled to Russia and replaced by

men loyal to Putin or Putin's allies. With the exception of a few officers in my section, the same thing happened to those at FSB headquarters who had knowledge of the dossiers. Generally, they were
reassigned to unimportant duties, often away from Moscow to places
where contact with foreigners was virtually impossible. One day, a
colleague would have a nice apartment and a good job in Moscow.
The next day, he could be running a security detail at a radar site on
the Arctic Circle. Those were the lucky ones. Some officers who complained that the oligarchs were looting Russia just disappeared.

"What remained of my section became a training unit for Putin
loyalists. We knew that as soon as they had a thorough knowledge of
our operations, they would take over and we would be out. My career
was over," Novak added wistfully. He raised his glass.

I poured him another vodka. "Was that when you decided to defect?"

"Yes."

Ever on target, Sherri asked him again, "How did you get Walldrum's material out?"

Novak smiled and tapped his temple. "I have a photographic memory." He downed the vodka and sighed. "When I was a boy, my father
gave me the best advice I ever got. He said, 'Vasili, never tell anyone
about your ability to remember things. There is a camera in your brain.
Possession of a camera is a threat to the state. If you become known as a
threat, the state will kill you. Keep your memory a secret and trust no
one with it, not even those you love.'" Novak looked from me to Sherri.
"That was good advice under the Soviets. It's good advice today, yes?"

Sherri again. "Tell us how you got out of Russia and survived the
plane crash."

"You're well informed. I think you are CIA." Novak smiled. "Excuse me, *ex*-CIA."

He continued, "While I was training those *Putnicks*—as we called
the president's lackeys—to take my job, I realized that I had to find a

way out of Russia and to the West. It was not easy. We were being watched and evaluated for our loyalty. So, the easiest way to leave Russia was to take Putin's spies with me and, then, elude them.

"At the time I made my decision to defect, we had targeted for subversion an important technology executive. He was an American CEO, trying to raise cash for his company, but he would not come to Russia. On overseas trips, he would route himself through Cape Town because he preferred black women as sex partners. Fortunately for us, he was a married white Southerner. We were planning to entrap him during one of his Cape Town orgies. I suggested that I take my *Putnicks* to South Africa to show them how it was done. To my surprise, the trip was approved. Eight of us flew to Cape Town. We never made it. The plane crashed and everyone aboard was lost and presumed dead."

"Including you, Colonel Bogdanovich," I noted.

"Including me, but now I'm Lucas Novak, retired engineer and British citizen."

"How did you escape the crash?" asked Sherri.

"Why do you care, young lady?"

I answered. "In order to verify the dossier for our employer, I need to account for all the details."

"For your employer? You said you were freelance."

"I am, but I consider the man with the ten-million-dollar reward my employer. I want to be thorough, should these questions arise."

Novak gave me a skeptical look. "If you were thorough, your research would have told you that I was a parachutist in the Red Army before being recruited into the security services. I left the plane several minutes before it crashed into the sea."

"Why didn't the *Putnicks* stop you?"

"Sadly, everyone on the plane—except me—inhaled a lethal gas before my exit."

Sherri wanted to know, "What was your route for defecting to the Brits?"

"I had arranged for MI6 to have a boat waiting near the coordinates where I planned to jump from the plane."

"Why did you go to the Brits? Why not the Americans?"

"In Moscow, the Americans were closely watched. It was easier to contact the British. Besides, the British needed a win, don't you think?" He smiled at us.

Sherri, keeper of the calendar, noted, "You defected in 1998. The Ironside Dossier on Walldrum didn't surface until 2016. Why the delay?"

"And why," I asked, "did the Brits leak the dossier through a retired MI6 officer?"

"You'll have to ask the British why they chose Mr. Ironside. The timing of the release was my doing. I didn't inform MI6 that the FSB had *kompromat* on Walldrum until he announced he was a candidate for your presidency."

"You didn't tell MI6 about Walldrum during your intake debriefings?"

"That is correct."

"Why not?"

"I needed insurance that MI6 would resettle me, not wring me dry and abandon me. I gave them many dossiers during my year of debriefings. I also warned them that I knew of others and would reveal them only if I was given a fair resettlement. Periodically, Ironside—I didn't know his real name until I read it in the papers last year—would come here and I would dictate dossiers to him."

I looked at Sherri. She rolled her eyes.

"There are specific allegations in the Ironside Dossier. I want the names of people who have firsthand knowledge that those allegations are true."

"You're going to Russia to interview them?" Novak was incredulous.

"I have to."

We took a break. Sherri and one of our security guys napped in Novak's guest room so we would have fresh drivers for the trip back to London.

I got pen and paper and sat with Colonel Bogdanovich—alias, Citizen Novak—as he wrote a list of dates, locations, deeds, sources, and their jobs, while he drank enough vodka to give a Clydesdale permanent brain damage. When he finished, I put him to bed with a promise that we wouldn't blow his cover, if he kept quiet about talking to us.

*　*　*

On the way back to London, Sherri drove, but I couldn't sleep. I was worried. It was easy to tell Bogdanovich that I was going to Russia to interview the sources he gave me. It would be hard to get into that country, find the sources, and convince them to talk to me. I needed a plan. About an hour from the city, one began to take shape in my mind. I drifted off to sleep stretched out on the back seat.

CHAPTER 9

THE NEXT DAY we all slept late and I had brunch with Sherri Layton at her hotel. I needed advice. When we were sipping our last coffee, I asked her, "What did you think of Novak?" We had agreed not to use his real name. "Was he credible?"

"His eye movements and body language said he was telling the truth. We should've done a voice stress analysis. Did you test his photographic memory while I slept?"

"He memorized and correctly repeated the serial numbers on ten bills in my wallet."

"That's as close as you're going to get to credibility without a voice stress analysis or polygraph. Do you want to go back for those?"

"No. MI6 may be moving to protect him."

"Well, now, you have to go to Russia and track down the sources." She shook her head slowly. "It's been three decades since the Russians first compromised Walldrum. Even if you find the sources Novak gave you, they may not remember, they may lie, they may be afraid to talk to you. Worst case, they turn you in to the FSB."

"I got smoke, if I don't go to Russia. My first problem is getting in. Any thoughts?"

"You could fly, but you're in their computers. Not a good idea. You could sneak in through Finland."

I nixed that idea. "It would involve too many people on both sides of the border."

"You could parachute in, like they did in the OSS." Sherri smiled at her ridiculous suggestion. Turning serious, she recommended, "Go in by cruise ship. No individual visa application is required. The downside of cruising is, once you land, you have to slip away from your tour, do your business, and rejoin the tour undetected. That's possible, but risky. A tour guide might report you. The ship will, if you don't return before it sails."

"A cruise might get me in, but it won't give me enough time to contact sources."

"You'd have time if you had a look-alike to replace you on the tour and return to the ship posing as you. If you were still with the Agency, that might be possible. Even so, getting out of Russia after the ship sails is a whole different problem."

"I'll have to give that one some thought." I was thinking about Rodney.

"Max, what's with Rucker?" On the drive back from Dumfries, I had told Sherri that Jill Rucker was joining the team. "How come you didn't use her at the warehouse or take her to Dumfries? Is there something I should know?"

"Jill's management; we're labor. If management knows what we know, they don't need to pay us. Besides, I don't trust her. She's too eager. It's a gut thing."

"Well, if you went the cruise route to St. Petersburg, a couple would attract less attention than a lone guy in his thirties. Jill could pose as your traveling companion . . . and you can keep an eye on her."

I didn't relish traveling with Jill Rucker, but Sherri was right. "If I travel with Jill, I want backup. You and one of your security guys apply for Russia tourist visas. Fly into St. Petersburg. We'll meet you. After

Jill and I finish our business there, we all take the train to Moscow. I'll give you details as I work them out."

"What business do you have in St. Petersburg? The only thing Walldrum had there was failed attempts to start businesses and sex with prostitutes. Everybody knows he chases women. What's the point of sourcing it? The money laundering sources are in Moscow. That's where you should focus."

"I disagree. Novak said the KGB documented their first compromising information on Walldrum in St. Petersburg during the 1980s. If the Russians have had the capability to blackmail him since then, that's significant. I need verification."

"What are you going to do, Max, knock on whorehouse doors and ask if anybody knows the prostitute Walldrum screwed in 1987? That's not a plan. That's suicide. The mafia and the FSB will be all over you on Day One. Besides, Novak's information is fifteen years old. What's the source of the current information in the Ironside Dossier? The infighting among Kremlin players about whether or not to meddle in our elections. Putin's firing of advisors because of blowback when the Kremlin's meddling was exposed. That didn't come from Novak. We're flying blind in one eye. If Ironside didn't go to Russia, he had other sources. Who are they?"

With that question in mind, I went to my hotel and called Langley on the sat phone.

Rodney came on full of good cheer. "Max, what a surprise."

I asked, "Do you remember that cancer study you asked me to verify?" *Spyspeak: cancer study meant the Ironside Dossier.*

"Progress already?"

"To a point. As best I can tell, the principal researcher never left the U.K. while he was writing the study. For all the statistics before 2000, he relied on a database provided by his former employer." *Spyspeak:*

Ironside got the pre-2000 dossier dirt from MI6. I dared not mention Novak on the phone.

"You're absolutely sure about that?" Rodney sounded alarmed.

"Ninety percent."

"And the post-2000 research?"

"There's the mystery. The post-2000 studies are from a different database, recently updated. If those studies are accurate, I'd say they were made available to the researcher during the past year, possibly by someone from a competing firm and here in London. Do we know anyone like that?" *Spyspeak: Ironside got his post-2000 information on President Walldrum from one of two sources: a recent Russian defector to MI6, or a MI6 mole in Russia's employ. The source must have come to London during the past year.*

"I don't know if we are aware of anyone like that," replied Rodney. "I'll try to get an answer for you, but everyone here is busy on high priority work at the moment. If I find anyone, I'll call you on Sunday." *Spyspeak: This is high priority and I can't talk about it on the phone. Sunday means I'll get back to you in twenty-four hours. I'll pick the time and place.*

While I was talking to Rodney, another piece of my plan to find sources in Russia fell into place. "Rodney, there's one more thing, I need you to update my Doyle identity. Make me a solid citizen, no government connections, and no foreign travel, except for my current trip. Doyle's profession should be something easy to discuss, maybe a schoolteacher. I need the legend yesterday."

"For what purpose?"

"For what I came here to do. 'You either trust the guy you put in the field or you don't put him there.' Those are your words, remember?"

CHAPTER 10

OF COURSE, SHERRI was, in the main, correct. I didn't have a plan for St. Petersburg. What I had was the name of one of the prostitutes who allegedly arranged Walldrum's alleged romps when he visited the city. The hard evidence—no pun intended—was on film and in Putin's safe. I did have an idea as to how we might get a leg up in St. Petersburg. I didn't tell Sherri. Where we were going, the more compartmented the operation, the better the chances of everyone coming home.

For the St. Petersburg part of my plan, I started at the U.S. Embassy in London. Inside, I approached a civilian security officer, easily identified by the wire in his ear. "I need to speak to the FBI liaison agent."

"Your passport, please."

I surrendered it for the third time since entering the compound. The security officer gave the document and me quick looks. "Just a minute, please." Holding on to my passport, he walked away, talking into his sleeve mic.

Minutes later, a brunette in pearls and a tan pants suit emerged from the inner sanctum and walked toward me. On the way, she executed a brush pass with the security officer, who handed off my passport with a deftness suggesting they had done it before.

The lady came to me and announced, "I'm Special Agent McNair. How can I help you,"—she glanced at the passport—"Mr. Dolby?"

"My business is confidential. May I see your credentials?"

McNair showed a moment of irritation, followed by a hint of a smile. She flashed her creds long enough for a speed-reading and returned the wallet to her pants pocket.

I took a furtive glance around the room and asked, "Could we speak in private?"

"Follow me." McNair led me from the reception hall to a small interview room.

We sat at a table and I told her, "I'm working undercover in London for the CIA. I'm not interested in current or future FBI operations. I need some really old background on Russians who might live in or near London."

"Why aren't you routing this request through your London station chief?"

"Because he has no need to know I'm here. I report directly to Langley."

That produced a frown.

I said, "There's an emergency number in my passport. It will get you Langley. Ask for Rodney. He'll vouch for me."

McNair gave me a skeptical look and departed. She returned in a short time and handed over my passport. "What do you need, Mr. Dolby?"

"I have a profile of the kind of person I'm looking for. I'd like you to tell me if there's a Russian criminal in London who fits that profile."

"Come with me." McNair led me to an elevator, up to her floor, and down a corridor to her office. I sat in the guest chair. She sat at her desk and fired up the computer. "Give me the profile."

"He's maybe Russian mafia, in London or near the city. Pimped Russian women to foreigners in St. Petersburg—it was Leningrad then—in the late 1980s and early 1990s. He may have had KGB connections."

As I watched her fingers dance over the keys, I wondered if it was the intent of the digital revolution or effective use of the taxpayers' money to transform a law school graduate into a clerk-typist.

"We have a hit," announced McNair. "Your man is Viktor Lukovsky, sixty years old. He ran a prostitution and human trafficking ring in St. Petersburg from the mid-1980s until 1996. He couldn't do that without a green light from the KGB."

McNair peered at the computer monitor. "Here's an interesting tidbit. Lukovsky's operation overlapped the years when Putin was deputy mayor of St. Petersburg, 1994 to 1996. Odds are that Putin knew him. When Putin left St. Petersburg for Moscow, so did Lukovsky."

"What did Lukovsky do in Moscow?"

"That's a blank in his resume. He came to London a few years ago claiming to be a retiree, living off investments and a pension from the Russian government. The Brits and Bureau like him for money laundering, but nothing sticks. He has no visible connections to the Russian mafia, other than a public dinner once or twice a month with some hometown mobsters. They get drunk, sing, tell Russian stories, and chauffeurs drive them home. The Brits can't even nail Viktor for DUI."

"I need something from this guy. Give me an *in* to him. What are his wants and weaknesses? What's the personal side of his life like?"

"He seems to have everything he wants. He owns a yacht. Hangs with expensive call girls. He doesn't shop them; they're his personal harem. Viktor has either a very active libido or a very active imagination."

"Or a very large wallet," I suggested.

"Could be the girls like all three. He has plenty of money and spends it."

"Family?"

"He bought three penthouse apartments in the building where he lives, one for himself, one for his wife, and one for his mother."

"A separate apartment for his wife? What's that about?"

"She leads a separate life, with a monogamous, live-in boyfriend. Viktor doesn't seem to care. She ignores his harem."

"Children?"

"No."

"What about his mother?"

"Her name is Elena Lukovskaya. She loves England and English culture. Most days, she has high tea at Fortnum & Mason. She attends lots of plays and does charity work for London's poor.

"Viktor has a three-hour dinner with her—just the two of them— every Tuesday and Thursday. Every other Sunday, he takes her yachting on the Thames."

"Sounds like mom is the soft spot in Viktor's armor."

"He's devoted to his mother. Involve her at your peril."

"I don't have another choice."

"Then be careful. Don't be put off by his *good ol' Ukrainian peasant* act. Viktor Lukovsky is a made man in the Russian mafia and a stone killer."

* * *

With that chilling thought to keep me company, I went back to visit Sherri in her hotel room.

"Sherri, I'm working a plan to get more precise information on the St. Petersburg source. I need your help."

"What do you want me to do?"

"There's a woman here in London named Elena Lukovskaya. This is her address and photograph." I got them from Agent McNeill. "This woman goes to Fortnum & Mason most days for high tea and she is addicted to stage plays. I want you to accidentally make her acquaintance. Try to steer the conversation to why you're in London. Tell her that you're with a friend who's on his way to Russia to find his mother, who he has never met. That's step one."

"What's next?" Sherri was warming to the task.

"Once she's hooked, the two of us will accidentally bump into her. You introduce me. I'll take it from there."

"Why are we doing this?"

"Elena Lukovskaya has a son who might be able to help me locate Ironside's St. Petersburg source. I need Ma Lukovskaya to introduce me to her baby boy."

"When do you want me to start?"

"First thing tomorrow. Use your security team, if you need them for surveillance. And, Sherri, be careful. This woman is connected to the Russian mafia. So, don't force the interaction. If she suspects she's being played, no telling where this could go."

CHAPTER 11

I WENT BACK to my hotel intending to have an early dinner in the hotel restaurant and spend the evening planning my approach to Mob Mom, Elena Lukovskaya. I was into the soup course when Jill Rucker slid into my booth on the other side of the table.

Pulling her chain, I asked, "Did I call you?"

"No. Mr. Bowen called me. He wants an update."

"Tell him to call me."

"We've already had that conversation. He doesn't want to talk to you directly."

"And I don't want to talk to him through you."

"He's paying your bills and he wants a progress report."

"Have you read my contract?"

"No."

"Bowen did and he signed it. It says I get paid for results, not progress reports. Refresh his memory when you talk to him."

"Next time I call him, what do I say about your progress?" She *was* persistent.

"Tell him there is no progress."

"What about your trip to Dumfries?"

"Who told you about Dumfries?"

"An unnamed source. I guess you forgot to tell your team I was an intern."

There was one thing I didn't forget. That was, there was no one on my team, except Sherri, who knew Jill Rucker existed, and Sherri would not have told Jill about Dumfries.

I tried to sound disappointed. "Dumfries was a dry hole."

"I don't believe you. You were gone for most of the night."

"Look into my eyes. Can you see that I don't give a shit what you believe?"

"Give me a break, Max? I'm just the messenger."

"I don't know if you are Bowen's messenger. You pop up here and introduce yourself as my new contact with Bowen. My line to him is out of service. I can't verify that Bowen even knows you. Since you have an open channel to Bowen and I don't, tell him this operation comes to a halt in two days unless the retainer he promised is deposited in the escrow account and I have proof. Can you do that?"

A reluctant "yes."

"Good. Tell Bowen that I would consider that progress . . . and it would prove to me that you are actually in touch with him."

Her tone became conciliatory. "Why are you busting my balls? I'm the middle man here. I'd rather be helping you than sitting in my hotel room and playing gofer for Bowen. Give me something to do."

I didn't trust Rucker as far as the restaurant door, but idle hands and minds are dangerous and I was thinking about taking her to St. Petersburg. "If you want to be helpful, get me brochures on Baltic cruises sailing in the next three weeks."

* * *

I spent the evening writing out my strategy for approaching the retired mobster, Viktor Lukovsky. That was the easy part. What I couldn't figure out was how to approach his mother and convince her to introduce me to her son. I decided to postpone dealing with that problem until Sherri made contact with Mob Mom. I went to bed and dreamed of having a yacht in Monaco and a penthouse overlooking the marina.

The next morning, I arose early, went through my exercise routine, and had breakfast in my room to avoid running into Jill Rucker. My pursuit of dossier sources was at a standstill until I heard from Sherri, or Rodney told me who Ironside's second U.K. source might be.

As I considered Ironside's travels, I realized my premise of a second U.K. source might be faulty. As a U.K. citizen, Ironside could travel anywhere in the European Union without a passport. He could have met with Russian sources all over Europe. Knowing how good Ironside was at tradecraft, he would have financed any European travel with cash to cover his tracks and protect his sources. Maybe he had a third passport that he used for travel to Russia. This mission might be more complicated than I first thought. Was Sherri right? Should we focus on Novak's Moscow leads? All those possibilities gave me a headache. I was getting an aspirin when someone knocked on my door.

"Room service."

I opened the door to a waiter standing behind a table set with a flower arrangement, snacks, and a bottle of cooling champagne. "Compliments of Mr. Rodney," the waiter announced as he rolled the cart into the room. "Would you like me to uncork the champagne, sir?"

"No, thank you."

The waiter handed me a sealed envelope. "Mr. Rodney said you should open this straightaway. It contains your theater tickets."

I went to the dresser for my wallet.

"No, thank you, sir. Mr. Rodney is a generous tipper."

As the waiter departed, I tore open the envelope. Instead of theater tickets, I found a note. *Trafalgar Square at the monument base, now. I'll find you.*

I took a cab to the Square, went to the base of the monument, pulled out a tourist map, and tried to look lost.

Rodney passed by and said, "Join me on the tour bus. I have your ticket."

I waited a few beats and followed him to the bus, a red double-decker job with an open second deck. The first deck was populated, but not crowded.

"Upstairs," commanded Rodney.

"It's as cold as a witch's tit up there."

"True, but the witch has no ears. Get up here."

I couldn't argue with that. I followed him up into the elements and we settled into a seat near the back. The deck was empty except for a few hardy souls near the front. They were huddled behind a plastic windscreen that shielded the first few rows from the wind.

I didn't want to spend much time up there. So, I opened. "You've come a long way from Langley in a short time. You must have something important for me."

"I do, but first, tell me about Bogdanovich."

"He's Ironside's source for events alleged to have occurred before 2000."

"How is that possible? Bogdanovich died in 1998."

"He's alive. He faked his death and defected to MI6. Before that, his job with the KGB and FSB was creating situations to blackmail Western visitors to Russia. When Bogdanovich defected, he brought over dossiers on his victims and gave them to MI6. One of those dossiers was on our president, Ted Walldrum."

"You got this directly from Bogdanovich?"

"Yes."

"Where is he?"

"I'm receiving you weak and distorted, over." That's what you tell a guy when you don't want to hear his question or he shouldn't be

asking. Secrecy was Bogdanovich's only protection. However, my eva-
siveness wasn't much protection. I was sure Rodney had connected
my questions about the Dumfries house to Bogdanovich.

Rodney shifted his focus. "Why didn't the Ironside Dossier surface
before 2017?"

"Bogdanovich didn't give MI6 everything when he defected. He
fed the dossiers to the Brits over the years to be sure they wouldn't
dump him. He didn't give up Walldrum until 2015, when Walldrum
announced he was running for president."

"Why didn't MI6 give us the dossier as soon as Bogdanovich gave it
to them?"

"Maybe they wanted to verify the allegations before passing the
dirt to us."

Rodney picked up the thread. "And they either couldn't—or
didn't—verify before Walldrum won the Republican primary. At
that point, they couldn't tell us without appearing to meddle in our
election."

"Sounds right. They probably believed Walldrum didn't have a
chance. So, they sat on the dossier and prayed."

"But," said Rodney, "when Walldrum won the White House, the
Brits knew they were holding the pressure plate on a ticking time
bomb. They couldn't let go and they couldn't hold on. So, they used
Ironside as a cutout to pass the dossier to the FBI."

"That, minus a few details," I said, "but, yeah, that route allowed
the Brits to give us the dossier without admitting they sat on it."

Rodney fell silent, apparently digesting the disaster.

Interrupting his thoughts, I said, "Your turn."

He explained, "When we spoke on the phone, I couldn't answer
your question about Ironside's second source for obvious reasons. I'm
here to answer it now." He gave me his serious look. "You realize that,

by exchanging this information, we're breaking laws in the U.S. and the U.K.?"

"I knew that when I asked you for a name."

Rodney pursed his lips. "Boris Kulik. He's the likely source for the post-2000 material in Ironside's Walldrum dossier."

"Who is Boris Kulik?"

"Number two man at the Russian embassy in London. He's a young rising star in Putin's universe, with oligarch connections. Before coming to London, he handled personnel issues for Putin's office. Knows where a lot of bodies are buried, who buried them, and why. He saw the Russian Federation rotting from the inside and was disillusioned. Kulik was posted to London in 2016. He contacted MI6 and offered his services as a mole."

"In return for . . . ?"

"Langley is not privy to his compensation."

"What did he bring to the table?"

"His teaser was a thumb drive of secret Russian documents, two pages of the SVR phone directory, and pieces of the SVR organizational chart." SVR are the initials of the Russian Federation's Foreign Intelligence Service.

"Whatever MI6 gave him, we'd have paid more. Why didn't he come to us?"

"Russian defectors won't come near the Agency since Walldrum was elected. They think Putin has a pipeline into the White House and the CIA."

"So, how did the Agency find out about this Mr. Kulik?"

"The Brits are a decent lot when it comes to sharing. MI6 invited us to a Kulik debriefing. Langley had to promise that the CIA station chief in London would be out of the Kulik loop. In return, we were allowed to observe the Kulik debriefing through a one-way glass and give our questions to a MI6 officer who asked them over the intercom. That way, Kulik heard a Brit accent, not an American one."

Rodney shivered against the cold wind as the tour bus meandered through the streets. He had a brandy flask and shared it with me as he continued the story.

"Kulik's no dummy. Based on the questions, he must have guessed that CIA reps were behind the one-way glass. He terminated the session and told his MI6 handler he wanted no contact with the CIA."

"Did Kulik give the Agency or the Brits any of the compromising allegations about Walldrum that showed up in the Ironside Dossier?"

"Not while we were listening," said Rodney. "Since MI6 was already sitting on their take from Bogdanovich, they probably told Kulik not to mention our president. I'm sure they wanted us in the dark until they figured out how to handle the allegations.

"Come to think of it," mused Rodney, "if MI6 told Kulik not to mention Walldrum, that might have alerted Kulik that the CIA was in on his debriefing."

Rodney shook his head in wonder or disgust. "Involving the Agency in the Kulik interview was well intentioned, but it was a screwup from start to finish."

A new name had been added to my sources. "Any idea how I can get to Kulik?"

"Yes. Moscow gave Kulik the additional duty of recruiting Brits to spy for Russia. MI6 created a cover story along those lines so they can debrief Kulik without arousing suspicion," he added, "if, indeed, one can do anything that does not arouse Russian suspicions."

"What's Kulik's cover."

"That he has a romantic relationship with the secretary for a White-hall intelligence cell the Russians want to penetrate. For SVR consumption, Kulik is cultivating her as a mole or an unwitting source. They meet once a week for lunch or sex at the same hotel. That's where he passes intel to MI6 and they debrief him. There is a strict routine for these meetings that does not vary. Consistency is bad tradecraft, but it seems to work."

London's sights streamed by as a metallic voice from the bus loudspeaker described them. Rodney's nose turned red. He shivered and put his gloved hands into the armpits of his overcoat. I couldn't feel my nose and there wasn't a coat warm enough to deflate my chill bumps. It occurred to me that this was nothing compared to a Moscow winter. If the Russians were following us, they were probably in Bermuda shorts.

Rodney described the routine Kulik, the secretary, and MI6 followed for their meetings. I listened with the urgency of a man dying of hypothermia, while Rodney droned on in the same slow cadence he used in the warmth of a Langley briefing room. "Based on Kulik's schedule, the only place you could meet him without alerting Brits and Russians is at the hotel, when he's supposedly banging the secretary."

"Any surveillance on the lovers?"

"Not by MI6. Occasionally, the Russians tail both of them. It's random."

"What about the Agency?"

"No."

"How do you know the details of Kulik's meetings? Brits don't share that stuff."

Rodney hesitated. He was either going to lie or spill some beans he would rather leave in the pot. "Kulik is a potential intelligence gold mine. We wanted to prepare for the day when the Agency might have to tap into that mine without the knowledge or assistance of our MI6 cousins. Since we agreed to keep London Station out of the loop, we brought in a surveillance team from Langley to document how the Brits were handling Kulik. Now, we can get to him, should the need arise. Bearing in mind the delicacy of this arrangement, you must devise an elegant solution for your contact with Kulik."

I had heard *elegant solution* before. It was Rodney's code for mission impossible. He confirmed that assessment.

"When you contact Kulik, neither the Russians nor the Brits can know. If the Brits find out, they won't take kindly to us approaching their asset. The special relationship between our two services would be damaged."

"I'm not with the services anymore, remember?"

"You know that won't fly. There'll be hell to pay at Langley. Those of us who supported your efforts here will likely join you in the unemployment line . . . or in a cell."

Maybe that was true, but I knew Rodney, and it was more than likely that he would tell the Brits and his Langley boss that I found out about Kulik through unauthorized access to some top-secret file while I worked at the Agency. Anyway, the subject was exhausted.

I said, "What about the legend I asked for?"

"Luckily for you, I was able to rush it through to fit your specifications." Rodney took a cloth pouch from the inside pocket of his overcoat. I opened it with my near-frozen fingers. It contained a passport and wallet, complete with credit cards and driver's license in my Dolby identity.

Rodney said, "Your company has a website. The address and password are in the wallet. Would it be asking too much for you to tell me why you need a legend?"

"Bogdanovich gave me a lead on one of his original sources. I need the help of a Russian mobster to find the source. I can't be a recently fired CIA officer."

Rodney nodded his understanding and, to my surprise, informed me, "I'm staying in town to manage any blowback from your meeting with Kulik. You can contact me by leaving a message with your hotel concierge. I gave him a generous tip to get that champagne lunch up to you." He added, hopefully, "Will you keep me informed of your talks with Kulik and the mobster?"

"No."

I left the bus at the next pub sign and went in to drink up and thaw out.

CHAPTER 12

THAT EVENING, IN Sherri's hotel room, she briefed me on her encounter with Viktor Lukovsky's mother, Elena. "I followed her to the theater and we struck up a conversation over drinks during the first intermission."

"What was your impression?"

"Nice lady, but she drinks vodka like a true Russian."

"Did you work me into the conversation?"

"Yes. I told her I was visiting London with a friend who was trying to find his Russian mother and that I heard her Russian accent when she ordered a drink."

"Was that moving too fast?"

"I think not. She was interested, but intermission ended before we could get into you. I avoided her for the second intermission so she wouldn't get suspicious."

"What's our next move?"

"Tomorrow, we go to Fortnum & Mason for high tea and *accidentally* bump into her. You tell her your story and ask for an interview with her son, the Russian mobster."

"How do you know she'll be there tomorrow?"

"I checked. She has a reservation."

* * *

The next day, a taxi dropped Sherri and me at Fortnum & Mason. All the way there, I worried over how to smoothly parlay our *chance* meeting with Ma Lukovskaya into a meeting with her mobbed-up son, Viktor, while not making the whole thing appear contrived. This woman had lived most of her life in Soviet Russia's underworld, where survival depended on her talent for spotting mob intrigue, government lies, and secret police spies. It was more than likely she had a finely tuned bullshit detector and that I would not fool her into thinking her theater encounter with Sherri, bumping into us at tea, and me asking for an audience with Viktor were coincidental. If she distrusted me from the start, I wouldn't get near Viktor or, if I did, he might be the last person on earth I'd see. Neither outcome would get me closer to ten million dollars.

I was still wrestling with the problem when we entered the Fortnum & Mason tea room. As we were shown to our table, Sherri whispered, "Black hat with yellow flower at eleven o'clock."

I stole a glance at the woman under that hat. She was heavyset with broad peasant features and looked younger than her eighty-plus years. A long black fur coat was draped over one of the three spare chairs at her table. I looked away, but before we got to our table, Lukovsky's mother yelled a delighted, "Sherri!" and waved us over.

Ma Lukovskaya enveloped Sherri in a bear hug, and said, in her thick Russian accent, "Sherri, darling, you surprise me!" They did a kissy-face routine after which Sherri said, "Mrs. Lukovskaya, this is Richard, the friend I told you about." We shook hands and exchanged pleasantries.

Ma Lukovskaya issued orders: "Come, sit here."

We sat. I pretended interest while Sherri and Ma reprised their theater experience. Finally, Viktor's mother addressed me in so-so English. "Sherri tell me you looking for mother."

To ease the conversational strain on her grammar and my ears, I replied in Russian. "Yes. My mother lived in St. Petersburg when I was born."

I saw a slight stiffening in her expression and posture when I mentioned St. Petersburg. I figured I had just a few sentences to establish my credibility. I continued in Russian, "This is embarrassing, but my mother worked the streets. My father was American and she was his mistress. I'm on my way to Russia to try and find her. I have been looking for Russians in London who might help me. I was told that your son, Viktor, was a businessman in St. Petersburg when I was born. So, meeting you is not an accident. I was hoping you would ask Viktor if he could help me."

Mom Lukovska stared at me, her body perfectly still.

"I'm not a policeman. Here's my business card." I placed it on the table in front of her. "I would be very grateful if you would ask your son to meet me, at his convenience. I'm staying at the Savoy. Thank you. Excuse me."

I stood and put a hand on Sherri's shoulder, signaling her to stay. I left.

I tried all evening to contact Sherri. She didn't answer her phone and her crew didn't know where she was. Worried, I finally drifted off to sleep.

I didn't know what magic Sherri worked with Viktor Lukovsky's mother, but I received a call early the next morning that Viktor's Rolls-Royce would pick me up at 10 a.m. The car arrived on the dot. The driver opened and closed the door for me and didn't say a word until we got to South Dock at Canary Wharf in East London. He stopped the car, looked in the rearview mirror, and said, "Go with Ivan."

A tall crew-cut bruiser in a dark overcoat opened the car door for me. As he did, I glimpsed some serious artillery under his coat and noted a receiver in his ear. Ivan motioned for me to follow him. As the

Rolls rolled away, Ivan—Mr. Silent-but-deadly—led me up the gang-plank of a stunning eighty-foot yacht. The hull and superstructure were black, contrasting beautifully with the blond wood decks. If this is how the mafia rolls, where do I sign? The problem is that the mafia, like any society, has its princes and paupers. Lukovsky had risen to princely status by climbing over lots of dead bodies. I was damned sure I didn't want to sign up for that.

Awaiting me at the top of the gangplank was another big fellow in white from head to toe, hair to shoes. His white hair was slicked back into a ponytail, accentuating a broad face that matched his prizefight-er's body. He smiled and extended his massive hand. "Richard, I'm Viktor Lukovsky. Welcome aboard the good ship *Payback*."

"Thank you for seeing me, Mr. Lukovsky."

"Viktor! Nobody calls me *Mister* except servants."

"Call me *Ricky*." I picked a nickname that was soft and non-threatening.

Viktor led me under the shelter provided by an extension of the superstructure. A table had been set for two just out of the sun and there were sleek electric heaters to keep us comfortable in the chilly breeze. We paused to enjoy a great view of the harbor.

"Usually on Sundays," explained Viktor, "I take my party girls sail-ing. I make exception today because my mother asked me to see you." Viktor, like his mother, did not embrace articles—such as "an" and "a"—as essential elements of English grammar.

"I never deny my mother anything." Viktor looked past me into an unpleasant memory. "When I was boy—after my father died—my mother slept with brutal KGB scum to put food on our table. I knew this asshole was sleeping with women all over Leningrad." For my benefit he added, "Today, it's St. Petersburg.

"I followed him one night and waited for him outside another woman's house until two in the morning. He came out drunk and pussy-whipped. I cut his throat and left him in the street with his fly open and the smell of her still on him. I made promise to myself that my mother would never want for anything again, no matter what I had to do."

He came back to the present and gave me a stern look. "If my mother had told me to kill you because you interrupted her tea, you would be dead now."

I believed him. "I'm glad I didn't displease her. I approached your mother because I'm desperate. I would like your help—"

Viktor waved me off. "We talk business later. First, we eat. I have good Russian dinner for us." He smacked me in the gut with the back of his hand. "You could use few more pounds."

Viktor sat on a padded bench along the rail, his back to the water. I sat across from him. He performed some magic invisible to me. A couple of stewards in white jackets appeared and served dinner. Both wore earpieces and jackets loose enough to conceal guns. Neither was Ivan. If this meeting went badly, the odds were at least four to one against me. Pray for peace.

The first course was a hot appetizer: mushroom caps, baked over with cheese and served in a crème sauce. The garden salad was served with feta cheese, olives, sliced hardboiled eggs, and homemade— yacht made?—Russian dressing. The entrée consisted of pancakes with sour cream, green onions, more chopped hardboiled eggs, and salmon. All good, but nothing to drink. According to Viktor, "Drink interferes with your full appreciation of the food."

Throughout the meal, Viktor gave me a verbal tour of the posh London marina. "Ever been to the docks before, Ricky?"

"This is my first time."

"Not many yachts here now, but you should see this place when the rich and famous sail in. Me, I like small, intimate boats. I want to enjoy all of my guests. Some of these yachts are ridiculous, floating hotels. One Russian guy got yacht with two helipads, two swimming pools, ballroom, thirty cabins with bathrooms, service staff, and security. With all those people around, how you gonna know who's on board? Fucking Jason Bourne could be hiding in a food locker, waiting to put a bullet in your head. You'd never know it until he whacked you." Viktor uttered a short laugh.

"You Americans, almost as bad. Paul Allen, the Microsoft guy, his yacht cost $170 million." Viktor went on to regale me with his descriptions and disgust of the super-rich.

As I listened, I'm thinking, *I hear you, Viktor, but we're sitting on an 80 WallyPower yacht and I'm guessing this baby cost slightly south of ten million, maybe more, depending on the custom fittings.*

After dinner, Viktor said a jovial, "Come inside, Ricky. We have drinks."

I followed him into the cabin. We sat at a large driftwood cocktail table that didn't match the décor, but if you own this boat, you can have whatever you want.

Again, through the miracle of invisible communication, a jacketed staff member appeared—this time, Mr. Silent-but-deadly—with a decanter and a plainly visible belt-holstered Glock. He put the decanter on the table. "Vodka" was carved into the crystal.

Viktor said to him, "Give the boys a couple of hours on the dock."

Ivan disappeared below deck. Minutes later, the stewards who had served dinner left the boat. Witnesses were jumping ship. Ivan and his Glock were still aboard. What did that mean?

Viktor poured us shots of vodka and raised his glass. "To the best president Russia ever had . . . Ted Walldrum." He downed his vodka and laughed like a mental patient. I was still holding my shot glass in the air while Viktor convulsed and turned red. Between gasping for breaths, he managed to say, "You . . . you should see your face!"

Well, ha, ha, ha. I smiled and downed my shot.

Viktor poured us another couple of rounds and downed his shots in one gulp. There was a brown leather box on the table, the size of a laptop computer, but two inches thicker. It had two covered compartments that ran the length of the box. One was long and narrow.

My host pressed one of two brass buttons on the side of the box. The top on the narrow section popped open to display a row of cigarettes and Cohiba cigars. Viktor took a cigar, snipped the end, and lit it with a gold lighter. He rotated the box to me.

"Smoke?"

"Thanks. I don't."

Viktor rotated the box toward himself, popped the top on the larger compartment, and removed an automatic pistol with a silencer attached. He blew smoke into my face and said, "Secondhand smoke can kill you just as quick." He wasn't laughing.

I raised my arms in a gesture of surrender. "I'm not here to cause trouble. I just wanted to ask for your help."

"You can bullshit my mother. You don't bullshit me. Give me your wallet."

I rotated my left hip toward him so he could see that I was going for the wallet. As I slid it across the table, Ivan appeared. He was leading Sherri by the arm. Her hands were bound behind her and she was gagged. Ivan sat her in a chair next to me. She appeared intact, but there was concern in her eyes, not panic.

"Are you okay?" I asked.

She nodded that she was.

Viktor tossed Ivan my wallet and he took it below. As I sat there looking at Viktor's gun, the words of FBI Special Agent McNair came to mind: "Don't be fooled by his *good ol' Ukrainian peasant* act. Viktor Lukovsky is a made man in the Russian mafia and a stone killer."

Viktor wasn't talking. I guessed he was waiting to receive my credit score from below deck. I began inspecting as much of the yacht as I could see.

Viktor asked, "You like this boat?"

"It's very nice." I was looking around for something to throw at Viktor, if Ivan returned with bad news.

"This?" He looked around it with some disgust. "This just payback."

"For what?"

"Everything. In 1933, Stalin starved millions of Ukrainians to make political point. My grandparents died, so did my wife's. Friends took in my mother and father and fed them. Ten years later, my father fought Germans at Stalingrad. He was hero. A year after war, agents from Ministry of State Security came to our home. They accused my father of being counter-revolutionary. They take him away. We never see him again. My mother was afraid. She moved us to Leningrad where secret police screwed us again." Viktor looked around the yacht and made a grand wave with his cigar. "That's what this is for."

I sat in uncomfortable silence until Viktor addressed me in Russian, "My mother tells me you speak good Russian. Where did you learn?"

I answered in Russian. "For as far back as I can remember, I had Russian nannies and Russian tutors. My father wanted me to be able to speak to my mother in her native tongue . . . if I ever met her." That was my legend. The truth was, I studied Russian for three years in college and another year at the CIA, adapting it to the spy business. That CIA year was prep for my posting to Moscow Station.

Ivan reappeared. He gave Viktor two sheets of paper and put my wallet on the table . . . in front of Viktor.

Switching back to English, my host said, "So, you are CEO of auto parts supply company?"

My legend is holding. Good old Rodney. "No. I'm a schoolteacher. My father was the CEO. He died. I'm running the company until we find a CEO who knows the business."

Viktor gave Ivan a satisfied nod. Mr. Silent-but-deadly withdrew.

"What you want from me, Ricky?"

"Help me find my mother. She's Russian. She lived in St. Petersburg in 1987. You were there then."

"Why not go to Russian embassy?"

"My situation is complicated."

"Make it simple," ordered Viktor. He was listening, but held the gun steady.

"My father worked in St. Petersburg in 1987. He frequently used the services of a prostitute . . . the same prostitute. She got pregnant and had a child . . . me. My father made plans to smuggle me and my mother out of Russia. Someone found out and my father had to leave the country in a hurry. He smuggled me out in a suitcase and promised to return for my mother. The Cold War was in full swing. He couldn't get back into Russia because of the politics. Even if he could, my mother couldn't get into the States with a record of prostitution. My father tried for years. He was unsuccessful. Finally, he gave up and married my stepmother. On his deathbed, my father made me promise to find my mother and bring her to the States."

"What your father doing in St. Petersburg in 1987?"

"He never talked about his work, only about my mother."

Viktor took a thoughtful drag on his cigar and said, "So, you came looking for a Russian who was pimping flesh in St. Petersburg in 1987?"

"Yes."

"There's plenty of old Russian pimps in New York City and it's closer to your home. Why you don't go there?"

"I don't have police contacts there. Even if I did, it would be dangerous to ask about Russian mafia in New York."

"And not dangerous here?" He thumbed the safety off his pistol.

"Less so. I have friends here."

"How did you find me?"

"As I said, I have friends here. I told one of them the kind of . . . experience I was looking for. My friend knows a policeman, who knows someone at Scotland Yard." I was making up the lies as I went along. "Some money changed hands and I was told that you might be able to help me."

"Who are these friends?"

"I promised not to reveal their names."

"Maybe if I shoot Sherri, you tell me?"

If there's one thing mobsters hate, it's an informer who gives up his friends. Even if I gave Viktor a phony name, I was a rat, and he might kill us both. If he didn't kill us for giving up our friends, I doubted he would help me.

"Viktor, I promised my friends that I would not say who helped me—"

Viktor pointed his gun at Sherri's head.

I put my hand between his gun and Sherri. "Please don't. We came here for your help. We are not interested in your business or your friends. It's not in your interest to kill us. If we die or disappear, there'll be an investigation. It would be a self-inflicted wound. You don't want that. You don't need that."

Viktor kept his gun pointed at Sherri, but his ice-blue eyes shifted to me.

I took that to mean that my argument was making sense to him and pressed on. "People in London know I'm here. Please don't do this. Help me."

"Help you find whore from thirty years ago?"

"Help me find my *mother*!" I faked the anger. "I want to know if she's alive. If she is, where? I want her address."

Viktor engaged the safety on the gun and laid the weapon on the table within easy reach. Sherri relaxed.

Thoughtfully, Viktor said, "If your mother is alive, she could be married, have family. Maybe she left St. Petersburg. She could be in another city, another *country.*"

"Maybe she's not married," I countered. "Maybe she's single or sick. Maybe she's waited all these years, hoping that my father or her son would come for her." I leaned across the table. "Viktor, I promised my father, on his deathbed, that I would try to find my mother. Will you help me keep that promise?"

He stared at me for a long time before asking, "What's in it for me?"

"I can't pay you and you already have every material comfort. But, if you find my mother, I'll give you something money can't buy. I'll meet your mother for high tea at Fortnum & Mason and tell her what you did for me and my mother. That will make your mother very happy."

He took his time putting the gun back into the case. "What your mother's name?"

"Tatyana Kedrova." I gave him her last known address, according to Bogdanovich.

CHAPTER 13

AFTER A TENSE few minutes with Viktor and his gun, Ivan untied Sherri and removed her gag. Viktor apologized for his caution and sent us back to my hotel in his Rolls. On the way, Sherri filled me in on what happened between the time I left her with Viktor's mother and our meeting with Viktor's gun on the yacht.

Sherri told me that Ma Lukovskaya was sympathetic to my quest for my fictional mother, but suspicious. That was probably due to her history with the Russian security services and the Russian mob. Leaving Sherri at the tea table for a trip to the ladies' room, Ma Lukovskaya called Viktor for advice. Viktor responded with assistance. When Sherri and Ma left tea time, a couple of hoods took them in hand and escorted them to Viktor's yacht. Ma Lukovskaya got to explain my plight to her doting son. Sherri was cross-examined about me and invited to spend the night on the yacht—or else. Viktor was a gentleman, but when Sherri explained that I was a friend, not her lover, he tried to hit on her. She declined. Next day, enter me, in Viktor's Rolls, for dinner and deception. Tying and gagging Sherri was more to intimidate me than to restrain her. In the end, Viktor was satisfied that we were not a threat, we went home, and it appeared that my first engagement with the Russian mob was a success.

* * *

While Viktor was trying to locate Tatyana Kedrova, I kept Jill Rucker in the dark about him and busy working on the Baltic cruise. Now, I had to find a way to interview Boris Kulik, MI6's mole at the Russian Embassy, without alerting the Russians or the Brits. To make that task more complicated, I couldn't tell my team—Sherri and her four-man *heavy metal band*—that they were interfering with a MI6 asset who might already be under surveillance. I did have to tell them enough to get the job done, but not the whole truth. So, I met the team in Sherri's hotel room and gave them the MI6 cover story.

"This man is your target." I showed a photograph of Kulik that Rodney had provided. "Call him Romeo. He's having an affair with this woman." I showed Rodney's photo of the secretary. "Call her Juliet. They meet the same day, every week, and have lunch or sex at this hotel." I provided the name and address.

"Their routine is predictable. If there's no sex on the menu, she waits for him in the hotel dining room. They hold hands. They eat, kiss, and go their separate ways." What I couldn't tell them was that when they hold hands, Romeo might slip Juliet a thumb drive of Russian secret documents.

I continued the briefing. "If sex is on the lunch menu, Juliet reserves a room in advance, arrives first to check in, and leaves a key at the desk for Romeo. If she's not in the dining room when he arrives, Romeo collects his key from the desk and goes to Juliet's room for sex."

I didn't tell the team that, according to Rodney, instead of secretary and sex, MI6 is waiting in the adjourning room. Kulik gives them the documents or a thumb drive, and they debrief him. After an hour or so, Kulik and the secretary come down, arm-in-arm, gazing at each other with loving satisfaction, and go back to work.

"I need an hour with Romeo in that hotel without anyone knowing, especially Juliet."

"Why the hotel?" asked Tony Davila, the leader of Sherri's heavy metal band. He was "Tony-D" to our team because we had another gun named Tony. "Why not snatch him and go somewhere else for a quiet hour's chat?"

"Because," I said, "he has a tight schedule and high profile. It has to be the hotel."

Sherri asked, "What's the game plan?"

"I want the team to set up a static surveillance at the hotel and verify their routine. Then, on a day Juliet doesn't make a room reservation for a tryst, we have to trick her out of the hotel, reserve a room ourselves, and lure Romeo up to the boudoir where I can talk to him. Your job is to confirm their routine and tell me how we can pull this off."

Sherri nodded an okay, but she was staring at Juliet's photograph. "This is a lousy picture. She's wearing that big hat, probably a wig, and oversized sunglasses. She doesn't want to be recognized." Sherri said, "Tony-D, see if you can get a better shot of her. Let's see what she really looks like."

Tony-D called my attention to another problem. "You said *static surveillance*. If you want to get Juliet out of the hotel, you need to know what buttons to push. We need to follow her and find something that would make her stand Romeo up."

That was risky, but it had to be done. "Okay, but be aware that both Romeo and Juliet are married. Either of their spouses might suspect the affair and have private investigators following them. If you spot any surveillance, break off." I was really concerned about Russian or MI6 tails. The PI story was my way of alerting and protecting Sherri's team.

* * *

Now, I had two pokers in the fire: Viktor-and-St. Petersburg, and the Romeo-and-Juliet surveillance. If I got lucky—or unlucky—both leads would take me to Russia. It was time to figure out how to get into that country without getting caught. I turned to the annoying Jill Rucker, who had been researching Baltic cruises.

At her request, we met in her room—which was nicer than mine—her rationale being, "I don't want to drag all this cruise stuff down to your room."

When I arrived, Jill poured us each a double scotch, my favorite brand. Coincidence? I believe in the Easter Bunny, too.

Jill suggested, "Let's look at our options." She directed me to a table where I expected to find piles of cruise brochures, because, she had said, "I don't want to drag all the stuff down to your room." The *stuff* was one brochure. I gave her a quizzical glance.

She smiled. "The scotch was here in my room." Without skipping a beat Jill added, "Almost no one cruises the Baltic in winter, Max. The only cruise I found was for academics during the school holidays."

"What's the itinerary?"

"It originates in Stockholm and terminates in Southampton."

"Ports of call?"

"Seven, but the one you're interested in is St. Petersburg, three days, two nights."

"How many passengers aboard?"

"About a thousand, and the ship has vacancies. Are we going to take a cruise?"

"Maybe." That depended on Viktor Lukovsky. "Do you have a problem with us traveling as a married couple?"

"Business or pleasure?" She gave me a seductive smile.

"Strictly business."

"Too bad." She looked me up and down, took a drink of scotch, and licked her lower lip. "What's our mission?"

"I'll tell you when I know."

"Do you want me to make a reservation for us?"

"Yes, for Mr. and Mrs. Richard Dolby."

"Do you have passports for the happy couple?"

"I'll take care of it. Get yourself a set of passport photos."

"Then what?"

"Buy warmer clothes and a good pair of boots. Russia is cold this time of year."

Jill went to the living room, flopped into a chair, and crossed her legs. "Sit a while, Max. Since we're going to travel as a couple, we should get to know each other. We might be questioned by the Russian police. They could ask you, 'What's your wife's favorite color?' or 'What kind of underwear does she like?' How would you answer?" She smiled mischievously.

I laughed. "I'd say that your favorite color is green, for money, and that you like your underwear off. Good night, Jill."

Following Rodney's instructions for setting up a meeting, I left a sealed message with the hotel concierge: *Are there any tickets left for tomorrow's performance?* Then, I went to bed and dreamed of the tantalizing Jill Rucker and my ladylove back in D.C., Claudia. Freud would have had an orgasm interpreting that dream.

* * *

The next morning, I got Jill out of bed. Over breakfast in the hotel restaurant, we made a list of what we would need in Russia. We were at the stores when they opened and returned to the hotel in time for lunch. There was a note from Rodney: *Pick up your tickets at the same place, 2 p.m.*

I told Jill I was going to meet someone who would help us with the Russia cruise. Because I have a suspicious nature, I also called Sherri to set a trap. While Sherri was getting into place, Jill and I dressed in our Russia tour clothes and took photographs of each other. I made prints at the hotel business center, dropped a few other items into a zippered pouch, and headed for my rendezvous with Rodney.

It was a cold walk to Trafalgar Square, but a good way to flush a tail. When I was halfway to my destination, I called Sherri on the mini-mike clipped to my scarf.

"Are you there?"

Sherri's voice came through my earpiece, "A block-and-a-half behind you."

"See anything?"

"The paymaster"—Jill Rucker—"has been on your tail since you left the hotel."

"Anyone with her?"

"Not that I can see."

"Let's check. I'm going into that movie theater up ahead. Let me know if she's working with a team."

I purchased a ticket, went directly to a fire exit door, and waited.

Sherri said, "She didn't talk to anyone. She bought a ticket and followed you in."

"Pick me up at the far side exit." I pushed the door open and walked into the street.

Sherri radioed that she saw me. A few blocks closer to the Square, she called again. "You lost your tail at the theater. Looks like she was working alone."

"Okay. Break off. See you at the hotel."

Rodney picked me up at the Nelson Monument. To my happy surprise, we passed up the open-air tour bus and took a taxi to a safe house.

After we filled our brandy-laced coffee cups, Rodney said, "So, why are we here?"

"I'm going to Russia." I gave him Jill Rucker's photos. "She needs a passport to travel as my wife, Mrs. Dolby. I also want a set of fake FSB credentials for each of us and the items on this list." Rodney took the list from me and looked down his nose at it.

"What's your plan?"

"We're taking a Baltic cruise." I gave him a brochure with the cruise details. "When we get to St. Petersburg, we're going to slip away from our shore tour and track down a source." I handed Rodney photos of what we would be wearing when we left the ship. "We need body doubles to replace us for the three days and two nights we're in St. Petersburg, and for the remainder of the cruise."

"Why do you need replacements after you leave St. Petersburg?"

"We're not returning to the cruise ship. We're going on to Moscow."

Rodney set his coffee mug aside and laced his fingers over his vest. "Now that I know what you want, let's talk about what I want. I want to know what you got from Kulik and your mobster."

"No, you don't. You're asking about progress. What you want—what you *need*—is product. You'll get the sources and their statements when I have them." I could have told him that I had nothing from Kulik or Viktor, but why twist his little brain.

Rodney was annoyed. "I get what I want or you don't get the documents."

I reminded him of CIA procedures. "One day soon, Langley is going to strap you to a polygraph machine. When that day comes, the less you know about what I did and how, the better it will be for you."

Rodney knew I was right, but he didn't like it. "You'd better deliver."

* * *

After my meeting with Rodney, we waited: waited for Viktor Lu-kovsky to find Tatyana Kedrova, waited for Rodney to deliver our cruise documents, waited for an opportunity to interrogate Boris Kulik. At the end of the second week of surveillance, it looked like we were going to get a shot at Kulik. Sherri called me and the team, minus Jill Rucker, to a meeting in her hotel room. Tony-D briefed us.

"Last week, Romeo and Juliet had lunch. This week, they had a nooner." He turned to me. "If what you told us about their schedule is accurate, they should have lunch at their next meeting. That looks like a good time to corner Romeo for a talk."

Sherri, who had left the planning to her surveillance team, asked Tony-D, "Have you found a way to get Juliet away from the hotel before Romeo shows for lunch?"

"We think this will work." Tony-D explained the plan and ended by suggesting to me, "When Juliet arrives at the hotel, Sherri should be the one who tells her Romeo isn't coming. She might get suspicious if a man makes the approach."

"That makes sense," Sherri agreed, "but I still don't know what Juliet looks like without her disguise. Did you get a good photo of her?"

"We did." Tony-D handed Sherri a head-and-shoulders shot of the secretary, without her hat and sunglasses. Juliet was sitting at a table in the hotel restaurant. Sherri looked at me. There was concern in her eyes.

"Okay," I said to the team. "Good job. Sherri and I need to discuss the plan. Take a thirty-minute break in the lobby bar."

When the team had gone, I asked Sherri, "What's wrong?"

"You tell me." She was confused and angry. "Juliet is no secretary. She's MI6. Her name is Sydney Swope-Soames. I met her at a security conference a couple of years ago. Why are we interfering with a MI6 operation? Who is Romeo? What have you gotten us into, Max?"

"You know damn well that it's better for you if I don't answer those questions."

I wanted to kick myself. I should have known MI6 would use a professional for an operation like this, not some clueless secretary. Still, Tony-D's plan might work.

Sherri wasn't having it. "We've been on some dicey missions together, Max, but you always told me the score. I don't like being deceived and I'm not going to disrupt a MI6 debriefing, which is what this looks like. I have a child and a sick mother to care for. I can't be doing hard time in Wormwood Scrubs."

The Scrubs is a London prison, with a nasty name and a worse reputation. I could have told Sherri that the Scrubs is for male prisoners, but I got her point.

Sherri made an observation vital to our success. "Your *Juliet* might recognize me. That would blow the operation and get us all into trouble. So, count me out."

"Can I use your team?"

She folded her arms. "I hired them. I'm responsible for them." She didn't say, "No."

"I need the team, Sherri. Unless I talk to Romeo, my investigation hits a dead end."

She looked at me thoughtfully. "You tell them enough about what they're getting into so they can make a good decision . . . and give them a bonus, if they want to play."

"Done, but you don't get to hear my pitch. I don't want you tainted."

The team returned and Sherri departed, probably to replace them at the lobby bar. I didn't level with the team. Too much was riding on my hoped-for conversation with Romeo. I did tell them we could get into trouble with the British government and maybe go to jail if the op went bust. And I dangled a bonus, *if* we separated Juliet from Romeo and *if* I got what I needed from Romeo. I had worked with these guys before. They trusted me. So, I skipped the "for God and country" speech. All four signed on.

Now, I needed to get Jill Rucker to replace Sherri on the op. Jill had pestered me to give her a bigger role than paymaster. So, it was easy to enlist her without divulging anything other than the Romeo-Juliet cover story. I still didn't trust her, but if she was involved, I could keep an eye on her. The downside was she could keep an eye on me.

* * *

On Thursday, at a quarter to noon, the team was in place and our radio signals were five by five—the best. Juliet arrived and sat at her usual table in the hotel dining room. She placed her purse, holding her cell phone, on the floor beside her chair.

Pretending to read a newspaper in the lobby, our guy alerted the team. "Juliet's here. She didn't make a room reservation."

That was the *go* signal for our operation. Our hacker entered the dining room. As he passed Juliet, he disabled her cell phone with some electronic magic in his briefcase.

Juliet ordered lemonade and told the waitress she was waiting for someone.

A few seconds later, Jill Rucker approached Juliet. Jill was wearing a black wool blazer with a set of borrowed concierge's crossed keys on her lapels. She smiled and said, "Excuse me. I believe you are waiting for a gentleman."

Juliet was surprised, then wary. "I am. How did you know?"

"You told the waitress you were waiting for someone. Your gentleman friend called the hotel and said you would be in the dining room. He asked us to tell you he's been delayed by friends from home."

We hoped Juliet would interpret that to mean Kulik was tied up with someone at the Russian Embassy and couldn't keep their lunch date at the hotel.

Jill continued, with a smile. "Your friend requested that you meet him at a restaurant closer to his place of employment. He said it was urgent. He sent a taxi for you."

As we had anticipated, Juliet went for her cell phone, maybe to call Romeo or her MI6 colleagues. That's why our hacker had disabled it.

After Juliet's second try at reviving the dead phone, Jill Rucker said, "Your taxi is waiting, ma'am." Jill extended a hand in the direction of the door. "Please follow me." Juliet threw the useless phone into her purse and followed Jill to a taxi at the curb, motor running. The driver was one of Tony-D's guys with orders to get Juliet lost for an hour.

As the taxi pulled away, Jill removed the concierge insignia from her lapels. She went to the desk, made a reservation, and left a key for Kulik. Not knowing what name Kulik used, she described him to the desk clerk.

The man gave her a sly smile. "I know the gentleman. I'll see that he gets his key."

Minutes after Juliet departed in the cab, our man in the lobby radioed the team. "Romeo just arrived. He picked up his key at the desk and he's on his way up." With humor, he added, "Turn down the bed. Turn up the heat."

Kulik unlocked the door and entered the suite. The first thing he saw was the back of a chair with Jill Rucker's naked leg draped over the arm. As he advanced toward the chair, I entered from the adjoining room, accompanied by Tony-D. Kulik halted, his eyes registering surprise.

"Don't be alarmed." I didn't want the team members to know his name. "Your friends don't know that you are here with us. We'd like to keep it that way."

"You are Americans. What do you want?"

"An hour of your time, as usual. Then, you're free to go."

"I want to go now." He turned and headed for the door. One of Tony-D's guys—the biggest one—stepped out of the bathroom and blocked the exit.

I said, "You can talk to me or you can explain to your ambassador what really goes on in these rooms when you meet your secretary here."

That got his attention. He turned back to me. "What do you want?"

"As I said, an hour of your time . . . and no one need know you talked to me. This way, please." I directed him into the bedroom. Tony-D and his assistant followed us into the room to reinforce the perception that we were in control.

The blinds were drawn. There was a table and two chairs in a window alcove. Kulik and I sat down. I said, "I want to discuss your conflicting loyalties. Am I correct in assuming that you would prefer this to be a private conversation between the two of us?"

His eyes darted from Tony-D and his teammate to me. He said a nervous, "Yes."

I asked my muscle team to wait in the next room. When the door was closed behind them, I said to Kulik, "We have very little time before you will be missed. So, let me tell you what I know, what I want, and how I can help you. Agreed?"

He said nothing, but he didn't make a dash for the window.

"I am," I told him, "the only one on my team who knows where you work, your real reason for coming to this hotel, and who you meet here. Those are not my concerns. I will not expose those arrangements, if you give me the information I need."

"What information?"

"First, let's deal with the lady you were supposed to meet for lunch. In your name, we called the concierge and left a message that you were delayed at your embassy and asked that she meet you at a restaurant close to your work." I gave him the address and phone number. "You sent a taxi for her and she's on her way as we speak."

I continued, "When we're finished here, call her cell phone. Say you have to cancel. You have urgent business at the embassy. If her phone's not working, call the restaurant and tell her. That will cover you with your British friends. Do you understand?"

He looked at the restaurant phone number, then at me. "Yes."

"Now, to business. I should tell you that we—you and I—want the same things, to preserve the freedoms of the West and to protect Russia from plunder by Putin and the oligarchs. Therefore, I won't use any of the information you give me to harm Russians, British, or Americans."

"Are you CIA?"

"No. I represent a well-financed group of American patriots who want to know if the allegations in the Ironside Dossier are true."

"How do I know that you don't want to discredit the dossier?"

"American fake news media are already doing a good job of that, don't you think?"

His eyes searched mine for something. I guess he found it. "What do you want to know?"

"Tell me about your meetings with Jeffery Ironside in 2016." That was a guess.

"I don't know any Jeffrey Ironside."

Here we go again. Ironside's face had been around the world in papers and on TV.

"Our time together is limited. Please don't waste it. Even if you didn't talk to him, you would know who he is. His face has been on television constantly regarding the dossier's allegations of President Walldrum's ties to Russia. I'm sure that's a topic of interest at the Russian Embassy. Should I call your ambassador to confirm it?"

Kulik sighed. "That won't be necessary. I met with Ironside. I didn't know his name until I saw him later on the television news."

"Did you meet here, in the hotel?"

"No. The secretary and I spent a romantic weekend in the city of Bath. That was the cover story for Ironside to interview me."

"Why did he come to see you?"

"He knew that I worked in Putin's office, the Presidential Administration. It is similar to the West Wing of your White House."

"How much time did Ironside spend with you?"

"About four hours."

I had fifty minutes. I needed to establish priorities. "In your meetings, what subjects were of most interest to him?"

"He wanted to know about the FSB's dossier containing *kompromat*—compromising information—on Walldrum that could be used to blackmail him."

"Did he know about the compromising dossier before he talked with you?"

"Yes."

He knew because Bogdanovich had briefed him.

Kulik continued, "Ironside wanted to know if the dossier existed or if it was FSB disinformation. If it was real, what did it look like? Where was it located? Who maintained it, and so forth?"

"What did you tell him?"

"The dossier exists. I have seen it. I have not read it."

"How do you know it was Walldrum's if you didn't read it?"

Kulik paused and lit a cigarette, maybe taking time to gather his thoughts, or compose a lie. "When I worked in the Presidential Administration, I assisted the—you would call him—staff secretary. Most documents that went to Putin crossed the secretary's desk. I saw many of them, but there were documents the secretary did not control or see. Two, in particular, were the dossiers on Ted Walldrum and his opponent in the election. They were controlled by Petrov, Putin's spokesman. Petrov kept the dossiers in his safe and removed them only when Putin directed him to do so. Petrov, himself, would carry the dossiers to Putin's office. The only other times they were out of the safe was when documents were being added."

"The dossiers were not updated electronically?"

"No. I was told there are no digital copies of these two dossiers. Putin is afraid that your NSA might hack into our computer system and destroy them."

Tony-D opened the door and pointed to his watch. The taxi carrying Sydney Swope-Soames in circles was getting close to the restaurant. My time with Kulik was running out.

"If you didn't read Walldrum's dossier, how do you know it exists?"

"One Friday, Putin was reviewing the dossiers. He was also preparing for a trip, but he was called away for an emergency meeting on some military matter—Syria, I think. Petrov was away from his desk. So, the dossiers remained in Putin's office, awaiting Petrov's return. Putin did not return to his office. He sent an aide to collect documents for his trip. The aide took everything on Putin's desk, including the dossiers. He went to the airport and accompanied Putin on a flight with the dossiers in a case chained to his wrist. The problem was the dossiers were marked to be handled only by Petrov and were not to be taken out of the Presidential Administration. Putin's aide had ignored the markings.

"When Petrov returned to his office, he received a phone call from Putin instructing him to secure the dossiers in the safe. Petrov searched Putin's office, but couldn't find them. He panicked. We had to stop work and search for the dossiers. Of course, Petrov had to tell us what we were searching for and he showed us a copy of the special cover attached to such dossiers. That is how I was made aware of their existence."

Kulik described the cover in detail and continued his story. "When the dossiers were not found, security was called. The office was locked down. We were interrogated and searched. Petrov was beside himself. He threatened us, but I think he feared what would happen to *himself* when he told Putin the dossiers were missing. Hours later, Putin called to say he had the dossiers. That was a happy ending for everyone, except Putin's aide. We never saw him again, only his replacement."

That story accounted for two dossiers. There could be others. Ironside reported that Walldrum was supplying Putin information on Russian oligarchs' businesses in the States. I played a hunch. "Are dossiers on oligarchs also kept by the Presidential Administration?"

"Yes. They are kept in an archives office, staffed with FSB personnel. Special permission is required to enter. My superior would call the archives and ask for the dossier on a certain oligarch. The FSB officer would bring the file to my superior, who would take it to Putin's office immediately. Dossiers could not be left unattended."

Time was running out. I had to focus Kulik on what I needed. "Ironside's dossier made reference to a number of sources, some in the Kremlin, Russian Foreign Ministry, intelligence agencies, and among émigrés. Do you know the names of those sources?"

Kulik said, reluctantly, "No."

I was about to remind him that we could expose his relationship with MI6, when my security timekeeper knocked again, stuck his head in, and held up his wristwatch.

"Are there sources in Russia who would help me verify the Ironside allegations?"

Kulik stalled, grinding out his cigarette, maybe trying to decide how much to tell me. "I am concerned that Russians will die if I answer that question."

"Freedom may die if you don't. Isn't that why you talked to Ironside? Isn't that why you put yourself in danger by offering your services to MI6?"

He studied me with sad eyes before admitting, "Inside the kleptocracy that is stealing Russian resources, there are good men and women who risk their lives to work against Putin, the oligarchs, the secret police, and the mafia. They are a secret society." He gave me a tired smile and added, "We Russians are drawn to secret organizations. One such organization is the Omega Group, or simply Omega. Some members, like me, hold positions of trust within organs of the state. Ironside asked me how to contact Omega."

"What did you tell him?"

"There is a market in Moscow. You go to a certain shop during the same hour for two consecutive days. You carry a certain shopping bag and you buy something. If you are not being followed, someone will contact you. The contact might happen in the market or elsewhere. It will be somewhere in the open while you are walking. In Moscow, you must assume there are microphones everywhere, even on park benches." I wrote down the remaining contact procedures as Kulik dictated them.

I asked, "Is there a procedure for contacting this Omega Group in other cities?"

"No. You must make contact in Moscow. If you are going to other cities, your Moscow contact will tell you how to contact Omega at your destination."

"What about St. Petersburg?"

"St. Petersburg is difficult for Omega. It is Putin's hometown. He was deputy mayor there in the 1980s. Putin has many allies there, many admirers, much as Mussolini is still admired in parts of Northern Italy. They say, 'He is a bad boy, but he is our boy.'"

"Was Ironside going to Russia after he talked to you?"

"Where else would you go in pursuit of the truth, if not to the heart of the lies?"

At that moment, Tony-D burst into the room. "Screwup. Our taxi driver called. Juliet got her phone working. She's sending someone here to see if Romeo showed for lunch."

CHAPTER 14

THERE IS A saying among combat veterans that the battle plan goes out the window when the first shot is fired. That's not always true, but it's a reminder that if success depends on everything going according to plan, you're planning for failure. You're planning for a miserable failure if success rests on precision timing and the dependability of twenty-first-century electronics—as my Romeo interview did. The immunization against failure is to have a Plan B. I had one.

The success of my plan depended on keeping Juliet away from a phone until the cab dropped her at the new luncheon rendezvous. So, I had gamed Plan B, in case she got phone access en route. She had. In her place, I'd call Romeo to verify that he changed the lunch location. No answer? I would proceed to the new location. Romeo might have another thumb drive to drop off. I would also call my MI6 colleagues and send them to see if Romeo was at the hotel. This scenario and Plan B required that I give Kulik a new set of instructions to save himself.

"MI6 will be here soon to see if you kept your usual meeting schedule. Don't lie to them. Go down to the restaurant. Call your lunch date. Tell her you're here. Ask where she is. Tell her you have a problem. Of course, you won't discuss it on the phone. When MI6 shows up, tell the truth. There was a key for you at the desk. You came up to the room. You were met by a fellow with a British accent, but you think he was an American. He had security men with him. He asked you about the Ironside interview. They will be suspicious. Don't lie. They will check to see who reserved this room, who sent the cab, everything. Sometime soon, they may give you a polygraph test. If you fail, everything you give them afterward will be suspect."

My final instruction to Kulik was, "Tell your MI6 handlers that if they try to find me, I'll expose you to the Russians."

I wouldn't do that. In any event, I knew my threat wouldn't keep MI6 from trying to track me down, but it would give them pause. By the time they decided what to do and how, I'd be on my way to St. Petersburg.

Kulik went down to the restaurant. We headed for our respective hotels.

* * *

When I opened the door to my hotel room, Viktor Lukovsky was sitting cross-legged on the couch. His hair was out of the ponytail and down on his collar. He was wearing a charcoal gray suit with chalk stripes, and a paisley tie. Ivan—Mr. Silent-but-deadly—was sitting in a chair by the window. There was a large sample case on the floor at his feet. When I entered, Ivan stood up slowly and positioned himself between me and Viktor, but to one side. Viktor gave him the slightest nod. Ivan took his sample case and departed.

On the end table beside the couch, I saw an empty shot glass next to an empty miniature whiskey bottle from my cabinet. What riveted my attention was the leather-bound gun box on Viktor's lap, the one from his yacht. There was an envelope on the couch. Viktor picked it up and offered it to me. I walked to him, took it, and read the card inside. Written in block letters were Tatyana Kedrova's name and St. Petersburg address.

"Thank you, Viktor."

"Thank me when you get back . . . if you get back. You going to dangerous world. You sure you want to do this?"

"I have to."

Viktor gave me a long, speculative look before he popped the top on his gun box. My heart stopped. Instead of a pistol, he withdrew another envelope and handed it to me. "Something to keep you safe."

I looked at the red wax seal. "What's this?"

"You know Russian tattoos?"

"No," I lied.

"Not necessary for you to know. *They* will know. My phone number is in there. You get into shit you can't handle, give them that envelope. Tell them call me, collect."

In the Russian underworld, tattoos separate the bad asses from the jackasses. I was getting a safe conduct pass from a mafia don. "Thank you, again."

He waved off my thanks. "You get your ass killed, my mother's going to be disappointed in both of us." With, sadness he added, "But life is full of disappointments."

Viktor snapped his gun box shut and gave me a look that was chilling. "When you eat and drink on my boat, you leave lots of DNA. I keep some samples. A friend in St. Petersburg get sample of Tatyana Kedrova's DNA. I had lab here in London compare your DNA to DNA from Tatyana. Guess what. They don't match."

Viktor collected his gun box and got up from the couch. He walked to me and stood uncomfortably close to deliver his conclusions. "So, your father lied to you . . . or you lied to me. Either way, you're fucked . . . *Ricky.*"

CHAPTER 15

I SHOULD HAVE been happy or, at least, grateful. Viktor Lukovsky, my new fairy mobfather, had taken time from his busy schedule of money laundering—or whatever it was the Brits couldn't nail him for—to bring me the location of a source and a written guarantee of safe passage through the Russian underworld. Instead of gratitude, I felt anger. Seeing Viktor in my hotel room, sitting on my couch, and drinking my whiskey reminded me of my bad old days in Russia. When I was assigned to Moscow Station, we lived with one overriding reality, the suffocating intrusiveness of the FSB. They would enter your home when you were out, bug it, and leave you little reminders that you had no privacy, usually something out of place or broken. Unless you were in the embassy SCIF—secure compartmented information facility—you had to assume that you were always bugged, recorded, and photographed by the FSB.

It was clear from the mismatched DNA and his goodbye warning that Viktor didn't trust me. Naturally, he would want to know what I was up to. Which brought me to Ivan and his sample case. Had he forgotten to open it and show me his collection of shrunken heads, or was the case a bugging tool kit? A prudent deduction was that Viktor and Ivan had bugged my hotel suite while waiting for me to arrive.

We should have left London that night, because threats to my operation were multiplying. By now, MI6 had my description from Kulik, and the police would be trying to find the crew that burglarized Ironside's home-office. Ironside would have guessed burglars were looking for his sources. He would have gone to Dumfries to check on Colonel Bogdanovich—alias, Lucas Novak. The colonel would have given him descriptions of Sherri and me, which Ironside would have passed to MI6 and, maybe, the police. If that was not enough bad news, Viktor might be having second thoughts about helping me. If so, he could be planning another meeting for Sherri and me aboard his yacht, more likely, under it. The only reason for staying in London was to get a briefing from Rodney on how to meet our Baltic cruise body doubles in St. Petersburg.

In light of these threats, we had to take precautions for our safety. Sherri divided her "band" into two surveillance teams, one to follow her and one to follow me, when we were on the streets. They couldn't intervene directly if the police were on our tails, but they could warn us and discreetly help us avoid capture. Or so we thought.

Another obvious precaution was to relocate. Viktor would be looking for me at the Savoy, and one of the police lines of inquiry would begin with foreign hotel guests who checked in around the date of the burglary. Also, if Viktor had bugged my Savoy suite, I didn't want to plan the St. Petersburg trip with him listening.

After Viktor left my suite, I departed, too. Taking nothing but my hat, overcoat, and scarf, I exited the hotel. On the way out, I gave the concierge a message for Rodney, telling him that I was relocating and where. Assuring myself that I was not tailed, I checked into a downscale hotel several blocks from the Savoy. The desk clerk gave me a "no luggage?" look as he handed over my key. I made two calls from my room. The first was to Sherri to give her my new address and tell her to relocate with her team. The second was to Jill, inviting her to a meal in my new hotel's restaurant.

Over dinner, I told Jill, "A problem developed. I solved it by relocating our team." I didn't tell her that Viktor might have bugged my rooms at the Savoy. "Don't go to my suite. I want us to have as few visible connections as possible. Have a bellhop pack my belongings and take them to you in the lobby. Check both of us out and pay my bill. Go to the train station, switch cabs, and come here."

"What's going on, Max?"

"You don't have a need to know."

Jill was angry. "I helped you pull off the Romeo interview, didn't I? Why are you keeping me in the dark?"

I was still smoldering over Viktor's uninvited visit to my hotel and I remembered that Jill followed me when I went to meet Rodney. I blasted her. "I told you when we met that you were an intern. So, you're out of the loop until I need you to speak Russian, shoot somebody, or kick my ass."

"You may not have long to wait for the last two." Glaring daggers at me, she got up and left the restaurant.

Ah, the joys of command.

*　*　*

Hours later, Jill arrived and checked into the adjoining room I reserved for her. There was a noticeable chill in her demeanor. We unpacked our belongings and went to bed without a goodnight kiss. Jill locked the door connecting our rooms.

While I waited for Rodney to brief me, Jill and I needed to get to know each other well enough to pass as husband and wife. In the event we were subjected to a cursory interrogation by Russian authorities, we had to be able to answer questions like, "What color is your husband's eyes?" or "What is your wife's favorite color?" If we couldn't answer questions like that for, say, an immigration officer, we were headed for a serious interrogation by the FSB.

If we were going to do this right, I had to heal the rift with Jill. So, the next day, over lunch in my room I told her, "Internship is over, but we need an understanding. I have nothing personal against you, but you were a surprise. I don't like surprises. Bowen could have told me you were going to be his cutout. When people make unannounced changes on an operation like this, I wonder if I know their real game plan."

"Just what kind of operation is this, Max?"

Either she really didn't know or she was playing me. "Whatever Bowen told you, this ain't no research project and he's probably not paying you enough. You're involved in an investigation that could get you locked up in three countries. I kept you in the dark so that if you got caught, you'd have deniability." That was partially true. I just didn't trust Jill Rucker, for reasons I couldn't explain.

"I can't give you that protection any longer. We're going to Russia with fake IDs to interview people who might not want to be interviewed and we could encounter people who might try to stop us. We could get killed by the Russian mafia, or locked up, tortured, and shot by the FSB. If that bothers you, now would be a good time to buy a ticket home. If you stay, I'll assume that you're committed to the mission and you're on my team."

"Who else is going in with us?"

"At this point, it's better if you don't know."

She nodded her agreement.

*   *   *

As the days passed, we took most of our meals together, but kept the talk small and nonintrusive. Jill stopped locking the door between our rooms and we moved back and forth freely when it was open. I discovered that Jill was from Chicago and learned Russian from her grandparents, who lived into their nineties.

There were a few times when we strayed from our false bios and she let me see behind her woman-of-mystery façade. On one occasion, we were having a drink in her room after a long day of sightseeing together followed by a heavy dinner. She was relaxed.

I asked, "What was that fatmouth about when we met? You can 'kick my ass'?"

"You were rude. I had to draw a line. Besides, I do have a black belt in karate." She stuck out her chin, as if daring me to throw a punch at it.

"What's a girl like you doing in a belt like that?"

My question must have revived an unpleasant memory. Jill got a fierce, faraway look in her eyes. "In high school, I was a cheerleader for the football team. The players wanted my body, but didn't want to ask. So, I got the belt." She released that memory and gave me a faint smile. "Call it a black chastity belt."

"Did you do any damage?"

Her smile broadened. "Enough to get kicked off the cheerleading squad and referred to counseling for 'aggressive tendencies.'"

"After high school?"

"The Army. I volunteered for airborne and became a parachute rigger."

"Was that a good outlet for your aggressive tendencies?"

"Hoo-yah, master sergeant!" She laughed from her gut, a first with me. "After the Army?"

The smile disappeared. "Sorry, you're not cleared for that."

"What about now?"

"Now, I'm on your team."

That was too cute.

She tilted her head to one side. "What about you?"

"I didn't play high school football, if that's what you're asking." Both of us smiled. "I went to college and joined the Navy after." That wasn't true, but I knew enough about the Navy to fake it, if she had questions. "After the Navy, I worked in private security." That was partially true at the moment, but mostly a lie.

"And . . . ?"

"Sorry, you're not cleared for that." That ended our verbal self-disclosures.

There were other disclosures that didn't require words. Before and after our personal revelations, I had seen Jill in the hotel pool. She was a smooth swimmer and lifted herself out of the water with powerful-looking arms and shoulders that had just enough muscle definition to make her attractive. She had a generous chest, flat stomach, and nice legs, with the exception of her calves. They were like muscular bowling pins, hard-looking, with sharp definition. I assumed that was why she always wore pants.

Jill had an attractive face to match her body. It was framed by short, thick, blond hair. Her eyes seemed to peer out at you from some knowing place and gave the impression that she could read your mind. The defining feature was a wide, wicked smile. I could see why those high school football team hormones went into overdrive. Truth be told, my hormones weren't exactly oblivious in her presence. Jill Rucker was a babe.

The morning after my peek into Jill's real world, I checked at the hotel desk. There was a note from Rodney. We met at the usual place in Trafalgar Square and went to his safe house. Over breakfast, Rodney gave me the passports that would get Jill and me into Russia, the fake FSB IDs I had requested, and a briefing packet of details—burn after reading.

"Tell me about the couple we swap identities with when we get to St. Petersburg."

Rodney cleared his throat. That was his "tell" that things were screwed up. When he smiled, I knew things were really screwed up. "We're having trouble finding a double handsome enough to replace you."

"You don't have a couple yet, do you?"

"I'm working on it. It's complicated. It's not like walking into an alley with a Russian on your tail and giving your coat to another guy who diverts the tail, while you hide behind the trash bin."

"I don't care about the complications. What happens if we get to St. Petersburg and you haven't finished *working on it?*"

My attitude irritated him. "In that case, you take the advice of the Marine Corps: 'adapt, improvise, and overcome.'"

I had no intention of walking away with a non-answer like that. If we disappeared from the tours or the ship without doubles to substitute for us, the Russians would be on our tails within hours. I stared at Rodney until he told me his plan.

"The first stop on your cruise is Tallinn, Estonia. Meet me at the Café Kinsky. It's a couple of blocks east of the cruise terminal. Come as early as you can and come alone. I'll have things sorted out by then. If not, you'll have to abort or find another way in."

Peering at me over his coffee cup rim, Rodney asked casually, "Any exfil plans?" Rodney was asking if I had an exfiltration plan to get Jill and me out of Russia.

"Depends on what you tell me in Tallinn." I was deliberately vague. I had a plan, but Rodney didn't have a need to know, and the less he knew about it the more secure I felt. He already knew too much.

*   *   *

Back at the hotel, I spent the afternoon with Jill finalizing plans for the cruise to St. Petersburg. Our ship was scheduled to sail from

Stockholm in two days. We were going to fly to the Swedish port the following afternoon.

As for Sherri, my original plan was to have her and Tony-D fly to St. Petersburg as our security and backup, then, follow us on to Moscow. After Kulik told me about the Omega Group, another plan formed in my mind. I went to Sherri's hotel and briefed her and Tony-D on their roles for the Russia trip.

"After Jill and I leave for Stockholm tomorrow, I want you to fly to Moscow and make contact with this Omega Group." I explained the contact procedure as Kulik described it. "Tell them I'm coming to Moscow to verify the details of the Walldrum dossier. I need to talk to these people"—I gave Sherri a list—"and anyone else with firsthand knowledge of Walldrum's business dealings and sexual misconduct. If Omega is for real, I want them to locate the sources, do a reconnaissance, and tell me the best time and place to conduct a private interview. I don't want any other Russians present."

After everyone was briefed, we decided to split the teams and go out for our last night of London R and R. I was going to tighten the bond with my new, make-believe wife, Jill Rucker. One of Sherri's security guys was watching our backs. Sherri and Tony-D went to a play, with the other two members of our security team watching them for tails.

Before we went out for the evening, I called Claudia. It's crazy how you can want to be with someone and, at the same time, be mad as hell at them. That's how I felt about Claudia. She had ruined my career at the CIA, but the work tempo in London had hit a lull and I missed her. Weeks had passed since I arrived in England and I had not called her on purpose. Strangely, I felt the need to call her before I hit the streets with Jill.

"Hello?" Claudia answered.

"It's me. I miss you."

"You should improve your aim." She *didn't* say, "I miss you, too, lots." Instead she asked, "Are you on your way home?"

"Not yet."

"Where are you?"

"Here."

"Oh. There, again." That was a jab at my work absences for the Agency.

"How are you?" I asked.

"Fine." She was, too—a former beauty queen, and with brains enough to study law. Which raised the question, *why was she with me?* That mystery teased my mind as our conversation meandered through banalities.

Finally, I closed with, "See you soon," thinking, *if the Russians don't catch me.*

Her parting words, with a hint of detachment, were, "Take care of yourself."

*   *   *

After taking in a show together, Jill Rucker and I had a late dinner at an Indian restaurant. We were walking the few blocks to our hotel on a street with little vehicle or foot traffic. The sidewalk was narrow. A couple approached us, arm-in-arm. As we got closer to them, I sensed movement behind us. I glanced to the side. My peripheral vision picked up another arm-in-arm couple. They were close, too close.

I yelled to warn Jill and pivoted to face the pair behind us. The woman lunged for Jill. The man was bringing his arm down, aiming a blackjack at my head. I ducked, blocked the blow with my left forearm, and kicked hard to my rear, catching the guy from the other couple in the gut.

Jill shouted and another woman screamed. Go, karate!

I had blocked the blow to my head, but the guy with the blackjack was fast. He threw an uppercut with his left hand that snapped my head back. I couldn't stop his follow-up blow with the blackjack. My head exploded with pain and my knees turned to jelly. From behind, someone dropped a bag over my head and two guys threw me into a van. Before the sliding door slammed shut, I heard a woman yell, "Don't let that bitch get away!" There was pain in her voice. Jill must have done some damage. I struggled to get away, too, but went down for the count when I took another blow to my head.

When I came to, the van was rolling to a quiet stop. The driver's door opened and closed. I heard him walk around to the van's sliding door. It opened and the driver and the guy with the blackjack dragged me out of the vehicle and into a building. Wormwood Scrubbs came to mind, but I didn't hear prison sounds.

I estimated there were five people on the snatch team: a driver and the two couples. One couple and the woman in pain had taken off after Jill. That left the driver and a man from one of the couples. So, the odds were just two to one against me, if I didn't count the blackjack. I might have a chance against two kidnappers, unless there were more in the building.

They didn't tie me to a chair. They threw me on the floor and emptied my pockets. I could hear my pocket litter being dumped onto a table. Someone went through it while one of the guys from the van kept a foot pressed into my back. I assumed that someone gave a nonverbal signal. Two men picked me up and shoved me into a chair. One of them ripped the bag off my head. I was in the warehouse where my team had gone through the take from Ironside's office, home, and garage. Ironside, himself, was sitting in a chair facing mine, less than two feet away. The two guys who had dragged me from the van took up positions behind my chair, out of my field of vision.

Ironside peered at me as though he was looking at a strange specimen in biology class. "Max Geller." He shook his head slowly. "Have you lost your bloody mind?"

That was a rhetorical question. I looked around the room. In the far corner to my right, Tommy Leeds, my contract burglar, sat handcuffed to a chair. He was bruised and his clothes were in disarray. Behind Ironside, a man and woman leaned against the wall with their arms folded. They had positioned themselves for an unobstructed view of me while I answered Ironside's questions. I didn't recognize the man, but the woman was definitely Kulik's make-believe lover and MI6 contact, Sydney Swope-Soames.

Ironside asked, "Why did the CIA have you break into my place? What were you looking for?"

"I didn't break into your place." Technically, that was true, but one of the van guys slapped me hard with the blackjack. I saw stars.

Ironside turned and looked at Tommy, who addressed me. "I'm sorry, mate, but I warned you this couldn't come back to me."

Again, Ironside asked, "What does the CIA want from me?"

"I don't know. I don't work for the Agency anymore." I figured that would slow the interrogation and give me time to come up with a strategy.

My statement surprised everyone, except Ironside, who didn't miss a beat. He came right back at me. "Going the plausible denial route, are we?"

"No. I was fired a month ago for writing bad opinions of President Walldrum in an office email. I'm a freelancer, trying to verify the dossier allegations." That was the truth . . . almost. It was also consistent with what I told Bogdanovich, and Ironside would have questioned the colonel by then.

My free agent claim did slow things down. Ironside looked over his shoulder at Swope-Soames, who snapped her fingers at the man on the wall. He unholstered his cell phone, went into the office, and closed the door.

Ironside said to me, "So you had Tommy burglarize my place to get my sources?"

"No, Tommy offered the material. He knew what I was doing. He contacted me and said he could provide documents that would help. I didn't know how he had come by them."

"He's a bloody liar!" shouted Tommy.

I was, but Tommy had rolled over on me. Turnabout was fair play. Screw him.

Ironside stayed focused. "How did you find Bogdanovich's address?"

"Who is Bogdanovich?"

The guy behind my chair hit me hard enough to make my nose bleed.

Ironside gave me his handkerchief. "You visited the defector, Vasili Bogdanovich, and threatened to give him to the SVR. Are you working for the Russians?"

"Of course not. Come on, Jeffrey. We worked the Russians together. Why would you accuse me of being a traitor?"

Swope-Soames came off the wall with ice in her voice. "Enough! We know you're a traitor because two of our Russian assets were killed almost immediately after talking to you." She walked over to my chair, the harsh lights bouncing off her black leather jacket, pants, and boots. A black turtleneck sweater completed her sinister attire.

Swope-Soames took over my interrogation. "Bogdanovich told us that you questioned him and threatened to reveal his whereabouts to the Russians, if he didn't keep silent about it. He didn't and you burned him."

"I don't know any Bogdanovich."

"We have digital video and voice recordings of you and a female companion interrogating Bogdanovich at his home in Dumfries."

I didn't think so. If they had recordings, they would have played them for me to cut through my bullshit. She was bluffing. I said, "I don't know what you're talking about."

"Did you know that Bogdanovich and his daughter were attacked with a military-grade nerve agent last night? That's a Russian trademark hit."

The guy with the cell phone returned to the room and nodded "yes" to Swope-Soames. Someone had verified my departure from the CIA.

"What do you know about Boris Kulik?" she asked.

"Never heard of him."

"Really? Kulik was our London-based asset at the Russian Embassy, *was* being the relevant word. Thursday, last, your escaped dinner companion lured me away from my meeting with Kulik, allowing you to interrogate him in the hotel suite. You threatened to expose him to the Russians if he revealed your conversation. A few days later, he was recalled to Moscow, briefly tortured, and executed at Lubyanka Prison. Are you seeing the pattern we see? You threaten. People you threaten refuse to do your bidding. You give them up to the Russians. They die."

She craned her neck in my direction. "I want to know how many other MI6 assets you've compromised and how you identified them. I want to know right now. If you and friend, Tommy"—she shot him a glance—"do not give me what I want this night, both of you are going to vanish without a trace."

She looked over my shoulder and raised her chin. The blackjack hit the side of my head so hard I heard an explosion, but it wasn't my head exploding.

Besides the loading dock door, the warehouse had two exterior doors, one at either end of the building. Both exploded inward simultaneously. I dropped to the floor. My first thoughts were: *Here comes the cavalry! Good old Sherri!*

Two masked men ran into the room through each entrance. They weren't Sherri's cavalry, because they were firing Russian PP-09-01 submachine guns with integrated silencers. The teams moved into the room, firing their weapons in short bursts. When the shooting stopped, they had taken down everyone but me and Tommy. He had broken free from one arm of his chair. Tommy must have figured he was a goner, because he swung the remains of his chair at the nearest gunman. The guy dropped him with two chest shots. As the shooter was putting a third bullet into Tommy's head, another member of the hit crew screamed, in Russian, "No, you idiot! We wanted him alive!"

They wanted me alive, too. For the second time that night, someone dropped a bag over my head, while another someone flex-cuffed my hands. Then, two guys grabbed my arms and pushed me outside. The night air hit me and we took a few steps. Then, I heard a quick succession of "thunk-splat-scream" noises. It sounded like people were getting shot with silenced weapons. The men on either side released my arms and I heard their bodies hit the pavement. I followed them down to avoid the gunfire. A few seconds later, someone stood me up and ripped the bag off my head. It was Jill Rucker.

She smiled. "I just shot somebody. Now, all I have to do to complete my internship is speak Russian, and kick your ass, *nyet*?"

Jill cut off my flex cuffs and hustled me away from the warehouse to a stand of trees concealing our Mercedes sedan and the phony DSL truck. Behind us, I could hear muffled shots and shouts as my cavalry tidied up the Russians.

Minutes later, the "heavy metal band" came running. The four of them sped away in the truck. Tony-D took the wheel of the Mercedes and blasted us out of the trees. Over his shoulder he said, with disgust, "One of the damned Russians got away, but we got photos of the others."

"Any survivors?" I asked.

"Not now," replied Tony-D.

"How did you find me?"

Tony-D explained. "Nick was shadowing you and Jill, as planned. When the kidnappers grabbed you, Nick followed them. Jill got away and alerted the team. Nick called and told us they were holding you in the warehouse. We came to the rescue, but the Russians were already there, surrounding the building. We let them go in."

"They could've killed me."

"They didn't," was Tony-D's matter-of-fact reply.

"Where's Sherri?"

"She's moving us out of our hotels and taking our bags to the airport."

"What's the plan?"

"She wants the team out of London tonight. We'll take the chartered jet and drop you and Jill in Stockholm. The rest of us will take the charter from Stockholm to an airport in Eastern Europe." He was vague for Jill's ears. "Sherri and I will fly commercial to Moscow. The rest of the team will fly the charter to the States. By the time the Brits and Russians figure out they're after the same crew, we'll be vapor."

CHAPTER 16

AT HEATHROW AIRPORT, our team boarded the executive jet Sherri had chartered and we took off for Stockholm. We were in close quarters, but there wasn't much talk. The warehouse shootout and escape made all of us murderers or accomplices. After Stockholm, we were going our separate ways for different purposes. No one needed to know more about the man or woman next to him than he did already.

Stockholm was colder than London, but, thankfully, there was no police heat awaiting us when we arrived. After we pulled into the hangar, I took Sherri aside.

"Thanks for Plan B. Sorry you got involved with the rough stuff."

She shrugged. "We've been here before with the Russians, but interfering with MI6 . . . That worries me."

"It's too late for worry. I have some tasks for you." I gave her the sat phone Rodney had loaned me for emergencies. "Send this and my computer back to the States with one of your guys. I don't think they'll help us in Russia." I added, "Tony-D took mug shots of the Russian-speakers who grabbed me from MI6. Before my computer leaves for the States, use it to send those photos to Rodney for IDs."

"Who's Rodney?"

"The guy who emailed us background on Bogdanovich. Also, I need you to confirm my meeting with Rodney. It's scheduled for three days from now, early morning, at the Café Kinsky near the cruise terminal in Tallinn, Estonia." Tallinn was the first stop on our cruise and the last one before St. Petersburg. "Tell him to call me on the cruise ship if there's a change."

"More?"

"Do a background check on Jill Rucker . . . and I still need one on Bowen. Bring whatever you have on them to Moscow.

"Last task. When you get to Moscow, remember to contact the Omega Group. Ask if they can find us a safe house and the people on that witness list I gave you."

"Won't they check with Ironside?"

"He bought it when the Russians hit the warehouse."

Sherri looked worried. "How reliable is the skinny on this Omega Group? I don't want hard time in Lubyanka Prison any more than I wanted it in Wormwood Scrubs."

"I got it from a MI6 asset, but be careful. He's dead and the FSB has a talent for infiltrating opposition organizations."

The worried look didn't vanish. Sherri said, "Max, you shouldn't use your hotel reservation here. MI6 might pick it up. Let me send Nick to town with you. He didn't leave a paper trail in London. He'll pay for a room in his name. You and Jill can hole up there until your cruise sails for St. Petersburg."

Jill, Nick, and I took a cab into Stockholm. Nick got us into a hotel near the cruise terminal. Exhausted, Jill and I collapsed on our beds as soon as we got to the room. It was the letdown that followed the adrenaline high of my kidnapping and rescue.

During the next thirty-six hours, we kept a low profile: no mission discussions, no unnecessary interaction with hotel staff, all meals consumed away from the hotel, and everything paid for in cash. Otherwise, we stayed in the room and read novels or Russian grammar books to brush up on our language skills.

Eighteen hours into this routine, I was bored and in need of conversation and information. Propped up against the headboard of my bed, Jill against hers, I asked, "Did you tell Bowen you were going to Russia with me?"

Jill looked up from her Russian language novel. "Yes."

"What did he say?"

"Don't go."

"Why?"

"He said I could support you better from London."

I suggested another reason. "What he meant was, if I asked you for support and you had to call him to arrange it, the Russians could trace your call to his doorstep."

"I'm sure that was on his mind."

"What did you say?"

"I told him I was going to Russia with you, posing as your wife, and I wanted hazardous duty pay."

"Hazardous duty pay because of the Russians or me?"

"Both." She didn't smile.

I laughed. "Did he give you instructions?"

This time, she smiled mischievously. "He told me that I was just your make-believe wife and not to sleep with you. He said you had enough problems at home already."

"And you said . . . ?"

"I hung up." Jill went back to her novel.

I went to wondering how Bowen knew that Claudia and I were having problems . . . and why he told Jill.

*   *   *

The next noon, we took a cab to the Stockholm cruise terminal. With only carry-on luggage, we quickly processed aboard our ship, along with a thousand other passengers. Our roomy balcony cabin had double beds, a Jill Rucker request. We unpacked and settled down to enjoy a bottle of champagne, provided by the thoughtful staff. A few hours later, we sailed into a gloomy Baltic evening. Our Russian adventure had begun.

As in the Stockholm hotel, we maintained a low profile, keeping to our cabin and taking meals at the buffet. Our goal was that passengers and staff would have only a vague recollection of us after we jumped ship in St. Petersburg. Our first night on the water was the Stockholm-to-Tallinn run. After dinner, we read in our cabin until boredom overtook us again.

Jill broke the silence. "Lawyers make lousy domestic partners, Max. They work long hours and they speak a language designed to confuse us mortals."

"How did you know my girlfriend was a lawyer?"

"You talk in your sleep."

"I do not."

"How do you know, if you're asleep?"

"I record all activities in my bedroom."

Jill laughed. "Got any hot footage? I'll post it on the Internet and make you a star."

"What makes you think I'm not already a star in my little world?"

"According to Bowen, you and your lady lawyer aren't getting along. Most couples fight about money and sex. Which is it with you two?"

That was none of her business, but I wasn't going to say sex was a problem. "I lost my job last month."

"Well," she said, "if your lawyer leaves you, you won't have trouble finding a replacement. You're smart, fit, and good-looking."

I'm also going to be ten million dollars richer in a few weeks and I have a finely tuned bullshit detector, Ms. Rucker, but do continue.

She didn't. Instead, she announced, "I'm going to take a shower."

The running shower provided soothing background noise while I studied a street map of St. Petersburg, located Tatyana Kedrova's house, and checked a city guidebook for transportation and communications. I was using the documents to plot possible escape routes—if we needed them—when the shower noise ceased along with my interest in planning. My cruise hormones kicked in and I began to imagine Jill Rucker toweling her tanned, athletic body.

I didn't have long to imagine. The bathroom door opened and Jill walked out, naked from head to waist. She wore a towel, knotted below her navel, that covered her from hips to ankles. She hadn't dried herself completely and little droplets of water clung tantalizingly to her flesh, especially her lovely breasts.

I was sitting on the side of my bed facing Jill's. She sat down facing me across the short distance between us defined by the nightstand. She undid the knot and smoothed the towel out under her, presumably to keep her naked, damp bottom from wetting the bed. She gave me a silent, "So?" with raised eyebrows.

I watched as she bent over to clip her toenails. Her breasts were tight orbs that hardly moved as she leaned forward. Water droplets slid down from her shoulders, ran to her nipples, and plopped onto the carpet. I believe I counted them as I thought, *This is going to be one long freakin' night.*

After clipping all ten toenails, Jill sat up, crossed her legs, leaned back on her hands, and looked at me. She wasn't a bit put off by my eyes playing over her body. Maybe it was black belt confidence.

"How would you rate our chances of coming out of this in one piece—make that two pieces?" She gave me a little smile.

"Honestly, if I was a betting man, I'd bet on the other side."

"Why?"

"Too many maybes. Maybe we find the people we're looking for. Maybe they won't talk to us. Maybe the Russian mob or Russian police will get us."

She nodded her understanding. "Tomorrow night is prep for combat and rest?"

"Yeah."

"Well, since this is our last free night, let's not waste it." Jill Rucker got up from her bed and stood in front of me. I was looking into her navel and smelling the residue of shower gel on her body. She pulled the map from my hand and pushed me over backward on my bed. My prediction came true. It turned into one long, long night. No complaints.

*   *   *

Our ship made port in Tallinn after sunup. I left Jill sleeping and headed for my rendezvous with Rodney at the Café Kinsky, near the cruise terminal. The café was a small place that appeared to be the haunt of locals, not tourists. Rodney sat at a window table, nursing a coffee with a side of something in a schnapps glass. He looked unhappy.

Before he burdened me with his displeasure, I said, "Did you ID the photos I sent?"

"Yes. They *were* a Russian hit team. The Brits think Putin sent them to settle some old scores. Where did you get their photographs?"

"A source gave them to me."

"Did your source tell you those photographs were taken at a warehouse where Ironside, six MI6 assets, your four Russians, and one civilian were killed?" Rodney didn't wait for an answer. "The civilian had one wrist cuffed to what was left of a chair. His name was Tommy Leeds. I believe he's the fellow you used for some black bag jobs a while back. What the hell happened?"

"A misunderstanding."

"Understand this," said Rodney, lowering his voice. "The Brits have mounted a manhunt for you. They're showing a drawing of your likeness around London. They don't have your picture or real name, yet. If you want me to try and cover you, explain the misunderstanding."

Rodney had no incentive to cover me at his expense. In fact, it would be to his advantage to cut me loose if the Brits closed in, but this was my chance to set the record straight, sort of. I told Rodney, "MI6 kidnapped me. The Russians killed them and kidnapped me, again." Then, I got creative to protect my team. "The Russians put a bag over my head and were taking me out of the warehouse when someone—several someones—shot them. My new kidnappers kept the bag in place, shoved me into a car, and drove me to a field. They gave me the cell phone with photos of the Russians and told me to call a cab. I called my team instead and we flew out of the U.K. that night."

Rodney was quiet, evaluating my story. "These benefactors who rescued you from the Russians, what were their nationalities?"

"Only one spoke. He sounded like a Brit or Aussie."

"Why did he give you photographs of the dead Russians?"

"He said, 'You might want to know who's after you, mate.'"

"How generous of him." Rodney sounded skeptical.

I tried to divert him from evaluating my story. "Are the Russians looking for me?"

"There's nothing in the ether, but if they snatched you from the Brits, I assume they want you."

Rodney emptied the schnapps glass into his coffee and took a long swig. I signaled a waiter and ordered what my companion was drinking.

"How did MI6 find you?" Rodney asked.

"Tommy hit Ironside's place for me. Somehow, the Brits knew. They grabbed him and he gave me up. I'm wondering how the Brits knew about Tommy?" I figured Rodney had sources in MI6 or he had access to signal intercepts on that subject.

Rodney pursed his lips. "I think Tommy must have triggered a silent alarm during the burglary or even gotten his picture taken by a hidden camera. Maybe that's why Ironside left Ibiza in a hurry. The other possibility is that MI6 had Ironside's place under surveillance while he was in Ibiza. Either of those events would explain why MI6 sent a yacht to fetch Ironside from his vacation."

"That explains Tommy. How did the Russians find out about me?"

"Where have you been that Russians might have seen you?"

Bogdanovich's home or the meetings with Kulik and Viktor Lukovsky. I dismissed Viktor. He could have delivered me to the Russians twice, if he had wanted to.

I said, "MI6 told me Bogdanovich was dead. Maybe the hit team had his house staked out when I got there."

Rodney picked up the thread. "Or they could have had Kulik under surveillance when you hijacked him at the hotel. By the way, what did he tell you?"

That sounded like a progress report request and, with both of my London sources dead, according to MI6, I was not about to give Rodney a memory dump. "Kulik gave me nothing. I threatened to expose him to the SVR. He called my bluff."

"*Did* you expose him?"

"No." I waited for Rodney to tell me that Kulik was dead; he didn't. Curious.

Anyway, that was history. My concern was the future. "What about our doubles?"

"Are you and Jill signed up for the city tour in St. Petersburg?"

"Yes."

"When you leave the ship, be among the first on your tour to clear immigration. While you wait for the rest of your group to clear, visit the gift arcade just beyond the immigration booths. Go to the restroom.

Knock on the door of the last stall and say, 'The city tour is leaving. Are you ready?'

"Your double will reply, 'I'm with the Hermitage group.' He will come out. His coat will be on his right arm if everything is okay. You discreetly exchange passports and IDs. I suggest you have those items in a plastic bag to facilitate the handoff, and don't forget to include your ship's ID card. Go into the stall, reverse your coat, and change your hat. Presto! The deed is done."

"What's the signal to abort, if there's a problem?"

"Your double will emerge from the loo with his coat over his left shoulder. Do nothing. The next day, take the Hermitage Museum tour. Your double will contact you there, in the restroom, at the end of your tour. That's the time of maximum confusion because of the crowds."

"Does Jill follow the same procedure?"

"Yes, but, of course, she will meet her contact in the ladies' room." Rodney smiled at his little joke.

"Weapons?" I asked.

"Your double will leave a bag in his toilet stall. It will contain two FSB-issue automatics with noise suppressors, and the address of your safe house in St. Petersburg."

Peering over his coffee cup rim, Rodney asked casually, "Any exfil plans, yet?"

"No." That was the second time he had asked me if I had a plan to get out of Russia. If I had one, it was a bad idea to share it with anyone who didn't need to know.

"Is that all?" I asked.

Rodney gave me an appraising look. "Sure you're up to this, Max? You look tired. Is married life aboard ship wearing you out so soon?"

Wearing? Jill Rucker was the vigorous lover that her robust physique promised. I felt like my limbs and loins had been drained by an energy vacuum cleaner. That was another thing Rodney didn't need to know.

* * *

When I returned to the ship, the remnants of a light breakfast littered the cocktail table in our cabin. Jill Rucker was facedown on the bed and naked. I admired her body for a time and draped a towel over her torso and tapped her on the shoulder. "Time to go to work."

"Again?" She threw off the towel and rolled over, treating me to a frontal.

"Put something on. I need to brief you on our arrival routine for St. Petersburg."

She gave me a feigned disappointed pout and got dressed. I relayed what Rodney told me and we rehearsed switching identities with our doubles until every move was second nature. Then, we had lunch. Afterwards, we read some and made love, a lot.

* * *

We missed dinner. I awakened at 1:34 a.m., according to the nightstand clock. Jill was curled into the fetal position beside me, close enough for me to feel the heat from her luscious body and hear her gentle breathing. I was where she had left me, on my back and physically drained. Fortunately, the mind I lost in her embrace had returned, alert and energized. I had that wonderful sensation that my brain was disembodied, free to roam with clarity and objectivity, unimpeded by physical need. I slipped out of bed and into jeans and a sweater. The hallway outside our cabin was deserted. I made my way to the all-night snack lounge two decks below. The place was empty except for the counter man who served me a double cappuccino. I took it to a table and studied my reflection in the window that separated me from the blackness of the Baltic night and churning sea. My restless brain went to work on the *Why mes?* lurking there.

Six months ago, I had a career and a girlfriend, Vanessa, whom I wanted to marry. Before I could pop the question, my life became a roller coaster of bad luck, followed by good, followed by more bad and good. This pattern began when Vanessa, also an Agency employee, got a three-year assignment to Australia. We didn't kid ourselves. Our relationship might not survive that time-distance barrier. We said a tearful farewell and, with support from my favorite scotch, I became more of a workaholic than usual.

As time passed, my boss, Rodney, noticed—in his fluent French—my lack of *joie de vivre*. "Max, you can't moon over your lost love forever. You need to get out, meet new people. I'm having a party at my place next weekend. Be there. That's an order."

Rodney's party was not the stodgy Georgetown cocktail affair I expected. It was lively, with people my age, a disc jockey spinning platters from my youth, and lots of dancing. That's where I met Claudia. As I recall, she asked me to dance. She was—and is—a lean, mean, raven-haired, dark-eyed beauty, with great legs, interesting conversation, and excellent diction, all of which turned me on. A month later, she was a regular at my place. Two months later, she moved in. Speed dating? Anyway, it was the perfect match. Both of us had demanding schedules and liked the same things. In retrospect, that was my first "too good to be true" experience on the road to Russia.

The only thing we didn't agree on was the President of the United States. Being a lawyer, she was in the innocent-until-proven-guilty camp. I, on the other hand, was from the impeach-now-before-he-ruins-us camp. Given the sensitivity of this conflict, we agreed to confine it to our home. That was working. Unfortunately, as the president's actions got more bizarre, our arguments became more heated.

One day, thanks to Claudia, my distaste for the Leader of the Free World spilled over into my office emails. I got fired as a result. For this president, loyalty was the gold standard and, in my case, the Agency enforced that standard. That was my first "too bad to believe" experience on the road to Russia.

After being rejected by the several organizations that needed my considerable skills and experience, I get hired for ten million dollars to prove what I believe to be true about the president—that he's a traitor. That was my second "too good to be true" event. The third came when Rodney, the CIA boss who fired me, helped me get the ten-million-dollar gig and agreed to help me.

Next, I'm on a Russian assassin's hit list and being pursued by MI6. That's my second "too bad to believe" experience.

My most recent good news was that, as I carried out my ten-million-dollar suicide mission, I'm assisted by Jill Rucker, my Russian-speaking lover, who is also a skilled pistol shot and karate expert. How did I get so lucky?

While reviewing the good fortune the roller coaster had sent my way, I was reminded of an Agency analyst who used to caution, "If it's too good to be true, it's too good to be true."

The follow-on thought was out of my case officer playbook. If I wanted to set up someone with my skills and experience to undertake this mission, I would do three things to the unsuspecting mark. First, take away the things most valuable to him, like his job and his girlfriend. Second, I would give him something to hope for, life with a woman like Claudia. Third, I would dangle before him the means to keep Claudia, a ten-million-dollar payday. The mark would be hooked. Then, I'd wind him up and send him to England and Russia in search of what I wanted. But why give the mark a Jill Rucker?

Before I could think through the answer to that question, the lady, herself, appeared at my table.

Smiling mischievously, Jill said, "I thought I put you to sleep?"

I smiled back. "You put me into a coma, and, yet, I rise."

"You certainly do."

Courtesy of the cruise line, Jill was wearing a white terry-cloth robe, tied at the waist. As she sat down facing me, she flared the garment to let me see there was nothing beneath it but Rucker.

CHAPTER 17

OUR CRUISE SHIP docked at the St. Petersburg terminal at dawn. Jill and I conducted a final rehearsal of the ID handoffs to our doubles and had breakfast at the buffet before the mob arrived. Afterwards, we returned to our cabin and dressed for debarkation, comparing our clothing to copies of the photographs I gave Rodney for our doubles. Then, we went to the lounge, got our tour ID stickers, and were off the ship at the head of our group. We presented our fake Mr. and Mrs. passports and entered Russia with only a cursory hostile glance from the immigration officer. While the remainder of our group negotiated immigration, Jill and I headed for the Russo-junk arcade restrooms.

The men's restroom was apparently empty. When I had finished with nature's call, I knocked on the door of the last stall and said, "The city tour is leaving now."

The guy inside gave the correct answer: "I'm with the Hermitage tour." He opened the door. I was surprised. He looked enough like me to be my twin and we were dressed exactly alike, down to the shoes. As he came out of the stall, I entered. We executed a brush pass, swapping plastic bags containing our IDs. I heard him wash his hands and leave. If it was a trap, now was the time for the FSB to come out of the woodwork and scarf us up. Nothing happened.

I reversed my coat, exchanged my hat for a cap, and checked the IDs my double had given me. My new Russian passport said my name was Oleg Stasevich. I had all the other papers and a credit card to prove it. My other ID said I was Colonel Nikolai Usenko, an officer in the FSB. The credentials looked good, but it had been a while since I had seen authentic FSB creds. I hoped this stuff wasn't from a Russian spy museum. I also had a U.S. passport for emergencies. There was a cloth bag beside the toilet. As promised, it contained two FSB-issue SPS automatic pistols that had been modified and fitted with short-barrel silencers. You don't want to be trying to screw on a silencer when you need one. Our thoughtful armorer had also provided three 18–round magazines and a pancake holster for each gun. We were loaded for the Russian bear. The trick was to avoid him.

To avoid getting caught together on camera in our new personas, Jill and I caught separate cabs and gave the drivers an address one street over and two blocks away from the one Viktor Lukovsky had given me for Tatyana Kedrova. When I met Jill at our rendezvous address, she was wearing a wig, a different hat and scarf, same coat. Thankful for our boots, we crunched through old snow to a massive Stalin-era building. It had no elevator. We walked up four flights to Tatyana Kedrova's apartment. Above us, the stairs continued up to the vanishing point. Maybe they went to Communist Heaven or the Dustbin of History.

I stood out of sight to the side of the door while Jill Rucker knocked and spoke in Russian. "Tatyana Kedrova, I have a message for you."

The female voice in the apartment asked a hostile, "Who are you?"

"A friend of a friend," replied Jill.

I stooped and slipped a hundred-euro note partway under the door.

The note disappeared. The woman asked, "What friend?"

Jill said, "A friend with money for you."

I fed another hundred euros into what was becoming a reverse ATM.

"If I came to hurt you," said Jill, "I would have kicked the door in by now."

After a pause, we heard locks being released and the door opened enough for us to see a tall blond in her fifties, an age that would make her about right for a 1987 tryst with Ted Walldrum.

"What's the money for?"

"Information," said Jill. "We can pay more, if you help us."

Saying *we* and *us* was a mistake. Tatyana took a quick peek outside and saw me. She tried to slam the door. Jill blocked it open with her boot. This time I offered her a five-hundred-euro note.

Tatyana paused before issuing a hostile invitation. "Come in."

Over her protests, I conducted a quick search of the messy little apartment while Jill kept her occupied. When I was sure we were alone, the three of us sat down at her kitchen table.

Tatyana wore her blond hair in a ponytail. She had large eyes, a straight nose and sensuous mouth, and dimples in her cheeks and chin. She had what Rubens fans would describe as ample breasts to fill out her turtleneck sweater and her tight pants revealed long shapely legs. She had been a beauty in her youth, but time and the street life had added a hard edge to her good looks.

One at a time, I laid three more hundred-euro notes on the table, side by side.

Tatyana eyed the money greedily. "What do you want?"

Jill told her, "We're Americans. We were told that you provided sex services for Theodore Walldrum during his visits to St. Petersburg in the 1980s. What do you remember about those visits?"

"That was long time ago," she said, in broken English. "I don't remember him."

Jill stood and began looking around the apartment. Tatyana tried to keep an eye on her. I laid down another five hundred to focus her attention on me. "Are you telling me that you don't know the President of the United States?"

She eyed my bankroll and I added another five hundred, for an even two thousand.

Tatyana swept the money off the table top into her lap and sneered, "I remember him. He was a pig."

"That's a good start, but it's not worth two thousand euros. I need details, if you want to get rich today." Under her greedy eyes, I counted out another five hundred, but held the stack in place with my fist.

Jill asked, "Toilet?"

"Through there." Tatyana nodded in the direction of her living room.

"What did Walldrum like?" I asked.

"Tall girls," she said, grudgingly, "with low voices, heavy accents, long hair, long legs, big tits. More than one girl at a time."

That narrowed it down to half the male population on Planet Earth. "And . . . ?"

"And what?" She shot a glance at Jill, who had paused in the living room to leaf through papers on Tatyana's desk.

"Do you remember how many times he came to St. Petersburg?" I asked.

"Three times, I think."

"Did you service him?"

"Yes, when I was available."

"What services did he like?"

"Rough stuff. He liked to hurt the girls."

Jill called out, "Is that why you called him a pig?" and pretended not to listen while she opened the drawers of Tatyana's desk.

"He liked to watch them pee . . . on each other. He wanted to take every opening. He liked back door. He was rough there. Some girls didn't like that. There was trouble on his first visit. Pyotr tried to protect us, but KGB told him give Walldrum whatever he wants. Next time, Pyotr find girls who don't mind rough sex."

"Who is Pyotr?" I asked.

"He was house manager where we worked."

"Was the KGB filming Walldrum having sex?"

Tatyana said a fearful, "I don't know about such things."

Jill came over and stood behind Tatyana. "How do you remember Walldrum and what he liked so clearly after thirty years?"

"I . . . I see picture on television . . . and I remember him."

Jill grabbed Tatyana's ponytail, yanked her head over the chair back, and gave her a sharp tap on the throat. "You're lying about remembering what he likes. You saw Walldrum on television and went to the archives to refresh your memory."

When Tatyana stopped choking, she gasped, "No! I tell you truth. I swear."

Jill yanked her hair. "Where's your 'john' book?"

"What you say? I don't know what is 'john' book."

"The book with the names of your customers and what they like. Where is it?"

"I have no book. I just remember."

Jill yanked her hair again. "What color was my scarf?" Jill had removed it and stuffed it into her pocket.

Tatyana hesitated.

"You can remember a john from thirty years ago, but you can't remember what I was wearing when I came in a few minutes ago? Bullshit!"

Jill got in her face. "I think you saw Walldrum on television. You recognized him and realized you had valuable information. So, you went to your john book and looked him up. That's where you got all those details. Either that or you are lying to us. Now, you show us the book, or we take back the money and kick your ass for wasting our time." Jill yanked Tatyana's hair and tapped her on the windpipe with a two-fingered blow. Tatyana lunged forward again, clutching her throat and gagging.

I chimed in as the good cop. "If we see the book and it's real, you get the jackpot."

With a raspy voice she said, "Book not here. I hide it. I think someone would come to take it away."

"Get it," Jill hissed.

Tatyana said to me, "You come back tonight, seven o'clock."

Jill pulled her hair again. "Bitch, if you don't show up tonight, I'll make sure your name and address are on the front page of every Western newspaper in the world. When that happens, the FSB will come here and that will be a very unpleasant visit for you."

Tatyana pulled her hair free of Jill's grip. "I come here tonight. You bring ten thousand euro."

*   *   *

We needed to kill time before our next meeting with Kedrova and decided to check out our safe house. My double had given me the address when we swapped IDs at the arcade. The cab dropped us near the place and we did a walk-by reconnaissance. It was another Stalin-era monstrosity-cum-apartment building with no good escape routes if the police or FSB cornered us. We decided to skip it and went to the train station. While having lunch, Jill and I observed the layout. We bought tickets for a late train to Moscow, downscale luggage, and some typical Russian clothes.

With more time to kill and the need to get lost in a crowd, we went to the Hermitage Museum and wallowed in the decadent Western art that had become jewels in the crown of Soviet Communism. When our cultural tolerance was exhausted, Jill and I had dinner in a nearby restaurant. We put together Plan B to deal with Kedrova, in case Plan A—exchanging euros for her john book—went wrong. I had no intention of walking into a prostitute's lair with ten thousand euros, hoping she would be honest enough to hand over a piece of political dynamite that would prove our president had been susceptible to blackmail since the 1980s.

As we were finishing the meal, I slid my lock-picking kit across the table to Jill. "Do you know how to use this?"

She inspected the contents. "Sure."

That answer was a relief because its use was essential to Plan B. It was also disturbing. Where did Jill learn to pick locks? I filed the question in my memory for later consideration.

Jill took the kit and went off to execute her part of Plan B. I killed more time in the restaurant and held my table by reading a newspaper and ordering shots of cheap vodka that I poured into my water glass. I needed a clear head for my meeting with Kedrova.

Half an hour before our scheduled meeting, I had a cab drop me a couple of blocks from Kedrova's apartment and walked the rest of the way through a light snow.

I knocked on Kedrova's apartment door. No answer. I knocked again. "Tatyana?"

A door creaked open down the hall. I turned to see an elderly, white-haired woman peering at me. She shut the door quickly and I heard the lock fall into place.

I knocked again. Nothing. I turned the knob and pushed. The door opened and I stepped inside. The door slammed shut. The guy behind the door with the gun said, "Tatyana's not here." He was big, bald, dressed in all black, and very serious . . . and, yes, he wore a heavy gold neck chain. It looked almost fashionable against his black silk shirt.

He motioned me toward the living room, which looked like it was in the process of being searched.

Another man was standing at Tatyana's desk. He was smaller than the door guy, with a narrow face and dead eyes. He had a gun, too, but his clothes didn't scream "pimp." He wore a camel's hair sports coat over a tan shirt, paisley tie, and brown wool slacks. He said, "Did you bring the money?"

"What money?" I asked the question in Russian.

"Search him," ordered the living room guy.

The door guy patted my overcoat pockets and removed two stacks of five-hundred-euro notes. He smiled at his colleague and tossed the money onto the cocktail table. Both men gave me a nasty smile. The door guy continued to pat me. "What have we here?" He pulled the gun from my holster and carefully placed it next to the money.

The boss in the paisley tie smiled and rephrased a line from Glen Frey's "Smuggler's Blues." "He always carry weapons 'cause he always carry cash." Both of them laughed.

The humor vanished when the door man found my fake FSB credentials. I thought I might have to change his diaper. He went pale and handed the creds to his boss. Maybe I was going to need two diapers. These guys were freaking out, which meant they weren't FSB. That was good.

"No need to panic," I assured them. "This is the new Russia. There's plenty of money for everyone. You keep the cash. Give me Tatyana. Is she in the kitchen?"

I kept my arms in the surrender position as I glanced toward the kitchen and moved in that direction. As I had hoped, they reoriented themselves to face me with their backs to the rest of the apartment. Both of these guys were in a temporary state of shock, but it wore off quickly.

The boss said, "I know the FSB men in this area. Why don't I know you?"

"I'm on special assignment from Moscow. Where is Tatyana?"

"She's gone," said the boss. "Where's your partner?"

"Behind you," Jill said, stepping out of the bedroom with her pistol leveled at them. "Drop your guns."

These guys moved like they had worked together before. The boss turned, stepping away to his left. The door guy turned to his right, stepping away. Those moves increased the distance between them, presenting Jill with more separation between her targets. That didn't help these guys. Moving to his right, the door guy would be able to bring his gun to bear on Jill first. Jill shot him first. Her silencer gave a little "thunk" and his head exploded. I kicked the boss off balance and Jill shot him once in the gun arm and once in the gut. He went down. I clamped a hand over his mouth so he couldn't scream.

Jill knelt and pointed her gun at his head. "Did you find Tatyana's book?"

He hesitated. Jill whacked his kneecaps with her pistol.

Through his pain and my fingers, the pimp screamed, "Fuck you!"

Jill shot him.

"Are you crazy?" I whispered. "Now, we've got nothing, no Tatyana and no book."

"We couldn't leave them alive. Besides, he was dead when I gut-shot him. Let's get the hell out of here. Somebody might have heard his screams."

She was right, but so was I. Without one of these guys telling us where Kedrova was, all we had to show for our St. Petersburg trip were two dead hoods and our faces on a wanted poster. I retrieved my gun and bribe money from the table.

Calmly, Jill told me, "Tatyana's dead. These two killed her. I heard them talking about it. And they didn't have Tatyana's john book.

They were searching the apartment for it when you got here and interrupted them."

I said, "I'm not leaving empty-handed. We'll take ten minutes to search this place."

We divided the rooms, searched the likely hiding places, and found nothing. I returned to the living room to see Jill was taking a watch off one of the dead guys.

"What the hell are you doing?"

"If this looks like a robbery, the police are less likely to call the FSB."

Good idea. Jill and I emptied their wallets and took the rest of their valuables.

We eased into the hallway and I closed the door to Tatyana's apartment. Both of us turned as, again, a door creaked open down the hall. The white-haired lady who eyed me when I arrived was gesturing for us to come to her.

Jill and I looked at each other. I'm sure one word occurred to both of us: witness. My second thought was, *Are we going to whack this old lady?* That was the ten-million-dollar question. *She had better have a damn good reason for opening her door.* As we walked toward the elderly tenant, my mind spun through ways to deal with her.

She put a finger to her lips for silence and opened her door wide. We entered and found ourselves standing in an apartment that was the twin of Tatyana Kedrova's. Our hostess was wearing a flowered flannel housecoat, wool socks, and ratty slippers. She closed the door quietly, and we spoke Russian.

She addressed me. "Tatyana said you have something for her."

"Tatyana has something for me. What happened to her?"

"I don't know," replied our elderly hostess. "After your visit this morning, Tatyana went out. She was gone for two hours and came back. Two men came to visit her. Later, they all went out together.

Then, your friend"—she glanced at Jill—"came and let herself into Tatyana's apartment. After that, the two men came back to the apartment without Tatyana. You came soon after they did."

The chronology of comings and goings at Tatyana's apartment was all very interesting, but the cops might arrive any minute and we needed to get out of there.

Before I could whack this busybody, she said, "You came for Tatyana's book. I know where it is. You have something for Tatyana?"

I reached into my pocket and gave her a packet of bound euros. The old lady flipped through the bills like a Vegas casino cashier and announced, "This is half, I think."

I smiled and gave her the other packet. She took the money, went to another room, and returned with a diary. The old lady said, "Tatyana left this with me before the two men come to see her. She said I was to give it to you only. I think she was afraid the men would take it from her."

I leafed through the book while Jill looked over my shoulder. It was a diary and john book. Time to go.

We had been speaking Russian and I got an inspiration. I flashed my FSB creds and said, "You have the thanks of state security. Keep the money. Stay in your apartment. You saw nothing. You heard nothing. You will speak to no one of this."

She gave me a fearful nod, but wouldn't look me in the eye after seeing the FSB ID.

The odds were that Tatyana's elderly neighbor would spill the beans at some point. Two murders down the hall, a visit from a couple of bogus FSB agents, a mysterious book, and ten thousand euros were just too much for a busybody to keep quiet about. So, it would be smart for us to get out of St. Petersburg as soon as possible.

Jill and I walked far enough away from Tatyana's building so as not to be identified with it. We rode the Metro to the railway station and caught the 10:50 train to Moscow. Jill and I took sleeping compartments in separate coaches. If the authorities knew about us, they would be looking for a couple.

Alone in my compartment I had time to think about my partner, and what I thought was not comforting. Jill Rucker was a total professional during the shootout at Tatyana's apartment. When she got the drop on the two Russians, she stood sideways, making herself a smaller target, anticipating they might turn on her. When they did, she dropped the guy who presented the greatest threat first, one round in the side of the head. She shot the second guy twice in the gun arm and once in the gut so we could question him, and kneecapped him when he wouldn't talk. Bowen hadn't sent me just a paymaster and logistician. He sent an assassin—a very good one. With those unpleasant thoughts, I drifted off and awakened in the morning as we neared Moscow.

CHAPTER 18

Regional FSB Headquarters, St. Petersburg, Russia

WITH MAJOR IPATEV at his heels, Lieutenant Colonel Konstantine "Kostya" Zabluda was livid when he charged into the operations center. Though in civilian clothes, his height, muscular physique, determined stride, and obvious anger commanded the attention of the staff as he marched past their desks and consoles. The focus of Zabluda's ire was the FSB regional commander, Colonel Dragonov.

Dragonov, a slim, compact man and a head shorter than Zabluda, was in uniform and talking to one of his staff officers when Zabluda interrupted with, "What kind of surveillance report is this! They went to the restrooms! They joined the tour group. He asked questions about the Italian masters! There's nothing here!"

"Because there's nothing to report," replied Dragonov, with smug satisfaction. "It looks like your American master spy came to St. Petersburg to see the sights."

The officer who had been talking to Dragonov moved away.

Zabluda threw the report on the floor. "Geller didn't come here to see the fucking sights! He came to gather information from traitors, enemies of the Russian Federation! I want to know who he contacted. Who did he talk to besides members of his tour group and the waiter at lunch! That"—he jabbed a finger at the papers on the floor—"is not surveillance, it's nonsense! Who did he talk to!"

Calmly, Dragonov replied, "He talked to the tour guide, but he's one of our informants." Sarcastically, "Maybe our guide is your traitor?"

Struggling to control his temper, Zabluda asked, "When did Geller leave the tour group?"

"He didn't. Did you even read the report?"

"What about his traveling companion, Jill Rucker? Did she leave the group?"

"No."

"How did you organize the surveillance?" demanded Zabluda.

Dragonov calmly replied, "Mobile teams in different cars followed the tour bus from the beginning of the tour to the end. Static observation teams were posted at every stop on the tour, including inside the restaurant where the tour group had lunch. Finally, the subjects were under constant observation on the tour bus. I had a couple of agents join Geller's tour. They pretended to be on the cruise. The male agent surveilled Geller; the female agent surveilled Rucker. They were with your *spies* all day."

"I want to speak to those agents now."

"They went home after they completed the report you filed on the floor."

"They have cell phones, don't they?"

"Of course."

"Recall them."

Reluctantly, Dragonov gave the recall order to a subordinate.

Zabluda said, "In the meantime, I want the immigration photographs of Geller and Rucker distributed to every police officer in the city. Start with transportation terminals first. If Geller is still in the city, he'll be leaving soon.

"Radio the cruise ship. The ship's photographer is our informant. Tell him to send us current pictures of Mr. and Mrs. Richard Dolby. Geller and Rucker are traveling under that cover."

Dragonov listened passively while Zabluda paced, issuing orders as they came to mind. "I want every piece of video footage that could have covered Geller: from the cruise dock, from the immigration booths, from every street and shop camera within a five-mile radius of the cruise terminal. Interview every taxi driver and bus driver working within that radius from the time Geller and Rucker cleared immigration until noon. Set up the necessary staff and equipment here to review the video coverage." Zabluda added, "This is first priority, Dragonov. Put your St. Petersburg organization on full alert. Work your people on twelve-hour shifts until we find out who Geller and Rucker contacted."

"That is not *my* first priority," replied Dragonov. "It is *your* first priority. My superior in Moscow decides what the priorities are here."

Zabluda got very close to Dragonov as he said, "I work for the superior of your superior's superior. If calls are made to Moscow, I will make one to tell my superior that your surveillance team lost two American spies. I don't think you want that going to your chain of command until you've had a chance to find them.

"You think I don't know what happened here? You went to your friend, the deputy director, and had my surveillance team replaced with yours. You wanted part of the credit for my operation to improve your chances for promotion. Well, you screwed things up and, now, *you* have a problem."

Just then, a man and woman in civilian clothes entered the operations center. The man addressed Dragonov, "You wanted to see us, Colonel?"

"No. Colonel Zabluda wants to see you."

Zabluda demanded, "What were your orders regarding the surveillance of subjects Geller and Rucker?"

As team leader, the male agent answered. "Keep them in sight at all times. Report all contacts they had with anyone, especially Russians and persons not on the city tour."

Zabluda turned to the female agent. "And your orders?"

"The same, Colonel."

Zabluda addressed the male agent, "Walk me through your surveillance. When did you acquire the target, Geller?"

"When he came off the cruise ship. We"—he nodded to his partner—"were on the pier pretending to be on the cruise and with his tour group. We were taking photographs of ourselves with the cruise ship in the background.

"The subjects, Geller and Rucker, came down the gangplank and went directly to the immigration booths and were cleared for entry. Then, they went to the souvenir mall. We followed at a discreet distance."

"Were they in your view between the immigration and the souvenir mall?"

The agent hesitated. "We were delayed for several minutes at the immigration booth because the officer who checked our passports was confused."

"Confused about what?"

"When she checked our passports against the database, she saw that we were FSB and wondered why we didn't show our credentials to pass immigration. She called a supervisor for assistance—"

Zabluda said, "And Geller and Rucker got out of your sight."

"Only for a short time," protested the male FSB agent.

"Why didn't you go to the supervisor before the cruise ship docked and arrange to be cleared promptly through immigration?"

"We . . . we were told that this surveillance was most secret and we were not to involve anyone not part of the operation."

Zabluda shot a withering glance at Dragonov.

Turning back to the two agents, he asked, "What happened after you *lost sight* of the subjects?"

"We followed them into the souvenir hall and—"

"Correction. You didn't follow them into the souvenir hall. You went looking for them in the souvenir hall."

The two surveillance agents were sweating and the male's voice was shaky. "We . . . I . . . as I approached the men's restroom, Geller was coming out. He stopped to buy a Russian doll. I turned away and pretended to be looking for a souvenir to purchase."

"When Geller came out of the men's room, did he see you?"

"Yes."

"When he stopped to buy this doll, did he turn away from you?"

"Yes, sir."

"Did you get a good look at him?"

"As I said, he turned away to buy something."

"How do you know it was Geller?"

"By his clothes. I recognized what he was wearing when he left the cruise ship."

"Did you recognize his face as the man who came out of the restroom as that of the man who got off the cruise ship, or just his clothing?"

"I didn't get a good look at him as he came out of the restroom, Colonel. He turned away to purchase a gift . . ."

"You followed the decoy." Zabluda turned to Dragonov. "He followed the damned decoy."

Zabluda turned back to the agent. "Were you told that Geller would use a decoy?"

"No, sir. I was told that he would change identities with another man."

"Who told you that?"

"Colonel Dragonov."

"And how did you interpret that information?" asked Zabluda.

"That Geller would exchange papers with someone so he could move about the city with a Russian identity." The agent shifted his puzzled gaze between Zabluda and Dragonov.

Zabluda questioned the female agent next. Her story of the broken surveillance was essentially the same as her partner's.

Addressing the two agents, Zabluda said a frosty, "Thank you. You're dismissed."

Zabluda turned to Dragonov. "For you, promotion is now out of the question. You want to keep your job? Get those videos and find Geller! I'm leaving my second-in-command, Major Ipatyev, here to monitor your search and to keep me informed."

"Where will you be?" asked Dragonov.

"In Moscow. We are sixteen hours behind two American spies. They may have already contacted the traitors here in St. Petersburg and be on their way to Moscow. I'm going there to try and catch them. For your sake, pray that I'm successful."

Zabluda was still fuming. He walked away from Dragonov. Then, he came back to the colonel and pointed a finger at him. "Understand this, Dragonov. I was sent here to kill people. Right now, the only people worthy of my services are in this building. Find Maxwell Geller!"

CHAPTER 19

THE SAYING GOES, "When in Rome, do as the Romans." When in Moscow, follow Moscow Rules, a set of Cold War guidelines developed by Western spies for survival in that hostile city. The rule of immediate concern to me was, "Go with the flow, blend in." Accordingly, we had taken a train that arrived at Moscow's Leningradsky station at 7:55 a.m. to coincide with rush hour.

I left Jill at the station with instructions. "Take a cab. Ask the driver where you can get a good breakfast. Eat slowly. Meet me back here in two hours."

"Where are you going?"

"You don't need to know."

"What if you don't come back?"

"Sherri will meet you here at 4:00 p.m."

"Did you make that arrangement in Stockholm?"

"Yes,"

"And you didn't tell me?"

"I just did."

She was pissed. "Suppose the FSB had grabbed you on the train?"

I smiled. "You would have shot them and we would have escaped."

* * *

I took a cab to a years-old rendezvous point, hoping to meet an asset who worked in Russian intelligence. In times past, he dropped his daughter off at a private school and walked to a nearby café for his morning coffee.

Sergei was on his way to the café when I approached him. His eyes widened in momentary surprise. Then, he glanced at the paper cradled under my left arm, the sign that I wanted a meet.

He said, "A good morning to you." That was the signal that it was okay for me to meet him at the coffee shop.

I circled the block scanning for surveillance. Detecting none, I met Sergei as he was leaving the café, coffee cup in hand. We walked to his car—a black Lada Vesta—and slid into the front seat.

"What the hell are you doing back in Moscow?"

"I'm happy to see you, too, Sergei."

"I read that the CIA fired you for criticizing Walldrum. That wasn't smart. Maybe I bet on the wrong political system when I gave you Mother Russia's secrets."

"You don't believe that. Democracy is the best political system in the history of mankind."

He gave me a stern look. "I believe that, but you Americans better get your shit together soon or you're going to be a dictatorship. Putin doesn't like democracies."

I changed the subject. "How are you getting along with your new case officer?" Sergei was still spying for the CIA.

"His Russian is not as good as yours, but he's smarter than you."

"Based on your product, you deserve the best."

Sergei smiled. "So, what do American spies do after they're fired?"

"They become private investigators."

"Working for . . . ?"

"Working for what you and I always worked for, to free Russia from Putin. That's why I came to see you."

"What do you want, besides the opportunity to get yourself killed in the shadow of the Kremlin?"

"I want to verify a claim in the Ironside Dossier that Ted Walldrum cavorted with prostitutes at the Riga-Ritz Hotel in Moscow. I need original sources, people who saw things with their own eyes, heard things from the mouth of the speaker with their own ears. Rumors won't cut it. So, who should I talk to at the Ritz and who should I avoid?"

Sergei sighed. "Why are you doing this? Your government has already verified many of the allegations. Nobody cares if prostitutes pissed on a bed at the Ritz."

"Walldrum cares. He keeps denying it. Did it happen?"

Sergei massaged his forehead. After a while he said, "Okay. Avoid the hotel manager. He's FSB, so is the security staff. If you want eyewitnesses, you have to find the maids who serviced the room and the laborers who moved the mattress. There's your problem. Those people have been bought off, moved off, or killed off. A maid was murdered for talking to a reporter about this. The reporter was killed, too." Sergei looked at me with concern. "That's all I know and I got that secondhand."

"How would I get a roster of hotel employees at the time of the alleged incident?"

"I doubt there is one. If I had to cover up the incident, the second thing I would do—after getting rid of the witnesses—would be to delete the names of those witnesses from the personnel roster or replace the entire roster with one that was bogus."

Sergei was silent for a few beats. "If you're serious about this, you need to stay off the radar of the security services. No hotels. Check Moscow obituaries from six months to a year after the incident. Find a hotel worker and a reporter who were killed about the same time and you have a lead. Then, you track down the hotel worker's family and find out who he or she worked with and where. Even if you do all that, and find the people you need to talk to, they may not want to talk to you. You could do a lot of work and end up with nothing."

"I could be successful and end up with a hand grenade."

"Ah, but who would pull the pin on your grenade and throw it into the political arena? How many times have we intelligence professionals given politicians the ammunition they need, only to have them squander the opportunity to use it?"

That was a depressing thought. I moved on. "Have you heard of the Omega Group?"

Sergei said a thoughtful, "No. What is it?"

I gave him a polite smile.

He nodded his understanding that I couldn't tell him. "So," he said, "this is how it works—I tell you what you want to know and you tell me nothing?"

"If I told you what I think it is, you would have to do something. That would hurt your cause and mine."

"Well, if the Omega Group is an organization whose interests conflict with those of the Russian Federation, the FSB has probably penetrated it. We're very good at placing our agents in opposition groups, remember? If you get involved with this group, be very careful." Sergei looked at his watch. Our time together was running out.

I requested, "Two more topics?"

Sergei nodded his okay.

"I have information that Walldrum was laundering money for oligarchs as far back as the nineties. Who would have firsthand knowledge of that?"

"One or two senior managers during that period at the Moscow branch of Allgemeine Volksbank—our Kremlin kleptocracy's hometown bank of choice. The problem is, senior managers in that era are retired. Your best source would be the bank's records. You need someone on the inside with access to the archives, if they haven't been destroyed."

"Do you know someone with access to those archives?"

"It would take someone with a long nose and a short life expectancy. The only one who comes to mind immediately is you." He didn't smile.

"Last subject. Do you know General Alexei Grishin?"

"He retired before my time, but he's a FSB legend. Old-timers call him 'The Ghost.'"

"Why?"

"His career was rescued from the graveyard more than once. Grishin ran the FSB version of your Pussy Posse, setting honey traps to get *kompromat* on enemies of the state."

"Or anyone passing through the state," I added.

Sergei ignored me. "The story goes that Grishin was marked for oblivion when Putin became head of the FSB and started replacing Posse staff with his own people. In the 1990s, Prosecutor General Yury Skuratov opened a corruption investigation targeting President Yeltsin, his family, and political cronies. Grishin saved the day by producing a tape of Skuratov in bed with two young women. Putin put it on TV. Skuratov resigned. The investigation died and Putin became a Yeltsin favorite. Unfortunately, the tape didn't make Grishin a Putin favorite. To Putin, Grishin was just doing his job. Grishin resumed his slide into the career graveyard.

"After Putin left the FSB, Grishin again rose from the grave. He caught a drunken Chechen in a honey trap, telling a prostitute about a plot to blow up the Moscow Metro. That was the beginning of a string of successes. Grishin kept dropping well-timed sex tapes of the regime's opponents and got his long overdue promotions. They say he still holds a grudge against Putin for not promoting him early in his career."

"Where is Grishin on the political spectrum these days?"

"He has supported political opposition figures, including Boris Nemtsov."

"Why didn't Putin's hoods kill Grishin when they murdered Nemtsov?"

"Russians understand if you kill your political opponents. If you start killing people who helped you rise to power and kept you there, your current supporters might begin wondering if they're next. That can destabilize a regime."

"If it came to a hard choice, would Grishin be with us or Putin?"

"Ask him."

"Where does he live?"

"He has a dacha in the country and a Moscow apartment in the Presnya district." Sergei gave me directions to both.

I knew about the Presnya apartment. The address and Grishin's name were listed in an Internet phone book. My question was a test to see if Sergei was still batting for our team.

He started the engine. "Time to go. I have a job and I'm late."

"Thank you, Sergei. I wish you well."

"I wish you hadn't come back, my friend. You're like a man fighting a bear with a hot poker. You better hope the bear gives up before the poker burns your hands."

CHAPTER 20

I GOT BACK to the Leningradsky train station late. Jill was unhappy. Too bad for Jill.

As we checked our suitcases into a fresh set of lockers, she demanded, "Well?"

"I have a couple of leads. I'll tell you later."

"Why are you keeping me out of the loop, Max?"

"For your protection. If the FSB picks us up, you can't compromise anyone because you don't know anyone. It's that simple." It really wasn't. Hopefully, when I met Sherri later, she would be able to tell me just how complicated my relationship with Ms. Rucker really was.

"Now," I diverted her attention, "we need to buy a few more items of typical Russian clothing so we can blend in when we need to."

With Jill in stony silence, we took the Metro to the Partiyanskaya stop northeast of Moscow center and headed for the shopping center. My suit and boots were expensive enough for a FSB colonel, but I bought a good fur coat and an expensive fur hat, appropriate to my rank. I also purchased a set of cheap clothing in case I needed a common man's disguise. Jill's purchases matched mine.

When we returned to Leningradsky Station, I called General Grishin's Moscow apartment on a pay phone. Good news. No answer. Jill and I packed our suitcases with clothes to sustain us for a few days and took a cab to Grishin's apartment.

Presnya is a quiet, pricey, residential neighborhood with easy access to the center of Moscow. The residents are affluent Russians and expatriates working in the Tverskaya Street business district nearby. There were enough restaurants, bars, shops, and Metro stops for us to move about without attracting attention. The area had been yuppified since I was stationed in Moscow. Lower-class housing had been razed and replaced by luxury apartment buildings. Grishin lived in a ten-story version of one. There was no doorman. A uniformed concierge sat at the lobby desk. His name tag read, "Dmitri."

He started to speak, but I took the initiative. "Has General Grishin returned yet?"

"No."

"Good." I flashed my phony FSB creds. "I am Colonel Usenko, FSB. My wife"—I nodded to Jill—"is the general's grandniece. We've just arrived from St. Petersburg. Which apartment is the general's?"

"It's 1004, Colonel."

"Thank you. We have a key. We'll wait for the general."

The concierge looked confused momentarily. He recovered and opened a leather-bound book. "Would you sign the guest register, Colonel?"

Before the book was open all the way, I closed it gently on his hand and gave him a sinister smile. "We want to surprise the general. You won't expose us, will you?"

He straightened his back. "Of course not, Colonel."

Jill gave him a friendlier smile. "Thank you, Dmitri. What is your family name?"

"Yolkin."

She wanted to leave Dmitri with the unsettling knowledge that a FSB colonel knew his full name. Later, to our peril, we would discover that his real family name was Grishin.

The brass and glass elevator took us to the tenth floor where Jill stood guard while I picked the lock on apartment 1004.

Inside, I used my handy-dandy laser detector to check for hidden cameras, while Jill used an equally handy RF sweeper to find listening devices. The place was clean.

Grishin's apartment was compact, but comfortable, befitting a general. There was a small kitchen, expansive living room, master bedroom, and a smaller guest room with twin beds. Jill and I unpacked our belongings in the guest room.

"We're staying here?" she asked.

"Until we can't."

"What about the meeting with Sherri at the train station?"

"If we don't show, she or Tony-D will come back each day until we make contact. It's called 'tradecraft.'"

"I know what the hell it's called. I don't like being kept in the dark. Why are we here? I thought Sherri was going to find a safehouse for us."

"This is Moscow. The people Sherri is dealing with might be compromised. If they are and they get Sherri, she can't give us up."

"You're a cold-blooded son-of-a-bitch."

"Those are the sons-a-bitches who stay alive in this business. Aren't you glad I'm on your side?"

She grunted and turned back to her suitcase duties.

After the heat went out of the conversation, we raided Grishin's fridge, cooked dinner, and worked out a sleep-watch schedule. Jill crawled into one of the twin beds and went to sleep immediately.

I took first watch in a living room chair near the door, with my gun handy. It was 6 p.m. I figured I'd give Jill four uninterrupted hours of sleep. In the cold, dark silence of the apartment, I tried to analyze why I was being such a jerk with Jill Rucker. The answer came to me. I was back in Moscow, with its rules for survival, honed by foreign spies over decades of the Cold War. I was following Moscow Rules. Rule

Number 2: never go against your gut, and my gut was telling me not to trust Jill Rucker. She was a dead shot, a karate expert, and a fluent Russian speaker who had never been to Russia. There was also something dancing just out of focus in my mind that connected Jill to Moscow. Those thoughts were interrupted by an overwhelming desire to sleep, but I was on watch and I couldn't sleep . . . and what was that smell?

*   *   *

I woke up when someone slapped my face. I expected to see an irate Jill Rucker. Instead, I saw my gun pointing at me. Dimitri, the concierge, was doing the pointing. Across the room, Jill, in pajamas, sat on the couch. A man in his late thirties stood behind her pointing a gun at her head. Behind him, windows were open and the room was freezing.

Dimitri gave me a smug smile and explained, "I put something in the ventilation system to help you sleep."

Keeping his eyes on me, Dimitri spoke to the younger man. "Pavel, close the windows. I think our little sleep-inducer has dissipated."

Pavel shuttered and closed the windows.

Jill's ankles were tied to a leg of the couch with what looked like a bathrobe sash and her hands were behind her back. I was lashed to the back and legs of my chair with electrical cord. Dimitri sat in a chair just out of lunging distance. The only sound in the room was him cocking and uncocking my gun.

I needed these people talking, not shooting. Searching for an ice-breaker, I noticed something familiar about Pavel. "You must be Vasili Bogdanovich's son. I saw a picture of him when he was about your age. You could pass for his twin."

Dimitri jumped up and whacked me across the face with my gun. "No talking!"

Pavel wasn't getting the memo. "Who is Vasili Bogdanovich?"

To me, Dimitri snarled, "You will not talk." In a less hostile tone he told Pavel, "This man is a spy. All spies lie. The general has been trained to interrogate spies. He wants them kept quiet until he arrives."

Pavel disagreed. "That's what *you* said, Uncle Dimitri. That's not what my father said." He pointed his gun at me. "Who is this Bogdanovich?"

"You'll find out soon enough." That promise was being made by a stocky, white-haired man of about seventy who was entering the apartment. He hung his overcoat on a rack near the door and added, "But first, we need to know who our guests are."

He went to Jill and announced, "I'm General Grishin. You're pretty, but you're not my grandniece."

Grishin came to me and inspected the gash on my cheek, courtesy of Uncle Dimitri. "You are not so pretty and you are not my grandnephew-in-law. Who are you?" His head swiveled between me and Jill.

Dimitri answered. "Maybe they lost track of who they are, with so many identities to remember." He pointed to the dinner table where our credentials were neatly laid out. The general flipped through our U.S. passports, phony FSB credentials, and the Russian identity papers provided by the couple who replaced us on the cruise in St. Petersburg. Luckily, I had left my letter of transit from Viktor Lukovsky in a locker at the train station. That was one less item for me to explain. Still, the appropriate term for this situation was, "Busted!"

Grishin came to me. "Who are you? If you're lucky, you'll have to tell your story just once. So, make it a good story and it had better ring true."

I believed him. "I'm Maxwell Geller. The lady tied to the couch leg is Jillian Rucker. We're not spies. We're freelancers, private investigators hired to authenticate some documents."

Grishin glanced at our IDs. "You have exceptional support for freelancers."

"I'm former CIA."

"Have you worked for the CIA in Russia?"

"Yes, but I was fired for criticizing President Walldrum."

Grishin gave that some thought. "Why did you come to me?"

"Vasili Bogdanovich suggested I contact you."

"Bogdanovich is dead." Grishin put his gun to my forehead. "Did you kill him?"

"No. I went to him for information. I got his location from MI6."

"Why did Vasili send you to me?"

I shot a questioning glance at Pavel and Dimitri. The concierge looked bored, probably just wanting to shoot us and get rid of the bodies before his shift ended.

"Dimitri and Pavel are family. You can speak in front of them."

"Bogdanovich told me that you helped him defect to the British." That was true. "He also said you supported Boris Nemtsov and other politicians who oppose Putin." Actually, Sergei told me about Nemtsov as we sat in his car, but I couldn't out my source. "Bogdanovich said you might help me."

"Help you how?"

"You've heard of the Ironside Dossier on our president?"

"Who hasn't?"

"I was hired to find out if the dossier allegations are fact or disinformation. I can't do that without Russian help. I want to interview people who have firsthand knowledge of Walldrum's activities in Moscow before he became our president."

Pavel interrupted. "And I want to know about this man, Bogdanovich!"

Grishin sighed and ignored Pavel. He asked me, "Do you have children, Maxwell?"

"No."

"One of the ironies of parenthood is that parents go through life seeing their adult children as their subordinates, while children go through adulthood seeing themselves as their parents' equals."

In a soft voice, Dimitri said to the general, "It's time to tell Pavel the truth."

"Time to tell me the truth about what?" demanded Pavel.

To me, Grishin said, "Another irony is that people with no children give you advice on how to manage yours"—he glanced at Dimitri—"but sometimes they know what they're talking about."

The general turned to Pavel. "This is not the time or place I would have chosen for this conversation, but it seems fate has chosen for us."

So, with the three of them standing around holding guns and Jill and I lashed to the furniture, the Russians decided to have a family therapy session.

General Grishin said, "Vasili Bogdanovich was an officer who worked for me. He was also engaged to my daughter, Galina. Vasili wanted to defect and convinced Galina to go with him. Vasili planned to fake his death in a plane crash during a flight to Cape Town. There was no way to get Galina on the plane. So, we arranged with MI6 to smuggle her out of Russia through Finland and on to England. Galina was to leave for the Finnish border the day Vasili's plane left for South Africa. At the last minute, she refused to go. She wouldn't tell me or her mother why.

"When Vasili's plane went down—presumably with all hands—Galina told us she was pregnant. Vasili didn't know. Galina was afraid to go to the West in her condition. She wanted to have her baby here in Russia with her mother attending.

"Everyone thought the plane crash was an accident. As Vasili's fian-cée, Galina would normally be grief-stricken. I sent her and my wife to live with friends in the Urals for a year to 'get over Vasili's death.'

"While they were away, Galina gave birth to a son. She died in childbirth." He jammed his gun into his belt and took Pavel by the shoulders. "That son was you."

Pavel was speechless. He turned pale, then red.

The general continued. "Your grandmother and I didn't want you to go through life carrying the double burden of knowing your father was a defector and your mother died giving you life. Besides, if the state discovered that Bogdanovich was alive in England, his name would have doomed you to harassment or worse.

"When my wife returned to Moscow a year later, we told everyone that you were our child and that Galina had died of pneumonia. I gave you my name and we raised you as our own. We could do no less for you."

Pavel was enraged. "Why didn't you tell me this before now!"

"What good would it have done?"

Pavel had tears in his eyes when he turned to me. "When did you see my father?"

"Three weeks ago, in Scotland."

"Is that where he lives?"

"He *did* live there. I'm sorry to tell you he was killed shortly after I visited him."

Pavel was seething. "Who killed him?"

"The British think it was Russian assassins."

Pavel stood in the center of the room, his arms limp at his sides, staring into the lie that was his past.

Grishin went to the bar, poured two shots of vodka, and brought them to Pavel. "Drink this," ordered the general. "It will help you digest the truth."

Uncle Dimitri, the family cynic, declared, "In Russia, vodka is the only antidote for truth."

Pavel swallowed the vodka with robot-like detachment. He asked Grishin, "Why did my father defect?"

"He was a FSB officer in a politically untenable position and he knew too much. He was going to be replaced by someone loyal to Putin and sent to an insignificant post that would end his career. He had pride. So, he defected. Had he stayed, he would have fought the system and been destroyed by it. I could see this in him." Sadness crept into Grishin's voice. "Take care, Pavel. I see those same self-destructive inclinations in you."

He added, "Last week in Scotland, Putin's assassins killed a man called Lucas Novak. His real name was Vasili Bogdanovich, your father."

All during the therapy session, good old Uncle Dimitri had kept his gun trained on me and his eyes on Jill. He reminded Pavel and the general that a decision had to be made. "Now that we all know the sad history of Vasili Bogdanovich, what are we going to do with these two?" He was referring to me and Jill.

The general looked us over. "I have no affection for the United States. Why shouldn't I turn both of you over to the FSB?"

Jill spoke up. "We want the same things for our people that you wanted for your daughter and Bogdanovich: truth and freedom from tyrants."

"How do you know what I wanted?"

"You were willing to let your daughter defect with Bogdanovich and risk your neck by helping them. You may have no affection for the West, but you had faith that there was a better life outside of Russia. Otherwise, why would you support Putin's political opponents?"

Grishin said to me, "You have a good partner, Maxwell Geller, but she is not persuasive. If I help you, it might mean trouble for my family. If I turn you over to the FSB, that's the end of it."

"No, it's not!" declared Uncle Dimitri. "They are spies. Connect us to American spies and that's not the end of this. It's just the first step into hell. The FSB will want to know why they came to this building on their first day in Moscow. Next, there will be a surveillance van parked down the street. The FSB will want a rent-free apartment here so they can monitor who comes and goes. You, of all people, should know how they think. You were one of them."

"What are you proposing, Dimitri?" asked the general.

"I say get rid of them in a way that they can't be traced back to us. We don't want to get involved with the security services."

It was time for me to redirect the conversation. "Maybe Pavel would like to know the names of the men who killed his father. Maybe the general would like to know, too."

That got everyone's attention, including Jill, who wasn't privy to my last conversation with Rodney.

"How could you know that?" The general was skeptical.

"I was kidnapped by the Russian hit squad after I visited Bogdanovich."

"How do I know you are not lying?"

"Jill helped rescue me from the Russians. Take her into the bedroom. Ask her what happened. Dimitri and Pavel can question me here. Compare our stories. If they're the same, you'll know I'm telling the truth."

Jill and I were grilled separately for about ten minutes, after which everyone returned to the living room. Jill was dressed. Dimitri tied her ankles to the couch leg and the Russians compared notes out of earshot. Then, they turned their backs on us and a discussion in harsh whispers ensued.

Dimitri made an angry statement punctuated with gestures, and Pavel countered with frowns and pleading hand gestures. The general said, "Enough!" for all to hear. "Pavel, bring the car to the back door."

Dimitri looked pleased.

Pavel shouted, "You lied to me all of my life. Now, you deny me the names of my father's killers!"

This exchange suggested that Jill and I were not getting a lift to the Ritz.

Grishin gave Pavel a red-faced response. "You are my son! You will do what I tell you! Bogdanovich has brought enough suffering to this family!"

Dimitri said, "Leave the spies tied until we come back. I'll go with Pavel." They left the apartment together. I guess Dimitri didn't trust his nephew to do as he was told.

The general sat at the dining room table and kept his eyes on us while we waited.

It wasn't long before Pavel returned and announced, "Dimitri is waiting for us in the car. He said we can get rid of their luggage later."

Pavel scooped up our IDs from the table and dumped them into a plastic bag. Then, he untied me and Jill, and threw our overcoats, hats, and boots at us.

"Why are we wasting time with that?" the general wanted to know.

"It's freezing outside, Papa. Anyone not dressed for it will attract attention. You need to put your coat on, too."

The general shoved his gun into his belt and was taking his coat from the hall rack when Pavel made his move. He snatched the gun from the general's belt and jumped back out of reach.

"What are you doing!" demanded the general.

"We're not killing these people, Papa."

"What are you going to do?"

"It's better you don't know." Pavel said to me, "Tie and gag him."

Jill and I happily cooperated in that task.

"What now?" I asked.

"Pack your suitcases and be quick."

Fifteen minutes later, we were in the car headed out of Moscow with Pavel at the wheel. I was riding shotgun, Jill was in the back seat, and we had our guns back.

Jill asked Pavel, "What happened to Uncle Dimitri?"

"I locked him in the garage. He'll get out soon enough. The windows are high, but large enough for him to squeeze through."

"Then what?"

"He'll go to the apartment and release the general. That will be the end of it."

"No police?" I asked.

"Uncle Dimitri avoids drawing attention to the building."

"Is he doing something illegal?" asked Jill.

"No." Pavel smiled grimly at the windshield. "If his activities were illegal, he might have the protection of the mafia or the FSB. Dimitri is a retired soldier. He pooled money with other retirees to buy the building. Most of the owners live there. They rent the other apartments. They're concerned that if the building gets negative attention from the authorities, there might be interference from the city administration."

Jill was incredulous. "He was going to kill us to avoid drawing attention to his building?"

Pavel sighed. "If you're on the wrong side of Moscow politics, they will find a legal way to take your property. The general's political views have already focused unwanted attention on the building. Dimitri is a man in transition. He's a capitalist who craves democracy, but he fears the Kremlin kleptocracy. So, he avoids publicity that would offend the hand that steals from him."

We drove for a while before Pavel asked, "Do you have a place to stay?"

"No." I didn't tell him that Sherri might be working on that.

"I'll take you someplace safe. You tell me who killed my father, and I will help you with your dossier investigation. I approve of what you are doing, but it is very dangerous."

Jill observed, "Helping us is also dangerous. General Grishin said you have self-destructive tendencies, like your father. Are you taking us to join the resistance . . . or Pussy Riot?"

Pavel smiled at Jill in the rearview mirror, but said nothing.

Pussy Riot is a protest rock group that opposes Putin and advocates for feminism, LGBT rights, and other issues unpopular with the state.

Since our lives were now in Pavel's hands, I took time to appraise him. Physically, he had his real father's good looks, but not Bogdanovich's compact body. Pavel had inherited General Grishin's ramrod-straight stature. Though he was wearing drab civilian clothes, I had no trouble imagining Pavel in one of the many uniforms on Moscow's streets. More importantly for us, Pavel was both emotional and decisive. He had shown those tendencies by his reaction to the facts of his birth and how he had moved against the general and Uncle Dimitri. If those were the traits that defined Pavel's personality, I could see why the general had labeled him self-destructive. That could be bad for us.

After we passed Moscow's outer ring, we drove for an hour until we came to a farmhouse. Pavel told us, "I have friends here. Speak Russian. Your train tickets showed you came from St. Petersburg. Do you know the city well enough to discuss it?"

"Yes," I answered.

"Be polite. Avoid conversation. If you must talk, limit the topic to St. Petersburg. They don't expect you to give details about who you are or what you do."

We didn't have to talk to anyone. Pavel went into the farmhouse, returned shortly, and led us to a room on the second floor of the barn. It was windowless and warmed by electric heaters and heat from cattle bodies beneath us. There was a long wooden table with equally long wooden benches on either side, three sets of bunk beds, a closet, and wash basins. The place had the feel of a harvest season bunkhouse.

Pavel told us, "Many hotels are monitored by the FSB. You can stay here until we find more suitable housing or until you complete your work. There is a shower at the back of the main house. Signs are posted.

"I would like to discuss our arrangements now."

Jill asked, "Could we have a pot of hot tea and some vodka?"

Pavel went to the farmhouse to get us drinks. As soon as he left, we broke out our gear and swept for bugs and cameras. We found none. Pavel returned with a bottle of vodka, a pot of tea, and three mugs. We drank and began negotiations by candlelight.

He opened. "You are the professionals. How do we do this?"

I told him, "I'll give you the name of one of your father's killers and three more when we complete our mission here."

"What do you want in return?"

"What do you have to offer?"

I wanted to know if Pavel was a player or a talker, but he was cagey. He shifted his gaze between me and Jill. I assumed he was trying to assess whether or not he could trust us. In his shoes, that's what I'd be doing. I guess we didn't pass his test.

"I have another idea," Pavel said. "Tell me what you need. I tell you if I can help."

"Okay." I went for overload to see how he would react. "We want the names of the prostitutes who were allegedly in Walldrum's room at the Moscow Riga-Ritz in 2013, the staff who serviced his suite, and the FSB men who taped Walldrum with the prostitutes. I want a copy of the *kompromat* tape, maintenance records for Walldrum's suite the next day, and the hotel bill."

"That was five years ago."

"I can count, Pavel. Can you help us or not?"

"It's possible."

"Immaculate conception is possible. If you can't help us, don't waste our time. I'll give you one of the names you want and we'll be on our way."

Pavel sat back from the table and glared at me. I thought I detected some steel in him I hadn't seen before.

"What else do you need to complete your investigation?"

"Walldrum's name has been tied to allegations of money laundering. The Moscow branch of Allgemeine Volksbank has been mentioned. I want the bank's loan records for the 1990s, the entire decade, in digital form."

"You want a lot."

"I can pay well."

"How much is a man's life worth?"

"Only the man who does the work can answer that question."

"In that case, I want two names to begin work."

"I'll give you one now and one after we conduct our first usable interview with any person you identify."

"The name?"

I gave him the name of one of my Russian kidnappers who Sherri's team had killed outside the London warehouse. We established two-way communications procedures and Pavel departed, promising to return the following evening.

Jill was concerned. "What happens when Pavel discovers that you gave him the name of a dead man?"

"We'll know that Pavel has good sources. That dead man's orders to assassinate Bogdanovich and take out those MI6 officers at the warehouse had to come directly from the Kremlin."

CHAPTER 21

THE NEXT DAY, Jill and I found a farmer headed for Moscow and got a ride into the city. We killed time eating and cruising department stores until rendezvous time with Sherri at Leningradsky train station.

We were in Moscow. You had to assume the opposition was always tailing you or the person you were meeting. That made meetings potentially dangerous. Jill and I worked out a plan to find out if Sherri was being followed. I got to the train station before Jill, bought a coffee, and found a seat that gave me a good view of the meeting point. Sherri was already there with a suitcase, looking expectant and impatient. She saw me but we didn't acknowledge each other.

Ten minutes later, Jill arrived to meet Sherri. They embraced like long-lost sisters and went off to the cab stand laughing. I stayed with them to the curb, watching their backs. No one was taking their pictures or talking into his lapel. No cars pulled away from the curb to follow them.

I knew their destination: a restaurant Sherri and I had agreed on before we parted in Stockholm. Tony-D would be there providing overwatch for that meeting. I grabbed a cab and took a shortcut to the restaurant. I was seated when Jill and Sherri came to join me at my table. No one followed.

Sherri and I did the kissy-face routine for the benefit of anyone I missed. We ordered our meals and got down to business. I briefed Sherri on our adventures since we parted in Stockholm. She brought us up to date on what she and Tony-D were up to.

"Tony-D and I arrived in Moscow four days ago. Our cover story for the Russians is we're here for the Moscow Winter Festival. We're staying at the Blue Hotel in the Arbat district. It has plenty of museums and other public places where we can meet our Omega Group contact without arousing suspicion."

"You made contact with Omega?"

"Yesterday. I told our contact that we were journalists working undercover on the Ritz story. I asked if Omega could help. He declined. He said all the witnesses are gone and the only staff at the hotel who might have direct knowledge of the incident are FSB. Approaching them would be like asking for a ticket to the interrogation room."

That tracked with what Sergei told me the previous day. "Okay. Stay away from the Ritz and Omega. Let's try a different approach. My Moscow source said a hotel staff member was killed after discussing the Ritz incident with a reporter. The reporter was killed, too. Find a way to check the Moscow obituaries since 2013. See if you can find a reporter who died around the same time as a hotel employee. If we can identify the hotel employee, we might be able to locate some coworkers."

"That sounds like a good start," agreed Sherri.

There was an awkward silence until I said, "Jill, Sherri and I need a couple of minutes."

Jill headed for the ladies' room in a huff, cut out of the info loop again.

I asked Sherri, "What's the lowdown on Bowen, my employer?"

"William Bowen graduated from a third-tier law school, went to Panama during Noriega's regime, and opened a practice. He's been there ever since."

"If he was there during Noriega's time, he's probably a crook. Got a client list?"

"No list. He's Executive Director of the Global Democracy Initiative—GDI—a Panama-based private foundation. Its mission, as stated on its website, is to support democratic candidates for government around the world. It's interesting that this foundation was established a week after the news media revealed the existence of the Ironside Dossier, with its allegations about President Walldrum."

"Why then?"

"Either the allegations really upset some guardians of democracy or . . ."

"Or what?"

"Or substitute your favorite conspiracy theory."

"My employment contract isn't with GDI. It's with Panama Essential Consultants, LLC. What do you know about that company?"

"Essential Consultants is a subsidiary of GDI."

"Where does a Panamanian LLC get ten million dollars for one job and how did they find me?"

"My sources say Bowen makes lots of trips to D.C., but not who he visits. He keeps those cards close to his vest. His finances are also a black box. *You* would have to break some banking laws to get his financials."

I caught her emphasis on *you*. "What about Jill?"

"The mysterious Ms. Rucker," said Sherri, with a snort. "We found plenty of Jill and Jillian Ruckers, but not ours. She doesn't exist. I had my hacker tap every online phone book and database he could access. He didn't find a Jill Rucker who matches the profile of our Jill. As a last resort, he reached out to a friend at the IRS and asked if anyone with Jill's name and age range had filed an income tax form in the past five years. He got a zero. Our Jill isn't who her driver's license says she is."

I gave Sherri directions to our farm in case she needed to contact me or hide out. We agreed on communications procedures as Jill returned from the ladies' room.

Jill asked, "Finished discussing my future?"

I said, "We were discussing our elusive employer, Mr. Bowen. Sherri's staff was unable to find him. Any ideas?"

Jill gave Sherri a nasty smile, but spoke to me. "Maybe you should hire a better researcher."

On that happy note, Sherri left, with Tony-D still watching her back from a distance.

It was approaching rush hour. So, I called Pavel for a ride back to the farm. He arrived thirty minutes later with a battered green van and three sour-looking helpers. The van had three rows of seats. Pavel was driving. One helper rode shotgun beside him. The other two helpers sat on the last row. Pavel got out, opened the sliding door, and ushered Jill and me into the two middle seats. There were no introductions.

This was Moscow. My survival instincts kicked in and I started computing the odds in a fight. They were obviously four-to-two, but higher with two of the four sitting behind us. I was hoping Pavel hadn't consulted with Uncle Dimitri about this ride.

Pavel announced, "We're going to meet friends. We need to blindfold you." With that, the shotgun rider turned and pointed a real sawed-off shotgun at us. The men behind us reached around, relieved us of our guns, and dropped black hoods over our heads.

We drove for ninety minutes to a very quiet place. The Russians pulled us out of the van and shoved us into a building. They took our hoods off and we were standing in a car repair shop. There were two new guys waiting for us, bringing the odds to six-to-two, or if you liked division, three-to-one. The shotgun rider appeared to be the only one armed.

Near the back wall of the shop, I saw a table accommodating a group that looked ominously like a tribunal. There was one woman in her late twenties or early thirties and four men, ranging from the thirties to late middle age. I recalculated the odds in the room as too-many-to-futile.

On the wall behind this group there was a Russian Federation flag with a black-and-white military-like patch sewn to its center. The patch contained an eagle claw holding a globe with an arrow embedded in it. The banner underneath contained one word: Omega.

Pavel pointed to the table. "Sit."

We sat. The muscle from the van joined us on either side, except the shotgun rider. He had traded his shotgun for our pistols and stood a safe distance behind me and Jill.

The studious-looking younger man in a heavy sweater brushed dark hair away from one eye and peered at us across the table. "We represent Omega. Have you heard of us?"

"A Russian friend gave me the name of your group. He said you might help me connect Walldrum to the Ironside allegations."

"What's your Russian friend's name?"

"It doesn't matter. We talked in London. Not long after, he was sent back to Moscow and executed. I wouldn't reveal his name any more than I would yours."

"If he's dead, there's no reason for you to withhold his name."

I agreed, but these people were patriotic conspirators. They, like the mafia, hated informers.

There was a woman across the table, a redhead with piercing green eyes. She leaned toward me and said in a harsh voice, "Understand this, the only reason you're still alive is that we believe you can help our cause by disrupting certain Kremlin plans that have come to our attention. We need to know that we can trust you. You need to trust us. Give us the name."

"Boris Kulik. He worked at the Russian Embassy in London."

They all turned to a tough-looking fellow. He announced to the group, "Boris Kulik was executed at Lubyanka Prison two weeks ago." To me, he said, "Pavel tells us you have in your possession FSB credentials. Explain, please."

"They're forgeries, part of my plan to get out of Russia when I finish my work."

He gave me nothing in return. My guess? He was some kind of cop, there to assess our trustworthiness.

Jill spoke for the first time. "Tell us about Omega."

The redhead responded with fire in her eyes. "Omega is a group of patriots dedicated to taking back Mother Russia's wealth from the apparatchiks, the oligarchs, and the mafia, and bringing them to justice. We have Omega members at every level and sector of society, government, banking—even in the security services and the mafia."

She pointed to the wall. "This is our flag, the Omega flag—the claw, globe, and arrow, superimposed on the flag of the Russian Federation. The arrow signifies pursuit—pursuit of the thieves who have stolen Mother Russia's wealth. The globe shows that they have hidden that stolen wealth around the world and we will follow it to those hiding places. The claw symbolizes our global reach and our intention to claw back that wealth, return it to Russia, and punish the thieves."

Apparently, she was the group ideologue and probably designed the flag.

Jill pressed her. "Why do you call yourselves the Omega Group?"

"Omega is the last letter in the Greek alphabet. For us, it signifies the time when the pillage of Mother Russia's resources ends. When that time comes, the corrupt political system will crumble and the thieves will flee to the ends of the earth to enjoy their ill-gotten gains. We will pursue them. We will find them. We will take back what

belongs to Mother Russia. We will destroy them and any who bene-
fited from their thievery—the families, the bankers, the politicians,
the mafia—all of them."

She looked at me, her eyes burning with patriotic intensity.
"Which brings us to you. You want to follow the money, like your
special prosecutor."

"That always works," I told her. "I want to see the Allgemeine
Volksbank records of all oligarch wealth management funds, and the
money transfers in and out of those funds. Can you help me?"

"That is not possible. Those records are inaccessible."

"What does inaccessible mean to you?"

"Since the world press has drawn attention to those records, they
have been taken offline. They are now managed in stand-alone computers in a secure room at the bank. Therefore, they are not susceptible
to hacking and any attempt to copy them would alert the cybersecu-
rity staff. That is what inaccessible means to me."

Pavel spoke soothingly to me. "We understand that you want to
document the precise origins of the money to follow its trail. Records
are useful, but we know the money is being stolen and who is stealing
it. Omega's first priority is to understand the systems for laundering
Russian money. Then, we identify the destinations. When the time
comes, we will get it back."

He added, "If you understand how the money is moved, I think
you will then know what specific records you need in order to follow
the money to Walldrum and on to its ultimate destinations. If you are
interested in *how*, we can help you."

I wasn't very interested. I wanted the damned wealth fund records,
but I didn't want to offend our hosts, especially the shotgun rider
standing behind us with my gun. Nor did I want Pavel—the apparent
organizer of this little gathering—to lose face. After all, he had saved
us from Uncle Dimitri's final solution. I announced, "We're all ears."

"Good." Pavel gave me a little smile of appreciation. "There are many illegal operations and simultaneous activities. A great deal of wealth is laundered through real estate transactions in foreign countries. To understand that aspect of the laundering process, we examined one real estate project in detail. With the information we uncovered"—he looked at me—"some of it hearsay, we developed what we think is one of the money laundering protocols. I will use Walldrum Tower in Panama as an example, because it is the project about which we have the most information . . . and the best guesses.

"Assume that oligarchs steal a billion dollars. They deposit the money into a wealth management account at their favorite Moscow bank—Allgemeine Volksbank, AVB. Next, they need to get the money out of Russia. They can't wire it to another country without triggering alarms throughout the banking system. The authorities—bank regulators and tax people—will ask where did this money come from? To whom does it belong? How did the owner earn it? What is the purpose for sending it here? The thieves don't want those questions asked. Also, if they are under sanctions, the money or any assets purchased with it might be seized. So, the money must be laundered in such a way that it can't be traced to the source—the oligarch funds.

"To achieve this, the oligarchs conspire with a legitimate-looking real estate developer in the States—like Ted Walldrum—to move money. The developer applies to the bank—AVB—for a loan. Both the oligarchs and the bank want to keep the source of funds secret. So, the bank transfers the money out of the oligarch's account and merges it with the bank's pool of cash available for loans. They loan the developer four hundred million dollars to build a high-rise condo hotel in Panama. The developer builds the high-rise and furnishes it in lavish style, but at a cost of just three hundred million dollars. On paper, it costs four hundred million because a quarter of his expenses are supported by bogus invoices for materials and services never delivered."

The redhead interrupted him. "There is a unit here in Moscow that prepares phony invoices for each real estate project. If there is ever an audit of the expenses, there will be a paper trail and no apparent irregularities."

I asked Pavel, "What happens to the money the developer didn't spend?"

"He transfers it to a *real estate development fund*. Usually, the fund is in a third country where banking secrecy is tight and banking morals are loose. No one questions this transfer because real estate development requires lots of cash. Once the money is in Country 3, it's moved through a series of corporations, with hard-to-trace ownership, until it ends up in an LLC controlled by the oligarchs who funded the original loan. Then, front men for the oligarchs use that hundred million to buy condos from the developer in the Panama high-rise.

"The developer reports the hundred million in condo sales in his income tax filing. He deducts business expenses and, if he has a good accountant, he pays no taxes on that money. He might even get a credit. After taxes, the developer has somewhat less than a hundred million dollars in laundered Russian money. He takes a small percentage and transfers the bulk of the hundred million to an offshore account in Country 4, also controlled by the oligarchs who loaned him the original four hundred million. Since the developer paid taxes on the money, it's clean."

Jill asked, "When does the developer repay the four-hundred-million-dollar loan?"

Pavel smiled. "That's the magic in this transaction. Never."

"*Never?* How does the bank balance its books?"

"It doesn't. AVB falsifies the books to show the loan has been repaid. The oligarchs don't care. Their goal was to move the money out of Russia. It's been moved."

I expected Jill to be dumbfounded, but she was clinical. "What about bank regulators and audits?"

"The AVB branch in Moscow is regulated by the Kremlin. If an honest auditor discovered that money is missing, who would he report it to, the Kremlin?"

The room was silent until Jill broke the spell with an observation. "I calculate the oligarchs lost three-fourths of their four-hundred-million-dollar loan on the deal. That's expensive money laundering."

Pavel disagreed. "It's not as expensive as you think. They have a hundred million in laundered cash, plus another hundred million in condos. Those are just the first two phases of the operation. The big money moves during the third phase."

"What happens then?" Jill was taking over my interrogation.

"Remember, on paper, the building cost four hundred million. Since the developer has sold a hundred million in condos, the building is worth more. Through their front men, the oligarchs buy the building from the developer for six hundred million, using the hundred million in laundered cash as the down payment. The developer claims the sale on his taxes and recycles the down payment back to the oligarchs, after taking his laundering fee.

"Now, the oligarchs have about a hundred million in cash, and they own a six-hundred-million-dollar building, with a hundred million in condos inside the building. The building is a condo hotel. So, they also get the proceeds from the sale of condos and rents generated by the hotel."

I asked, "How do the oligarchs pay off the building?"

"More magic. The one hundred million is recycled through the developer and oligarchs until the building is paid for."

"What does the developer get for all his risk?"

"A percentage of each laundering transaction, he's paid to put his name on the building, and he earns an annual fee for managing the hotel."

I needed to get to the bottom line. "Once the smoke and mirrors are gone, how much wealth has been moved?"

"When the down payment is recycled back to the oligarchs, they have laundered two hundred million on this one project and they own the building. Multiply the cash and property in this transaction by the number of Walldrum towers in the world and you begin to grasp the magnitude of the thefts and the scope of the money laundering activities."

That was a lot to grasp and it caused a few gasps. Evidently, this was news to some of the Omegas. Or were they Omegans?

Pavel added, "If you really want your mind numbed, understand that Walldrum is just one of many real estate developers involved in operations like this."

It was time for me to exercise a little diplomacy and refocus this group on my needs. "That was an impressive education on money laundering, but without documentation, that part of my investigation is dead in the water. I need copies of those *inaccessible* bank records. The paper trail always catches the criminals."

"Not this time, I think," said Pavel.

"Why not?"

"It won't work because—if I may paraphrase one of your television personalities—you are playing checkers. Putin is playing three-dimensional chess."

"What are you talking about?"

"The Ironside Dossier stated Putin was getting reports from Walldrum on the business activities of oligarchs in the States. Why would he care? Once Putin rewards them by letting them steal money, why would he care what they did with it—care enough to get periodic reports on their business activities?"

"I'll give you that, it doesn't make sense. He could get Russian intelligence to check on the oligarchs."

"That's true, but you're missing the point. Why would Putin *want* reports from anyone on the oligarchs?"

Suddenly, I knew. "Because it's still Putin's money. It's not theirs."

"Exactly."

I asked, "Why didn't Putin stash the money in countries with strict banking secrecy laws and put his name on the accounts? Why give it to the oligarchs to hide for him in their names?"

The cop spoke up. "Putin was, is, and always will be KGB. The KGB never wanted its fingerprints on an operation, except to intimidate someone or an institution. During the Cold War, the KGB used assassins from Soviet satellites, like the Bulgarians, to do their dirty work. Today, it's little green men—Russian soldiers out of uniform—fighting in the Ukraine. Deniability is in Putin's DNA. He does not want his fingerprints on the billions he's moving out of Russia."

The redhead came at us, full of passion. "If the Russian people found out Putin had billions in foreign bank accounts, in his name, they would drive him from office. That would be the end of the kleptocracy, Omega Day. So, the accounts are in the names of oligarchs. And if Putin needs a sacrificial lamb for political purposes, he can burn an oligarch, confiscate his wealth, and maintain his status as a champion of the people."

"So, what is Putin's chess game?"

Pavel answered me. "As you know, U.S. sanctions are blocking Putin and his oligarchs from their stolen money and property. Putin wants those sanctions lifted and he sees Walldrum as his best hope for that outcome. Therefore, he wants Walldrum in power as long as possible and will do whatever is necessary to keep him there. To do that, Putin must ensure that Walldrum is not tainted with money laundering for Russians. That's the key. There is a scheme"—Pavel paused for effect—"to sever connections between the oligarchs' money and Walldrum."

He looked down the table to a man who had the demeanor and dress of a mid-level bureaucrat. "Arkady."

Arkady leaned forward, resting his forearms on the table. "There is a special records unit at the Allgemeine Volksbank, an entire floor of accountants and clerical staff working around the clock to develop a second set of bank records that exonerate Walldrum." Arkady smiled at me and Jill. "We learned from your master fraudster, Bernie Madoff."

I struggled to understand. "Didn't U.S. investigators request the AVB records?"

"That is correct."

"Did AVB provide them?"

"Not yet. AVB will surrender the records only if your government issues a subpoena."

"So, what's the point of fabricating a set of phony bank records?"

Another member entered the conversation. He had tried to dress down with a worn, stained leather coat, but the expensive shirt beneath the cashmere sweater sent a different message. He was a neat, white-haired man with a cultured voice. I guessed he was with the Russian Foreign Ministry, but changed that assessment to Economics Ministry or banking as he spoke.

"When the request came for the bank's records, a meeting was called to determine how to respond to it. One course of action was simply to deliver what was requested. It was clear that delivering the documents would provide your prosecutor evidence of money laundering.

"A second course of action was proposed: burn the Moscow branch of AVB to the ground, destroying all records. That was rejected as too obvious.

"Consideration was also given to having AVB refuse to provide any records, using banking privacy as a cover. That option was debated, but discarded because the U.S. would have sanctioned the entire AVB banking network. That would further cripple the ability of oligarchs to move money out of Russia or access their stolen funds abroad.

"It was decided that AVB would deliver all subpoenaed documents, but a countervailing strategy would be employed."

Jill interrupted him. "I'd like to know who attended that subpoena meeting."

"Senior representatives of the president's office, the bank, the ministries of Foreign Affairs and Economics, and the FSB. There was also representation from the oligarchs who have money in wealth management funds at AVB."

Jill insisted. "Names would help us confirm that the meeting took place."

Us? What's up, Jill?

The white-haired gentleman was adamant. "We will not provide names."

That didn't work for me. "Without names or corroboration from someone at the meeting, all I have is hearsay."

"We are not operating in a U.S. court of law where hearsay is inadmissible. You claim to be an intelligence professional. Have you never taken action based on hearsay?"

"I am not getting paid to report hearsay."

"And we are not getting paid to talk to you! We are here at the risk of our lives. Do you want to listen to us or not!"

Tension was high in the room. I asked, "Is there any vodka here?"

Everyone relaxed a notch. A guy in coveralls with dirt under his fingernails went to the office and returned with a fifth of vodka and a collection of mugs, glasses, and jelly jars. The bottle made one trip around the table and came back half empty.

Pavel interrupted our moment of togetherness by announcing, "It's getting late."

I asked, "What's the strategy to deal with the records AVB plans to deliver to our investigators in response to subpoenas?"

Arkady, who had been sidelined by the subpoena discussion, resumed his story. "As I said, there is a records unit at the AVB developing a second set of bank records that exonerate Walldrum."

"If our investigators get copies of the originals, what's the point of making a phony set?"

"To discredit the originals. If Walldrum is tried or impeached, there will be a discovery process, yes? Your prosecutor must provide copies of the subpoenaed AVB records. Walldrum's attorneys will ask AVB for the same records given to your prosecutor. AVB intends to provide the forged records. Therefore, the special prosecutor's records will be different from the ones Walldrum's defense team gets from AVB. The defense will claim that your special prosecutor altered their copies to falsely implicate Walldrum."

I finished his scenario. "And, at best, the jury will be convinced there's a conspiracy against Walldrum. At worst, they'll be confused. Americans won't know who is telling the truth. The case will be dismissed and Walldrum remains in the presidency doing Putin's bidding."

"Yes," agreed Arkady.

It was mind-boggling, but what about the past year wasn't. I said, "I need proof. If I can't have names, I want to see samples of documents AVB will provide in response to the subpoena and the same documents that have been altered."

Arkady was prepared. "I have documents. Pavel said you would want proof."

The group cleared half of the table and Arkady laid out copies of original money transfers and other bank records side by side with the altered ones. I pulled out my pocket-size tourist camera and took photographs.

As soon as I snapped the last frame, Arkady scooped up the documents, threw them into a trash can, and put a match to them. The fellow who had delivered the vodka grabbed the can and left the room.

"Convinced?" asked Pavel.

I was ... almost, but Moscow Rule Number 3 is: everyone is potentially under opposition control. Arkady—and this whole group, for that matter—could be selling me a boatload of snake oil at the direction of the FSB.

I told Arkady, "I want to visit the unit that prepares the fake records."

He was shocked. "That is impossible."

For a group conspiring against oligarchs, the mafia, and the might of the Russian Federation, these guys had a narrow conception of what was possible. I had to change that or go around it. "Why is it impossible?"

"The floor," Arkady replied, "is restricted to workers, a bank supervisor who oversees the operation, security staff, and a FSB officer, who visits regularly."

"How often does the FSB officer come?"

"Once every two weeks. He gets a progress report from the floor supervisor."

"Does the same FSB officer come each time?"

"Usually. Sometimes his supervisor is with him."

"When was the last FSB visit?"

"Yesterday."

"Tell me about your unit: location, access procedures, floor plan, work routine, and names and ranks of the FSB officers who visit the unit."

Pavel interrupted me by announcing to the group, "Sorry, but it's time to go, everyone." The group dispersed and began loading into vehicles parked in the shop.

I took Arkady aside. Jill made a move toward us. I gave her a wave off. She raised her eyebrows and stayed put, while Arkady gave me some quick answers to my questions.

When he finished, I promised, "I'm coming to see that unit, Arkady."

He saw I was serious. Arkady took a digital storage thumb drive from his pocket and showed it to me. "Buy two of these. They must be exactly like this one. If you come to the bank, bring them with you. I will try to have two identical drives on my desk. You must exchange yours for mine without attracting attention." He gripped my forearm. "Make this work. Omega is depending on you to get this information to your investigators. It is very dangerous for all of us."

Roger that, Arkady.

He got into a sedan. Someone turned out the building lights and opened the bay doors. We watched the vehicles quietly roll out of the shop, headlights off. The shotgun rider returned our pistols.

Jill and I climbed into the van with Pavel and he drove us to the farm. We didn't talk. There was plenty for everyone to think about. The Omega Group had exposed itself to us, but my concern was that Jill and I had exposed ourselves to them. If there was a FSB informant in that shop, he—or she—knew about us and saw our faces.

Outside of our bunkhouse, I let Jill start for the door and said, "Go on up. I'll be there in a minute. I need a word with Pavel."

Jill glared at me, turned, and went into the barn.

Standing in the darkness I said, "Pavel, after I visit that records unit, the FSB will be onto Jill and me. I need to plan for our departure. Do you have any hackers in Omega?"

"Of course."

"I need one to hack into your airline flight and crew schedules."

"You want to hack into Aeroflot?"

"Yes."

Pavel sighed and looked at me like I was out of my mind, but he nodded.

At last, I had asked for something that wasn't impossible. Progress in small steps.

"What do you want to know?" Pavel asked.

"I want a list of flights leaving Moscow for Panama City during the next two weeks and names, addresses, and photographs of crew members scheduled on those flights."

"Yes, and I want a new Mercedes with a good heater and air-conditioning."

Old Pavel had a sense of humor. He just shook his head and got into the van. Before he drove off, he leaned out of the window and said, "First, we try without the hacker. We have friends at Aeroflot. Give me a couple of days."

When I got up to the bunkhouse, Jill was pacing and angry. "What were you and Pavel talking about?"

"It doesn't concern you, yet."

"Why are you still keeping me in the dark, Max?"

"I'm not keeping you in the dark. I'm telling you what you need to know when you need to know it." I had something else to set Jill straight on. "You asked questions that interrupted the flow of my conversation with the Omegas. Don't do that again. I'm a trained listener and interrogator. I know how I want to guide the conversation. Bowen assigned you as my assistant. You're not my partner."

"You didn't mind me being your partner in St. Petersburg when those two pimps had the drop on you at Tatyana's apartment."

"You did what was necessary to get us out of there. As I remember, you wrote your job description the day we met: crack shot, karate chop, and resident ass-kicker. You're the muscle here, not the master-mind. Stick to your specialties and we'll get along fine."

Jill didn't reply. She made a show of checking her pistol, jacked a round into the chamber, and shoved the gun under her pillow.

CHAPTER 22

THE NEXT MORNING, we had a breakfast of eggs, sausages, bread, and tea, delivered by a middle-aged man in farm work clothes. He ignored Jill and said to me, "Pavel called. The message from your sister is that your mother is better. You can visit her today at the hospital near Gorky Park."

That was a message from Sherri. She wanted to see me.

Later that morning, the farmer drove Jill and me to the nearest Metro station and we rode the train to Gorky Park where the crowds were large enough for us to blend in. As we left the train, Jill peeled off to watch my back. When I got to the park, Sherri was walking near our prearranged meeting point. I didn't see Tony-D, but I was sure he was there watching her back. I sauntered over to Sherri. There was excitement in her eyes. We made a show of the long-lost greeting and walked hand in hand down the path.

"What's up?" I asked.

"I connected a reporter to a hotel maid, Anya Koslowskaya. Both were killed about the same time by persons unknown. I used the information in the maid's obituary to locate her family. They were angry that Anya's murder was never solved. Her mother was eager to help when I told her we were looking into it. She told me that Anya worked at the Riga-Ritz until a few weeks before she was killed. She gave me the name of Anya's best friend, Yulia. Yulia was also a maid in the Ritz, same floor, same shift as Anya. Both of them were reassigned to another Intourist hotel on the same day."

"For the convenience of the government," I suggested.

"Right."

To clarify the sequence of events, I asked, "All this happened in 2013?"

"No. The reassignments and murders happened in June 2015."

"Right before Walldrum announced he was running for president?"

"The maids were reassigned two days after."

I laid out a likely sequence. "Day one, the Kremlin called a meeting to decide how to cover Walldrum's tracks at the Ritz. Day two, they fired everyone with knowledge of the incident and doctored the hotel's records."

"Sounds right to me," Sherri agreed.

For the benefit of suspicious eyes, Sherri squeezed my arm and kissed me on the cheek. And I don't think she minded that it might piss off Jill Rucker. "But that's another story," as Lou Jacobi said in the movie.

"Tell me about Anya's friend, Yulia."

"She lives in the same building as Anya's mother. I visited Yulia, but she was reluctant to talk. I offered a thousand U.S. dollars. Can you pay her?"

"If she has worthwhile information, sure. When can I meet her?"

"See that lady in front of us, green coat, pushing a baby carriage? That's Yulia. So, get your money ready. This lady is pay-to-play, all the way."

I detoured into a public urinal, took ten hundred-dollar bills from my money vest, rolled them into a tight cylinder, and secured it with a rubber band. When I came out, Sherri was talking to the lady pushing the carriage. I joined them.

Sherri introduced me. "Yulia, this is my friend. He's also a reporter."

We shook hands and I palmed her the roll of hundreds. She saw zeroes on the top bill and pocketed the money. Yulia was thin, dark, and sullen, an unhappy toiler in the fields of Putin's paradise. "What do you want to know?" she asked.

"Tell me about the incident at the Ritz in 2013 involving Ted Walldrum and prostitutes."

We strolled while Yulia told her story in broken English. "The morning after . . ." she screwed her face into a mask of disgust ". . . after the nastiness, my friend, Anya, and I went to clean suite where Walldrum stayed. Mattress was soaked with pee and stinking. I call housekeeping supervisor. Men came and took away whole bed. Later, they bring new one. We don't think more about it, until day we are fired."

"When was that?"

"Two years later, 2015."

"How did you know your firing was about Walldrum?"

"Supervisor call meeting to remind us of nastiness in 2013. He tell us not to discuss with anyone. He say it is state secret."

"Did you see Walldrum or the women in the room?"

"No."

"How do you know Walldrum was there?"

"I see pictures of Walldrum in room and women standing on bed peeing."

"Where did you see these pictures?"

"I know man who worked at Ritz. He was FSB and make movies of guests in their rooms for *kompromat*. He take other pictures for himself."

"For what purpose?"

"He want to give pictures to CIA so they can see who is victim of FSB *kompromat*. In return, he want to leave Russia with family. Go to United States."

Sherri and I exchanged glances. We knew this could be big.

Yulia continued. "The day Walldrum say he is running for President of United States, this man come to me and Anya. He is very excited. He say he had way out of Russia and show us pictures of Walldrum and women in the middle of the nastiness. Next day, everyone on our floor must leave Ritz.

"Anya love working at Ritz. She is very angry. Later, she talk to reporter about the nastiness. They kill her . . . and reporter."

There were tears in Yulia's eyes. I let her run with the grief for a while and we didn't talk. The baby whimpered. Yulia gave it a little reassuring pat on the cheek and a loving smile. I nodded for Sherri to continue.

"What happened to your FSB friend?" asked Sherri.

"They send him to Tula, far away from Moscow. No opportunity there for him to meet Westerners and sell photographs." Suddenly, she was energized. "But you are here now. You are not reporter. You are CIA, yes?"

Moscow Rule Number 6: stay within your cover. I repeated, "I'm a reporter. My paper has CIA contacts. I need to speak to this man with the *kompromat* pictures?" I didn't believe he was in Tula. If so, this conversation would have been pointless.

Yulia raised her arm. Up ahead, a tall man in a fur hat and dark overcoat waved back with his newspaper and started toward us. He needed a shave and—judging from his scowl—and an attitude adjustment.

Yulia said, "That is man with pictures."

"You said he was in Tula."

"He is on holiday, in Moscow for Winter Festival."

Whatever. I hope he's in Moscow for a show-and-tell with the Walldrum photos.

Sherri and I had our own signals with our shadows, Tony-D and Jill. We looked back and got all-clears that we weren't being followed or walking into an obvious trap.

The Tula visitor did kissy-face routines with Yulia and Sherri, and gave me a big hug and a frisk. Any listening devices? No. Just friends meeting in the park.

He kept his voice low, speaking excellent English, switching to Russian and safe subjects when anyone came close. He got right to business. "You are looking for photographs of a certain hotel guest?"

"Yes."

"I will give them to you, if you get me and two other people out of Russia."

I was sure he was talking about Yulia and the infant in the carriage. He declared, "You are CIA."

"I'm an investigative reporter working for a newspaper in the States."

"You're also wasting my time. Do you want the photographs or not?"

"I want them. Why haven't you traded them before now?"

"I've been in fucking Tula for two-and-a-half years. Even Russians don't come to Tula. Forget about MI6 or the CIA.

"Here's a sample." He pulled back the baby's blanket revealing an 8-by-10 photo of Ted Walldrum looking on with a smile, while three women urinated on the bed. Over Walldrum's shoulder, on a desk, I could make out the hotel logo on a leather-bound services book, and a copy of the *International Times*. The newspaper date could be pulled up without much technical effort. Someone—probably one of Walldrum's Russian companions—had done a masterful job of setting up the future President of the United States. Or was someone setting me up? Hey, that's Moscow.

Leaning over the carriage, Mr. Tula shuffled through five more photos while he cooed at the baby and smiled for the benefit of any surveillance cameras. When he thought I had seen enough, he pulled up the baby's blanket. "Satisfied?"

"I need to see the negatives."

He laughed derisively. "What century are you from? They're digital photos."

"Then, I need the camera card."

"You get the camera card when I get to New York."

"It doesn't work that way. If you're FSB, you know that. Nobody's going to buy retouched pictures from you. Give me a couple of photographs and the card. If they stand up to technical analysis, you can negotiate a way out."

"Without the photos and the card, I have no bargaining power."

"Don't you have photographs of other Westerners you've compromised?"

"Maybe."

"Well, if you convert 'maybe' to 'yes,' there's your bargaining chip. Your move."

"No. It's your move. You want the photographs. Figure out how to protect my interests. Put some effort into it. I could make an anonymous phone call to the FSB and you would be in an interrogation cell by midnight."

I gave him a hard stare. "If that happened, the first thing I'd give up is Yulia's name and address. Your description would be the second. It won't be hard for the FSB to find out who was taking dirty pictures at the Ritz in 2013."

Sherri intervened. "Let's not threaten each other. A compromise is possible. You"—she addressed the Tula guy—"have valuable photographs, but they're worthless unless you find a buyer. We're buying. Suppose we buy the pictures and the camera chip from you. We can deposit the purchase price in a Swiss account. That way, if the CIA won't smuggle you out, you may be able to bribe your way out."

Tula hesitated. "How much money?"

Sherri looked at me.

"Seventy thousand Swiss francs." I made it sound like a first and final offer.

"How do I know I can trust you?"

Sherri asked, "How do we know the photographs are genuine? We don't. We have to trust each other to get this deal done."

"If you are not CIA, where would you get seventy thousand francs?"

Sherri smiled and stayed with our cover. "Do you know how many newspapers we would sell around the world with one of your photographs on the front page?"

"When will you deposit the francs?"

I answered. "As soon as we authenticate the photographs, three weeks."

"That's too long."

"It's not. I have to smuggle the photographs out, get a technical analysis, and make arrangements for your payment."

"How will I know when the francs are in my account?"

"Your newspaper." I pointed to the one under his arm. "In four weeks, there will be a job announcement in the *International Times* for a forensic accountant. The job number will be your numbered account at the WorldCorp Bank in Geneva. The code at the end of the job description will allow you to access your funds."

"What about my way out of Russia?"

"If your photos are authentic and an exit is possible, someone will contact Yulia."

"I don't like these arrangements."

"Can you think of better ones?"

Tula looked off into the distance, probably considering his options. Then, he laid his newspaper in the carriage and pretended to focus on the baby. He stuffed the photographs into an envelope and folded the newspaper around it. We all walked awhile in silence. Abruptly,

Tula turned to me and shook my hand. There was a camera chip in his palm.

"Goodbye, Mr. Reporter. I hope to see you soon. Now, kiss Yulia and don't forget to say goodbye to the little one."

I bear-hugged Tula, did the kissing routine with Yulia, patted the baby's cheek, and took the newspaper and envelope. Sherri, Yulia, and Tula gathered around the baby carriage to shield me while I slid the newspaper under my overcoat.

Sherri and I broke off and walked a few blocks. I had Sherri signal Tony-D to join us. Jill lagged discreetly behind us on overwatch.

When Tony-D arrived, I said, "Nice job, you two. Your work is done here. I need you to pack up in Moscow and go to Panama City."

Tony-D wanted to know, "Florida or the Canal Zone?"

"The Canal Zone."

"What's in the Canal Zone?" asked Sherri.

"I've got a lead on how Walldrum's money laundering scheme works. Informants told me that Walldrum got a four-hundred-million-dollar construction loan to build the Panama Walldrum Tower. He skimmed off over a hundred and fifty million and laundered it for the Russians."

Tony-D whistled. "I was in the Panama Walldrum Tower on a VIP security team once. Every item I saw there was top quality. I worked at my uncle's architectural firm for three summers and I can tell you that a luxury forty-five-story condo-hotel averages out at seven-to-twelve million dollars per floor. Forty-five floors at the minimum of seven million a floor comes to well over three hundred million. There's no way Walldrum built his Panama Tower and skimmed a hundred and fifty million off the construction loan."

Sherri asked, "What if he used cheap labor and substandard construction materials?"

"Walldrum couldn't build it and skim that much money if he used slave labor and plywood." Tony-D asked me, "Are you sure about the size of the skim?"

"I'm sure about what I heard."

Tony-D gave us his assessment. "Well, the numbers for the construction loan, the quality of the building, and the amount of skim don't add up. There's something fishy about this whole thing."

I asked, "Do we know any experts on Walldrum's business in Panama?"

"The reporter David Sanchez," said Sherri. "He did a TV special on the Panama Papers. He's an authority on financial corruption in Panama."

"Get on down to Panama and find him. See if you can set up an interview for me."

Sherri wanted to know, "When are you leaving?"

"As soon as I make a withdrawal from the Allgemeine Volksbank."

* * *

Sherri and Tony-D went on their way. Jill and I took lunch in the Arbat district. Afterwards, we walked to our rendezvous with Pavel. It was cold, but I wanted to see if we were being followed. I checked behind us in store windows and sideview mirrors of cars. That was breaking Moscow Rule Number 4: Don't look back; you're never completely alone.

Why did I sense I was being followed when there was no one behind me?

Sherlock Holmes said, "When you've eliminated the impossible, what remains, no matter how improbable, is the truth."

Maybe the person following me was beside me. Moscow Rule Number 2: Never go against your gut.

Jill distracted me from those dark thoughts with annoying questions. "Get anything good in the park?"

"It's too early to tell." That was true. The rest was to throw her off the scent. "The guy at the baby carriage knows a guy who might know something useful. The baby carriage guy will contact Pavel if the guy with the information wants to talk."

"Any names for these guys in case you need to contact them?"

"There are things I don't want to know. You can't give up names you don't know."

"What was that cluster at the baby carriage about?" She was sharp.

"That's none of your damned business," was what I wanted say. Instead, I lied, "The baby threw up."

"Who was the woman?"

"Just a prop, as far as I could tell."

Jill stopped asking questions. My guess? She wasn't buying any of it.

*   *   *

We connected with Pavel and he drove us to the farm without any substantive conversation. When we arrived at the barn, I thanked Pavel. Jill and I headed inside.

Pavel said, "Max, a word?"

"Sure. About what?"

"Vasili Bogdanovich." Pavel couldn't call Bogdanovich "father" after believing that General Grishin was his father for all those years.

I told Jill, "I'll be up in a few."

She kept walking to the barn, and I heard her footsteps going up to the bunkhouse. To get away from the bitter cold, I slid into the front seat next to Pavel.

He asked, "How much time did you spend with Bogdanovich?"

"About eight hours."

"What was your impression?"

"He was smart. He played his hand with his British handlers strategically. He made sure they would take care of him."

"Was he a moral person?"

"That's hard to know in the short time I spent with him. I can tell you that your father gave MI6 the *kompromat* material on Walldrum as soon as he heard Walldrum was running for president. I consider that a moral act."

Pavel was silent for a while. "Did he mention my mother?"

"I didn't ask about his personal life before or after he defected. We had a lot to cover in the time I was with him."

"And he didn't mention me?"

"No."

Pavel said, "The name you gave me—one of Bogdanovich's assassins—I found no record of him. Are you sure . . . ?"

"I'm sure. He worked directly for the Kremlin. His record is probably secret. My CIA contact identified him after he was killed in London."

"You said there were others involved."

"Also killed in London." I didn't tell Pavel about the one who escaped. I wanted to give him closure.

"Did you kill them?"

"No, but I know who did."

Pavel looked away and nodded sharply as if the matter was finally settled.

I asked, "Do you have a family, Pavel?"

"I have a son. He is with my wife. We are divorced."

"I'm sorry."

"So am I, but it was for the best. I had to make her divorce me. The work I do with Omega is dangerous. If I am caught, they would try to use my family against me. The divorce was to protect them. My wife knows that. It was hard, but she agreed that my work is important."

"Do you get to see your family?"

"From a distance. I can't make contact if I want to protect them."
Pavel turned and looked at me. "As I said, the work is important."

It was getting dark. Pavel turned on the overhead light. He took a
briefcase from the floor and placed it on the seat between us, removed
a manila folder, and handed it to me. The folder contained Aeroflot
flight schedules, along with crew names and their photographs cross-
referenced to flights.

He said, "There are no direct flights from Moscow to Panama. I
recommend you take a Moscow-to-Paris flight. It's only three and a
half hours. If our security services are after you, that flight gets you
quickly to the West. Then, take Air France to Panama City. In the
next few days, there are several flights from Sheremetyevo Airport to
Paris." He pulled another list from the folder. "Here are names and
addresses of the crews on the Paris flights. Do you intend to contact
any of these people?"

"That's possible."

"International flight crews are subject to surveillance by the security services. You should not go to their homes."

"Where would you suggest?"

"Because of rest requirements before an international flight, these
crews spend the night before their flights at this airport hotel." Pavel
pointed to the name and address he had printed at the top of a flight
schedule page. "The hotel would be a good place to catch them."

I looked through Pavel's documents and found a pair of crew members on the same flights that conformed to profiles I had in mind—a
male flight engineer who resembled me, a female flight attendant who
resembled Jill Rucker.

I decided to push my luck. "If I give you our photographs, can you
get Jill and me airport security passes?"

"I think not. Too many people would be involved."

"Anyway, good work," I told Pavel. "Thank you."

He smiled. "You're welcome . . . and no hacker required." He remembered something and took several folded sheets of paper from his pocket and gave them to me. They were hand-drawn floor plans of the Moscow branch of the Allgemeine Volksbank.

We said good night and Pavel drove away.

CHAPTER 23

Moscow, the Minister's Office

THE MINISTER SAT at the desk in his cavernous office overlooking the square. He wore his olive drab general's uniform with yellow and red lapel piping. Pinned above three rows of ribbons on his left breast was a gold star dangling beneath a ribbon of white, blue, and red—the flag colors of the Russian Federation. The medal signified that he was a Hero of the Russian Federation who had shown "conspicuous bravery . . . in the service of the state."

Lieutenant Colonel Zabluda and Major Ipatyev strode up to the general's desk and saluted.

The general returned their salutes and looked at them with hooded blue eyes beneath heavy white eyebrows. In a gravelly voice he ordered, "Succinctly, without the sauce, tell me why you have not found the American spies, Geller and Rucker."

Zabluda replied, "Sir, my men were in St. Petersburg, ready to execute the mission. I had two teams, one for surveillance and one for wet work. As a courtesy, I informed the FSB sector commander, Colonel Dragonov, of the outlines of my operation and requested minor assistance.

"Colonel Dragonov is ambitious. He saw an opportunity to enhance his reputation by taking over part of my operation against the

Americans. He called his benefactor, the deputy director. The deputy ordered me to stand down my surveillance team, and gave the surveillance mission to Dragonov.

"Dragonov bungled it. He lost Geller and Rucker minutes after they left the cruise ship. I ordered Dragonov to take emergency measures to find the subjects and—"

"*You* ordered?" The general reminded Zabluda, "Colonel Dragonov outranks you."

"I gave him the option of taking my . . . recommendations or I would expose his incompetence."

The general pursed his lips and stared at Zabluda, who continued, unfazed.

"While I attended to other matters, Major Ipatyev stayed in Colonel Dragonov's operations center to monitor implementation of the measures I recommended."

The general shifted his steely gaze to Ipatyev.

The major related the efforts to find Geller and Rucker. "Sir, Colonel Dragonov's staff reviewed video recordings of every conceivable location where Geller might have been, but was unable to locate him. They also interviewed taxi drivers and bus drivers who may have transported the subjects, but were unable to find or track Geller and Rucker."

"Not even a trace?" asked the general.

"A trace, yes, sir. We found two abandoned suitcases in lockers at St. Petersburg's Moskovsky train station. The suitcases contained clothing and other personal articles belonging to a man and a woman. Security camera footage shows the subjects putting their suitcases into the lockers and, separately, purchasing one-way tickets to Moscow."

"When did they travel to Moscow?"

"Four days ago, the same day they arrived in St. Petersburg by cruise ship."

Zabluda spoke up. "The timing suggests they made contact with their sources in St. Petersburg soon after their arrival and acquired the information they came for."

"Where were you, Colonel Zabluda, during this Dragonov dragnet?"

"I left St. Petersburg for Moscow as soon as I discovered that Dragonov had lost the subjects. I assumed Geller might be in Moscow already or on his way. I came here to organize the search."

"Are Geller and Rucker in Moscow now?"

"Yes, sir," answered Major Ipatyev. "They took the overnight train to Moscow the same evening they purchased their tickets."

"Where are they?"

Zabluda answered. "The trail went cold after they got to Moscow. We know they arrived on the train during morning rush hour, very clever. They separated and took several cabs to throw us off the scent. Later that day, security cameras recorded them at Partiyanskaya Metro station. They were gone before we could establish surveillance. I'm sure they vary their travel modes and patterns. Good tradecraft," observed Zabluda.

"What about the doubles who replaced Geller and Rucker on the cruise? Have you arrested them?"

"No, sir."

"Why not?"

"Because arresting them might alert Geller that we're tracking him."

"How would he know that the doubles were arrested?"

"All it would take is passing a few hundred dollars and a cheap cell phone to a member of the ship's crew, a cabin boy or a low-level member of the security staff. That's how I would do it. So, I don't want to signal Geller that we know he's in Russia. I need him to be comfortable until I'm ready to take him down."

The general was not pleased. "So, Geller is comfortable and moving freely about Moscow while you are doing what?"

"I'm following leads, General. Two days after Geller and Rucker arrived in Moscow, our technical support unit alerted me that someone initiated an Internet search for two obituaries. One was for a former maid at the Riga-Ritz. The other was for a newspaper reporter who was investigating certain activities at the Ritz. Both were murder victims and the cases remain unsolved."

The general grumbled, "That again? Who was reading those obituaries and why?"

"It was an American woman, Sherri Layton. She arrived in Moscow on a tourist visa, two days before Geller and Rucker. She and her boyfriend were here for the Winter Festival."

"That is their cover," surmised the general.

"Yes, sir. Layton used the obituaries to identify the maid and find her mother. Layton questioned the mother about her daughter's death. We know this because we followed the same path and interrogated the mother yesterday."

"Was the mother cooperative?"

"Fully cooperative. She told me Layton claimed to be a reporter, seeking information about the maid's death because her murder was never solved."

"And never will be, if you do your job. Is the Layton woman working with Geller?"

"Yes. We have video footage of Rucker meeting Layton at Leningradsky train station three days ago."

"What did the maid's mother tell Layton?"

"The little she knew. Her daughter worked at the Ritz. She was transferred without explanation and killed in a robbery weeks later."

"Where is the Layton woman now?"

"She left the country yesterday, one day after she talked to the maid's mother."

"These Americans seem to be a step ahead of you every time. Layton's gone and you can't find Geller."

"Geller is very good at his job."

"It sounds like he's better than your best, Zabluda. Is he?"

"Not better, sir, just faster, thanks to the head start Colonel Dragonov gave him in St. Petersburg. And, so far, Geller has been lucky."

"How do you intend to change *your* luck, Colonel?"

"First, we will pursue any clues to his whereabouts. Second, every plainclothes and uniformed officer in Moscow has his picture. We may get lucky and catch him moving about in the city or on his way out."

"You've alerted the transportation authorities?"

"Of course, but Geller would have anticipated that. We can't expect to catch him with something as routine as an airport, seaport, or train station security check. In his shoes, I would have planned something unique for my escape."

"You may have to, if you don't find Geller." The statement was not meant to convey humor. The general added, "There is no margin for failure on this mission."

Zabluda was not one to be intimidated by rank or threats. He continued with a professional demeanor. "Without the sauce, General, I may not be able to establish surveillance in Moscow. Geller lived and worked here. He knows the territory. I'm sure he has contacts here and even friends who might hide him and help him move about. I have little hope that we will find Maxwell Geller or his partner before they leave Russia. And, as I said, I assume Geller has an escape plan that gives him a better-than-average chance of getting out of the country."

"What is your plan to deal with that eventuality?"

"We know where Geller will go when he leaves Russia. I plan to be there waiting for him and I will complete my mission."

CHAPTER 24

IT SNOWED THE next day, not enough to bring Moscow to a halt, but enough to stay at home if you had no pressing business in the city. Farmer Boris—I never knew his real name—came to wake us with a breakfast of stew, black bread, and tea. Following Pavel's advice, I rewarded Boris with an envelope full of rubles. He nodded, but said nothing and left.

After Jill and I ate, we settled down to plan our visit to the records counterfeiting room at the Allgemeine Volksbank using the hand-drawn floor plans Pavel had given me the previous evening. We sat next to each other on a bench that ran the length of the wooden table, on which I laid the floor plans. We devised and rehearsed scenarios to convince the bank manager to take us to the counterfeiting unit on the third floor. Once we had those cold, we gamed every conceivable question and event that could prevent us from getting out of AVB without shooting anyone or getting shot.

My interactions with Jill were mission-focused, but there was palpable tension between us from many sources. Jill resented me for keeping her in the dark about aspects of the operation. I was tense because I didn't know who she was. According to Sherri's research, the version of Jill Rucker with me had almost no history. I was angry that Jill was trying to deceive me, with so much riding on my success.

There was also sexual tension born of close quarters in the snowstorm and abstinence since our hot sex on the cruise ship.

By evening, we had exhausted all foreseeable scenarios and gamed all of our responses. Simultaneously, we turned to each other to speak. Looking into each other's eyes, the tensions exploded with animal ferocity. We went at each other with a face-sucking, button-popping, zipper-ripping, crotch-grabbing lust. We propelled ourselves into one of the lower bunks, but it was too confining. We tore two mattresses from bunk beds, threw them and each other to the floor. We caressed and lunged at each other until there was a second, more exhausting explosion of tension. And a third. Until we lay naked and exhausted on the mattresses and the cold of the bunkhouse threatened us with hypothermia. I pulled quilts off all the bunks and made a warm nest for us on the mattresses. We lay there and slept the sleep of the dead until early morning.

We showered, dressed, and checked our pistols. Pavel came early to take us to Moscow. The sky was slate gray and the snow was passable.

The Moscow branch of the Allgemeine Volksbank was in a renovated building of classical style, high exterior steps, and massive columns designed to project strength and engender confidence. Depending on what side of the legal divide you were on, that confidence was a good cover or misplaced. An indicator of the extent of the bank's criminal activity was that its parent organization had recently been fined five hundred million dollars for money laundering. Management just reached into shareholders' pockets and paid the fine without batting an eye or admitting guilt. Nobody is guilty. Nobody goes to jail. Nobody gets screwed, except the shareholders. Welcome to the wonderful world of capitalism.

Jill and I were armed. Our guns triggered a buzzer and flashing lights as we passed through the screener. We flashed our phony creds.

I said, "FSB," and we kept walking.

A guard scrambled to block our path. "Sir, it is forbidden to take your firearms into the bank. You can leave them with us. We will return them when you leave."

I gave him a hard look. "What if we're here to arrest someone?"

His mouth fell open. We walked past him, past the protesting secretary, into the manager's office. The manager was a rotund guy who had consumed too much borscht or vodka. We walked to his desk and flashed our FSB credentials.

I announced myself as, "Colonel Usenko. This is Major Yukovka. We're here to inspect the special records unit. Please show it to us."

The manager was surprised. I anticipated he would try to clear our visit with the FSB officer who normally visited the unit. I was right.

He sputtered, "I . . . I'll have to call Colonel Kozar."

"Do you have his number at Lubyanka Prison? He was arrested this morning."

The manager turned pale. "For . . . for what?"

"Are you considering a career in the security services?" Jill sneered. "You would make an excellent interrogator." Both of us gave him deadpans.

The blood drained from his face. While he was still on his mental heels, I said, "I require a list of the personnel assigned to the special unit." He was glued to his spot and shaking. "Today, if you please!"

That snapped the manager out of his trance. He sat at his computer and printed a copy. I handed it to Jill without looking at it or her. "And one for me."

He printed another. To really mess with his head, I made a show of reading down the list, pointed to a random name, and showed it to Jill. She nodded, having no idea what I was up to. I folded the list and put it in my pocket. I thought the manager might go into shock.

"Take us to the unit. I require an operations briefing."

The three of us got into an elevator. The manager inserted a key and took us to the third floor. He led us down the hall to a large window-less room. It contained a staff of about forty people. There were no desks. Individual staff members sat at long worktables strewn with documents. Each table had two computers, a printer, and scanner. My quick assessment of this operation was that copies of original documents destined for the U.S. investigators were in one computer. Workers would look at the original and create a phony document on the second computer.

For this to work, there had to be a staff of accountants to identify which documents had to be altered and how. Otherwise, this was just an exercise in chaos that any decent forensic accountant in the States could shoot down in flames.

As those thoughts crossed my mind, a door opened near the back of the room and out popped a group of men and women with clip-boards. They began to circulate among the tables checking work and giving instructions. They were better groomed and dressed than the worktable staff. These were the accountants leaving their coordina-tion meeting.

One of them saw us and rushed up. The manager introduced him. "This is Burkov. He is head accountant and supervisor of the special records unit."

Burkov looked puzzled.

The manager picked up on it. "Colonel Kozar is—"

"Is not available," I said, cutting off any discussion of the colonel's whereabouts.

"This is an impressive operation," I told him. I surveyed the room, rotating slowly so that my hidden body camera could take in the work area. I asked Burkov, "Is there a quiet place where you can brief us on the operation? That room you just left might do."

"Yes, of course," said Burkov. "This way."

The bank manager turned to leave.

I stopped him. "Please join us. This unit is one of your responsibilities, is it not?"

As we walked toward the conference room, I noted that each table contained a nameplate identifying the worker. Arkady from the Omega meeting was sitting at one of those tables. He shot me a brief glance and turned away.

When we were in the room with the door closed, I laid down the parameters of the briefing: fifteen minutes, purpose of the operation, goals, timelines, progress, completion date, and obstacles.

The accountant accommodated me while my body cam recorded his presentation. When he finished, I said, "Major Yukovka has some questions for you. I have some for the staff."

The manager rose half out of his seat to accompany me.

"Please stay for Major Yukovka's questions. They may be instructive."

I walked out into the work area, personnel list in hand covering the two thumb drives Arkady told me to purchase. There were cameras covering this floor. I knew it and Arkady knew it. The switch could be tricky. I walked the room, stood in front of each worker, placed the personnel list on his worktable, asked one or two questions and checked his name off the list. When I arrived at Arkady's table, his two thumb drives were there in plain sight.

I read from his nameplate, "Arkady Abramov. What is your job here?"

"Sir, I am not allowed to discuss my work. Please speak to my superior."

"That is the correct answer, Arkady Abramov." I laid the personnel list over the thumb drives and put a check mark by his name. Beneath the paper, I dropped my two thumb drives and palmed the two Arkady had prepared for me. It looked like a good switch, but you never know. If it came up shaky on the security camera, Arkady was going to take one for the team. I knew it; so did he.

I moved on to other workers, repeating my routine to give Arkady cover. I was approaching the last row of workers when the door burst open and two guards rushed into the room, guns drawn, pointing at me.

"Hands up!" both shouted.

The bank manager heard the commotion and left Jill to investigate. "What's going on!" he demanded.

"He"—meaning me—"took something from that man's desk." The guard pointed to Arkady.

I said, "I took my personnel list, you fool. I'm FSB."

"His list?" said the manager, obviously confused by the whole scene.

"No!" answered the guard. "He took thumb drives. We saw it on the security camera."

I announced, "I'm FSB. Let me show you my credentials."

"Hands up!" The guard was in panic mode. "I don't want to see your credentials. I want to check your pockets. Turn around."

As I was about to turn, I saw Jill Rucker step out of the conference room. I crouched and Jill fired. The guard screamed. I grabbed his gun arm and pushed him into the second guard.

Jill ran along the wall to get me out of her line of fire. I was pushing the second guard backwards with the body of the first guard when she fired again. Both guards fell to the floor dead or dying with head shots.

I yelled, "Jill, they got us on the security cam! Elevators!" I grabbed the manager by his coat collar and dragged him to the door. Jill stopped at Arkady's worktable and fired two shots into his chest and one into his head.

My first thought was, *WTF!* My second was that Arkady was on a recording swapping thumb drives with me. A triple-tap was the best thing he could hope for.

We ran down the hall to the elevator, dragging the manager with us.

I told him, "When we get off the elevator, act surprised. Go to the front entrance. Ask the guards what's happening."

I had my gun out. Jill shoved a fresh clip into hers.

As we exited the elevator, an alarm was shrieking and two guards were closing the front doors. We abandoned the manager and dashed for those doors, firing as we ran. The guards went down, people screamed, and the alarm was still making a racket.

We ran through the doors and were halfway down the steps before we saw them. Evidently the bank had a quick reaction force. On the sidewalk at the bottom of the steps stood three men in guard uniforms, pointing AK-47s at us. We stopped and threw up our hands. I said, "FSB! FSB!"

They weren't buying. All three screamed instructions. "Drop your guns! Hands behind your head! On the ground!"

It's not a good idea to drop a cocked pistol on cement steps. Jill and I bent to lay our weapons down. At that moment, the van that had taken us to the Omega meeting pulled up behind the guards. Masked men leaned out of the curbside windows and mowed the guards down in a hail of automatic weapons fire.

The shooter in the shotgun seat beckoned us to run for the van. We snatched up our pistols, ran down the steps, leaped over the guards, and scrambled through the van's open sliding door. Other masked men pulled us inside and slammed the door shut as the van skidded away from the curb.

We went for a short, fast, twisty, no-talking drive, during which the masked men relieved us of our guns and dropped bags over our heads.

What is it with this hood-over-the-head thing?

After about ten minutes, our captors hustled us into another van and we sped away. The next leg of our journey took about forty minutes in fast traffic. I guessed we were heading away from Moscow.

The van stopped. I heard a gate squeak. The van rolled forward until we entered some enclosure that smelled of hay and manure. I knew we were inside because it was warmer and the wind no longer lashed the van. The van door opened and strong arms pulled me outside.

A voice said, "Walk. We will guide you."

A man on either side took my elbows in vice-like grips and propelled me forward. We walked out into the cold. A few paces later, someone opened a door.

"One step up," said the voice of authority.

We entered a kitchen. I could smell the lingering aroma of eggs and sausages. As we moved through two other rooms, I could hear Jill's footfalls behind me. I estimated there were five or six men holding us: one in the lead—the voice—two each guiding me and Jill and maybe a sixth man bringing up the rear.

Beyond the kitchen, the rooms were warm and I smelled wood burning. We passed through a heavy door into a room that was colder, larger, and smelled of burnt wick and candle wax. The floor was stone. Voices and footfalls echoed. I was shoved onto a wooden bench. Jill was pushed down beside me. Our hoods were removed. We were sitting in the first pew of a church and alone, except for our masked escorts.

One of the masked men took a head scarf from his pocket and handed it to Jill. "Put this on." He gestured toward an alcove housing a statue of the Virgin Mary. "Go light a candle and say a prayer thanking the Virgin for your deliverance at the bank. Take your time. I'll tell you when you're finished."

Jill shot him a hostile glare, but did as she had been told.

On the opposite side of the church, another masked man stepped out of the gloom and snapped his fingers once.

The man who had given Jill the scarf asked me, "How long since your last confession?" I thought I heard some humor in his voice.

"I don't confess."

"This is a good day to begin." He pointed to the confessional with his AK-47.

I didn't spend time in churches when I was assigned to Moscow Station, but I knew that Eastern Orthodox churches didn't have confessional booths. So, we were in a Catholic church. In spite of persecutions by various regimes, there are well over a hundred thousand Catholics in Russia.

The interior of the confessional was dark except for a dim light on my side of the grill. My confessor could see me; I couldn't see him.

The man on the dark side of the grille spoke English, with a slight Russian accent. "You've had a busy morning . . . and a lucky one. Did you get what you were after at the bank?"

"I went to the bank to cash a check. There was a misunderstanding."

He laughed. "I'll take that as a 'yes.' What you got from Arkady may—or may not—help your cause, now that we Russians know you have it. Putin is playing many games. The AVB documents is just one of them."

"Who are you?" I asked.

"Think of me as the man who saved you from a firing squad."

"How did you know we would be at the bank this morning?"

"We didn't know what day you would choose. After Arkady invited you, I put the bank under surveillance. Frankly, I wasn't sure you had the guts to try. I'm glad I was wrong."

He changed subjects. "Arkady?"

"He got caught in a crossfire. He didn't make it."

There was a short silence on the other side of the grille. "Are you injured?"

"No."

"Your partner?"

"She's fine. Why did you rescue us? What do you want?"

"I want you to deliver a message to Washington."

"Why me?"

"Before Ted Walldrum was elected your president, we could entrust certain people in the CIA and elsewhere in your government with information that would be useful to them. Now, there is such rapid turnover among your officials and the people we trusted are gone or not accessible. We were not sure who to trust with our *contributions* to the well-being of the United States. Then, suddenly, an honest man comes to Russia looking for truth at the risk of his life. That's you. That's why we selected you."

"I'm in this for the money."

"I've studied you, Maxwell Geller. You're a proud man. You want to redeem your reputation. So, let's get to the task."

He continued, "I'm going to tell you a secret and hope you have the good judgment to pass it on to someone who can act on it. Is your judgment good?"

"You saved us. I owe you the truth. Lately, I've come to question my judgment."

"In our line of work, it's good not to get too comfortable with our judgments or the people around us."

Enough with the philosophy. "What's the secret?"

"Putin invited Kim Jung-Un to Moscow recently."

"That's public knowledge. Kim cancelled because of *domestic concerns*."

"That's what Kim told the world. What did your Agency sources say about the purpose of Kim's trip and why he cancelled?"

"I won't discuss Agency sources. Let's just say I had no knowledge of Kim's visit beyond what I read in the papers."

"Fair enough. My sources told me the purpose of the meeting was to develop a peace plan for the Korean Peninsula. China was left out, found out, and forced Kim to cancel. China's President Xi told Kim and Putin there would be no Korean peace plan without Chinese input and approval. China is Kim's principal benefactor. Kim had no choice but to decline Putin's invitation."

I was confused. "The meeting never happened. What's the secret?"

"The secret is that another peace plan meeting is scheduled and the plan is designed to deceive the United States. The devil, as you say, is in the details."

"I'm listening."

My confessor struck a match and I could see his outline briefly, but he had turned away. I smelled tobacco burning and the match went out. He must have turned back to me because I could see the glow of his cigarette when he inhaled.

He said, "Your President Walldrum has boasted that he could bring peace to the Korean Peninsula where his predecessors have failed. Putin's plan is to let Walldrum succeed."

"And those devilish details . . . ?"

"The plan involves a summit meeting of Kim and Walldrum. Kim will agree to begin negotiations with the U.S. to halt his missile development, denuclearize the Peninsula, and normalize relations with South Korea. For his part, Walldrum will agree to suspend joint military exercises with South Korea and begin a phased withdrawal of U.S. troops from the peninsula."

There was something not quite right about that. I needed clarification. "Even if Kim was serious about giving up his nukes—which he isn't—China and North Korea are the parties that gain by having U.S. troops out of South Korea. Putin gets nothing and the deal might backfire. We could pull our troops out and send them to Europe to reinforce NATO. Putin wants NATO weaker, not stronger. What does he get out of this plan?"

"He gets Walldrum a Nobel Peace Prize—which your president's ego demands—and that's Walldrum's ticket to reelection in 2020.

Understand that Putin's goal is to keep Walldrum in office as long as possible so that Walldrum can continue to disrupt the U.S. government and the Western alliances."

"Assuming Walldrum is elected, what happens to the peace plan?"

"Now, you're thinking like Putin. Kim will back out of the plan."

"What does China get out of this scheme?"

"That's one of the secret details. China gets nothing." He blew smoke through the screen at me, maybe for emphasis. "Xi will approve this plan, believing he has a chance to reduce U.S. forces in the Far East. Putin's plan is to make a side deal with Kim."

"What's the deal?"

"In return for entering into these phony negotiations with Walldrum, Putin will secretly supply whatever North Korea needs to become a nuclear-armed nation, with ICBMs, by the time Walldrum stands for reelection in 2020. At that point, Kim is assured the survival of his regime. He will be less dependent on China and have the support of his new friend, Russia. Putin will have checkmated Chinese ambitions by installing a nuclear-armed North Korea on the Chinese border and by leaving thirty thousand U.S. troops in South Korea."

No doubt, responsible people in Washington needed to know that the peace plan, if it materialized, was a fake. "When will this meeting take place?" I asked.

"Kim is planning a secret trip to China in March 2018. Ostensibly, it's to consult with President Xi Jinping. The truth? It's a four-party meeting involving Kim, Xi, a senior official from the Russian Foreign Ministry, and a senior officer of the GRU," Russian military intelligence. "They will work out the details of a Korean peace plan."

"Why is the GRU at the meeting?"

"The GRU officer will plan clandestine measures to support Walldrum's 2020 reelection campaign."

"What are the names of these Russian officials?"

"The fact that there will be a meeting and the officials involved are closely held secrets in my government—if I gave you names, sources would be exposed and killed."

"How did you find out about this meeting?"

"My answer is the same. Sources would die."

"I need more than a church confessional rumor to sell that story in Washington."

He hesitated. "For your purposes, say it was divulged during pillow talk of two homosexual lovers close to Putin." My confessor chuckled. "If that gets back to Moscow, Putin will tear out what's left of his hair. He hates gays." My confessor's voice turned serious again and impatient. "Your Washington contacts have satellites. Tell them to see if Kim's special train goes to China in March.

"Speaking of going, I assume you have a plan to get out of Russia. Now is a good time to execute it. You know too much. You and your partner are the primary targets of every policeman, border guard, and FSB agent in Russia."

I didn't tell Rodney what my exfiltration—exfil, for short—plan was and I certainly wasn't going to share it with some faceless guy in a confessional. Misdirection is often best. I told him, "When people are expecting you to run, laying low is a good idea."

"If you were thinking of the farmhouse—"

I wasn't.

He continued, "It's no longer safe for you there. My men collected and packed your belongings. Your suitcases are here, even the money you hid under the floorboards."

How does he know about the farmhouse, and why isn't it safe?

"That was thoughtful of you," I said. "We'd like to change clothes, and could you have someone without a mask and AK-47 take us to Leningradsky Train Station?"

It was almost 4 p.m. when we left the church. Moscow daylight was fading fast and I was happy to have darkness to cover our travels. Three blocks from the station, Jill and I got out of the sedan provided by my father confessor. Jill took a direct route. I took a longer one at a slower pace, to give her time to complete some tasks.

At the station, I put my suitcase—minus what I needed to get out of Russia—in a locker and purchased one ticket to St. Petersburg. If cameras and the FSB were watching for a couple on the run, that might throw them off. Casually, I strolled outside.

Jill was standing beside a cab she had hired. "Oleg! Over here!" she shouted at me.

I slid into the back seat beside her and off we went. We would change cabs twice more before heading for our destination, a hotel at Sheremetyevo Airport, but first we had to make a hospital stop.

CHAPTER 25

I HAD NEVER met Dr. Zhukov, but his medical services were an important part of my get-out-of-Russia plan, all of which I had withheld from Jill Rucker. She was not happy about that. For reasons of self-preservation, I was. And, I must admit, the closer we got to leaving Russia, the more paranoia I felt.

At the hospital, we slipped past busy administrative gatekeepers and went directly to Zhukov's office on the second floor. His door was open. The doctor wore the obligatory white coat and was examining a medical file through thick, rimless spectacles. He had a graying beard, but looked to be about the same age as Pavel. Resistance is a business for young people.

I knocked and said, "Cousin Pavel sent me about my back. I was in an accident."

Without a word, Zhukov bounded out of his chair and closed the door behind us. Giving me and Jill a worried appraisal, he said, "Your accident is all over the news. You were lucky to survive." He didn't sound happy that we had.

"It was an unavoidable tragedy," I explained.

He ignored that. "Please sit over there on the examining table."

With Jill looking on, wondering what the hell was happening, Zhukov quickly, expertly, and silently applied bandages to my forehead, the left side of my face, and the bridge of my nose. I was sure that no one could identify me from the Russian wanted posters that were probably circulating. Jill recognized what we were up to and patiently awaited her turn.

Zhukov gave me a satisfied appraisal and turned his attention to Jill, helping her into a dark wig and applying unattractive false moles to her upper lip and chin. Our disguises completed, Zhukov went to a closet and rolled out a folding wheelchair for me. "Please sit here." He also provided a cane.

To Jill he said, "Would you go to the elevator and hold it for us?"

As soon as she left his office, Zhukov gave me three hypodermic needles in their paper and plastic shipping cases. "Take two and don't call me in the morning." He smiled for the first time. Turning serious, he added, "One for each person, in the neck, and a spare, if you need it."

Zhukov pushed me to the elevator and turned me over to Jill. "There is a car waiting for you downstairs in the name of Egorshin. Take the chair with you. Your driver said it might come in handy at the hotel. Good luck."

On the ground floor, Jill wheeled me out of the elevator and toward the hospital exit. Just inside the door, a thick, middle-aged fellow pushed himself off the wall and approached us. It was the cop who had interrogated me at the Omega Group meeting.

"Mr. Egorshin?" he asked, as if he had never seen us before,

"Yes."

"Your doctor called a car for you. I'm Yuri, your driver."

He addressed Jill. "Do you need help with the wheelchair?"

"I can manage. Will you take the luggage?"

The luggage was in my lap and there wasn't much to take. We were traveling with a couple of overnight bags of items taken from our suitcases before ditching them in lockers at Leningradsky Station.

I played the cripple, struggling into the front seat of the car with assistance from my cane and Jill, while Yuri folded my wheelchair into the trunk. Jill rode in the back seat, literally and figuratively, because Yuri addressed most of his comments to me during the trip.

Once we were in the traffic flow, Yuri said, "The security services are tearing Moscow apart looking for you. You are wanted for bank robbery and murdering guards in the process."

"Bank robbery?" asked Jill.

"Yes. You got away with several hundred thousand rubles, didn't you?"

"That's a lie," she protested.

"Of course, it is," admitted Yuri. "What did you expect them to say, that you stole forged documents that would destroy your government's case against Ted Walldrum?"

I asked, "Are there really rubles missing from the bank?"

"Yes. They probably went into secret retirement funds for the bank manager and the FSB officers investigating the robbery. This is Moscow." Yuri looked at me and shrugged. "There's nothing you can do about it except get out of Russia."

"Where are we going?" Jill directed the question to no one in particular.

Yuri looked at me again.

I answered. "To an airport hotel. Pavel made a reservation for us in our Russian names and checked us in. I have a room key. We don't have to stop at the front desk."

Everyone was quiet until Yuri began to brief us. "The guests where you are staying are mostly Russians. Room surveillance by the FSB is less extensive than at the high-end and Intourist motels where foreigners stay. At your hotel, surveillance begins when you make a reservation. If the FSB wants a look at you, they assign you to certain floors where the rooms have audio and video surveillance capabilities."

I asked, "Is our room being monitored?"

Yuri gave us the bad news. "We don't know all the floors and rooms that are under surveillance. Once you're in the hotel, assume your conversations and actions are monitored and recorded."

I processed the implications of that out loud. "That means we have to take out the FSB surveillance suite before we go after our targets."

"What targets!" Jill was alarmed.

"Tell you later," I said. I thought I could feel the heat from Jill as she went into a slow burn. Left out again.

I asked Yuri, "Where's the FSB monitoring suite located?"

"On the sixth floor." Yuri gave me the suite number.

"Can we avoid violence? Why not interrupt power to the FSB suite for thirty minutes while we take out the targets?"

"Not possible. A power outage would be suspicious. The FSB might lock down the building and check every guest and every room. That would not be to your advantage."

"What's the best time to take down the FSB surveillance team?" I asked.

"They change shifts at 3 a.m."

"That's an odd hour."

"Selected with care," Yuri informed us. "It's the hour when sex and other guest activities of interest to the FSB have usually been completed."

"How many on the surveillance team?"

"Two men on shift and two coming in to replace them. The two of you will have to deal with the four of them."

Outnumbered again. Great. "Tell me about the targets, Yuri."

"The engineer is in room 524. The flight attendant is in room 526. A door connects their rooms. We have reliable information that they are lovers. At 3 a.m., it's likely they will be sleeping in the same bed, probably hers. That should make your task easier."

"Good news at last. Anything else we should know?" The *we* was to make Jill feel part of the team, even if she didn't know the game.

"The lovers usually take breakfast together in one of their rooms, before they leave for the airport. The pilot also has a room in the hotel. He leaves early on the hotel shuttle and eats at his favorite airport restaurant. The lovers join him and the remaining crew members at the gate and they all board the plane."

Yuri had no additional information and I had no more questions for him. No doubt, Jill had questions, but was disciplined enough to wait until I was ready to read her in.

It was late when we arrived at our destination. Yuri got my wheelchair out of the trunk and bid us farewell. I sat in the chair with our luggage on my lap, waiting for Jill to push me into the hotel.

She hesitated. "Are you going to tell me what's going on or wait 'til we're inside where the FSB can hear you?"

"We got into the country by switching places with a Russian couple. We're going out the same way."

"Only, this time, the couple is not volunteering," surmised Jill. "Who are they?"

"A female flight attendant and a male flight engineer. They're our targets."

Jill restated our problem. "And we can't approach them until we take out the FSB surveillance team?"

"Right."

"Where are we going?"

"Into the hotel. I'm freezing."

"You know what I mean. Where's our flight going?"

"Los Angeles," I lied.

Jill was angry. "I've earned the right to know your plans when they involve me."

That statement was really a question. I tried to answer it without telling Jill I didn't trust her because she had lied to me twice and that, from our first meeting, I had a gut feeling that she was not to be trusted.

Instead of those truths, I told her, "I was in the field for seven years, working alone most of the time. For survival, I didn't share my plans with colleagues until there was a need for them to know. It's an old habit. I'm comfortable with it and it's hard to break. You won't have to put up with it much longer. Tomorrow, we'll be in the States."

Jill didn't reply.

We entered the busy lobby and she pushed me to the elevator, attracting little attention, and we rode up to the sixth floor. On the way to our room, we took notice of the door to the FSB monitoring suite. I let us into our room with the key Dr. Zhukov had given me at the hospital. To my surprise, we had a two-room suite. For the benefit of our FSB watchers and listeners, I complained about being in too much pain to sleep and I took first watch in the living room, watching television. Jill made tired noises and went to bed.

My decision to take first watch allowed the roller coaster that had become my life to deliver yet another load of good-news-bad-news. The RT—Russian Television—commentator was reviewing and ridiculing indictments in the Walldrum-Russia collusion case, claiming they were attempts by the "deep state" to unseat a duly elected U.S. president. The program showed videos of indicted Americans from Walldrum's inner circle at various locations. The video that caught my attention was recorded at a posh Moscow hotel. It showed a retired U.S. general, President Walldrum's future national security advisor, sitting next to Vladimir Putin, at a gala dinner celebrating the tenth anniversary of the Russian Television network.

I had seen still photographs of that seating many times. This was the first time I'd seen the video. Someone in the background looked familiar. Over Putin's shoulder, a woman at another table looked directly into the camera. She appeared annoyed, rose from her chair, and walked out of camera range. That woman was the person I knew as Jill Rucker, crack pistol shot, karate expert, and Russian speaker, the Jill Rucker who told me she had never been to Russia.

Was Jill there with the American general? Was she his bodyguard? Was she there with the Russians as a guest or bodyguard? Whatever her role, I knew one thing for sure. Jill Rucker was a liar.

At 2:15 a.m., I began my act for the benefit of our FSB monitors, if they were listening. "Olga! Wake up!"

Jill came out of a sound sleep. Her look said she was not quite with the program, but she adjusted quickly. "What's wrong?"

"I'm having chest pains. Get my medicine. It's in my coat pocket."

Jill brought me the bottle of aspirin provided by Dr. Zhukov.

"Water," I said with fake pain in my voice.

Jill got water from the bathroom and I used it to wash down a couple of pills.

Playing the role, she hovered over me with feigned concern. After a few minutes, she asked, "Are you feeling better?"

"Worse. I think I need to go back to the hospital."

We dressed hurriedly, but taking care to draw out our departure until a few minutes to 3 a.m., when the FSB shifts changed. I got into the wheelchair and Jill pushed me into the hall. It was empty. Not what we wanted, but we had prepared a contingency.

"Olga, I forgot my cane."

Jill returned to the room and stalled as long as she could before bringing the stick out and hanging it on the back of the chair. Just then, the elevator announced its arrival with a little "ding" and two plainclothes FSB hoods stepped into the hallway and came toward us. I slumped forward holding my chest. "Olga, please, the elevator is here. Let's go."

One of the FSB men went back and appeared to press a button to hold the elevator for us.

Jill pushed me at just the right speed so that we were directly opposite the surveillance suite as one of the FSB men slid his magnetic key through the slot and unlocked the door.

As soon as the door was open slightly, Jill shot him twice. He fell forward blocking the door open. I shot the younger man who had held the elevator for us, proving once again Clare Boothe Luce's warning, "No good deed goes unpunished." I felt sorry for him as he fell into the room, stumbling backwards over his downed partner.

Jill leaped over them and into the suite. I followed her. A fellow monitoring the bank of TV screens was half out of his chair when Jill shot him. We turned in opposite directions scanning the room for the fourth man. He was absent.

Where was he? In the bathroom, and he came out fighting. Jill was pivoting toward the bathroom door, but hadn't completed the turn when the guy struck. He brought his left fist down hard on Jill's gun wrist, and used his right hand to rip Jill's gun from her hand. At the same time, he kicked Jill's legs out from under her. Then, he focused on me.

The move to get Jill's gun was brilliant. Knocking her down was a mistake. Jill had been in my line of fire. When she fell, I had a clear shot at her attacker. I fired three bullets into his chest and he went down. Jill snatched her gun from his dead hand.

I searched the bodies and found a master key that would let us in to surprise the lovebirds. Meanwhile, Jill pulled my wheelchair in from the hall and disabled the console that allowed the FSB to spy on guest rooms. On our way out of the suite, I spiked the electronic lock to delay entry into the suite and discovery of the bodies. That done, we ran downstairs to the lovers' rooms.

According to Yuri, the flight attendant was in Room 526 and the lovers would spend the night in her bed. He made a good guess. Using the passkey, we slipped in without waking them. Moonlight defined their bodies for us. I motioned Jill to the attendant's side of the bed. I went to the other side, peeled one of Dr. Zhukov's needles out of its plastic case, and plunged it into the sleeping engineer's neck. I sat on his chest while he struggled briefly and went limp.

Unfortunately, his struggle awakened his lover. She bolted upright with a scream in her throat. Jill clamped a hand over her mouth and I plunged the needle into the target's neck. Her eyes rolled back, she sagged, and fell back onto her pillow.

"What's in those needles?" asked Jill.

"Dr. Zhukov didn't say."

"How long will they be out?"

"Until the Second Coming."

She chewed on that for a while. "What else haven't you told me?"

"I picked this flight attendant because she resembles you, physically. She's your new identity and your ticket on a plane to the States." I took a paper from my pocket, unfolded it, and handed it to Jill. "That's her bio. Study it. Know what's in her purse and luggage. Put on her uniform. Wear her jewelry and perfume. You have to be her until we get through airport security this morning."

"Do I need to know anything about the duties of a flight attendant?"

"No. Once you're on the plane, you're a FSB major. No one will question you."

I checked my watch. It was almost 4 a.m. I advised Jill, "You've got about ninety minutes to transform yourself into that flight attendant . . . and make sure there's nothing in her luggage that will hang us up at the security check." It was not unheard of that some flight attendants had a sideline of smuggling.

I had my own transformation to make. I removed Zhukov's mummy wrap from my head and face, shaved and showered. Afterwards, I went through the flight engineer's belongings with an eye for anything that should be discarded before the security check. Everything passed muster. I put on his uniform and ID badge, and checked myself in the mirror. Not bad.

A room service waiter delivered the lovers' breakfast. I had him leave it in the hall. After we ate, we hung "do not disturb" signs on the doors of both rooms and took the shuttle to Sheremetyevo Airport.

When we arrived, I addressed a question I'm sure was on Jill's mind. "I haven't told you why the pilot will let us onto his plane. We'll meet him in a few minutes and I'll run down the con. You just listen and go along."

"Don't I always?" She gave me a nasty look.

Just as Yuri said, we found the pilot having breakfast at his favorite restaurant. I recognized him from the photo Pavel had given me. He was a thin man with a full head of gray hair and a smug expression.

"Captain Federov?"

"Yes?" He looked up, frowning, probably annoyed that a three-striper interrupted his breakfast.

"I'm Colonel Usenko, state security." I flashed my FSB credentials. "This is Major Yukovka, also of state security." Jill and I sat down.

Federov pushed back from the table, concern on his face. His eyes widened as they moved from our unfamiliar faces to the familiar name tag of two of his flight crew.

I noted his concern. "Don't be deceived by our uniforms or name tags. We are working undercover and require your cooperation to observe—and eventually catch—a group of smugglers."

"How can I help you with smugglers?" Again, he glanced at our uniforms. "Is my crew involved?"

I smiled. "No. You and your crew are not in difficulty."

"Where are my engineer and flight attendant?"

"They agreed to let us take their places so that we do not alert the criminals. We believe the smugglers have been successful because they have accomplices in flight and ground operations, as well as other elements of the Aeroflot organization. This, of course, is a state secret, not to be discussed with anyone else."

"I understand. What can I do?"

"The suspects, a man and woman, are traveling in coach. We want to keep them under surveillance until we arrive in Paris."

Jill's eyebrows arched when I said "Paris." Earlier, I told her we were flying to Los Angeles. The more I learned about Jill Rucker, the less I trusted her. Deception is one way to keep an operation from being compromised, and getting out of Russia was the difference between life and death. Compromise was not an option.

I continued briefing Captain Federov. "Do nothing out of the ordinary. Follow your usual routine for this flight, with two exceptions. Major Yukovka—call her Natasha—will replace one of your flight attendants in coach so that she can observe the smugglers. I will replace your flight engineer in the cockpit."

The captain looked worried.

I explained. "I need to be in the cockpit because we believe these criminals have a unique communications system with the ground and service crew in Paris. I must be in position to observe those crews without attracting attention."

"What if there's an emergency and I need a flight engineer?"

"Captain, I have read your file. You were a qualified flight engineer, correct?"

"Well . . . yes."

"Then, I'm sure you can handle those duties for the relatively short flight to Paris. However, I have anticipated that you might need help in an emergency. There is a flight engineer aboard in civilian clothes.

If you require his services, I will identify him to you." That was a lie, well told. "Any other concerns, Captain?"

"No, Colonel."

"Of course, you will not discuss our duties with anyone except your first officer after we are cleared for takeoff. Please advise your flight attendants that Major Yukovka will supervise them in coach." I smiled. "Let's go to Paris, Captain."

We accompanied Captain Federov to security and breezed through without incident. Jill, cutting a fine figure in her Aeroflot flight attendant's uniform, ran interference for us. The security guys seemed more into checking her figure than her documentation. Federov and I followed in her slipstream. The three of us joined the remaining crew at the departure gate and boarded the aircraft.

With Jill trying to fake it, departure prep was a bit hectic, but everyone settled down once we were airborne. It was quiet in the cockpit. Ordinary Russians tend not to chat with FSB colonels.

Although we were off the ground, we were still in Russian airspace and I had a disturbing vision of MiGs escorting us back to Sheremetyevo if anything went wrong. What could go wrong? That depended a lot on who was traveling with us.

I broke the cockpit silence. "Captain, I would like to see the passenger list."

A flight attendant delivered one. I scanned it. "Captain, please identify the security officers," the Russian equivalent of U.S. air marshals. "I may need their assistance." *Or I may need to kill them.*

I had no doubt that, after the bank shooting, our pictures had been sent to every law enforcement officer in Moscow, especially the plane's security staff. Our only edge was they were most likely looking for us among the passengers, not the crew.

The captain pointed to a name. "This is your man."

The security officer had an aisle seat in the last row of first class, left side of the plane as you face the cockpit. That meant his right hand—his gun hand—was free for a clean shot at anyone trying to force his way into the cockpit. The window seat next to him was empty. So, no interference.

"Any other security personnel?"

"With the exception of you and . . . Natasha, no."

I doubted there was just one security officer onboard. Russian officials traveling outside of their country always travel in groups of two or more. It's insurance against defections. I scanned the seating arrangements in coach, looking for a likely colleague of the first-class security officer. There was a woman in the last row on the aisle. The window seat was unoccupied, same MO as the security officer in first class.

I pointed to her name on the manifest and asked, "Is she anyone special?"

"No. Just another passenger," said the captain.

Using the cockpit intercom phone, I called the flight attendants' station at the rear of the aircraft.

Jill answered, *Da?* We were speaking Russian, of course.

"This is Colonel Usenko. There is a woman alone in the last row of the coach section. She may be one of them. Watch her, but don't draw attention to yourself. You may have to follow her when we get to Paris."

That was my coded way of telling Jill that the woman might be an undercover security officer for our flight.

With potential threats identified, I turned my attention to the future. The engineer whose identity I borrowed had a computer in his carry-on. It wasn't password protected. When we were out of Russian airspace, I switched it to English, sent some emails, and made plane reservations.

An hour out of Paris, Jill called me on the cockpit intercom. "That woman in the last row, she recognized me. She was watching a video on her cell phone. It was from the bank. She gave me a good look and closed the phone when I approached her."

"You're sure about what was on her phone?"

"I heard your voice on the video."

"Don't let her contact anyone. Spill coffee on her if you have to. Move the other flight attendants to duties at the front of the cabin. I'm on the way."

"Problem?" asked the captain, showing a frown of concern.

"One of the criminals may have recognized Major Yukovka. I'll handle it quietly. We prepared for this eventuality." *Like hell we did. Adapt, improvise, and overcome! Semper Fi!*

Leaving the cockpit, I grabbed a pillow and a stack of blankets from the first-class overhead. As I moved down the aisle, I held them high enough to block the security officer's view of my face. At the front of coach, I squeezed past attendants collecting trash and distributing snacks. Jill was waiting in the rear, at the restrooms, trying to look over the security officer's shoulder.

I beckoned Jill to me, handed her a blanket, and whispered, "Give me some privacy."

Jill unfolded the blanket and held it across the aisle, pretending to check for holes or whatever flight attendants check blankets for.

I smiled at the security officer and said, "I see you're going on to Zurich with us. You might like to have a blanket before the mob gets on in Paris."

As she took the blanket, she looked up at my face. Recognition registered in her eyes, but too late. I plunged Dr. Zhukov's last needle into her shoulder and covered her face with a pillow. She gave up a little yelp. The woman in the next row tried to turn to see what was happening. Jill blocked her view with the blanket.

For the benefit of nearby passengers, I told the barely conscious security officer, "You'll be fine. Just relax." I laid her out on two seats, put the pillow under her head, and covered her with a blanket.

Jill smiled and announced to inquisitive passengers, "She's exhausted. She's been traveling for days. We'll take her to the airport clinic when we get to Paris."

"Call me when she wakes up." *If she does, I'm going to be very unhappy with Dr. Zhukov.*

Back in the cockpit, I told the captain, "We have to detain one of the passengers. She recognized Major Yukovka. After you and your crew leave the aircraft, Russian security officers will come aboard to take her into custody. The major and I will stay behind and see to the transfer."

Cautiously, the captain asked, "What about her accomplices?"

"Unfortunately, we have to abandon surveillance. We believe the woman used her cell phone to warn them. There will be another time. Criminals are greedy and stupid."

Four hours after our Moscow departure, we landed at Charles de Gaulle Airport. Before the plane came to a halt, I went to the rear to "see to the prisoner." The passengers deplaned, followed by the flight officers and crew. Jill sat the unconscious female security officer upright and posed her in a sleeping position. We were about to leave when I looked up and saw the security man from first class coming down the aisle toward us. Maybe the captain didn't know there was a second security officer onboard, but this guy did. They were a team.

Jill was between us and I told her who he was. She gave him a helpless look and whined, "She won't wake up."

The officer looked at Jill, first with concern. His second look was recognition. He reached for his gun. Jill kicked him in the groin. When he howled and doubled over, she twisted the pistol from his hand and drove her knee into his forehead. He stumbled backward. Jill followed up with two quick karate chops to his throat. He fell to the floor. Jill jumped on his chest and twisted his head until his neck snapped.

Cold as ice water she said, "Help me get him into a seat."

Minutes later, Jill and I hurried off the plane. We changed clothes in terminal restrooms and abandoned our flight uniforms and weapons in trash cans.

During our escape from Moscow, I had used the flight engineer's computer to book us seats on a plane to Marseilles, France, leaving in an hour. My idea was to get us out of the Aeroflot terminal and out of Paris before the manhunt began. We cleared immigration and customs using our U.S. passports. I collected our tickets and we headed for Terminal 2E and the flight to southern France. Along the way to the departure gate, Jill complained again about not being in on my plan.

It was a ninety-minute flight to Marseilles. I used the time to pump Jill for information on our employer, the elusive Mr. Bowen, the holder of my ten-million-dollar bounty. I didn't expect Jill to tell me the truth. I wanted her version of the truth.

I asked, "Where is Bowen's base of operations?"

"My sense is he goes where the action is hot, and the cash is cold and plentiful."

That was evasive. Sherri told me that Bowen had been in Panama since Noriega's reign. Jill would have known that, too.

"What else do you know about him?"

Jill shrugged and sipped her drink. "I know that he pays well and on time. That's all I need to know." She turned in her seat and gave me a professional appraisal. "I'm sure you can appreciate that, considering how you limited me to 'need to know' information in Moscow."

Did I detect a drop of venom mixed with the professionalism? I pressed on. "How does Bowen contact you?"

"By phone call or text."

"No face-to-face?"

"Rarely."

"How did he make contact with you the first time?"

Jill exhaled heavily and put her glass on the arm rest between us. "We met at a security conference."

"Where?"

"In a secure location."

"What were you trying to prevent at this security conference?"

"Among other things, conversations like this."

Bravo, Jill! That was a smooth "none-of-your-business" message.

She lapsed into a brief, hostile silence, which I interrupted by telling her what she needed to know about the rest of our escape plan.

"The Russians," I said, "and whoever they can persuade to join the hunt will expect us to be traveling together. So, we're going to split up in Marseilles." I handed her the airline ticket sleeve. "This is your flight to Mexico City."

"I thought we were going to Panama."

"We are, but first, we're going to Mexico City and take a detour for some well-deserved R and R in Cancun."

Jill gave me a broad smile. "Now, you're talking. How will you get to Mexico?"

"I'm flying Iberia to Mexico via Madrid. I'll arrive two hours after you. Take a room at the Hilton Reforma. Leave a note at the desk for me. I'll find you."

This time, Jill's smile was seductive. "It's nice to be in the loop again. Maybe we can get back in touch, too, in Cancun."

I smiled back, but said nothing. Jill had no idea how far she was out of my loop. Seeing the video of her in the room with Putin sent my trust level to zero.

When we arrived in Marseilles, Jill had an hour to catch her plane for the seventeen-hour flight to Mexico. We said a quick see-you-later and she made a run for the security line.

I had a small fortune in bribe money I hadn't used in Russia. In spite of what I told Jill, my actual plan was to use it to charter a private jet and fly directly to Panama City.

I called Sherri's office in Virginia and got Tony-D's phone number in Panama. It was about 11 a.m., his time.

He was concerned. "Max, are you out of the danger zone?"

"Affirmative."

"And your traveling companion?"

"Yeah. She's due to arrive in Mexico City on a flight from Marseilles in about seventeen hours from now. I want to know who meets her when she comes out of the arrival hall, and I want twenty-four-seven surveillance on her until I say stop. Can you manage that?"

"No problem. I know people in Mexico City."

"She'll be staying at the Hilton Reforma and expecting me to join her."

"When will that happen?"

"Never."

"Never?"

"Is there an echo on this line? Listen, Tony, expect unfriendlies to be in the area."

"Copy that. Is there anything else I should know?"

"See you when I see you." I broke the connection.

I gave Jill's plane an hour after departure before I used a burner cell phone to call the Russian Embassy in Paris and asked for a security officer.

"Yes?" came back a serious voice from Paris.

I spoke Russian. "I understand you are looking for a man and a woman who robbed the Allgemeine Volksbank in Moscow. Is there a reward?"

Hesitation and muffled conversation with someone on his end.

"There is a reward, ten thousand rubles. Who are you?"

"A good citizen of the Russian Federation. Where do I go to claim the reward?"

"If you are in Paris, come to the embassy. Ask for Yevgeny Torshin. Where are the fugitives?"

"On a plane to Mexico City." I gave him Jill's airline and flight number.

I broke the connection and used a second burner to call Bill Bowen's messenger at the number Jill wasn't supposed to give me in London. It was the number I bribed the Savoy's night man to pull off Jill's long-distance call record.

In Panama, a familiar voice answered.

"Can you get an emergency message to Mr. Bowen?" I asked.

"I can."

"Tell him that Ms. Rucker and Mr. Geller are flying to Mexico City as we speak." I gave him Jill's flight information and arrival time. "Tell Mr. Bowen they are carrying sensitive documents. He should meet their plane and bring his checkbook. If he's a no-show, his absence could trigger a bidding war."

"Who is this?"

"This is the guy who's hanging up on you."

Jill Rucker, or whatever her name was, would get a surprise when she arrived in Mexico City.

My chartered jet was ready for takeoff. I went to the private terminal, completed my clearances, and was in the air in no time. As I wallowed in the luxury of first-class seats, second-class food, and third-class champagne, I could feel my relationship with Jill Rucker coming to an end and that ten million dollars getting closer. But before I could touch the money, I had to discover the secret of President Walldrum's high-rise Russian money laundering machine, the Panama Walldrum Tower.

CHAPTER 26

TEN HOURS AFTER I departed Marseilles, my plane arrived in Panama City, a little after 8 p.m. local time. I had called ahead. Sherri met me at the airport wearing sandals, shorts, a polo shirt, and ponytail. She looked delicious and greeted me with a radiant smile.

"Glad to have you back among friends. How did you get out of Russia?"

"Through the OK Corral."

Sherri was alarmed. She blocked my way, thrust her hands inside my jacket, and patted me down. "Are there any holes in you?"

"Only the one in my head where Bowen planted the idea of going to Russia."

"Shush. We got the goods, didn't we? We'll get it in Panama."

"Did you locate the anti-corruption reporter you told me about?"

"David Sanchez, yes, but I had difficulty tracking him down. He's not strictly in hiding, but he's not an easy guy to get ahold of."

"What's the problem?"

"His reporting exposed politicians and crooks around the world. They sent their money to Panama to avoid taxes or corruption investigations in their home countries. Sanchez believes he's on the hit lists of some powerful and unpleasant characters."

"Is he going to talk to us?"

"Maybe. I spoke to him twice on the phone. He asked lots of questions about us. He wants to make sure we're the real deal. I pumped up our bona fides by telling him some of what we did in Russia. If he talks to us, he wants an exclusive when we nail Walldrum with rock-solid evidence of a crime. I gave him your word. That's the price of doing business."

"If he decides to talk to us, when will it happen?"

"Tomorrow night."

"Where?"

"He'll call me with the location an hour before the meet."

"He's a careful man."

"I would be. There have been two attempts to kill him."

As Sherri drove me to the hotel, she asked, "What's with Jill Rucker?"

"You were right. She's not who she claims to be. I saw a video of her sitting behind Putin at Russian TV's tenth anniversary gala."

Sherri's jaw dropped. "You're kidding."

"I never joke about my work, 006," I said, paraphrasing James Bond's legendary quartermaster, Q. "If the Russians don't grab Jill in Mexico City, she'll come here. When that happens, be on your guard. I'm not sure what her game is, but Jill Rucker is a killing machine."

Sherri had booked herself, me, and Tony-D into hotel bungalows in Panama's Bella Vista district near the Walldrum Tower. Tony-D said I should see what a four-hundred-million-dollar building looks like up close. At the hotel, Sherri showed me to my bungalow. I told her not to wake me until noon, and collapsed into bed.

The next day, I was up at 10 a.m. and had breakfast in my bungalow. Precisely at noon, Sherri and Tony-D arrived. We sat at my dining table and they briefed me. Tony-D looked worried.

Sherri looked happy and was carrying a stack of magazines, newspapers, and miscellaneous documents. She announced, "Good news.

David Sanchez has agreed to meet us this evening, time and place to be announced during his next call."

I asked, "Is there a time limit on the meeting?"

"No. He'll stay as long as we want. We should eat an early dinner and be ready to travel as soon as he calls. In the meantime"—Sherri pushed her pile of documents across the table to me—"here's your reading assignment on the Panama Walldrum Tower."

Tony-D didn't have reading material. He had a grave expression and photographs. "My surveillance crew set up at the airport in Mexico City a little after midnight. Jill Rucker's plane arrived on schedule.

"Two heavies from the Russian Embassy were waiting for her when she came out of the arrival hall." Tony-D passed their photos to me. "I'm guessing they're SVR," Russian foreign intelligence service. "My Mexican contacts are trying to get positive IDs. Jill was surprised to see them. They had a brief exchange. Something they said upset her."

"Did they take Jill into custody?"

"They didn't cuff her. They didn't strong-arm her. They escorted her out to a limo with Russian diplomatic plates and blacked-out windows. The heavies got into the front seat." Tony-D gave me the last photograph and continued. "This guy was leaning against the limo having a smoke. He got into the back seat with Jill.

"They talked for ten minutes. Jill got out of the car and it drove off. Jill took a cab to the hotel, as you said she would. She's in her room now, probably waiting for you."

Tony-D tapped the last photo with his forefinger. "This guy, the smoker, he's the problem."

"Who is he?"

"I don't know, but he was the lookout for the Russian team that raided the London warehouse, killed Ironside and the MI6 agents, and tried to kidnap you."

"You're sure?"

"Positive. I had overwatch for the warehouse operation. We were about to go in to rescue you from MI6, when the Russians drove up. This guy stayed outside to provide security. The other Russians went in, took down the MI6 people, and dragged you out with a bag over your head. We hit them before they could get you into their van. I watched this guy. Jill fired the first shot at him. He made a run for it on foot. She fired off a couple more rounds and missed. He was into the wind."

Tony-D added, "Expert pistol shot Jill Rucker missed this guy three times?"

I speculated, "Maybe he came to Mexico to thank her. Where is he now?"

"Last seen entering the Russian Embassy in Mexico City."

"Can you tell me where he goes, if he leaves the embassy?"

"Surveillance there is a waste of your money. He has a dozen ways to sneak out. Besides, the CIA and Mexican intelligence are all over that embassy. Our guys would just be under foot. I recommend we watch the airport to see if he or Jill takes a flight to some exotic locale . . . like Panama."

After Tony-D and Sherri left, I attacked Sherri's pile of research on the Great Man, Walldrum, and construction of his *fallicus erectus*, the Panama Walldrum Tower. I spent hours sifting through piles of news clippings and PR dross, searching for a clue to the frugality that allowed Walldrum to create his tower, while stealing millions from the construction budget. I found nothing. In late afternoon, I stopped reading and had a leisurely dinner in my room. I needed time to consider what questions I wanted to ask David Sanchez.

Sherri called at 6 p.m. to give me a heads-up that it was time to leave for our rendezvous with Sanchez. Ever vigilant Sherri had checked out our meeting place with a hotel staff member. He told her it was not wise for gringos to roam the streets in that neighborhood after dark. As a precaution, we had a cab drop us directly at the door of the appointed seedy saloon in a backstreet near Avenida Central.

Sherri and I got predatory appraisals as we entered and walked to the bar. I asked for Sanchez. The bartender nodded us down a poorly lighted hallway, past closed doors, to a room at the end. I opened the door and was confronted by a guy built like a downsized sumo wrestler. He wore khaki pants the size of a fest tent and the flowers on his tropical shirt were large enough to be mutants from an atomic blast. His shirt was opened to expose the huge automatic pistol in his belt. His eyes and body language indicated he was in prep mode for attack. He patted me down. I wasn't packing. He raised eyebrows at Sherri.

"She's armed," I said. "She's my bodyguard. She can come in or stay in the hall, but she's not giving up her weapon."

Mr. Sumo looked at Sanchez, the only other person present. The reporter was sitting in one of the room's four booths and had overheard the exchange. I was relieved when he said, "Mr. Geller, Ms. Layton, welcome." He waved us to his booth.

Mr. Sumo reverted to rest mode, but I never saw him take his eyes off the door.

David Sanchez was a small, compact man with slick black hair, and very telegenic. He wore a nice tan, tropical suit, and open shirt with a crisp collar.

"Thanks for seeing me," I said. We shook hands and sat down.

Sanchez apologized to Sherri. "I'm sorry I interrogated you on the phone. Some very bad people don't like my reporting on their corruption. They would love to have a private chat with me. I had to check you out." He looked at me and added, "And you, too, Mr. Geller." Sanchez smiled. "Anyone fired from the CIA for criticizing Walldrum can't be all bad . . . and your trip to Russia . . ." His voice trailed off. He shook his head and gave us an admiring smile. "How can I help you?"

I showed him Bowen's picture and business card. "Do you know this guy?"

"Wild Bill Bowen, cowboy boots and all, I know him." There was distaste in Sanchez's tone. "He's the resident fixer and bagman for one of Panama's less reputable law firms, Talcott, Ilyich. They help the rich— especially the unsavory rich—hide their money from tax collectors."

"Does his law firm do much business with Russians?"

"Definitely."

"Is there a connection between the Panama Walldrum Tower and Talcott, Ilyich?"

"What are you really after, Mr. Geller?"

"Information on Ted Walldrum's business activities in Panama, specifically the construction of the Panama Walldrum Tower."

"Tell me what you already know."

"A source told me that millions of dollars were skimmed from the Tower's construction loan and shipped offshore. If that much was really skimmed, Walldrum wouldn't have had enough money left to complete the Tower. I want to know if he skimmed it, how he did it, and how much."

"I hadn't heard about the skimming, but I'm not surprised. This is Panama," Sanchez reminded us, where corruption was routine. He continued, "As far as I know, Walldrum's firm paid the usual bribes to the usual politicians and labor leaders, and completed his building on schedule."

Sherri asked, "If our source was accurate, could Walldrum have gotten a loan to replace money skimmed from the original construction loan?"

"Do you know approximately how much was skimmed?"

"North of a hundred and fifty million dollars, according to our sources."

Sanchez shook his head. "To get a loan that size, Walldrum would have had to justify a second mortgage and give the lender a lien on his building. I found just one lien, held by the Allgemeine Volksbank, the bank that issued the original construction loan for Walldrum's building."

Sanchez continued, "Anyway, why would Walldrum steal money and take out a loan to replace it? He would incur another debt, with interest. It doesn't make financial sense. That would also create a paper trail for investigators like me to follow."

He gave it more thought. "The only reason you would do something like that is if you were going to take the skim and run to a hideaway on the far side of the world. The only thing Walldrum ran for was President of the United States."

The second mortgage sounded like a dead end. If money had been skimmed, there had to be another angle.

Sherri interrupted my thoughts with a question to Sanchez. "Did you uncover anything out of the ordinary about financial management at the Walldrum Tower?"

"I did. Walldrum admits his firm sold a lot of condos to Russians, all over the world, in fact. I looked into who was buying his condos in Panama and if there was a whiff of money laundering. I couldn't find laundering, but I did find odd patterns."

"Such as . . . ?" I asked.

"First, because people are superstitious, high-rise builders tend to skip thirteen when they number their floors. The numbering sequence usually skips from twelve to fourteen. Savvy builders have one set of elevators that go from the lobby to the twelfth floor and another set of elevators that go from the lobby directly to the fourteenth floor and above."

"But not the Panama Walldrum high-rise," I guessed.

"Right. Evidently, Russians aren't superstitious. They bought all of the condos on the thirteenth floor in the Panama Walldrum Tower, and it was the first floor to sell out.

"The second odd thing is the Russians bought the entire thirteenth floor before construction began and didn't get a discount. Normally, buyers get a discount if they buy in early and another discount if they buy on a less desirable floor—like floor thirteen."

"You're sure all the buyers were Russian?" asked Sherri.

"They tried to hide their identies behind LLCs—limited liability corporations—but they were sloppy. They're Russians, take my word. Talcott, Ilyich established many of the LLCs the Russians used to purchase condos in the Walldrum Tower."

I felt we were on to something. "What else can you tell us about the condos?"

"The majority of Russians who hid behind LLCs bought condos on the thirteenth floor or higher. They bought out entire floors and none of the condos on the all-Russian floors participate in the rental program. That's odd for a condo-hotel. One of the selling points is that owners get a return on the investment by putting their condos up for rent when they're away."

"What if the condo is the owner's permanent home?" Sherri wanted to know.

"That's the catch. The purchase contract doesn't allow owners to live in their condos year-round."

I was puzzled. "How does a condo-hotel make money if it can't rent condos?"

"My question, exactly," replied Sanchez. "I cultivated an informant on the hotel staff. He told me the hotel only rents condos on floors one through twelve and on the penthouse floors, even when they have a waiting list.

"I tried to get access to the Russian-owned floors, but that proved to be impossible. Security is tight."

"How tight?" Sherri, our security expert, wanted to know.

"Very. The security contract for the building is held by a Russian firm with mob connections. Security is divided into two divisions. Division 1 consist mainly of locals who provide security for those floors of the hotel where the owners allow their condos to be rented, basically the first twelve floors and some of the penthouse floors.

"The staff for Division 2 is exclusively Russian. They provide security for the grounds and the all-Russian floors. The Division 2 security force, the condo owners, and the hotel manager are the only ones with access keys to the Russian-only floors.

"Owners, renters, and registered guests on floors one through twelve have an elevator key that limits their access to those floors. For those same categories on the penthouse floors, their access is limited to the floor on which they're staying. They don't have access to floors above or below. Fire doors have a lockout system that prevents guests from gaining entry to other floors by walking up or down stairs, except in emergencies.

"I asked my informant to try for a look at the non-renting, Russian-only floors. One day, he texted me: 'I know why Russians don't rent their condos. You need to see it. Talk later.' On his way home that night, he was robbed and killed. Do you believe in coincidences, Mr. Geller?"

"Do you, Mr. Sanchez?"

Neither of us did.

Finally, I thought we were on to something. I told Sanchez, "I need to see those floors where they don't rent the condos."

Sherri wanted to know, "What's their perimeter security like?"

Sanchez shook his head. "You don't want to go that way. My informant told me that perimeter security is tight: cameras, infrared imaging, silent alarms, the complete package. Overkill for a hotel, but it's there."

I asked Sanchez, "How would you go about getting a look at those Russian-only floors?"

"I've thought a lot about that since my source was killed. I'd do it from the inside. Rent a condo on the twelfth floor and find a way to go up, or rent a penthouse condo and find a way down."

We called a cab and left David Sanchez with our thanks and the promise of an exclusive.

*　*　*

I had a lot on my mind as we rode back to the hotel. I knew it wouldn't be long before Jill caught on that I wasn't coming to Mexico City. She would guess I was either dead or in Panama, and she'd head for Panama. Her game was still a mystery to me, but whatever Jill was up to, I wanted to see Walldrum's all-Russian condo floors before she arrived. And there was the Russian hood, who had tried to kidnap me in London. Was he still after me? If so, what did he want? Would he come to Panama to get it?

However, I couldn't let those concerns distract me from my ten-million-dollar mission. Back at our hotel, Sherri called the Walldrum Tower and got us a twelfth-floor condo rental, beginning that night.

"We're arriving on a late flight," she told the reservation clerk.

To execute our assault on the Walldrum Tower, we needed a plan. The ever-resourceful Tony-D had begun planning before I arrived in Panama. He had employed his architectural chops and a serious bribe to get us the building's blueprints. Back in my bungalow, we went over them and Tony-D quickly reached the same conclusion as the reporter, David Sanchez: "This building is tight. The only way to get from the twelfth floor to the thirteenth floor is up the elevator shaft. We climb up the shaft and jimmy the elevator doors open."

I asked, "What if the doors are alarmed?"

"They might be," Tony-D admitted. "I'll check the doors to see if they're wired. If they are, I'll try to run a bypass."

"What if there's an alarm and we can't bypass it?" asked Sherri.

Tony-D suggested, "Let it ring. Security will think it's a short circuit. We go to one of the condos, pick the lock, and hide in a closet. It would take them all night to search every room on the floor. They'll check a few condos, give up, and reset the alarm."

"What if the condos have alarms?" I was playing devil's advocate.

"We pick the locks on as many as we can and let security think the electronics have gone whacko."

"That's not a very sophisticated plan, Tony."

"Maybe you should dismiss me and bring in the 'mission impossible' team."

"Go to hell."

Tony-D smiled. "I'll be happy to, as long as I'm properly compensated for the trip."

We weren't going anywhere unless we had the proper equipment. Tony-D compiled a list of what we needed. I called David Sanchez and asked him to find a willing supplier for us—at a generous premium over retail. Our equipment was delivered to the hotel two hours later.

We decided to keep our bungalows as emergency rendezvous positions, but we dressed like travelers, packed like burglars, and headed for the Panama Walldrum Tower.

It was 11 p.m. when we checked into our condo and swept it for bugs—audio and video. Finding none, Tony-D and I prepared our equipment for the climb up the elevator shaft. Then, all of us got some sleep.

We allowed for a security shift change at midnight and time for the incoming shift to make their first rounds. At 1:30 a.m., Sherri went down to the lobby on a pretext and brought one of the elevators up to the twelfth floor. Tony-D and I climbed through the roof panel, replaced it, and shinnied up the cables to floor thirteen.

Sherri stayed in the condo, our base of operations. She kept in touch with Tony-D by radio and followed our progress on two screens receiving feed from our body cameras. If we got into serious trouble, Sherri's job was to pull a fire alarm, creating enough chaos for us to escape.

Suspended in a safety rig, Tony-D examined the shaft side of the elevator doors and found no alarms. I jimmied the doors open and we entered the dark hallway of the mysterious thirteenth floor. We turned on our flashlights. The hall stretched to infinity both ways from the elevator. It was a mirror image of the twelfth floor: crystal chandeliers, textured wallpaper, generous molding, and carpet thick enough for a wild boar hunt.

Tony-D said, "This is top quality material."

"Let's look inside the condos," I whispered.

We turned our flashlights off in case we stumbled into an occupied residence. I picked the lock of the nearest condo door and waited for an alarm to announce us. Nothing. I pushed the door open a bit. No "beep-beep-beep," telling me to enter the security code into the key pad. We stepped inside. I didn't feel carpet under my feet.

The windows were blacked out, but even in the dark the condo gave off an empty feel. I flicked on my flashlight and examined the room.

Tony-D whispered, "What the hell?" and turned on his flashlight.

I said, "Let's check the rest of the rooms."

We went through the condo playing our flashlights over the floors and walls.

When we met back at the entrance, Tony-D suggested, "Let's check next door."

We did. The second condo was exactly like the first.

I told Tony-D, "We need to check more condos."

He grunted. "We need to check another floor. You finish down here. I'll go up to fourteen." Tony-D disappeared into the elevator shaft through the propped-open doors.

None of the condo doors were alarmed. Moving quickly from one unit to another, I popped the locks, walked in, and took a quick look. It didn't take long to see what I needed to know. Inside the thirteenth-floor condos, I saw no carpeting, no wallpaper, no crystal chandeliers, no molding, no appliance, no furniture. They were empty, concrete boxes with electrical cables dangling from the walls and ceilings. Some crook with a sense of humor had left yellow signs in the foyer of each condo: "Under renovation."

That explained how Walldrum could skim millions from the construction budget. He left whole floors unfinished. Although the Russians paid millions for those empty, concrete boxes, Walldrum wasn't scamming them. That's how he laundered their money.

"Hold it right there." The command came in Spanish from behind me. "Put your hands up and turn around slowly." Another voice repeated the commands in English.

I thought of dropping the flashlight and diving for a dark corner, but the guards had flashlights on me and I was unarmed. When I turned, they were momentarily caught in the beam of my flashlight. These guys looked more like a Russian version of Seal Team Six than security guards: combat load-bearing vests, fingerless black gloves, black fatigues, and boots. One had a Heckler and Koch submachine gun, the other had a pistol. Both weapons had flashlight attachments and the beams were on me.

A thick Russian accent demanded, "What the fuck are you doing up here?"

I responded in Russian. "Looking for a condo."

Something came out of the darkness and hit my head, knocking me flat on my back.

The guard behind the Heckler and Koch ordered, "Search him."

The searcher said, "On your knees. Hands behind your head."

He gave me a quick pat-down, but missed my body cam. He found my condo key. "Registered guest," he announced, surprised. "Condo 1202."

He tossed my cell phone on the floor and rummaged through my wallet. "Oleg Stasevich from St. Petersburg." That announcement was followed by a derisive grunt.

Beneath my undershirt, I wore a leather wallet secured around my neck with a rawhide string. The guard ripped it off me.

"What's this?" He holstered his pistol and held the wallet under my nose. In the glare of his partner's flashlight, he pulled it open and took out Viktor Lukovsky's envelope with the double eagle, red wax seal.

"Look." He showed his partner. I got a glimpse of the tattoo Viktor told me about.

"Where did you get this?" asked the guard with the Heckler and Koch.

"My boss gave it to me. Use my phone to call him collect if you have questions. His number's there with the tattoo. He calls me *Ricky*."

In spite of the flashlight's glare, I saw silhouettes of the guards turn toward each other. The one with the Heckler and Koch handed over his weapon to the other guard. "Keep him covered. I'll make the call." He took my phone and went into the hall.

I heard one side of a muffled Russian conversation drift in from the corridor. The guard came back inside and handed me the phone. "Your boss wants to talk to you."

I turned the speaker off and said, "*Da?*"

Viktor Lukovsky growled, "Am I on speaker?"

"*Nyet.*" I continued in Russian for the guards. Viktor spoke English.

"What the fuck are you doing in Panama?"

"Looking for a condo."

"Good. I told him you were scouting condos for me. Stick with that story."

"I'll take care of it right away. Any other instructions?"

"He said you're staying in the Tower. Go to your room, pack your suitcase, and jump out the fucking window, if you have to, but don't be there when the sun comes up." There was concern in Viktor's voice. He added, "You haven't heard the last of this. That guy's going to report you to his boss. When he does, people may want you to explain yourself to their power tools. So, get out of there, now! I mean out of Panama!"

He continued to grumble. "Even if you get away, I may have to spend a few million on one of those worthless condos to save your ass . . . and mine."

I smiled up at the guards. In fluent Russian, I said, "I'll take care of it right away, Uncle Viktor, but I wouldn't pay top dollar."

CHAPTER 27

AFTER VIKTOR LUKOVSKY broke the phone connection with me, the leader of the two-man guard detail asked, "What instructions did your *uncle* give you?" He didn't sound convinced that Viktor was my uncle, but whatever Viktor said to him, it had given his trigger finger pause. I decided to take Viktor's advice and stick with the condo story.

"He might want to buy a condo here. What time does the sales office open?"

"Nine thirty."

"Do I need an appointment?"

"I'll make one for you. Now, go back to the condo you rented and get some sleep. I'll post a guard outside your door to make sure you don't go sleepwalking."

"Thank you, but that's not necessary. My friends and I are sound sleepers."

"I insist. An open elevator shaft is a fatality waiting to happen. We would hate to lose you to an unnecessary accident."

That was when Tony-D hit the guy with a pipe. I think it was a pipe because it gave off a hollow sound when it bounced off the guard's skull. He fell like a sack of grain. The other guard tried to turn, but Tony-D hit him halfway through his pivot. He went down to the clatter of weapons and commo gear.

Tony-D radioed Sherri. "You seeing this?"

"Roger that. I've got it on tape."

"Pack up now and wait for us on the elevator."

I gave Tony-D a thumbs-up. While Sherri packed, Tony-D and I bound and gagged the guards with what they were carrying or wearing, and left them in the condo. We closed the elevator doors and slid down the cables. When we climbed through the elevator's roof panel, Sherri was waiting with our luggage. Tony-D and I peeled out of our burglar's gear and dropped it into a suitcase. The three of us were out of the Panama Walldrum Tower minutes after Tony-D dropped the guards.

It was 3:30 a.m. and I was in a hurry to leave town, but we owed David Sanchez an exclusive. I called the reporter as soon as we were in the car and had put distance between us and the Panama Walldrum Tower.

He came on the line groggy and grumpy. "Do you know what time it is?"

"Yes. It's time for me to deliver that exclusive I promised you. I need to meet you now and you need to bring a computer with lots of memory free. I have body cam video for you to copy."

"Can't this wait until tomorrow?"

"This *is* tomorrow. We're leaving the country. Do you want the exclusive or not?"

He cursed and promised to call me right back. He did, in half an hour, and told us to meet him at his newspaper office.

David Sanchez was accompanied by a pretty Panamanian woman named Daniella. She and David appeared to have a familiar relationship that went beyond professional. While she copied Tony-D's body cam video, and Sherri napped on a couch, Sanchez viewed my cam video on his computer.

Mesmerized by what he saw, Sanchez turned to me when the video ended. "This is great footage, but I need proof that you were actually in the Walldrum Tower last night."

"There are GPS and time tags on the tapes . . . and this." I showed him a copy of our registration form.

"Can I make a copy of that?"

"No. Some hotel personnel may have been injured. If that's the case, we don't want this form to fall into the wrong hands."

"Doesn't the hotel have a copy?"

"Yes, but their copy can't connect us to you. If you don't have our registration form, how these videos came into your possession remains a mystery, right?"

Sanchez smiled and let it go.

Daniella returned Tony-D's video chip. She made an impatient face when I insisted Tony-D check it. We needed to be sure that Tony-D had his undamaged original before I gave up mine. I follow the advice of writers, magicians, and casino owners: "Trust everybody, but cut the cards."

Daniella was insulted, but Sanchez understood. He raised his chin and gave her a nod that my request was okay. Tony-D's original was intact and I surrendered my chip to a sullen Daniella. While she made the copy, Sanchez questioned us about construction costs. Tony-D, our resident architectural expert, conducted the tutorial.

"A fully tricked-out condo floor in a place like Walldrum's Tower costs about twelve million dollars. So, you need only ten floors like the ones we saw last night to shave a hundred million dollars or more from the construction budget."

Sanchez got it. "So, Walldrum could be generating laundered money on both ends—construction and sales. He skims money from the construction loan from a Russian bank by not finishing several floors. Then, he sells unfinished condos to Russians for the finished price."

Tony-D suggested the math. "Multiply the number of condos per floor by the number of floors that are nothing but bare walls and you have some serious cash flowing into and out of the Walldrum organization."

While Tony-D schooled the reporter, I used Sanchez's computer to make myself a backup copy of the Tula chip. I considered giving it a movie title: *Dirty Pictures at the Ritz*, starring President Ted Walldrum. I discarded that title. It would be too obvious for any prying eyes searching my computer.

Sanchez turned to me. "Are you going to follow the skimmed cash?"

"I'll leave that to you. You want the Pulitzer Prize. I don't."

He didn't like that. Even reporters don't want to hear the truth sometimes.

Daniella returned with my chip. After I checked it, I announced, "That concludes our business. Thanks for your help."

Sanchez grabbed my arm. He was agitated. "Wait a minute. You promised me an exclusive on the photographs you collected in Russia."

"No. Sherri *told* you about the Russia photos. I promised you an exclusive, not a subject. Don't get greedy, Sanchez. Your career will go ballistic when you put those body cam images online."

*   *   *

We didn't return to our old hotel right away. We were hungry and needed a fast exit out of Panama. Tony-D located an Internet café across from a restaurant. Sherri and I had breakfast while he went to the café to nail down our escape plan. Sherri was returning to Washington. Tony-D and I were going to pay a surprise visit to Jill Rucker in Mexico City.

As Sherri and I were enjoying our second cup of good coffee, I asked her, "Do you know a techie you can trust to analyze the camera chip and photos the Tula guy gave us?"

"Sure. One of the hackers we took to London could do that."

"No. Don't use anyone from the London team. The Russians tried to kidnap me in London. That means they knew what I was doing there and they might have identified our team members. If they did, they'll go after our techies first."

"You're assuming the Russians know we have the chip and photographs."

"Assume the worst and you don't get nasty surprises. Who else can you trust?"

Sherri consulted her mental address book. "I have a friend who does computer forensics for a D.C. security firm."

I gave Sherri the package with the camera chip and the photographs of Walldrum and the prostitutes.

"You make one copy of those for safekeeping. I don't want the techie copying anything. Can you watch this guy the whole time he handles the package?"

"Yes, but it will cost you."

"Offer whatever it takes to keep him honest and keep his mouth shut. Tell him that he's the only one who knows about those photographs. If there's a leak from any source, I'll blame him. I'll find him and cut his balls off."

"Too late," Sherri informed me, with a smile. "*He's* a *she*."

"I don't care. I'm not kidding, Sherri. Tell her she's playing with the bad boys."

Before Sherri could comment, Tony-D joined us for breakfast and briefed us on transportation.

"Sherri, you're on a commercial flight to D.C. in ninety minutes. No time for you to go back to the hotel. I'll check you out. Actually, it's not smart for any of us to go back." Tony-D looked at me. "Those Walldrum Tower guards will have been discovered by now and people will be looking for us."

Between empanadas and gulps of coffee, Tony-D told me, "You and I leave for Mexico City on a charter flight at noon."

I wanted to pay Jill Rucker a little surprise visit before I asked Bill Bowen for my ten million dollars.

CHAPTER 28

TONY-D AND I were staying in hotel bungalows. As Tony-D said, there was risk associated with going back to check out, but both of us had things we didn't want to leave behind. We planned on a quick in-and-out: pack, check out, and gone.

It was after nine in the morning when I got to my bungalow. I walked in, dropped my suitcase full of burglar equipment, and looked into the barrel of Jill Rucker's gun. She sat in an easy chair pointing her newly acquired .22 caliber pistol at me. The gun didn't have much stopping power unless the bullet hit a vital organ. However, it used to be an Israeli favorite because it was quiet. You didn't need a silencer, but you had to be a good shot. Jill Rucker was an excellent shot. She looked both deadly and sexy in a polo shirt, cargo pants, and hiking boots.

"Hello, Max. Did you miss me, or did I miss you in Mexico?"

"You should have had a little patience. I just chartered a plane to come join you."

"Sure, you did." She didn't sound convinced. "Have you been to the Walldrum Tower yet?"

"Yes."

"What did you find?"

"Nothing," I lied. "It was just a normal condo-hotel."

"So, the Omega Group was wrong. There is no multimillion-dollar skim scheme." Jill sounded cynical.

"I didn't say that. I haven't been here long enough to find out if there is a skimming operation."

"And yet, you were leaving for Mexico City to see me. Why the rush?"

"I promised us R and R in Cancun."

Jill sighed. "I guess you're just going to lie until I shoot you. Where's the *kompromat* you collected in Russia on Waldrum?"

"I sent it to Washington."

"I don't believe you, Max. With ten million dollars on the table and Bowen's firm in Panama, I think you came here to collect. Where is it?"

I stooped to open the suitcase.

"No," she said, quickly. "Don't move. Just tell me where it is."

"Some of it's in this suitcase. I keep it with me for obvious reasons."

In reality, the suitcase contained equipment and the two screens Sherri used to monitor what our body cams picked up as Tony-D and I moved through the empty condos in the Panama Walldrum Tower.

Slowly, I took the suitcase key from my pocket and held it up. "Do you want to open it?"

"You open it." Jill got out of the chair, keeping her gun trained on me. She was about eight feet away.

I knelt and rotated the case so it was at a right angle to her line of fire. I got as much of me as I could behind the suitcase, planted my feet, and lunged, using the case as a shield.

Jill fired twice. I heard the rounds tear through the suitcase wall and smash a monitor. She was moving to my left and I knew her next shot would be at my legs. As I propelled myself toward her, I swung the suitcase in a roundhouse blow that knocked the gun from her hand. It hit the wall and slid across the floor away from us. I let go of the heavy suitcase, but momentum caused it to follow the gun across the room. It hit the wall, too, and crashed to the floor, spilling its contents.

Carried by the suitcase's momentum, I was off balance, rotating to my left, with my right side exposed. Jill was rotating to her left and delivered a painful blow to my right kidney. I buckled and Jill kicked me in the same spot, sending me staggering across the room toward the suitcase.

Jill came at me kicking. I couldn't let her connect with another blow from those boots. I grabbed the empty suitcase for a shield. She kicked. I blocked. She grabbed a floor lamp by its shaft and swung the base hard enough to knock the suitcase out of my hands. Jill followed up with a blow to my ribs. I went down. She dropped the lamp and dove for her gun. I slid a monitor across the floor and sent the gun spinning out of her reach. I was on my knees, trying to get up, when she kicked me in the ribs. Jill had a knack for delivering those blows to the same spot.

I rolled in the direction of the floor lamp, grabbed it, and knocked her legs from under her. She went down. I jumped to my feet and swung the floor lamp, hitting her in the head with the base. Jill was stunned and bloodied. I hit her once more. She lay on her back, motionless and moaning. The fight was over.

I grabbed Jill's gun and sat on her chest, pinning her arms to the floor with my calves. I pressed the pistol against her temple with one hand and held her throat in a tight grip with the other.

Through the pain that was wracking my torso, I couldn't help saying, "Looks like you failed the ass-kicking event of your internship."

Her voice was labored and hoarse. "You . . . said you wouldn't . . . fight fair."

"I keep my promises and I promise you this. If you don't tell me your real name and your part in this game we've been playing, I'll kill you right now."

Her head was bleeding. "As far as you're concerned . . . my name is Jill Rucker. I'm working a counterintelligence investigation for the agency that fired you."

"Bullshit! You've been spinning me since we met in London." I cocked her pistol. "I'd better believe the next thing out of your lying mouth or you're going to die."

Jill moved under me.

"I'm feeling you tense up." I forced the gun in her mouth. "Try any of that karate crap on me and it's over. I mean it."

Jill relaxed. Clearly, she was considering her next words carefully.

I said, "Let's start with something easy. You told me you'd never been to Russia. What the hell were you doing at the tenth anniversary gala for Russian Television? You sat a couple of tables from Putin."

Blood was running from the gash in her forehead and pooling on the carpet. "I swear, this is true. I was on an undercover counterintelligence investigation. There were several Americans at that gala. My mission was to get close to one or more of them and try to discover Putin's plans to influence our presidential elections."

"You had a specific target. Who was it?"

"I can't tell you that. If I did, my career would be over. There were several U.S. presidential candidates and a former top U.S. spy at Putin's table, and they weren't the only Americans in the room. It was a target-rich environment for counterintelligence. If you had to pick one to investigate, who would it be?"

I'd pick the former top U.S. spy. Was he Jill's target? Did it even matter now? Hell, no. The only thing that mattered was if I believed Jill Rucker was being truthful.

She kept talking. "You saw the newspapers and you must have read Agency intel on Putin's efforts to subvert our election. We could have justified investigations on every American in that room."

It sounded like the truth, but if Jill was lying to save her life, her story had to ring true. Still, it was a long road from a Moscow gala to a shady Panama law firm.

"How did you get from the RT gala to Bowen's payroll?"

"When the pool of presidential candidates narrowed, so did the number of counterintelligence targets on my radar. I was reassigned. At the same time, there was growing Agency concern about Candidate Walldrum's financial ties to Russians. A lot of indicators, including sources inside the Omega Group—yes, the Agency knows about them—they told us that targeting the Russian money laundering machine in Panama might be worthwhile.

"Under my cover, I had previously worked for Bowen. So, when Langley put my counterintelligence target on the back burner, the Agency sent me back here to penetrate the Talcott, Ilyich money laundering operation. My goal was to get procedures, the client list, and find any connections between Candidate Walldrum and Russian money."

I prodded her with the gun. "Bowen hired me to see if the Russians had *kompromat* on Walldrum. Whose side is Bowen on?"

"Bowen's a bad guy. He works for Talcott, Ilyich. The lawyers at that firm have their hands into laundered money up to their Rolexes, and not just Russian money. Their services are available to anyone with enough wealth to make it worthwhile. Bowen is the traveling business recruiter. He finds crooks who require his firm's skills."

"How did you come to be my London contact?"

"While I worked for Bowen, I studied his operation. I convinced him that he was too visible and that, once he set up an operation, I could handle the logistics and be his cutout to clients and field staff. That would put me in position to know the clients, operators, and processes. That's where the Agency wanted me."

Jill continued, "The election happened, followed by a year of Washington turmoil, and you came along. I knew what Bowen wanted you to do, but I didn't know why or who was offering ten million to verify Ironside's dossier. Because of the sensitivity of what you were doing, I convinced Bowen to send me to London as his cutout, in case you screwed up or got caught."

Jill grimaced and squirmed. "Now, will you please get off of me?"

I didn't move. "Why did you want to come to London?"

"Your job was to find out if Russians had compromising information on Walldrum. If you accomplished that, it was way more important than exposing a Panamanian money laundering operation. It had national security tracks right into the White House. To be honest, being part of that would be a career-maker for me . . . and, I didn't trust you or Bowen. Even if you found evidence that Walldrum had been compromised by the Russians, I had no idea what you, Bowen, or his client would do with it."

She grimaced and squirmed again. "Now, either shoot me or get the hell off me. My arms are going numb."

"I'm going to let you adjust your position, but if you make one threatening move, I'll shoot off a kneecap. Copy that?"

She groaned. "Yes."

I let her free her arms. "Roll over on your back and put your hands behind you."

"We already did that position on the cruise ship."

"I think I should just start hurting you."

She rolled over. I kneeled on her forearms while I reached back and pulled the laces from her boots. They made a nice cord to bind her wrists together. I hauled Jill up by the collar and sat her in a chair. She gave me a look that combined fatigue and disgust.

I went to the bar sink and got a wet towel to wipe the blood out of her eyes.

She asked, "What now?"

"Now, tell me about the Russian who keeps crossing your path."

"What Russian?"

"The fucking Russian in the limo in Mexico City, that Russian!" A flash of anger seared me. I shoved Jill over backwards in the chair.

She rolled away from the chair and lay on her back looking up at me. "Max, you're a private citizen. I work for the CIA. I can't read you in on classified operations!"

"Yeah, I get it. You could tell me, but, then, you would have to kill me. Who do you think is most likely to get killed here? You need to reassess your situation. Nobody is coming to save you. Nobody's recording what you say. Either tell me everything about our time together since we met in London or I'm going to assume that you're a Russian spy and I'm going to shoot you."

I set the chair upright. Jill got up slowly and walked to it.

We sat facing each other. I laid the pistol on my thigh, barrel pointed in her direction. "I know way more about your stop in Mexico City than you think. Do you want to start over? Tell me about *all* the Russians."

Jill ran her tongue over her lips, stalling. I let her. "When I arrived in Mexico City, two Russian intelligence officers were waiting for me. They asked if you were on the plane. I said, 'no.' They knew we were the shooters at the bank in Moscow. They said that was not their concern. There were other considerations. They said someone wanted to speak to me. We went out of the terminal to a limo. There were two men in the car."

I showed her a photograph of the smoker by the limo. "Was he one of them?"

"Yes."

"Who is he?"

"His name is Konstantin Zabluda. His nickname is 'Kostya.' He's a colonel in the Russian special forces, on temporary duty with their military intelligence service. He runs a network of assassins. The Agency and MI6 believe he's leading a hit team that's been killing ex-Soviet spies in London on orders from Putin."

I warned her. "Think carefully before you answer my next question." I fingered the trigger. She noticed. "Where had you seen Zabluda before Mexico City?"

Jill hesitated, stalling, again. "He was with the Russian hit squad at the warehouse in London when we rescued you. Zabluda was the outside man."

"You fired three shots at him and missed. Why didn't you kill him?"

She took another long pause. "When I told my Agency boss that Bowen was sending me to London with you, he warned me that Zabluda was a threat. Langley believed Zabluda was in London for the same reason as you, to track down Ironside's sources. His job was to kill them, on orders from the Kremlin."

"How did Langley know why I was going to London?"

"Bowen told me. I told Langley."

"In London, you pretended not to know what I was doing. Why did you lie?"

"I wanted you to see me as an ally, not as Bowen's spy."

"So that it would be easier for you to spy on me?"

She didn't have to answer.

I was confused. "If Zabluda was a threat, why didn't you kill him at the warehouse?"

"I was told to avoid him. If our paths did cross, my orders were not to engage him."

"Why was Langley giving this guy a pass?"

"After the last Russian assassination in London, the prime minister was really pissed at Putin. She wants a show trial that ties Zabluda and his team to a specific hit on direct orders from Moscow. The Brits have cracked Zabluda's communications system and they want to keep him operational until they deliver the package that the PM wants."

"All right, let's hear about your meeting in the car with Zabluda in Mexico City. What did you talk about?"

"Nothing. He was in the car; he didn't speak. He listened. Bowen did the talking."

"Bowen?"

"Yes. Bowen thought you and I flew to Mexico together and you were bringing him the Walldrum *kompromat* from Russia. He wanted to know what you had."

"What did you tell him?"

"I lied. I said you didn't trust me enough to share your findings. You were afraid I would steal what you had collected and claim the ten-million-dollar reward."

"Did he buy that?"

"Did he have a choice? I told him you were meeting me at the hotel and we were going to Cancun for a quick vacation. He wanted me to stay with that plan. I left him and went to the hotel."

"Why was Zabluda there?"

"Why do you think? He was there to kill us after you gave Bowen the dirt on Walldrum."

"What's your assessment of the Bowen-Zabluda relationship?"

"Bowen obviously works for the Russians. I'm with Langley on that. I think the purpose of your ten-million-dollar reward was to have you smoke out Ironside's sources so Zabluda could kill them."

Jill gave me a hard look. "You suspected that, didn't you? That's why you sent Bowen and the Russians to meet me at the airport."

"I wasn't sure about Bowen. I thought you were working for the Russians. Maybe you are. Anyway, I wanted to see the reactions when all of you met in Mexico City."

Jill gave me a grim smile. "In your shoes, I'd have done the same thing. It's not personal. It's just business, right, Max?"

It felt damned personal to me when we made love on the cruise ship, but I've been criticized for being a romantic.

There was a knock on the bungalow door. "It's Tony-D. You ready to go?"

I opened the door. "Come on in, Tony. Meet the worst shot in London."

Tony-D glanced at me, the gun, Jill, and the wreckage that used to be my living room. He said, "I guess we're not going to Mexico City. What the hell happened here?"

I explained. "Jill failed her internship."

Tony-D's eyes held a question, but he didn't go there. Instead he observed, "Jill needs a few stitches to close that forehead wound."

Tony-D drove to the hospital with Jill and me in the back seat.

Jill kept up her pitch for God and Country. "Max, you've got to turn over the stuff on Walldrum to the special prosecutor."

"How much is the special prosecutor going to pay me?"

"He's not going to pay you anything; neither is Bowen. Bowen will take the Walldrum *kompromat*, give it to the Russians, and Zabluda's going to kill you."

Tony-D asked, "Who is Zabluda?"

I answered. "Mexico City. The smoker leaning on the limo."

Tony-D nodded.

Jill was agitated. "Were you listening to me? Zabluda was in Mexico to kill us."

"Stiffing me and putting a bullet in my head may be Bowen's plan. I have a plan of my own. Did anyone from Mexico follow you here?"

"No. There were a couple of surveillance teams sitting on me at the hotel, one Russian, the other local. I slipped by both when I left."

"Where's Bowen?"

"I don't know."

"I need some time. Give me twelve hours before you contact anyone here, in Washington, or Mexico."

"Why should I give you a head start? I don't approve of what you're doing."

I pressed the replay button on my body cam monitor. Jill saw and heard herself say:

His name is Konstantin Zabluda. His nickname is "Kostya." He's a colonel in the Russian special forces, on temporary duty with their foreign intelligence service. He runs a network of assassins. The Agency and MI6 believe he's leading a hit team that's been killing ex-Soviet spies in London on orders from Putin.

Jill was livid. "You bastard! You said you weren't recording me!"

"I also told you I play dirty, but I won't ruin you. Stay quiet for twelve hours, and I'll erase this video. If I think you contacted anyone, this goes to your boss at the CIA."

"That video could send me to jail."

"When you get out, you can work exclusively for Bowen."

Jill was smoldering. "How will you know if I stayed off the grid for twelve hours?"

"I'll just have to trust you and you'll have to trust me."

We dropped Jill at the *Hospital Regional Docente 24 de Diciembre* on our way to Tocumen Airport. I brought Tony-D up to date on my fight with Jill, and he called ahead to have our pilot file a flight plan to Washington, D.C. I had to get the Tula man's Ritz photographs from Sherri and figure out how to get my ten million dollars from Bowen.

CHAPTER 29

TONY-D AND I arrived at Dulles Airport six hours after wheels up in Panama. The twelve-hour clock on my grace period with Jill Rucker was half over. Tired or not, I had to move fast. I called workaholic Sherri at her office from a terminal pay phone.

She had good news. "Your chip and prints are the gold standard."

"How much is that info going to cost me?"

"Only our silence. The examiner wants nothing to do with your product. It's too controversial. She could lose clients. I don't know whether you're cursed or one lucky son-of-a-gun."

All of the above, so far.

"Sherri, I'm bunking with Tony-D tonight. Can you bring the chip and the photographs to his house when you leave the office this evening?"

"Can do."

"Make it late. I need some rest."

"We're all going to need some rest. My house is being watched."

"You sure?"

Sherri didn't answer me because that was a stupid question. I had no idea why anyone would be watching Sherri's house. But she was an experienced operator and if she said they were watching, I had to believe her.

Sherri ignored my question and told me, "There's something odd going on. Nobody followed me to the office. They're just watching my house. It's creepy."

"Any signs they entered your home while you were away?"

"No. All my tells were intact."

"Then, they're waiting for someone to show."

"Who?"

"Me."

"Why would they be looking for you at my place?"

"I need to think about that."

Sherri added, "Vanessa called me."

Vanessa was my Agency sweetheart, reassigned to Australia months before I lost my job. I hadn't heard from her even after I got fired. You would think that someone who had been that close to you would call and say, "Sorry to hear you lost your job." Maybe even, "Come to Australia. Let's figure out how we can be together."

Instead, Vanessa went dark, not a word.

Sherri snapped me out of my thoughts. "Did you hear me, Max? Vanessa called."

"Yeah. I'm just surprised. What did she say?"

"She wanted to know if you were out of bed yet?"

Code for, "Is Max still undercover?" What the hell was Vanessa talking about?

"You need to call her." Sherri gave me Vanessa's number and we broke off.

I used the same public phone to call Vanessa in Australia. When she answered, I didn't waste time on polite greetings.

"This is me. Are we on a clean line?"

"Yes."

"Why did you ask Sherri if I was out of bed yet?"

"I heard that you were leaving work temporarily for a serious operation and would be bedridden for several months. I heard Dr. Leamas is caring for you."

Dr. Leamas? What the hell is she—Then, I got her message. Alec Leamas is a Cold War fictional spy who, to appearances, was fired from MI6. In reality, he went undercover for the Brits so the Russians would recruit him. His mission was to give the Russians information that would lead them away from a MI6 mole in the East German security service. Had someone told Vanessa I'd gone undercover?

"Who told you about Leamas?"

"Your French-speaking colleague."

Fucking Rodney!

"When did he tell you?"

"In August."

That was months before Rodney fired me!

Vanessa continued. "Your illness was the reason I was sent to Australia. Your French-speaking colleague told me it would be better if I went away while you were in bed recovering. He made me promise not to tell you or contact you. I was promised that my posting here was temporary until you were no longer bedridden."

So, Rodney told Vanessa that I was going undercover and it would be best if she went away until my assignment was completed. Then, she would be reassigned to Langley and we could continue our relationship.

"Van, listen carefully. I'm involved with some bad people. They may try to use you to get information from me. You need to disappear right now."

"What? What about my job."

"Your job won't matter if you're not alive to go to work. Take sick leave. Did you keep your D.C. bank account?"

"Yes."

"I'll wire some money to that account. Withdraw it immediately. Pay cash for everything. Stay out of sight and off the grid.

"In ten days, call Sherri's office and give her a number where I can contact you. If there's no message from me, go to the Agency inspector general and tell him everything that my French-speaking colleague told you and what we discussed on this call." I hung up on Vanessa's protests.

I was concerned and a lot angry at Rodney. There were two possible explanations for his actions. One, he had permission from the Seventh Floor to run me in a deep cover operation without my knowledge. Or, two, he was in bed with Bowen, and that put Rodney in bed with the Russians. In the latter case, that meant there were three people who wanted what I had on Walldrum and all of them wanted me dead. I needed to know which door Rodney was behind. My live-in, Claudia, was the key to Rodney.

The clock on my twelve-hour grace period with Jill Rucker was ticking down.

Tony-D was making a purchase at the newsstand and must have picked up on my stress.

He ambled over. "Something wrong?"

"Yeah. Can you put a tap on my landline at home?"

"Sure. When?"

"Now, before my live-in gets home. She's usually there after seven."

Tony-D looked at his watch. He pursed his lips and exhaled. "Let me make a call."

We took a cab to Tony-D's townhouse near Crystal City and napped until his cell phone rang at 8:30 p.m.

Tony-D listened to his caller, broke the connection, and announced, "Your tap's in place. The bad news is your landline already had a tap. What the hell's going on, Max?"

"Damned if I know, but I'll tell you what I do know when Sherri gets here." My guess was that the first tap was Rodney's work.

Tony-D meticulously placed pepperoni slices on a frozen cauli-flower pizza and popped it into the oven. We had cold beer and pizza while we waited for Sherri. She arrived by the second slice. Tony-D gave her a beer and a plate, and we settled down to eat, while I told my story. I needed objective input.

"I think Claudia set me up so Rodney could fire me. Then, Rodney handed me off to Bowen who sent me—us—to England and Russia to find Ironside's sources."

"Who is Claudia?" Tony-D wanted to know.

"She's a high-six-figure D.C. lawyer. I met her at Rodney's after Vanessa—my girlfriend—was sent to Australia. Claudia sort of moved in six weeks before the three of us went to England."

Sherri asked, "How does one move in, *sort of*?"

I gave the obvious answer. "She spends more time at my house than at hers."

"Did she bring clothes and flowerpots?" Sherri was enjoying my discomfort.

Tony-D wasn't. He said, "I don't underestimate your charm, Max, but there's a lot of cash-connected testosterone in D.C. Why did she choose you?"

A bit too gleefully, Sherri said, "If it's too good to be true, it's too good to be true."

I admitted, "It was Claudia's email that caused the Agency to fire me."

Sherri asked, "Did the Agency fire you or was it Rodney? If Rodney conspired with Claudia, that was definitely a setup."

"Well," sighed Tony-D, "I'm giving odds that Rodney and Claudia set you up. The only question in my mind is, did Claudia know about Bowen and his Russians?"

I doubted she knew. "Rodney wouldn't have told Claudia she was part of a CIA operation. I just want to know if Claudia used her email to set me up so Rodney could fire me, or if her email was a coincidence and Rodney took advantage of it to fire me."

"Why do you care?" asked Sherri.

"I just need to know how badly I've been played."

"If Claudia deliberately set you up," said Sherri, "she had a motive. What would she gain by getting you fired? Does Rodney have something she wants? Are they lovers behind your back?"

I didn't believe either motivation. "Claudia doesn't need money. I checked her out when she moved into my house. Rodney has his own love life and Claudia is too busy to cheat on me."

Sherri uttered an unconvinced grunt.

Tony-D wondered aloud, "If Rodney has nothing to offer her, who does? Could she be doing that someone a favor by helping Rodney fire you?"

Sherri liked that argument. "Yeah. Maybe someone Rodney *knows* has something Claudia wants."

The possibility that Claudia knowingly set me up stoked my anger. "You're asking if there is something she wanted badly enough to sleep with me and destroy my career."

Sherri said, "This is Washington, Max. Don't make it personal. At the Agency when we were trying to turn somebody, we always asked, 'What would he sell himself for?' So, what does Claudia want badly enough to ruin you?"

Without hesitation, I said, "A partnership at her law firm."

Tony-D got enthused. "Now we're getting somewhere. Does Rodney know someone at Claudia's law firm who could improve her chances of becoming a partner? If there is such a person, he or she is the reason Claudia stiffed you."

Sherri reminded me, "You said you met Claudia at a party at Rodney's house. Was anyone else there from her firm?"

Rodney had introduced me to lots of people at the party. Under the watchful eyes of Sherri and Tony-D, I wrote down all the names I could remember, along with the name of Claudia's firm. Sherri called my list in to the night man at her office—she had overseas clients—and gave him instructions. He went to work on Internet searches. We finished off the pizza and Tony-D broke out a pristine carton of tiramisu-flavored ice cream.

By the time we finished our decaf Espresso—a culinary oxymoron—Tony-D's fax machine was spitting out the Internet search results from Sherri's night man. He had cross-tabbed Claudia and Rodney with all the names on my list and identified people connected to both.

Sherri read us the relevant facts. "There's only one person with a significant connection to both Rodney and *your* Claudia." She gave me a tight smile. "He's Lyle Palmer, the senior partner at Claudia's law firm. Rodney and Palmer went to Princeton together. Palmer worked in the Office of the General Counsel at the CIA before moving on to private practice. He also represented Rodney during his divorce and Palmer's wife is a partner at the firm. They could definitely influence Claudia's career advancement."

"Bingo!" announced Tony-D.

It wasn't hard evidence that Claudia had sandbagged me to get a partnership, but it was close. I wanted her confession. A confrontation wasn't going to work. Claudia was too good a lawyer to admit she engineered my firing.

I checked my watch. It was half-past ten. Claudia would be up working for another hour. I announced, "I need to nail this down. Tony, crank up your tape recorder. I'm going to call my house."

Claudia was there, pretending—or not pretending—to be happy hearing my voice. That happiness vanished quickly. I gave her enough information to raise concerns and trigger a call to Rodney, which she made, as soon as I hung up.

Rodney sounded drowsy. "Claudia, it's late. Is anything wrong?"

"Max called."

Sleep vanished from Rodney's voice, replaced by alertness. "Where is he?"

"In the D.C. area. He wasn't specific."

"What did he say?"

"He said you fired him so you could hire him out to the Russians. Is that true?"

Rodney ignored her question. "Was he angry at you?"

"What? No. He was angry at you for setting him up and firing him."

"The setup wouldn't have worked without you. If he knows I wanted him fired, he knows you were in on the plan."

"What *plan!*"

Rodney was composed. "Did he have anything for me?"

"Anger!"

"Cute. Did he ask for anything from me?"

"No."

Suddenly Rodney knew. "Damnit! He was playing you to get you to call me. Don't call me again. Stay by the phone. If Max calls, keep him on the line. Find out where he's staying."

Claudia was angry. "Rodney, I didn't sign up for this spy versus spy shit! I agreed to work with you as a favor to Lyle."

Rodney's response was cold. "You signed up to do a favor for your boss so I would tell him you did a good job on a national security matter. You wanted him to be impressed and recommend you for a partnership. In pursuit of that goal, you slept with Max. You baited him with your email and made it possible for me to fire him. You did whatever was required. Don't go innocent on me now that a little light is seeping into your dark corner."

"You told me I was helping you make it look like Max was fired so he could go undercover. You didn't say a damned thing about any Russians!"

"You need to stop using that proper noun."

I could almost hear Claudia's teeth clench. "I didn't call you for a fucking English lesson! I want to know what kind of mess you've gotten me into."

"Calm down. Max is lying to you. He bungled his assignment and he's looking for an out."

"I don't care about any of this! I'm going to tell Lyle Palmer everything and I'm finished with you!"

"That won't get you a partnership. Lyle knows nothing about what we're doing. You tell him you're involved with Russians and you'll be lucky if you're not fired. In any event, a bad recommendation from me will probably torpedo your partnership hopes . . . and I would have to tell Lyle you're lying if you mentioned Russians."

"You bastard!"

"At your service. Now, I'll tell you what you're going to do. If Max calls, keep him talking. We'll trace the call, get Max, and all of this will go quietly away."

"You'll trace the call! Is this line tapped!"

Rodney ignored her again. "Just keep Max talking. Ask when he's coming home. Tell him you miss him." With sarcasm, he added, "I'm sure you do."

Tony-D shut off the tape recorder. I'm sure Rodney went back to sleep. Claudia probably stayed awake.

Sherri was uncomfortable with the surveillance on her house. So, we all spent the night at Tony-D's. It was the first night since we arrived in London weeks ago that we could sleep soundly without the fear of someone crashing through the door. I slept well.

*   *   *

The next morning, Sherri left for home before anyone else was awake. My first thought when I awakened was that any lead time Jill Rucker had given me was used up. I showered and dressed. Tony-D and I had breakfast. I nursed my anger and killed time until opening hour at Claudia's firm. Then, I called her boss.

"Stratton, Radcliff, and Bowles," the receptionist announced. "May I help you?"

"I'd like to speak to Lyle Palmer. I have an urgent message from Rodney."

"And you are . . . ?"

"The urgent messenger."

"Just a moment." Well trained. She didn't hesitate. Maybe Stratton, Radcliff, and Bowles were used to urgent messages from anonymous sources.

There was a thirty-second pause before a cultured voice came on the line. "This is Lyle Palmer. I understand you have a message from Rodney."

"I have a message *about* your friend Rodney and your employee Claudia Navarro. They are about to become embarrassments for your firm."

Palmer was impatient. "Who are you?"

"If I wanted you to know my name, you would already have it. Do you want to shoot the messenger or hear the message? I can give it to the *Washington Post* if you're not interested."

He said, "Proceed."

"Claudia is involved in Rodney's operation to suppress information that would compromise the president"—to avoid confusion, I added—"of the United States. Rodney is working with Russian agents to make that happen."

"Is this a joke?"

"That's the wrong question. The correct question is, 'Do you have proof?' If you had asked that question, my answer would have been, 'Yes.' I have a taped telephone conversation of Claudia and Rodney discussing how their plan went wrong and how Rodney intends to cover it up with a murder. Mine."

"Are you trying to blackmail me?"

"No. I'm trying to do you a favor. Their scheme is going to be exposed. When that happens, Claudia Navarro's only other claim to fame will be that she works for your firm . . . assuming she still works for your firm when the story hits the newspapers."

"What's in this for you?" asked Palmer.

"A favor for a favor. It seems everybody in Washington needs a lawyer these days. When my time comes, I might need your services. I'll remind you of this favor."

"What happens to the tape?"

"It's my insurance. Maybe you'll accept it as your fee, if I ever need your services."

*　*　*

The mind is a funny thing. You have a question without an answer. You file it in your head, and while you're doing something unrelated, the answer reveals itself. I called Sherri.

"Sherri, I think I know why those guys are sitting on your house."

"You said they were waiting for you to show."

"Yeah, but why at your house. Why not mine? I gave you my sat phone in Stockholm because I didn't want to take it to Russia. What did you do with it?"

"I was going to Russia, too. So, I gave it to one of my hackers to bring back to the States. He dropped it off at my house when he got back to D.C. You think it's the sat phone."

"I'd bet on it. The phone is transmitting its location at your house and somebody's waiting for me to show up there."

"What do they want?"

"I'm going to find out. When you get home this evening, put the phone in a metal box to kill the signal and bring it to me at the Capital Yacht Club in Southwest D.C. Also, I need a clean piece with a silencer."

* * *

CIA lock-picking skills are like typing skills—you can use them anywhere and for a lifetime. After Sherri dropped off the sat phone, I used the cover of darkness and my CIA-acquired skills to bypass the marina gate lock and gain entrance to the yacht I was looking for. It was a 42-foot, Grand Banks Heritage Classic named *Envy*. It was a long way down the price list from Viktor Lukovsky's Wally moored at Canary Wharf in East London, but the name *Envy* served the purposes of the owner, who didn't sail her often.

Structure-wise, up the aft ladder from the entry deck, the boat had a spacious flybridge—cockpit to landlubbers like me. Down the aft hatch and below decks there was a plush lounge with a galley. A guest bedroom was forward and three steps down from the lounge. The master bedroom was three steps down from the lounge and aft. The craft was comfortable for sailing and perfect for an ambush. I took the sat phone out of the metal box, attached the silencer to my gun, and turned the lights off.

Two men came to the *Envy* a little after three in the morning. Good timing. The marina party animals had sucked up the last of their Simi Valley Cabernet and crawled into their berths to await the arrival of midmorning and headaches. Apparently, I was the only one awake, as two men in soft shoes and tight, black ninja outfits tiptoed down the steps to the lounge-galley of the *Envy*. Their silhouettes were visible in reflected television light from the forward bedroom. Muted talk show conversation wafted up to the lounge. They were drawn to it, as I had planned.

At the aft end of the yacht, the narrow entrance to the master bedroom was flanked on the port side by a shower. On the starboard side, there was a bathroom with a full-length mirror embedded in the door. I had propped the bathroom door open so I could view the lounge while I stood in the shower out of their view and line of fire.

As they crept toward the forward bedroom, the trailing man must have caught a glimpse of reflected light in the bathroom door mirror. He whirled and put a bullet into the head of his reflection with his silenced pistol. As the mirror shattered, he realized what had happened and whispered a harsh, "Go! Go!" Both of them scampered down the steps toward the light in the guest bedroom. After they checked possible hiding places, one said, "He's not here."

"He's behind you," I said. I was looking down from the lounge. They were standing in a small space between two beds, with no maneuver room. Fish in a barrel looking up three steps at me.

"Drop your guns."

The guy closest to me said, "I'm putting it down." He knelt, laid his gun on the carpet, and pushed it away. The move was a distraction to take my eyes off the man behind him. As the first man knelt, the second man raised his gun to shoot. His problem was that he had to raise his gun high to shoot up the steps. My gun was already pointing down at him. All I had to do was pull the trigger. My first shot nicked his chin and tore into his chest just below his neck. I put a second round in the same spot.

The first man was kneeling on the deck, trying to unholster his ankle gun. I shot him twice in the chest. He was a big man and he just fell back against his dead partner and kept clawing at his ankle holster. I assumed he was wearing a protective vest. I shot him in the head.

*   *   *

Rodney's Georgetown home had three levels. He lived on the second and third. The first level had been converted into a garage for his sixty-five-thousand-dollar Jaguar XF, with all the usual refinements, minus the 007 ejection seat, headlight-mounted machine guns, etcetera. Although, Rodney would have enjoyed showing them off had they been available. Having been a guest at Rodney's several times, I knew there was no way to bypass his security systems. I waited low in the back seat of my curbside rental car. Rodney pulled into his garage. I made a dash for the door as it was coming down. When he got out of his car, he was staring at me and my gun.

"You look surprised to see me, Rodney."

"I am. You don't normally enter my home by sliding under the garage door with a gun in your hand."

"Special circumstances. Let's talk upstairs."

Minutes later, I was sitting in Rodney's home office. The walls were lined with books and photos of Rodney with presidents and members of Congress. There was a Chinese rug on the polished hardwood floor. He was at the liquor cabinet holding a bottle of my favorite scotch poised above a crystal shot glass. "Drink?"

"I gave it up for Lent."

"You're not Catholic. You're a confirmed heathen."

"I want to be in good standing, if I convert."

Rodney looked at my gun and quit the banter. "Would you please put that away?"

"I'm more comfortable pointing it at you."

Rodney shrugged and took his drink to the antique desk. He removed his coat and hung it on the chair back. Deliberately, he walked to the front of the desk, leaned back against it, gripped the overhang, and crossed his ankles. Since I was seated, his position of superiority was established. He took a sip of his drink and said, "You mentioned special circumstances."

"You ruined me and used me. You lied to Vanessa and had her reassigned. You conspired with Claudia to set me up so you could get me fired. The purpose of all that was to destroy my morale and my finances so I'd be vulnerable when Bowen came to recruit me to work for the Russians."

Rodney smiled. "You don't know what you're talking about. I couldn't tell you, but you were involved in a legitimate operation. I grant you Bowen is shady, but he had money and we couldn't use CIA assets to verify the Ironside Dossier because of the politics here in Washington. And there was our strained relationship with the Brits. The Agency *had* to have deniability if the Brits or Russians caught you with your hand in their cookie jars. Our plan was to let Bowen fund your activities. We would keep whatever you found and leave Bowen holding the bag with the Russians. That's why we needed an Agency man leading Bowen's search for compromising information about President Walldrum. It was an off-the-books operation, but sanctioned by the Seventh Floor."

Rodney was telling me that the CIA director approved what I had been doing.

"The Agency," Rodney continued, "was prepared to take you back when you completed the mission. So, did you complete the mission?"

"Before I give anything to anyone, I want my status clarified. Pick up your phone and call the director. I want him to tell me he approved this operation."

Rodney didn't budge from his leaning position. "Don't be ridiculous. You know the director doesn't get involved at that level. We run operations like this all the time."

"Okay. Call the director of operations. Let him tell me."

"No. The Seventh Floor can't claim you, now. You caused one helluva stink in the U.K. and Russia. Christ, man, you left blood on the floor in London, St. Petersburg, and Moscow, and you robbed a bank. What the hell was *that* about? Couldn't you find an ATM?"

"I'm not a cowboy, Rodney. I did what was required to get what you wanted and get out. Which brings me to another issue—why did you give me a sat phone?"

"So I could provide support if you needed it, of course."

"What was I going to do with a sat phone in Russia, call in air strikes? I think that phone had another purpose. It sends a signal that you were going to use to track me in the U.K. and Russia. You passed my U.K. locations to a Russian hit squad. Is that how the Russians found Bogdanovich in Scotland and Boris Kulik in London?"

"You're delusional."

"Maybe. I think your sat phone tracking fell apart when I didn't take the phone to Russia. None of the Moscow sources died because you couldn't track me there."

"That's ridiculous on its face. What good would it do to kill sources after you got *kompromat* from them?"

"Not much, unless you killed me, too, and took the *kompromat*. The men you sent to kill me have been trying to use your sat phone to find me since I got back to D.C."

Rodney dismissed the idea of his involvement. "Anyone with suitable technology could track that phone and you know it. After the mess you made in Europe, it's probably MI6 or the Russians. In any case, I have no idea who might be tracking you."

"I think you do." I carried a large envelope to his desk and dumped out the wallets of the two hit men from the *Envy*. "Take a look. Tell me if anything is familiar."

Rodney stood motionless, glaring at me for several seconds before he picked up the wallets and examined their contents. "I don't know these men."

I shoved my gun into my belt, put on a pair of surgical gloves, returned the wallets to the envelope, and dropped the gloves in after them. Rodney understood the significance of my actions. His fingerprints—not mine—were on the wallets of a couple of dead men.

I told him, "I took something from one of those wallets you would recognize, your private phone number."

The master spy had a ready response. "You promised me the Walldrum documents. I hadn't heard from you since we met in Tallinn. Claudia told me you were in town. Didn't you expect me to look for you? I sent those men to find you. They meant you no harm."

"Well, they tried to harm me. One of those guys was carrying a backpack with duct tape and some nasty-looking cutlery. I think you sent them to torture me for the location of the Walldrum documents and put a bullet in my head."

"I'm not going to address your conspiracy theories. You ought to be on talk radio with an imagination like that."

"You were gambling that I hadn't gone home because I was carrying the Walldrum documents with me. You wanted to catch me before I had a chance to stash them or make copies. When it comes to dealing with the Russians, whoever has those documents is holding the trump cards. That person can negotiate almost anything."

I noticed that Rodney tried to avoid discussing things Russian. He moved on. "The only relevant issue for your future is that you found the sources and got verification of the compromising material on Walldrum. Where is it?"

"What's relevant to me is you ruined my career, my finances, and my relationship with Vanessa, and sent me out into the cold. How much did they pay you for me? What am I worth on the Russian market?"

"I don't know anything about the Russian market, but you're worth ten million dollars to Bowen if you have the *kompromat*. That's what your contract specifies. Take it and stop whining about what might have been."

"That's what I intend to do. I have what I was paid to get, the low-down on President Walldrum: his money laundering for the Russians, a Russian whore's diary listing his sexual preferences, compromising photographs of him with prostitutes in Moscow, and a lot more. Now, I want to get paid, but I can't find Bowen. That's why I came to you."

"How should I know where he is?"

"You sold me out to Bowen. You two want the same thing. I'm pretty sure you can find him when you need to, and right now, you need to. Here's a clue. He was last seen in Mexico City riding in a limo with Russian diplomatic plates. Go to your sources. I want to see Bowen sitting at Lenny's bar at noon tomorrow. He knows the place."

"Or what?"

I took the digital recorder from my pocket and held it up. "Or this recording of you telling me that my firing was sanctioned by the Seventh Floor goes to the Agency inspector general."

"And if, by chance, I find Bowen . . . ?"

"All I want is my ten million, but you're not off the hook. By now, Claudia is spilling her guts about her role in my firing to Lyle Palmer at Stratton, Radcliff, and Bowles. And there are a couple of dead men on your yacht and some bullet holes in the woodwork that need your attention."

"You're a real prick, you are."

I smiled. "You taught me everything I know." Not true, but I enjoyed saying it.

I had advice for Rodney. "If the SVR gave you a Russian passport, now is a good time to dust it off and call Aeroflot for a one-way ticket to Moscow. But your reception won't be a warm one unless you or Bowen deliver the *kompromat* I collected on Walldrum and a list of sources."

My parting reminder to Rodney was: "Bowen. Noon, tomorrow. At Lenny's."

* * *

I don't know what strings Rodney pulled, but at noon the next day, Bowen was at Lenny's sitting on the same barstool where I met him weeks ago. Same 260 pounds of him and expensive suit. Same cowboy boots and Rolex. Not the same air of self-assurance. Velma poured us scotch and we took our drinks to Lenny's private dining room.

I opened. "Thank you for coming." Politeness only costs ten million dollars.

Bowen was not polite. "Did you bring the documents?"

"They're in a safe place. We're here to talk about payment and delivery. Here's how it's going to go down. You and I are going to meet in Geneva, Switzerland, day after tomorrow. The one-million retainer fee you deposited in the escrow account; you keep that. I want five million wired to this account"—I gave him the number—"at the WorldCorp Bank, no strings. The money is to be released to me as soon as the bank opens for business on the day we meet in Geneva."

Bowen balked. "I'm not giving you five million dollars without inspecting the merchandise."

I handed him a copy of the Riga-Ritz photo. "Notice the clever FSB staging with the prostitutes and the future president in the foreground and the name of the hotel clearly visible over Walldrum's right shoulder. I have the camera chip and it's genuine."

I snatched the photograph from his hand. "As for the rest of the *kompromat*, I'm sure your stooge, Jill Rucker, told you about the prostitute's diary we picked up in St. Petersburg and some bank records that might be of interest to investigators at DOJ. So, do we have a deal on the five million up-front payment?"

Bowen said a reluctant, "Yes."

"My contract is for ten million. When you come to Geneva for the exchange, bring the other five million in cash."

Bowen looked stunned. "Do you have any idea how much five million dollars in cash weighs?"

"I know *exactly* how much it weighs. One million dollars in hundred-dollar bills weighs twenty-two pounds and fits into the average microwave oven. Five million dollars weighs one hundred and ten pounds and fits into two large suitcases."

Bowen sputtered, "What . . . what if a customs official inspects the suitcases?"

"Stop stalling, Bowen. An experienced operator like you wouldn't try to cross international borders with two suitcases of hundred-dollar bills. You'd wire the money to one of your crooked banks in Europe. How about the Allgemeine Volksbank? Isn't that the Kremlin's money laundry of choice in Moscow? AVB has branches all over the European Union. You can pick up the money at an AVB branch and bring it to me in Geneva without ever seeing a customs inspector."

Bowen looked deflated, like a man who had exhausted his excuses. That's where I wanted him. "Here's how it's going to work in Geneva. When you arrive with the cash, call the concierge at the Steigenburger Hotel and leave a message for me, with the name of your hotel and room number. I'll send a representative to check the money."

"And after your *representative* checks the money . . . ?"

"He'll take you to the bank of my choice, which will be revealed to you at that time. My banker will run the money through a counter, just to be sure it's all there, and verify that it's authentic. It would ruin my day if you paid me in counterfeit hundred-dollar bills." I gave Bowen a nasty smile.

I was sure Bowen's devious mind was conjuring other opportunities for mischief. To stifle them, I described my additional precautions. "The bank security staff will check for dirty tricks. So, don't screw with my money. No radiation or chip trackers. No dye packs. No invisible paint. No distinctive odors. And don't bother treating the suitcases with anything exotic. I won't be taking them with me. If the banker finds no problems with the money, I'll deposit it in the bank on the spot. It'll be transferred immediately to a non-European bank. I'll give you the dirt on Walldrum and you can leave the bank with your suitcases."

Sarcastically, Bowen asked, "Are there any other instructions?"

"Let's be clear. When my rep comes to your hotel, if he senses anything fishy about the money, if he even smells a double-cross or a Russian, the deal's off. I'll sell the Walldrum *kompromat* to the highest bidding newspaper or tabloid in Europe."

Bowen grunted. "They won't pay you ten million dollars. You'll take a loss."

"I'd rather take a loss than a bullet from your Russian friend, Zabluda."

His lips parted slightly, betraying surprise.

"Yeah. I know about the airport reception committee in Mexico City. You and Zabluda in a limo with Russian diplomatic plates."

"Jill told you." He said it with surprise and disappointment.

I protected Jill's CIA cover. "She didn't tell me a thing. I didn't trust her from Day One. That's why I got word to you and the Russians that Jill and I were on that plane. I had people watching when she landed. I wanted to see how she would be greeted. I guess you're all chums."

"Where *is* Jill?" asked Bowen.

"Last time I saw her, she was laying on the floor of my bungalow in Panama with a busted head. She tried to hijack the Walldrum stuff. We had a dispute. She lost."

"Why did you go to Panama?"

"I was looking for you," I lied. "You're a hard man to find. You really should stop changing your phone numbers. I came to D.C. because I thought Rodney would be able to find you . . . and here you are."

Bowen's thoughts went to our upcoming Geneva meeting. "About security for the cash. It's Russian money. They'll want to provide the security."

"No Russians, Bowen. Hire locals."

CHAPTER 30

Geneva, Switzerland, two days later

SHERRI STOOD AT the door of Bowen's suite wearing black slacks, a crisp white blouse, and a green blazer with the yellow WorldCorp Bank logo embroidered on the breast pocket. Above the pocket she wore a gold nameplate with her alias engraved in black letters, *Heidi Kemp*. To give her a severe, efficient look, she wore no makeup, rimless glasses, a short black wig, and green contacts.

She knocked.

A big guy opened the door. Sherri smiled and greeted him with, "*Dobroe utro,*" Russian for "Good morning."

"*Dob—*" The Russian, who wasn't supposed to be there—per my agreement with Bowen—caught himself and replied in German, "*Guten tag.*"

Sherri smiled and entered the suite. I followed her. The Russian who wasn't there searched us and looked through Sherri's tool kit. He missed the false bottom with the Glocks.

Bowen was in the bedroom with the other security guard. They didn't come out until the guy who had searched us gave them the okay . . . in German. *"Alles gut."*

Bowen was surprised to see me. "Max, I thought you were going to meet us at the bank."

"I thought I told you no Russians. I guess we both had a misunderstanding."

The two Russian money guards stared at me with dead eyes.

Bowen gave me an apologetic shrug. "Russian money, Russian security. I didn't have a choice."

"Well, I do. The deal's off." To Sherri I said, "Let's go, Mrs. Kemp. I'm sorry I wasted your time."

Sherri and I left the suite with Bowen in pursuit. He blocked us in the hall. "Wait!" he demanded in a harsh whisper. He asked Sherri, "Could you give us a moment of privacy?"

She went to the elevator and stood there without pressing a button.

Bowen turned to me and spoke in a low voice. "You already have five million dollars of their money. There are Russians in the lobby. They won't let you out of this hotel unless I say our deal is on. What the hell have you got against Russians, anyway?"

"You mean besides the fact that they tried to kidnap me in London and tried to kill me in St. Petersburg and Moscow?"

Bowen raised his palms toward me in a calming gesture. "Okay, I get it. You don't trust Russians, but there's five million dollars in there and the Russians aren't going to leave. Is there something I can negotiate with them that would make you comfortable enough to get this deal done?"

I pretended to consider his offer. I knew the Russians would be there. It was time for Plan B, Phase 1.

I told Bowen, "I don't want to be caught in an ambush coordinated by the Russians in the lobby and your money guards, while I'm sitting on the *kompromat* and five million dollars. If you want this deal to go through, here are my terms. The money guards keep their guns. They cannot communicate with their pals in the lobby. I want their radios and cell phones, and they can't use the hotel phone. When we leave the hotel for the bank, the lobby Russians can follow in their cars. They have to stay three car lengths behind us. If they come closer, I'm bailing out.

"You tell your Russians that we're on a strict timetable. If I don't show up at the bank by a certain time, someone somewhere is going to press the *enter* key and everything they want to keep secret about Walldrum goes on the Internet. After we make the exchange, if I am not at a certain location by a certain time, watch the Internet."

Bowen said, "Wait here. Give me a few minutes on the phone."

I made a point of checking my watch. "You're on the clock."

He went into the suite and returned five minutes later, smiling. "We've got a deal." Bowen gave me a plastic hotel laundry bag containing three cell phones, and two body radios with cords and earpieces.

"Where's your radio?" I asked.

Bowen raised his coat and turned around. He was clean.

"I want to check the guards, too."

"No problem."

"And I want to sweep the suite for microphones."

"The suite is not bugged," Bowen assured me.

"I believe that you believe that's true. If you don't mind, I'd like to be sure."

I gave Sherri a *wait* signal as Bowen and I reentered the suite.

I swept the sitting room. It was clean. The bedroom where the guards were keeping eyes on the money was an exterminator's paradise. There were bugs in the phone and every light fixture near the bed. I removed them one-by-one as the Russians watched impassively and Bowen watched sheepishly. I dropped the bugs into the toilet and flushed.

Back in the bedroom, I told Bowen and his guards, "I know there may be more bugs here that weren't activated when I did the sweep. So, I'm going to make a sweep periodically. If I find another bug, I'm gone."

The three of them looked at me and said nothing.

I said, "Bowen, ask the lady from the WorldCorp Bank to come in."

When Sherri was at my side, I said, "Let's see the money."

The cash was in two suitcases on a king-size bed in the king-size bedroom. The Russians stationed themselves on either side of the room. While we worked, Bowen sat in a big comfortable chair sipping orange juice.

Sherri donned rubber gloves, took a scanner from her tool bag, and found the suitcase trackers immediately. She used her Swiss Army Knife to cut the chips out of the suitcase leather and dropped each into a bedside crystal candy dish with a loud "clink."

I looked at Bowen.

He shrugged again. "Russian money, Russian suitcases."

Time for Plan B, Phase 2. I handed him the phone. "Call the concierge. Ask him to bring up the two suitcases I left at his station."

Sherri removed a special light and plugged the cord into the wall. The suitcases were smeared with Russian spy dust that stays on everything it touches for weeks. I expected that. I pulled on a pair of surgical gloves, opened the suitcases, and emptied the cash onto the bed. The money was in neat packs of hundred-dollar bills, mostly new. Sherri scanned the money for spy dust. It was clean.

A bellhop delivered the suitcases. The Russian guards inspected them. There was a money counting machine in one suitcase. The other contained bathroom scales.

Bowen eyed the equipment. "You're not leaving much work for your banker."

"You know the Swiss," I said. "Time is money and they don't like to waste either. Besides, they'll check all this again. Double checks are better than singles."

Bowen shrugged and got himself another orange juice from the fridge. The Russians maintained their state of alertness, carefully watching Sherri and me. I weighed the bills, one hundred and ten pounds, on the money, and examined each stack for trackers, die packs, and exploding-Russian-whatevers. Sherri fed the bills into a money counter that verified the amount and used magnetic and ultraviolet sensors to detect counterfeits. As Sherri finished the counts, I bundled the stacks and loaded them into the suitcases delivered by the bellboy.

When we finished, Sherri announced, in a fake accent, *"Gentlemen, I sink our buzziness here ist concludet. If you are zatisfied, vee can proceed to zee bank."*

Bowen said, "Let's go."

"Very well. Zee bank has zent an armored car to transport you to our fazility to complete zee tranzaction. Follow me, pleaze."

Bowen objected. "We have our own vehicle, thank you."

"Zat is not possible," Sherri announced, with the firmness of a mother superior. *"Once vee have examined zee money, it must remain under bank control. Othervise, zere will be furzer delayz at zee bank. I apologize if zis is an inconvence for you. Zee money must be transported in our car. Zat is our policy."*

I said, "Bowen, just call downstairs and tell your lobby Russians we're leaving in a bank vehicle."

We took the elevator to the lobby with Bowen carrying one suitcase and Sherri carrying the other. The Russians wanted their hands free for obvious reasons. For business reasons, they didn't want me touching the money until I delivered the dirt on Walldrum.

When we got to the lobby, the Russians I counted on the way in were gone. I could imagine them making a mad dash to the garage for their Putinmobiles.

Sherri had called ahead and our transport was waiting at the curb. It was a black Mercedes SUV with a discreet, green-and-gold World-Corp logo stencil on the trunk lid. Tony-D was behind the wheel wearing a chauffer's cap, a green blazer that matched Sherri's, and a name tag that read *Rolf Swisher*. He had a new moustache and gray hair protruding from his cap.

Sherri made a show of calling the bank on her cell phone. When her party answered, she said, "*Herr Huntsman, zey are leaving zee hotel momentarily.*" She broke the connection and made a slight nod to Bowen and me, in turn. "*Zank you, gentlemen. I vil zee you at zee bank.*"

The Russians loaded the suitcases into the SUV's cargo compartment and our party of four climbed aboard. I rode shotgun, next to Tony-D. Bowen sat in the back crunched between the two Russians. Tony-D put the SUV in gear, but one of the Russian guards laid a heavy hand on Tony-D's shoulder and kept it there, even after he said, in German, "Wait for our friends."

Almost as soon as he spoke, a white paneled truck big enough for a squad of infantry—or five million dollars and two hostages—pulled up behind us. The driver honked his horn.

The Russian money guard released Tony-D's shoulder. "You can go now."

Our short caravan took off into the streets of Geneva. It was near the end of morning rush hour. We had rehearsed the route for just two days, but you do the best you can with the time available. The truck with the Russians stayed three car lengths behind us, as agreed. Time for Plan B, Phase 3.

Sherri had left her tool kit with the Glocks on the floor near my feet. I put it on my lap. While the Russians were scanning the route for threats, I eased one of the guns out of its hiding place and held it on my lap, under the kit.

Tony-D approached the traffic light we wanted. There was one car behind, between us and the Russian truck. The light was turning amber. Tony-D slowed our SUV as though he would stop, and then floored the gas pedal as the light turned red. The large truck we had hired was just around the corner. Tony-D made a sharp right turn in front of it, drove into an alley, and stopped abruptly. As he did, a decoy SUV identical to ours—including WorldCorp Bank logo and passengers—pulled away from the curb and continued down the street. The Russian chase truck must have gone around the car at the light, onto the sidewalk, and turned down the street we had entered. The truck driver followed the decoy SUV that had stopped down the block to wait for him. Then, the two vehicles took off, with the Russians three car lengths behind—too far back to see that the occupants in the decoy SUV were not us.

Meanwhile, our SUV sat in the alley. I covered the money guards with the Glock. "Don't worry, gentlemen. This isn't a rip-off. You're going to get what you paid for and I'm going to get rich. No offense, but I don't trust your friends in the truck. I don't intend to end this day drugged and strapped to a gurney on a diplomatic flight to Moscow. Bowen, relieve your guards of their guns."

He gave me the guns and Tony-D drove us to our rented house outside of Geneva.

I gave Tony-D one of the Glocks to help me cover our guests and told Bowen, "Have your Russians bring the money inside." Unhappily, they trudged in with the suitcases.

"Is the product here?" asked Bowen.

I didn't answer.

We went into the living room where the protective dust covers had been pulled off some chairs and a long table. I said, "Make yourselves comfortable, gentlemen. This won't take long. Tony?"

Tony-D left the room and returned a short time later with a large briefcase. He put it on the table and went outside to provide perimeter security.

I told Bowen, "Check out your product."

Bowen went to the case and popped the locks with trembling hands. He took out a package and tore it open carefully. Inside, there were several smaller envelopes numbered consecutively. They contained compromising information in the order I had collected it.

The first envelope held the digital recording I made of my conversation with Bogdanovich in Scotland. I had it keyed to the part where Bogdanovich told me about the contents of the KGB dossier on Walldrum, the compromising sex activities and money laundering. There was also a transcription of the entire interview with Bogdanovich. Certain pages were tabbed and their ten-million-dollar passages underlined in red ink. The next envelope contained another recording and transcript. These were of my one-hour session with the late Boris Kulik, formerly of the Russian Embassy in London. Kulik's information verified the existence of a Kremlin dossier on Walldrum.

Bowen was too excited to listen to either recording or read the complete transcripts. He returned those items to the package and took out the St. Petersburg whore's diary and john book, Tatyana Kedrova's testament to Walldrum's debauchery. Bowen flipped to the juicy parts, guided by bookmarks I'd inserted. He looked up at me and smiled.

The Tula man's pictures of Walldrum and the prostitutes at the Moscow Ritz were next. Bowen didn't linger over them. I had shown him a teaser at Lenny's two days ago.

The next items were copies of the thumb drives Arkady gave his life to pass on to me. I had taped them to a one-page description of the counterfeiting operation at the Moscow branch of the Allgemeine Volksbank. That captured Bowen's attention. He read it carefully. When he finished, he looked concerned. Apparently, I had uncovered an operation even he didn't know about.

Bowen reviewed everything in the package, but everything wasn't in the package. I neglected to include contacts with Pavel and the Omega Group, the plot to get Walldrum the Nobel Peace Prize, and videos of the empty concrete boxes selling as multimillion-dollar condos at the Panama Walldrum Tower. It pays to have a few aces in the hole.

Bowen rummaged through the contents of the briefcase and looked at me, puzzled. "I don't see a list of your sources."

"You didn't pay for a list of sources. My contract calls for me to *find* the original sources and get firsthand evidence that proves or refutes the allegations against Ted Walldrum as stated in the Ironside Dossier. What you have in that package is proof of the allegations."

"Without a complete list of your sources, evidence is meaningless."

The Russians were giving Bowen disappointed looks and he was sweating.

I said, "Define complete. You have the names of Vasili Bogdanovich, Boris Kulik, and Tatyana Kedrova. They confirmed the major allegations against Walldrum."

"I need a list of all your sources, everyone you contacted in Russia."

"That was your goal all along, wasn't it? You were working for the Russians when you hired me. Moscow already knew what *kompromat* they had on Ted Walldrum. What they didn't have was the names of the people who gave Ironside the allegations he made in his dossier on Walldrum. You and Rodney set me up to find the sources so the Russians could kill them. The Russians were able to do that in England by tracking the location of my sat phone signal. They didn't kill my sources in Russia because I didn't take the sat phone to St. Petersburg and Moscow. So, you don't know who my Russian sources were. Well, that's your problem, not mine."

Bowen opened his mouth to protest as the sound of a suppressed shot ripped the air. He dropped to the floor with a bullet in his head.

In Russian, a voice behind me said, "Don't move and you may live." The man reached around me and took the Glock from my hand. "Sit facing the guards."

Another armed man moved into my field of vision. He was carrying a Russian pistol with silencer attached. He went to Bowen, checked for a neck pulse, and shook his head at the man behind me.

Behind me, the man—who spoke in Russian for most of this encounter—said, "The decoy bank vehicle was a very sophisticated ruse, but here I am. You're wondering how I found you." He chuckled. "You discovered all of my transmitters, except the one in the heel of Bowen's shoe. I'm surprised at you, Maxwell Geller, an old Russia hand, as you Americans say. The shoe transmitter is Cold War technology. A serious oversight on your part, maybe even fatal." He prodded me with his silencer.

In my peripheral vision, the man crouched behind my chair. Then, in my ear, *Pop! Pop! Pop!* went the silencer. I watched the two money guards as their heads snapped back and they pitched forward out of their chairs, blood streaming down their faces.

A couple of minutes passed while I watched Bowen and the guards bleed out and waited for my bullet. My only thought was, *This is a hell of a way for an intelligence officer to end his life: outfoxed by the competition.*

That final bullet didn't come. Instead, I heard the familiar rasp of metal-on-metal as a clip was being removed from an automatic pistol and the slide being pushed back to eject a round from the chamber.

The Russian behind me said, "Give me your right hand."

Okay, they're going to make this look like murder and suicide. My mind started to spin through the possible defensive moves I could make with one Russian standing in front of me with a gun and another behind.

I raised my right hand. The Russian behind me grabbed my wrist and put the automatic in my hand and forced me to grip it. Then, he gently opened my fingers and took the gun from my hand. He said to the man in front of me, "Ipatyev, check them."

Ipatyev went to the bodies of Bowen and the two guards and checked for life signs. After each check, he gave the man behind me a grave nod. All three were dead.

Konstantin Zabluda came from behind my chair and looked into my face. He had sharp features, brown hair, and brown eyes. There was a barely visible scar down his left cheek, probably from some long-ago battle. He wore a good suit and his tight silk shirt betrayed a lean, muscular body. There was an air of bottled-up energy about him, a vibe that I often got from certain soldiers and FBI agents. His partner, Ipatyev, had a similar build, but appeared more relaxed. I guessed they were chosen for their jobs, in part, because, absent a close inspection, they were unremarkable as they presented their fake passports and crossed international borders.

Somewhat amused, Zabluda said, "You were right on all counts in your analysis of our little scheme to find the sources for the Ironside Dossier, but a little late to your conclusions." He nodded to the dead men on the floor.

He added, "Still, you were a difficult man to catch."

"Why did you try to kidnap me in London? If you had killed me there, I wouldn't have led you to Ironside's sources in Russia."

"If I had tried to kill you in London, you would have been dead. We had you in our crosshairs when you visited Bogdanovich."

"Why did you come after me at the London warehouse?"

Zabluda looked puzzled. Then, he smiled. "You flatter yourself. We didn't come after *you*. My orders were to eliminate the MI6 cell that serviced Bogdanovich."

I grunted. "You were a couple of years late if you were trying to keep what Bogdanovich knew about Walldrum off the streets."

"I don't question the clocks in Moscow, Maxwell Geller. They seem to be a few decades behind these days, more Atomic Age than Digital.

Anyway, I believe the killings were supposed to send a message, not affect the flow of information."

He gave me a sad smile. "It was by chance that you were in the warehouse. One of my men must have recognized you from your visit to Bogdanovich. We were watching his house, you know. I guess my man decided to take you away for interrogation. He's dead. So, we will never know why he spared you."

Needlessly, I reminded Zabluda, "And then my crew rescued me from your team."

"They were good shots, too, all except the one who shot at me."

I couldn't tell him Jill Rucker had orders to miss.

Zabluda gestured to the carnage around us. "You think you know what happened here. Let me give you what your White House calls *the alternative facts*. He smiled at his gunman, Ipatyev. "I'll give you the facts according to Zabluda." They laughed.

"What I think happened is that you, a disgraced former CIA agent, collected some damaging information about your President Walldrum and you offered to sell it to a Russian government intermediary— William Bowen—in exchange for ten million dollars. Five million was deposited to your account when you showed Bowen proof that your information was credible. The second five million was to be paid in cash to you here in Switzerland upon delivery of the *kompromat*. When Bowen showed you all that cash, you got greedy. You killed him and disappeared with the cash and the *kompromat*."

Turning to his wingman, Zabluda asked, "Is that how our report will read when we submit it to Moscow, Ipatyev?"

"Word-for-word, Colonel." Ipatyev said it with a five-million-watt grin. He picked up one of my suitcases full of money and left the house.

Zabluda came to me and said, in a low voice, "Suppose an officer in the Russian security services offered to defect to the CIA and brought with him intimate knowledge of Kremlin assassination squads and five million dollars of his own money. What would you think about that?"

"I would think that Ipatyev is dead."

Zabluda threw his head back and enjoyed a belly laugh. "I haven't known you long, Maxwell Geller, but I'm going to miss you . . . if you're lucky." He laughed again.

Then, he turned somber. "We intelligence professionals are in a morally ambiguous business. Sometimes, we must do bad things—like killing Bowen—to prevent worse things from happening. For example, what bad things would Bowen have done with the *kompromat*? Buried it? Burned it? Sent it to Moscow? The Americans would never know the truth about Walldrum."

Zabluda went over to the table and picked up the package containing Tatyana Kedrova's diary and the Tula man's photographs from the Ritz. He hefted the package and studied it as if trying to make a decision.

He came back to me. "But we don't have to wonder what Bowen would do with this. Maxwell Geller escaped with it." He slammed the package against my chest and held it there until I took it. "And who knows what Maxwell Geller will do with it? Maybe he will sell it to the newspapers, as he threatened to do."

Zabluda picked up the last suitcase. "Or maybe," he speculated, "Maxwell Geller will take the *kompromat* to the prosecutor at the United States Department of Justice."

He gave me a serious stare. "But whatever happens, Moscow will know that Maxwell Geller escaped with the Walldrum *kompromat* and ten million dollars that belongs to the Russian government. That means that I—or someone like me—will be looking for Maxwell Geller for a long, long time, even in Atomic Age years."

Zabluda hesitated at the door and spoke to me in English. "As a former CIA officer, I'm sure you have committed many sins for which you should atone."

The voice was familiar, but I couldn't remember where I had heard it until he added, "When they least expect it, sinners can find absolution and sometimes salvation in the confessional. Have you ever had that experience, Maxwell?"

Zabluda smiled and left, carrying a suitcase with my two-point-five million dollars.

CHAPTER 31

TWO KREMLIN HITMEN had just walked out, each carrying two-point-five-million dollars of my money. Three dead bodies were bleeding out on the floor of my rented villa, and I'd have a Russian target on my back as soon as Zabluda made his report to Moscow. What else could go wrong?

Tony!

I'd last seen him when he went outside to provide security. That was just before Zabluda and his sidekick arrived. Tony-D was probably dead, but I ran out to look for him anyway.

The house sat on a little knoll. The front was level with the road. On the other three sides, the terrain dropped off abruptly and was supported by a semicircular brick retaining wall overlooking a garden five feet below. As I walked the wall searching for Tony-D, I looked down and saw him facedown in a flowerbed. I dashed to the front of the house, scrambled down the slope, and ran to him. When I turned Tony-D over, he was pointing his gun at my beltline.

"It's me, Tony!"

Tony-D grimaced in pain as he eased his gun into his belt holster. "I was hoping it was Zabluda coming to see if I was dead. Where is he?"

"Gone. Are you okay?"

"No," Tony-D hissed through clenched teeth. "Zabluda put a couple of rounds into my body armor. No penetration, but they knocked me off the wall and cracked some ribs, I think." Tony-D gave me an appraising glance. "How come you're still alive?" He sounded disappointed.

As I helped Tony-D up the slope, I told him about my encounter with Zabluda and Ipatyev. I wasn't sure why, but I omitted the fact that Zabluda left the Walldrum *kompromat* with me. The SUV's first-aid kit had what I needed to tape Tony-D's ribs while he sat in the luggage compartment with his legs dangling over the back bumper.

When I finished, he asked, "What now?"

"We need to get rid of the bodies. The police can't trace the SUV to us. Sherri used a fake ID to rent it and she's on a plane to the States by now. So, we load the bodies into the SUV, wait until dark, and leave it on a quiet street."

Tony-D gave me a skeptical look.

"What?"

He shook his head slowly and made a face. "I don't know. An abandoned SUV with two dead Russians and a dead American in Geneva, Switzerland . . . That's gonna to be a headline read around the world."

"You got a better idea?"

"Yeah. Milan is a three-hour drive south. We could abandon the SUV there. By morning, the bodies will have disappeared and the SUV will have a new paint job and a proud new owner. That's Italy. No questions. No headlines."

"You can guarantee that, right?"

"I have cousins in Milan."

* * *

Forty hours later, I arrived in D.C.'s Union Station, after flights from Rome to Atlanta and Atlanta to Philly followed by a brief train ride. No point in making it easy for the Russians, MI6, or the Agency to know I was back. I couldn't go home. That was the first place they would wait for me. I couldn't bunk with Sherri or Tony-D. Jill Rucker knew they were my teammates. I took a hotel room near the D.C. Beltway, close to a Metro line, had a meal in my room, and slept, off and on, for twenty hours.

I woke up with a clear head and the realization that I might not have long to live with the Russians gunning for me and MI6 a bit peeved by the results of my actions in London. It was time to set some things straight.

At a computer café, I emailed my banker in Belize instructions to make two wire transfers. One went to Sherri for what I owed her and her crew. The other sent seventy thousand Swiss francs to the account of the FSB agent from Tula, payment for the Moscow photographs of Walldrum with the prostitutes. I took an ad in the *International Times* to give the Tula agent his coded account and access numbers. Promise kept.

When I first met Jill Rucker in London, I had memorized her cell number. I dialed it from a pay phone.

"This is Jill." Her voice came through throaty and sexy.

"Ms. Rucker, you applied for an internship with my organization. Can we discuss that on this line?"

Her "yes" came back at me with surprise and enthusiasm.

"Good. You forgot the recording of our interview. I thought you might like to have it." I was referring to my recording of Jill revealing her undercover assignment to me. It could destroy her career. I knew damned well she wanted it.

"That's very kind of you. Would you like to send it to me or should we meet?"

"Let's meet. Can you be at the Farragut Square Metro Station, north platform, at seven this evening? I'd prefer you came alone. We have private matters to discuss."

"See you at seven." She broke the connection.

* * *

Jill Rucker was there on time. She was wearing a green, hooded parka, dark slacks, and a green-and-blue headscarf. I watched her from the south platform long enough to be sure she was alone before I dialed her number.

When she answered, I said, "Lenny's restaurant is two blocks north. Find it. I'll find you. No calls on the way. If you stop or talk to anyone, I'm into the wind."

I watched her leave the station before I ran to my waiting cab. When Jill entered Lenny's, I took her arm and steered her to the private room where Bowen had offered me a contract so many dead bodies ago. Jill and I sat facing across the only table.

"Here." I slid my body cam over to her. "It's the one I used to record our conversation. I didn't copy the memory card."

"Thank you." There was a question in her eyes.

I added, "I didn't want you to worry that I might show up some day, demanding favors and holding that recording over your head." Those last two words drew my attention to her stylish headscarf. She had skillfully wrapped it to hide the forehead wound I inflicted in Panama.

Jill saw where my attention was focused. "You marked me for life." It was a statement without rancor, just a fact.

"I'm truly sorry, but you were trying to shoot me."

"And I'm truly sorry that I missed." That was rancor.

I laughed. She didn't.

"Max, I still want the *kompromat* on Walldrum."

"We all want something. I want to know what happened to my old Agency boss, Prescott Hamilton, aka Rodney."

"Why are you asking about Rodney?"

"Curiosity. I haven't been able to contact him."

"Why do you want to contact the boss who got you fired?"

I smiled politely. "I have difficulty terminating relationships unless firearms are involved."

Jill didn't appreciate my humor, but she gave me an update on Rodney so we could get back to her favorite subject, the *kompromat*. "Rodney," she said, "stands accused of shooting two Russian illegals to death on his boat. There's no murder weapon . . . yet, but his fingerprints are on everything else that matters. Because of the Russian angle, the FBI took the case and quashed the news story. Rodney is being held in a secure location and interrogated by a joint CIA-FBI task force. He claims he was framed, but can't think of anyone with a motive.

"The task force is pursuing two lines of inquiry," Jill told me. "The first is Rodney's involvement with the Russians. The second is identifying people who had a motive to frame him. On the second issue, the investigators went thorough—among other things—Rodney's personnel actions. Your name rose to the top of the list of people with a motive. That's when the Agency pulled me into the investigation. Since I worked with you recently, the Seventh Floor thought my insights might be helpful."

"And were they, your insights, I mean?"

Jill ignored my question. She was doing a lot of that. "Speaking of people with a motive," she said, "where's your live-in, Ms. Claudia Navarro, the lady who initiated the email exchange that got you fired?"

"At my house or hers, I guess."

"Neither. She put her condo up for sale and cleaned out her bank and brokerage accounts. The forwarding address she left with her real estate agent is in Greece. We visited her workplace. Mr. Lyle Palmer, Esquire, of Stratton, Radcliff, and Bowles told us"—Jill raised her nose in the air and looked down it—"'Ms. Navarro has been let go due to an ethical issue involving one of the firm's clients.

Of course, we can't discuss it—with you. Attorney-client privilege,' 'cetra, 'cetra. Prick."

Jill continued, "It seems that Claudia Sleep-Over has vanished with the dawn like The Good Pussy Fairy."

"There you go. The guilty party is running. My money's on Claudia for the hit on the Russian illegals."

"Bullshit."

"Your language has gotten salty since you began discussing Ms. Navarro. I think you're jealous. How about a breath mint?"

"How about you kiss my ass."

"Didn't I do that on our cruise? Am I scheduled for an encore?"

"What you're scheduled for is a harsh interrogation at a safe house with lights shining in your eyes. The FBI has security camera footage of a man near Rodney's boat at the National Marina the night the Russians were killed. It's a partial profile shot, not enough to make an ID, but since you have a motive, a lot of people are looking for you."

"And here I am. Why didn't you turn me in when I called? You could have been voted CIA Employee of the Month."

She took too long to answer. "I didn't want anyone else to know about the body cam recording."

"That's partially true," I acknowledged. "The other reason you didn't give me up is that if I'm in custody, the focus will be on trying to nail me for the boat murders and 'case closed.' That's not what you and the Agency counterintelligence types really want. Is it? You want to know how Rodney was connected to the Russians. Right now, the Agency is looking at everything Rodney ever touched to see if he spied for the Russians. Am I right?" That was a rhetorical question. We both knew the Agency's mole hunt drill.

"Did you kill those Russians, Max?"

I smiled. "On the advice of counsel, I respectfully decline to answer that question on the grounds that it would tend to incriminate me . . . and make me a hero." I laughed. She didn't.

I decided to make things easier for her. "Here's a theory for you. Suppose Rodney sent those Russian illegals after someone, and that someone killed the Russians in self-defense. Maybe that someone left the bodies as bread crumbs that the Agency could follow back to Rodney, and find out what he was up to with the Russians."

"Is that what happened?"

It was my turn to ignore her. "That brings us to the other reason you didn't turn me in. You didn't get the *kompromat* from me in Panama. So, you came to this meeting, to talk me out of it, complete your mission, and get that little gold star next to your name."

Jill tried to be patient with me. "Max, I'm pretty sure Rodney screwed you and I know you're angry, but I also know you're a patriot. The American people need to see the documents we collected on Walldrum. Give them to me."

"What are you offering?"

"If your product is good, the Agency could give you back your old job. You might even get Rodney's job."

"What if I don't want an Agency job?" I was thinking about my five million in the Belize bank. "What I want is the same package the Agency would give a Russian defector who walked in with the goods on Walldrum. I want to come in from the cold with protection, a pension, and resettlement."

"That's not going to happen, Max."

"Your pay grade is way too low to make that call. Take my offer to your boss."

"And you'll deliver the Walldrum *kompromat*?"

"I can. Zabluda hijacked the *kompromat* and stole five million dollars from me. I think I know where to find him."

"Oh, Max, stop it! I know you're lying."

Jill was frustrated and done with me. She turned on the body cam and accessed the recording I made of her in Panama. For a few seconds, she listened to her voice telling me the things that saved her life and could ruin her career. Satisfied, she powered down the instrument and removed the memory card.

She said, "Get a new phone and text me the number. I may need to call you in an emergency."

Or track me using my cell phone. "What kind of emergency?"

"I told you, the FBI and the Agency are on your trail. I'll try to give you a heads-up if they get close."

"Why would you do that?"

"Professional courtesy. Maybe you'll want to deal the *kompromat* then."

Jill got up to leave and I gave her something to think about. "Just in case the people on my trail get lucky, they need to know that if I did have the *kompromat*, I'd have taken precautions to release it to the media if an accident should befall me or I just disappear."

* * *

I had no hope that the Agency would give me a defector package, but I had to ask. The Russians and Brits were after me. I needed cover. They were after Jill, too, but she had Agency protection.

At least my request would slow down the march of the bureaucracies while I attended to other business. Besides, given the then-current nature of D.C. politics, the CIA was far removed from people who made decisions about President Walldrum's future. I wanted to deal with the DOJ's special prosecutor's office. Unfortunately, my pursuers would view that location as a likely place for me to visit and have it under surveillance. I needed an intermediary.

Enter, Claudia's former boss, Lyle Palmer, Esquire, of Stratton, Rad-cliff, and Bowles.

"This is Lyle Palmer," his assured voice said into my cell-phone earpiece.

"This is the messenger who warned you about Claudia Navarro and your friend, Rodney. I hear you took my advice. Claudia's been dismissed."

"Resigned," he lied. "Thank you for the heads-up. Claudia explained the . . . ah . . . circumstances of her involvement in Rodney's scheme. I assume you're Max."

"I am."

"If memory serves, you said you might need a lawyer someday. Is this the day?"

"It is. When can we meet?"

"My first available appointment is at three this afternoon."

The environment at Stratton, Radcliff, and Bowles was all glass, teak, and soft leather, encasing soft-spoken, efficient men and women, sitting on even softer pillows. Lyle Palmer came for me before I could take the seat or the drink the receptionist in the white silk blouse and pearls offered.

A short walk down the hall and we were seated in the glass rectangle of a conference room, at a table that could accommodate the Last Supper and half an art class of Salvador Dali disciples.

Lyle gave me a perfect smile. "My firm owes you a debt of gratitude. May I call you Max?"

"Sure."

"Please call me Lyle. What brings you in today, Max?"

"I need someone I can trust to deliver items of value to the DOJ special prosecutor's office. I want to remain anonymous until I say otherwise. Can you handle that?"

"I have contacts with the special prosecutor. What's to be delivered?"

"Evidence that President Walldrum is susceptible to blackmail by Russia and is involved in activities not in the interests of the United States of America."

Lyle unbuttoned his Armani jacket, slipped it off over jade-and-gold cuff links and Patek Philippe watch, and draped it carefully over an empty chair. Thirsty Mr. Palmer went to a teak cabinet and withdrew a silver tray containing a decanter of scotch, two glasses, and a representation contract already made out for me. The representation fee was fifty dollars.

"I'm working for you pro bono. The fee is a formality. It pays for the scotch," he joked. My lawyer poured, loosened his tie, and unbuttoned his collar.

Lyle said, "Okay, Max, let's hear it."

I told him the *kompromat* story from my firing until my departure from Panama. I left out some details, the names of my teammates, and sources, U.K. and Russian.

When I finished, two hours later, Lyle shook his head, and poured us doubles. "How much can I tell the prosecutor's office about you?"

"Tell them to review the evidence and get back to you. If they're interested, we can talk about me."

"Okay. Let's see your evidence."

I gave him an inventory and summaries of each piece of compromising evidence, and copies of enough documents and photos to get the special prosecutor's attention. Lyle said he would call me soon. I took a cab to my hotel.

*　　*　　*

I didn't have long to wait. Lyle called the next day and asked me to come to his office. When I arrived at the conference room, he looked unhappy.

I asked, "What did your contact at the special prosecutor's office say?"

"He said, 'No, thanks.'"

"Why?"

"The special prosecutor's work is done. His staff is being reassigned. His report has been sent to the Attorney General. The AG will make the announcement in a day or two. It's over. Our timing was bad. We got to the prosecutor too late."

"I didn't know there was an expiration date on the truth. A lot of people risked their lives to get those documents, and some desk jockey tells me it's too late! To hell with that! I'll give it to the *New York Times* and the House Intelligence Committee."

Lyle spread his fingers and literally pushed back. "I would advise against those courses of action. If your story appears in media that have been unkind to President Walldrum, it will be viewed as a left-wing wet dream. You want the material to be taken seriously, don't you?"

"What about the House Intelligence Committee?"

"I'm not encouraged by the partisan environment in Congress at present. Anything sent there enters a political meat grinder. The president's allies will ask questions you can't or shouldn't answer.

"For instance, what if they ask you how you got the thumb drive containing those forged AVB documents? What will you say? You got it by impersonating a Russian colonel, escaped by shooting your way out of a bank, were trapped, and rescued by a faceless benefactor operating out of a church confessional, who told you about a Russian plot to get Walldrum the Nobel Prize? Do you hear how crazy that sounds? They'll drop a net over you."

"We've had two years of crazy since the election! Is my story that unbelievable?"

Evidently, Lyle thought it was. He exhaled loudly and offered, "I have a suggestion. If you refuse to give your information to the CIA, let me take it to the FBI's counterintelligence people. They understand how our spies operate overseas. They can vet the material, protect your sources, and—let us hope—your methods. They will package the facts for Congress so your story doesn't sound like the ravings of a madman. The FBI may even have sources that corroborate your findings."

I didn't like that much and my glare left no doubt.

"Max, may I take your information to the FBI? I think I can get an audience tomorrow morning."

"Take it, but tell your contact I'm not going to be stonewalled by, 'We don't discuss ongoing investigations.' I want updates, and if they don't get my stuff to Congress soon, I'll go to Capitol Hill myself and tell them the FBI is sitting on it. I'll go to the news outlets, too. I have copies of the digital files and certified true copies of the documents."

I called Lyle the next afternoon to get the Bureau's reaction and, to quote him, "The usually staid FBI is in a lather after seeing your product. They think it's dynamite."

That was good news, but the secret to moving dynamite through D.C. bureaucracies is to make sure you're not holding it when it explodes. When careers are at risk, explosives can end up on a conveyor belt to nowhere. Lyle counseled patience.

* * *

Meantime, I attended to unfinished business. I wired more cash to Vanessa's D.C. bank account and called Australia to tell her to go back to work.

"What about us?" she asked.

"Rodney's out. There's no one to honor his promise to bring you back to Langley. I'm out too, thanks to Rodney."

"You're out?" There was panic and disbelief in her voice.

"I'm doing consulting work in the same field, and in a bit of trouble."

Vanessa knew not to ask about my work. She just said a pitiful, "Oh, Max . . ."

"We said goodbye when you went to Australia. Maybe we should leave it there." That's where we left it.

A week went by. I changed hotels and logged a lot of TV time. The special prosecutor's report was stuck in the Attorney General's office and news outlets were in a feeding frenzy because of it. I called Lyle.

He hadn't heard from his FBI contact. "Max, you gave them a hot property. It may have stirred up another investigation, maybe more than one. It's going to take time to process. You have to be patient."

"No, I don't, Lyle. It sounds like the Attorney General is burying the special prosecutor's report and, for all I know, he's burying mine, too. Tell your FBI contact I want a progress report tomorrow or I go to Congress and the press."

* * *

Stan Herman was a friend. We did a tour in Moscow together. He reported the news for his paper. I ran Russian assets and collected intel for the CIA. We drank a lot of scotch together in those days. I had Stan's glass filled and waiting when he entered the bar.

He was a bear in corduroy and lumbered to my table with a broad smile and a hug. "Max! Great to see you."

"You, too. Sit. How's my favorite investigative reporter?"

"Still prowling the night, pen in hand. Hey, sorry about your job. I called a bunch of times to get the story behind *that* story. Why didn't you get back to me?"

"I've been away. I had consulting work in the U.K. and Russia."

Stan's eyebrows went up along with his antenna. "Oh?"

"I collected some documents about our favorite president."

Stan lowered his voice. "What kind of documents?"

"The kind that get you impeached. They confirmed allegations in the Ironside Dossier."

"You got them from Ironside himself?"

"Colleagues, eyeball witnesses to the dirty deeds."

"Ironside was killed some weeks ago. Are your documents linked to his death?"

"Yes."

Stan's lips formed a small "o." "Jesus, Max." He reached for the pad that was always in his jacket pocket. "Should I be writing this down?"

"Not yet. I notified the appropriate government agencies that the documents exist. I'm beginning to think they don't care. If I don't get a different vibe soon, I'm going public. Do you want the exclusive?"

"Does a bear crap in the woods? How many columns am I going to need?"

"A Sunday headline feature and some follow-on stories. Those should generate a boatload of leads for you."

Stan whistled. "Where have you been all my life and are you married?"

He calmed down and asked, "When will you make the decision?"

"Soon. There'll be a lot of sources and methods stuff that I can't tell you, but the documents speak for themselves. They meet the gold standard."

"They had better. I don't want the kind of flack that hit the Ironside Dossier when it went public."

I leaned into Stan. "Three governments are after me. If I go public, I'll have to do it fast and move. I need a code that gets me straight to you if I call."

"Sure. Say that you're Wilfred Jackson. If I get a call from Wilfred, the office staff will have instructions to interrupt me or find me right away."

"Who's Wilfred Jackson?"

"The guy who stole my high school sweetheart and married her. He's not likely to call and I'm not likely to forget his name."

"I'll need an address, too, if I can't deliver the documents in person."

Stan wrote an address on his business card and gave it to me. "What happens if your government friends decide to use your stuff?"

"In that case, I'll buy you drinks for a year and tell you stories you can't print."

Stan raised his glass. "Deal."

*   *   *

Early afternoon of the next day, I was using a rented computer to prepare a sanitized summary of the *kompromat* story for Stan Herman, in the event I had to go public. Jill Rucker called.

"Max, we need to meet. It's about our visit to the bank."

The only bank we visited together was in Moscow and we had to shoot our way out. My armpits began to sweat.

"Same place as last time?" I asked.

"No. Don't go there again. You copy?"

Lenny's was under surveillance. "Where?"

"You pick it."

"Hang on."

I connected to the Internet, found the website I wanted, and made reservations.

I told Jill, "Come to Union Station at 3:45 this afternoon. Meet me in the restaurant above the main floor."

I couldn't imagine what Jill Rucker wanted to tell me about the bank shootout. I was there. I don't know much about bank robbers. I know a lot about human nature. What I know told me that if one bank robber calls her accomplice weeks after the event and wants to discuss it, when they meet, there is a ninety percent chance that fifty percent of the robbers will be wearing a wire.

Jill had unfinished business with me. In Panama, I disfigured her forehead, kept her from getting the Walldrum *kompromat*, and secretly recorded her admitting she worked for the CIA. She might consider those grounds for a little payback, like her taping me talking about the bank shootout. I couldn't forget her admitting regret that she hadn't shot me to get what I had on Walldrum.

*   *   *

Jill entered Union Station at 3:40 p.m. She wore her hooded green parka, a green-and-tan headscarf, beige dress with buttons down the front, and brown suede boots to cover those muscular, not-so-attractive calves. From my perch above the main floor, I watched her stride across the lobby and up the steps to my level. She wasn't followed. That didn't mean she wasn't under surveillance.

Jill came to my table and surveyed the restaurant. "I hope we aren't eating here."

"Not to worry. We're taking a cab."

Not really, but if anyone was monitoring our conversation electronically, the shoe leather was headed for the cab stand outside.

My instructions to Jill were, "No talking at all until I say so."

She didn't protest. I grabbed the briefcase I had purchased for our meeting and guided Jill down to the main floor. Instead of heading outside to the cabstand, we went down one floor to the tracks and queued up in a short line for the Capitol Limited to Chicago and St. Louis.

I showed our tickets to the gate monitor and we boarded our train. I led Jill to the roomette compartment I had reserved for us. We entered and sat facing each other. I took a 10x6x9-inch Faraday bag from my briefcase and extended it, top open, to my companion. Jill's first look was hostile. Her second was disgusted, but she knew what I wanted.

She took the cell phone from her parka and dropped it into the Faraday.

"The watch and jewelry, including earrings."

She removed the items and dropped them into the bag. A Faraday bag has special insulation that prevents snoopers from connecting with your electronic devices to listen to your conversations or locate and track you.

The Capitol Limited glided out of the station. If Jill was wearing a wire, the guys waiting for us at the cabstand knew we were on the train, but it was too late to catch us.

"Why aren't you carrying a pocketbook?" I asked.

"I didn't know I would need one to fight off this assault."

"Where's your wallet?"

Out came the wallet and into the Faraday it went.

"Headscarf."

As Jill unwrapped it, she asked, "Do you want to admire your work?"

I passed on that one. "Now, the dress."

With a defiant look, Jill stripped to her bra, pantyhose, and boots. I examined the dress and laid it on my seat.

"Turn around, take off your bra, and give it to me."

She turned her back, removed the bra, and tossed it over her shoulder. I put it in the Faraday bag.

Jill faced me with a slight smile. "A bra with a microphone? What a novel idea. It certainly speaks to female needs. You should recommend it to tech services."

"They already have it."

"Do you want to inspect the rest of my apparel?" Her apparel consisted of black pantyhose and boots.

"No. I'm not doing this to embarrass you. I'm just trying to stay alive and free." I handed her the dress and parka. "Please put your clothes on."

As Jill buttoned her dress, she said, "Max, if I wanted to trap you, I would have suggested we meet at Lenny's."

"Maybe, but if you wanted to *en*trap me, you would let me pick a place where I'm comfortable and get me on the wire talking about a bank robbery."

"I'm not here about the bank. I lied because I knew the subject would get me a meeting."

"If you came to try and talk me out of the *kompromat* again, you're too late."

"The Agency already has it. The FBI gave it to us. I was asked to authenticate it."

"Did you?"

"The diary we got from Kedrova in St. Petersburg, yes. The rest, no. You kept me in the dark, remember."

"So, what are they going to do?"

"They've already done it. When the Agency got the *kompromat*, they gave it to a red team of analysts who aren't involved in the Rodney investigation. They had access to a lot of other sensitive Russian intel, but no knowledge of where or how the Walldrum *kompromat* was collected. Their mission was to identify the sources of the *kompromat* and assess its credibility. In record time, they rendered the opinion that info regarding the bank records switch and Putin's deal with North Korea were credible and originated from a source close to Putin."

"Did the red team identify the source?"

"No. They narrowed the field, but couldn't attribute to a specific individual."

Somebody in the Agency knew his identity. Normally, it would be one or two people at Langley and his handler at Moscow Station.

Maybe the source didn't trust Moscow Station after our election and used me to communicate with Langley.

Jill continued, "At that point, I was dropped from the task force and resumed my regular duties."

"What's the task force going to do with the *kompromat*?"

"That's what I came to tell you. They're going to bury it to protect the Moscow source."

"No!" I'm sure they heard me in the train corridor. "Why don't they use what can't be traced to the Moscow source . . . the Kedrova diary, the photos of prostitutes in the hotel with Walldrum? That stuff alone is enough to show that Walldrum was vulnerable to blackmail." I was beside myself with anger. "And what about the fake condos in Panama? That's evidence of money laundering!"

"They're burying all of it, Max."

"Well, they can't bury the money laundering operation in Panama. A reporter down there has the evidence and he's going to publish."

"They can't tie the money laundering operation to Walldrum."

"Why not?"

"Because the building doesn't belong to him. Four days after you and Tony-D left Panama, Walldrum sold the Tower to a Russian LLC. Bowen's law firm represented the seller and buyer, to make the transaction fast and smooth. Now, Walldrum's company just manages the place and rents out the president's name for the marquee."

"How do you know all this? You said you were dropped from the task force."

"The Panama discussion took place before I was reassigned. After I left the task force, I went back to regular duty. I had to analyze some data from another case. I needed a quiet place to think and write. I found a vacant conference room connected to a recording studio. I didn't want to sit at the table because someone might look in and interrupt me. So, I went into the adjacent recording studio, where I couldn't be seen. I spread out my papers and went to work. I'd been there for twenty minutes, when three people—two from the Rodney task force and one from the Seventh Floor—came into the conference room for a private chat."

Jill anticipated my question. "Don't ask me who they were, Max. Just telling you what they said could get me fired, but I owe you."

Jill continued, "So, these three people came in and what they didn't know, and what I didn't know, was there was a hot mic on the podium in the conference room. I could hear their conversation.

"They said the Agency and the Bureau agree that the *kompromat* is a can of worms and if they open it, everything will come out or people in high places will have to lie to protect the Moscow source. They don't trust Congress to handle this responsibly. Congressional committees want everything that might support impeachment. The politicians who support Walldrum will demand everything, sources and methods included, so they can discredit them. One of them said that some of Walldrum's allies in Congress may be on Moscow's payroll. They agreed that there's no way our *kompromat* is not going to leak if it goes to Congress. And nobody wants to risk losing the Moscow source or risk career suicide by lying to protect him."

That was bad logic. "What's the point in having a great source if you don't act on his product? Do they think he's risking his life so we can sit on what he gives us?"

"The decision's been made, Max. They're going to bury the *kompromat*. They said there's already enough evidence to impeach Walldrum. Congress needs to find the balls to do it."

"What if Congress can't find its balls!"

"If that happens, the consensus at the Agency and the Bureau is to let DOJ and the state prosecutors nail him on election fraud, money laundering, income tax issues, and his other crimes."

"That's not good enough. We risked our lives to collect that stuff and people need to know the president is batting for the other team."

"We have another risk to worry about now."

"What are you talking about?"

"One of the people I overheard in that conference room asked the other two about our *destiny*, yours and mine. At that point, one of them said, 'I don't want to be part of that conversation.' He left the room. The other two stayed and discussed whether or not they could rely on us to keep quiet about burying the *kompromat*."

"And . . . ?"

"I found out that I'm a 'ball-busting bitch,' but my ambition will keep me quiet and on the team. You, on the other hand, have a 'hard-on for the Agency' because Rodney sent your girlfriend to Australia and got you fired. That makes you a threat to the strategy for dealing with Walldrum. It would be better for everyone if you were 'removed from the equation.'"

"Were those the exact words?"

"Yes."

"Is there more?"

"No. After they left, I waited about ten minutes to be sure they had cleared the hall. Then, I left, but as I was closing the door, one of the two people who had been discussing our destinies came around the corner and saw me with my hand on the doorknob.

"He said, 'Were you in there?'"

"I said, 'No. I'm looking for a quiet place to work.' I don't think he believed me. I went back in anyway and spread my work on the conference table. He followed me in, looked around, and left. He came back about five minutes later, looked in, and left again.

"Then," Jill continued, "I got a strange phone call from Panama. The caller said he was one of the lawyers at Bowen's firm. I had heard his name, but never met him. He said he was helping Bowen with a case. That's unusual. The work is compartmented. I suspect they keep it that way because a lot of it is shady or downright illegal.

"First, he asked questions about things that were in my personnel file with his firm. His excuse was that he had never met me and had to be sure I was Jill Rucker. Then, he asked questions that he didn't have answers for."

"Like what?"

"'When was the last time you saw Zabluda?' When I told him, he rephrased it so I had to answer 'yes' or 'no.' His rephrase was, 'So, you say the last time you saw Zabluda was in Mexico City.' Is that correct?' He rephrased several questions like that.

"Max, I got the feeling the caller was giving me a voice stress test. The first set of questions established a stress baseline when I was telling the truth. He evaluated my answers to the second set of questions by comparing my stress level to my baseline. Can they do that over the phone from Panama?"

"I've never seen it done that way. It doesn't sound effective. There could be atmospheric interference that affects the electrical impulses on either end of the call."

I shifted gears. "You said the Panama caller wanted your help with one of Bowen's cases. What did he want you to do?"

"He wanted me to come to Panama right away so that he and Bowen could discuss the handoff with me."

The hair stood on my neck. "Don't go. It's a setup"

"How do you know that?"

"Bowen is dead. Zabluda killed him in Switzerland. I was there."

Jill slumped back against her seat, her expression showing shock and confusion. "You told me Zabluda took the *kompromat* and your money. You didn't mention Bowen. You had the *kompromat* and gave it to the FBI. I don't know if I should believe anything you say."

"Believe this. If you go to Panama, odds are it will be a one-way trip."

"I think both of us are in danger, Max. We need a plan."

My plan was to send the compromising evidence on President Walldrum to Stan Herman and let the free press do its job. Jill didn't have a need to know.

The conductor announced we were a few minutes from Martinsburg, West Virginia.

"My stop," I told Jill.

She looked surprised. "What are you going to do?"

"Get off the train."

Surprise turned to irritation. "I mean about the *kompromat* . . . and about us?"

"The *kompromat* has a life of its own now, and maybe a death. I've done my part—what you wanted me to do all along—deliver it to the Agency. I'm through. I have enough money to hide until the next election. I'm going to get into a hole and pull the hole in after me. Tell that to your colleagues at the Agency."

The train was gliding to a halt. "What am I going to do about you? Nothing. You need to separate your fate from mine. They said you're a team player. Go along. Do whatever is required to survive."

Jill's irritation melted into a plea. "Max, take me with you. We can watch out for each other. We're good together, professionally and personally. You know that."

"I do, but if we run together and they find us, we'll die together."

I gave Jill her ticket. "This will get you to St. Louis. Take the full ride and consider your options. Good luck." I dumped the contents of the Faraday bag into her lap.

When I got off the train, the chauffeured car I had reserved was waiting to take me back to D.C. As the big Lincoln glided southeast on the Charles Town Pike, I called my messenger service and instructed the manager to deliver a package to my reporter friend, Stan Herman. It contained the evidence Jill and I had collected on President Walldrum. I removed the SIM card from my cell phone and tossed both out the window.

For the rest of the ride, I thought about that hole I told Jill I was going to hide in. I wondered how to cover my tracks to it, and how deep and how far from Washington it would have to be to keep me alive.

CHAPTER 32

I SHOULDN'T HAVE done it, but I was tired. When you're tired, you make mistakes.

Irish had warned us many years ago during a training session at The Farm. "When the opposition is after you, you don't go where you normally go and don't see anyone you normally see. The only thing that can save your pitiful little ass is a swift exit." I should have listened to that advice.

Instead, I used one of my new burner phones to call Sherri.

"This is Sherri." Her voice was music to my ears.

"It's me. Just wanted to wrap up our last engagement. Are the troops paid?"

"Yes. Thank you. Let's never do that again sometime." She laughed.

"The SUV Tony-D was driving was in an accident. A big Russian truck, like the one at the London warehouse, jumped the median and hit the SUV. All three passengers were killed."

Sherri was alarmed. "Is Tony-D okay!"

"He escaped with minor injuries. His favorite vest was ripped in two places and he has cracked ribs. He's healing. He'll call when he's ready to go back to work."

"And the SUV . . . ?"

"Totaled. You might want to tidy up the paperwork." That was my way of telling her to destroy the fake ID she used to rent the SUV.

"Are you okay?"

"Yeah. I'm taking some time off. I need a vacation. Thanks for everything."

I sensed something and waited for Sherri to say it: "I've got bad news, Max. I have clients in the U.K. I read the London papers to keep up. Scotland Yard found Viktor Lukovsky's body floating near his yacht last week. The crew has disappeared."

It was time to run and I needed running equipment. The driver located an upscale shopping mall for me with his GPS. He waited while I bought luggage and warm-weather clothes to fill it. Then, we continued to Washington.

Considering my Farm training and Jill's warning, I should have gone directly to the airport, but there was the matter of the rented computer in my hotel room. I had tried to erase my digital tracks, but there are smart people in the FBI's cybercrimes unit. If they got their hands on the computer, they might be able to trace my instructions to the Belize bank. If they found my money, they would eventually find me.

I waited until after midnight before going to the hotel. I had an arrangement with the night desk clerk to let me in through the kitchen. I told him that I was in the middle of a nasty divorce and my wife had hired private detectives to find me. That story and a hundred-dollar bill was all it took to guarantee his services.

The lobby was empty, as it should have been at that hour. I took the elevator to my floor and went to my room. The automatic light didn't come on as I stepped inside. I sensed that something was wrong and stepped backward into the hall before the door closed. I got a hard shove from behind that propelled me into the room. The door slammed shut behind me. The floor lamp by the window came on. A man in a dark suit was sitting in the chair next to the lamp. He was holding a stun gun.

"I won't use this unless it's necessary," he told me. "Someone wants to talk to you. Will you come quietly?"

"Do I have a choice?"

"No."

I shrugged and raised my arms.

The man behind me patted me down for weapons. Finding none, he peeled off my trench coat and dropped it. He said, "Turn around."

I did. He cuffed my wrists in front of me and covered the cuffs with my coat.

We took the elevator back to the lobby. It was dark and the clerk was missing. A black SUV was waiting. They pushed me into the back seat with an "escort" on either side. We sat in silence until the driver exited the lobby and joined us. As we drove away, the lobby lights flickered to life.

The fellow who had patted me down produced a pair of blacked-out, wraparound sunglasses. "Hold still. I'm going to put these on you. It's better if you don't know where we're going."

"Better for who?" I asked.

No one answered.

There wasn't much traffic. We drove in silence, at a good clip, for over an hour to someplace rural. I heard crickets against an otherwise quiet night as they helped me out of the SUV.

My escorts led me up a gravel path, into a house with wooden front steps, down a hall, and downstairs to a basement. We walked down another hallway and stopped. A door opened. I was led into a room and pushed onto a cold metal chair. Someone removed the coat from my cuffs, but left the cuffs in place. Off came my blacked-out sunglasses.

Instinctively, I looked away from the harsh lights in front of me and saw Jill sitting in a bare metal armchair to my right. She wore the clothes from our train ride. She wasn't wearing cuffs or a headscarf. Her blond hair hung down in disorderly ringlets and there was a bruise on her chin. Evidently, she hadn't come quietly.

She looked at me. I saw anger and determination in her face.

We were in an austere box of a room. Halfway between our chairs and the desk in front of us was a large, circular drain in the floor with a perforated metal cover. My optimistic hope was that this was the shower room at Miss Hortense's Country School for Wayward Girls, and the reason we were there for our "talk" was because these guys couldn't afford upscale office space. I had to abandon that theory when I saw the walls. They were covered with spongy, burgundy panels consisting of vertical rows of sawteeth designed to muffle sound. The ceiling had the same paneling. I suspected the room had a more ominous purpose than girls' showers.

Someone turned down the harsh lights. I looked up and squinted. There, sitting on the edge of an ugly, gray, metal desk was Rodney. He wore a white, knit sweater with baggy sleeves and light gray slacks, white socks, and cordovan penny loafers. One leg dangled over the edge of the desk. The other was straight, his foot on the floor. He could have been at his country club's pro shop, casually holding a 9-iron. Instead, he was holding the ivory-handled .32 automatic I had seen in his collection.

He gave us his disarming smile. "Don't concern yourself with the gun. It's for my protection. You two have proven yourselves more-than-capable street brawlers. Whereas, I must rely on the gentlemanly art of shooting to defend myself, should the need arise. I hope it won't."

Rodney laid the gun on the desk between his right hip and an open package. He followed my gaze to the package and smiled, a triumphant little upturned crack in his patrician face.

"Yes, Max, it's what you think it is. We intercepted your package of presidential dirt before Stan Herman got his greedy reporter's hands on it. But look at the bright side. Now, we don't have to gouge out his eyes, cut out his tongue, and set him to wander in a wilderness of fake news." Rodney treated us to a grand smile. He was enjoying himself watching us watch him, while he enjoyed himself.

He moved on to his intuitive brilliance. "Because of your Moscow history with Stan, we guessed he would be your go-to guy if you went public with the *kompromat.*"

Rodney placed his palm on the package. "I assume there are others."

"Lots," I assured him.

"And should I also assume that, by a certain time, you must contact someone or appear in public to prevent the distribution of such packages?"

"*Absolument.*" I gave him a taste of *my* French. If I had to go, I was going in style.

Rodney sighed, "Humm." That was his usual "tell" that he had made a decision.

"You two should have guessed by now that the decision to fire Max and dangle him to Bowen was made on the Seventh Floor."

Like a lot of decisions made on the Seventh Floor, this one had unintended consequences. I didn't say that. It was my turn to listen and learn.

Rodney pressed on. Mainly for Jill—a relative newbie at the Agency—Rodney said, "Let me share some history with you. During his rise to power, Putin developed a list of enemies and marked some for assassination. High on that list were Russians who had defected to the West. Alexander Litvinenko was such a man. He was a FSB officer who defected and became a naturalized British citizen. In 2006, Putin had him assassinated in London by putting a radioactive substance in his tea. When the Brits failed to retaliate in a meaningful way, Putin was emboldened. He realized he could literally get away with murder."

Sarcastically, Jill added, "He could shoot someone down on Fifth Avenue and no one would care."

"Precisely. So, Putin ordered his military intelligence service to develop a network of assassins—a revenge squad, if you will—who would roam the world killing his enemies, with traitors at the top of the list.

"That didn't happen immediately," Rodney continued. "It took time to spin up the network: recruiting, training, organizing, and so forth. At the same time, Putin was busy with so many other activities: robbing his country blind, dealing with sanctions, killing off his domestic political opposition, invading Ukraine, annexing Crimea, the Sochi Olympics, not to mention meddling in the Middle East, European elections, and ours. We suspect that all of these concerns may have pushed his revenge squad to the back burner.

"Then, along came the Ironside Dossier, forcing the issue of disloyal Russians to the front burner of Putin's fevered brain. He was incensed that Russians, some apparently in his government, gave Ironside information that spoiled Ted Walldrum's smooth transition to power in the White House. Putin became obsessed with finding and killing Ironside's sources. So, the revenge squad was set loose, but not as you might imagine."

Rodney shifted his weight further back on the desk so that both legs dangled over the front edge. "You will remember that Putin is an expert in judo, a martial art that advocates using an opponent's strength to defeat him. It was Putin's idea to use this technique to unmask the traitors who helped Ironside. He planned to use a Western spy to find the traitors so the revenge squad could kill them. With the sources eliminated, no one could verify Ironside's allegations that Walldrum was compromised by Russia.

"Bill Bowen, a Moscow tool, was enlisted to find an ex-Western spy to ferret out the traitors. We found out about Bowen's project and wanted to control it to get the Walldrum *kompromat*, if there was any."

Jill was puzzled. "I was working for Bowen and I didn't find out what he was doing until after he had hired Max. How did the Agency know what Bowen was up to?"

Rodney turned deadly serious. "That is the secret that can never, ever be discussed again by the two of you. Understood?"

We both said, "Yes." At that moment, I also understood that we might not be going down that drain in the floor. Still, Rodney had the gun, I was handcuffed, and he could change his mind.

Not that it mattered in a soundproof room, but Rodney lowered his voice. "The Agency has a source very close to Putin. We share him with MI6. Let's call him Source Ivan, for the purposes of this discussion. Ivan gave Ironside some of the material for his dossier. When Ivan became aware of Putin's scheme to find Ironside's sources, he feared for his life. He knew that if Putin discovered his identity, it meant death for him and his family. Ivan got word of the scheme to the Agency and wanted us to pull him out. We wanted him to remain in place. To put Ivan's fears to rest, we had to sabotage Bowen's traitor hunt."

Rodney turned to Jill. "We knew you had infiltrated Bowen's money laundering operation, but we had no assurance that Bowen would let you join in the traitor hunt."

"That's where I came in," I concluded.

"Yes. To clear the air, I'll be brutally honest. I sent Vanessa to Australia under false pretenses. I set you up with Claudia to have you fired. I dangled you to Bowen. He took the bait and we were in business." There was no hint of apology in Rodney's tone.

I was angry. "You did a damn good job of ruining my life and my career."

"We're at war. Wars always result in collateral damage."

"Is that all Vanessa and I were to the CIA, acceptable collateral damage?"

"It wasn't that cold-blooded, Max. Our leadership agonized over how you would be treated. In the end, we determined that we needed you to be authentically pissed at the Agency and money-hungry. Our reasoning was that, should Bowen or one of his Russian colleagues give you truth serum or a polygraph test, you would pass and not end up on a garbage heap with your head and fingertips missing."

I let Rodney know I knew that wasn't the only reason. "And if I was really pissed and desperate, I might not let moral or legal restraints influence how I got the job done."

"That, too," he admitted without hesitation. "Again, Max, I remind you that we are at war, even if our Congress doesn't know it."

Something else was bothering me. "Why were you tracking me with the sat phone? Was that to let the Russians know when and where I made contact with the sources Putin wanted killed?"

"That is a convenient theory for your conscience, but incorrect. My sat phone didn't lead the Russians to Bogdanovich and your Russian Embassy contact, Boris Kulik. It was your sloppy tradecraft that led them to those sources.

"The Russians were about to burglarize Ironside's home when you showed up and beat them to the punch. They simply followed you to Bogdanovich and Kulik." Rodney couldn't resist a dig. "Better tradecraft on your part could have saved both sources."

I gave it some thought. Rodney's explanation raised another question. "How did you know the Russians were prepping to burgle Ironside's house before we got there?"

Rodney cleared his throat. "That's above your pay grade."

"I don't have a pay grade, remember. I think you know because Zabluda told you. He's quarterbacking the revenge squad and he's on the Agency payroll, isn't he?"

"Yes!" snapped Jill, her voice carrying triumph of an "ah-ha" moment. "That's why I was told to avoid him. It wasn't because the PM wanted to catch Zabluda getting kill orders from Moscow. He already had orders. The Agency didn't want me to take out its asset."

That raised another Machiavellian thought in my mind. "How does Zabluda work for the Agency and MI6, and make his bones with the Kremlin?"

Rodney didn't answer.

Jill did. She was on a roll. "They let Zabluda kill off a few old Russian defectors who had outlived their intelligence value and their shelf life on the pension rolls."

"Come on, Rodney," I needled. "You were going to be brutally honest. Zabluda has to be a double agent. He was the guy in the confessional who told me about the plot to get Walldrum the Nobel Prize."

Rodney was menacing. "Careful, don't talk yourself down the drain."

I didn't think so. "If you were going to kill us, we'd be dead by now. Besides, Source Ivan is the Agency's big secret. Zabluda is just convenient dirty laundry."

Jill had another ah-ha. "Zabluda is low-level. He wouldn't know about a Nobel Prize plot involving Walldrum, Putin, and Kim Jung-Un. Someone told him about it."

My light went on, too. "Source Ivan told Zabluda. Zabluda is Ivan's courier. In the confessional, Zabluda told me that, since the election, *he* couldn't trust CIA contacts in Moscow. Zabluda was just the mouthpiece. It was Ivan who no longer trusted Moscow Station."

The Zabluda cat was out of the bag and Rodney looked resigned to it.

"The London warehouse hit . . ." Jill recalled. "Zabluda was the team leader. Why was he standing watch outside? Why wasn't he inside supervising the action?"

Reluctantly, Rodney answered. "After Max left Bogdanovich, Zabluda's team killed the Russian. After, they watched to see if Bogdanovich's MI6 keepers would show up. They did, Ironside, Swope-Soames, and Jock 'What's-his-name.' Zabluda reported what he saw to Moscow. Back came orders to kidnap Ironside, make him ID his sources, and kill the others as punishment for aiding the Russian traitor.

"That put Zabluda in a bind," said Rodney. "He's sitting on an order to kill British spies, but the Brits know he's on our payroll. Zabluda's solution was to have his men execute the kill order while he stood watch. If he ever had to account for himself, he could claim to the Brits and to us that he wasn't a shooter at the warehouse."

The more Rodney told us, the dirtier it sounded.

I asked, "Why did the Russians kidnap me at the warehouse?"

"They killed Ironside by mistake when he drew a gun. Since they knew you had burglarized Ironside's home, I assume they thought you might know Ironside's sources. Zabluda would have left you had he not been standing watch outside."

Rodney gave his assessment. "Overall, the warehouse hit was potentially a huge screwup. If the Russians had taken you with them, you wouldn't have gone to Russia to collect the *kompromat*. Our plan, as well as Putin's, would have been trashed. Bowen would have had to start over."

"And you wouldn't have had another Max to dangle." I was seething with anger.

Rodney just gave me a sad look.

Jill asked, "Why is Zabluda working for the Agency?"

Happy to escape my hateful stare, Rodney explained. "Zabluda is a talented rogue and soldier-of-fortune, working both sides of the ideological divide. He's a friend of Source Ivan and the perfect courier. His job requires freedom of movement in Western nations. Ivan identified him to us for recruitment."

"Some friend," observed Jill.

With detachment, Rodney noted, "Zabluda is a pirate. Recruitment wasn't a hard sell, but we do prefer insurance. Zabluda has twin sons in the Russian Army. We compromised one of them while he was on R and R in Cuba. That's our hold on Zabluda and, of course, we could always out him as an Agency asset. Lastly, he likes money and wants to defect someday . . . if he's not promoted to general." Rodney smiled at me. "Now that he has your five million dollars, he may not wait for that promotion."

"If you want to ensure my silence about the *kompromat*, you could get my money from Zabluda and return it to me."

"That money is long gone down the rabbit hole, I'm afraid." Rodney lifted his chin and his voice. "We had something else in mind for you two. Jill, you did excellent work. Your reward is a promotion and the posting of your choice. The terms of your continued good standing with the Agency are that the words 'Source Ivan,' 'Zabluda,' '*kompromat*,' and 'Ted Walldrum' are never uttered by your luscious lips, written by your lovely hand, sent by you from a mountaintop with mirrors, or communicated in any manner whatsoever that connects one to the other. Agreed?"

Jill gave him a sullen, "Agreed."

Rodney slid down from the desk and inspected the bruise on Jill's jaw as if he hadn't noticed it before. He reached out with a forefinger and stopped short of touching her face. "I apologize for the roughhouse. The men I sent for you were warned of your prowess in karate. I fear they took every precaution to escape a disabling blow."

"Comes with the job," replied Jill. "I just hope I meet those bastards in a dark alley some night."

Rodney made a point of examining the scar on her forehead. "In a less emotional atmosphere, you might reconsider that aspiration. We don't want you to become the Agency's Salome, hiding your battle scars behind seven decorative headscarves." He glanced at me and gave Jill a nasty smile.

Jill glared daggers at him.

Rodney went behind the metal desk and pressed a call button. An intense-looking middle-age woman in a dark pants suit and white blouse came into the room. Rodney said, "Please escort Miss Rucker home."

Jill got up and left without a backward look. She had taken my advice and separated her fate from mine. It was the end of an interesting run for us.

Rodney gave me his full attention. "Max, you deserve a promotion and much more. However, because of the shooting on my boat and your attempt to frame me—"

"Rodney, I have no idea what you're talking about. I heard the FBI liked *you* for the shooting."

With a hint of admiration, he said, "Following the Agency playbook, are we? Staying with your cover story?"

"I don't have a cover story and don't need one."

Rodney was smug. "The Agency leadership believes my version of the shooting. Also, I have an alibi for the time those men were killed."

"Your alibi is someone from the Agency, no doubt."

"How ever did you know?"

"I used to be an intelligence officer, until I ran across a bad boss."

He didn't respond to that. "Those men on my boat were ours, not Russian illegals. We identified them as Russians so the FBI could take the case. We couldn't have them traced back to the Agency by the D.C. police. They were not going to hurt you. Their orders were to scare you into giving up the *kompromat*. They weren't even supposed to be armed."

"Well, they really screwed up, didn't they? I wonder who did them in?"

Rodney moved on with a cheery attitude. "By the way, Zabluda reported to Moscow that you killed Bowen and two Russian money guards. What happened to their bodies?"

"I don't know anything about that, but if you tell me the time and place they were killed, I have a witness who can give me an alibi. He's not even an Agency employee."

Rodney was enjoying the fencing match, but he had to conclude his business with me. "Anyway, because of the shootings and other circumstances, it is felt that you might hold negative attitudes toward the Agency that could affect your work. So, I can't offer you your job back . . . or any job."

"It's late, Rodney. What's the bottom line?"

"You asked for a defector package. I understand you have five million dollars somewhere in the world. So, a pension is out of the question. However, the Agency recognizes your recent sacrifices, and the fact that you're a target because Zabluda told Moscow you killed Bowen and made off with their money and the Walldrum *kompromat*. Therefore, the leadership has authorized me to offer you resettlement, a new identity, and the purchase of a new home. Of course, we will also assist in tidying up your local affairs. What do you think?"

I thought, *Nice bribe.* I said, "In return, you want me to either die in this room or stop those *kompromat* packages from being delivered to the media. And I must abide by the same restrictions you placed on Jill?"

"Precisely."

"Tell *the leadership* I'll stop the packages, and their secrets are safe with me. Convey my thanks for their generous offer, but no, thanks. I trusted the Agency to be straight with me and it destroyed the two most important things in my life. They don't get a second chance to screw me. I'm going off the grid until the next election—maybe forever—and I'm going to enjoy my five million dollars."

Rodney studied me for a long time before he removed his gun from the desktop and put it in a drawer. Then, he came to me and unlocked the handcuffs.

Relationships damaged by a breach of trust are never the same. Relationships battered by a misunderstanding can sometimes be restored. The day after my "talk" with Rodney, I booked a first-class ticket to Australia. For me, there was only one Vanessa in that country. I wondered how many Zabludas there were. Before leaving for Australia, I needed to get myself off the Moscow target list.

* * *

When I was a young boy, frustrated by some task I was trying unsuccessfully to perform, my grandmother would tell me, "There's more than one way to skin a cat." There was a cat out there named Zabluda, wearing my five-million-dollar fur. The best cat-skinners I knew were lawyers. I visited Lyle Palmer at Stratton, Radcliff, and Bowles.

Once again, I sat with Lyle at his teak conference table. Lyle owed me a favor for warning him about Claudia Navarro. So, he agreed to provide whatever services I needed. I told him as much about my work for Bowen as he needed to know, which wasn't a whole lot. I left out anything that would break my deal with Rodney and the Agency, and hit Lyle with the punchline. "I have a ten-million-dollar contract with Bill Bowen's Global Democratic Initiative to investigate the allegations against Walldrum in the Ironside Dossier." I gave Lyle a certified true copy of the contract. "Bowen paid me half before delivery. When I delivered the goods, Bowen was incapacitated and failed to make the second payment." I'm pretty sure being shot in the head and dead qualifies as incapacitated. "I want you to sue Bowen's firm for my five million."

Lyle frowned. "Wait a minute. You gave me the evidence you collected. I took it to the special prosecutor and the FBI. Why are you saying you delivered it to Bowen?"

"Because I did. After I delivered it, Bowen's associate, Konstantin Zabluda, gave it back to me. I'm not responsible for what happened after delivery. They still have an obligation to honor my contract and pay me."

Lyle warned me, "If you take this to court and GDI puts up a defense, you may have to reveal the compromising evidence on Waldrum."

"GDI is a Russian front, Lyle. The last thing they want is a public court battle. I'm betting they'll settle to keep this quiet and make it go away. What do you think?"

Lyle smiled. He was probably calculating his cut of my five million. Suddenly, he understood the rest of the story. "And the FBI and CIA can't get involved because they would have to admit knowledge that Walldrum has been compromised. That's brilliant."

He stopped salivating and got serious. "To make this work, you need proof that you actually delivered the material to Bowen and this Zabluda."

"Got a computer handy?"

Lyle had one delivered to the room. I inserted the thumb drive containing a digital record of Tony-D and me handing over the briefcase of *kompromat* to Bowen at the villa in Switzerland. The recording showed events from the time Tony-D and I arrived with Bowen and the money until Zabluda shot Bowen and the two guards. There was an obvious gap and the recording skipped to Zabluda leaving the room carrying a suitcase full of my money. Let Zabluda explain that in Moscow.

"What's on the missing segment, Max?"

"That's classified." Honoring part of my pledge to Rodney, I had deleted the segment that recorded Zabluda giving me the *kompromat* and our little talk about him defecting with five million dollars.

I think Lyle was shocked. He pushed back from the table and was quiet for a time, before asking, "How is it that you have this recording?"

"When I discovered Bowen was working for the Russians, I knew that the best way for him to wrap up his operation was to destroy the *kompromat* when I delivered it and kill me. If things went badly for me, I wanted to leave a record."

Lyle appeared thoughtful before asking, "By the way, who is Zabluda?"

"He's a Russian assassin."

"Fast company you keep. I don't think GDI will want to see this recording played in court." Lyle gave me a mischievous smile. "Where do I send the money?"

"I'll let you know."

ACKNOWLEDGEMENTS

Many people contributed to this book. All have my thanks. Some are recognized here.

Nelson DeMille and James Grady are thriller writers whose work inspired me. Kelly Gross (Lady Courage) is my friend and Russian and German tutor. Mr. T., a professional intelligence officer, made sure I didn't lose my way in the "wilderness of mirrors" that is the spy business. Lloyd, my lifelong friend, reminded me that "It ain't over 'til it's over." He looked Death in the face and said, "Not yet." On her deathbed, Ophelia made me promise to keep writing. Ophie, thank you. I miss you, but I'm in good hands.

Barbara is my politics junkie, cheerleader, book advisor, and all-around special person. She tolerated and encouraged my frequent descent into the dark world of spy fiction where I could not escape the dark world of our current reality.

Rebecca Shivvers, Bill Walker, Jenny Thouw, Jay and Hannah Harris, Betsy, Jerry, and Fred caught many of my mistakes, provided encouragement, and made suggestions. I ignored some of their advice in pursuit of artistic expression. Hence, errors of commission and omission in this work are my responsibility.

Finally, I am most indebted to Pat and Bob who saw something and said the magic words. Thank you.

AUTHOR'S NOTE

When the idea for *The President's Dossier* presented itself, I had no intention of writing a novel based on current events. One morning, I read a news article announcing that a magazine publisher had offered ten million dollars to anyone who could prove true certain unsavory allegations about our current president. The reward triggered story possibilities in my author's mind. What if someone accepted the publisher's offer? What would motivate such a protagonist? Where would the protagonist look for proof of the allegations? What if they were verified? A story began to form in my mind, but where were the twists? Readers—and writers—love surprises. What if the publisher had a nefarious motive? What if the allegations hadn't originated where the media said they had? As I answered these questions, *The President's Dossier* became a story I had to tell.

When I write, my goal is to give readers alternative and entertaining explanations for their beliefs. Since this book is rooted in current events about which readers may have opinions, I relied on recent news articles, testimony, and non-fiction books to provide authentic alternatives and background for the story. I also drew on my experiences as a soldier, my years of living and travel in Europe, and my engagement with—and research on—intelligence agencies.

In part, this story relies on the Russian tactic of ensnaring foreigners by recording them in compromising situations. An acquaintance once told me a story of her visit to Moscow. She was in her hotel lobby waiting for a tour guide. She returned to her suite to retrieve an article she'd forgotten. On the way, she passed a room adjacent to her bedroom. A man was there changing film in the camera used to record her bedroom activities. Should she become a person of importance, Russian intelligence had compromising or embarrassing photographs with which to manipulate her. It is doubtful that the Russians have abandoned this tactic.

For readers interested in Cold War Russian intelligence organizations and tactics, I recommend *Sword and Shield: Soviet Intelligence and Security Apparatus* by Jeffrey T. Richelson. The book describes activities that my character, Colonel Bogdanovich, narrates to protagonist, Max Geller. Bogdanovich would have worked in the KGB's Second Chief Directorate, an entity responsible for obtaining compromising material on visitors to Russia. In the 1990s, the KGB was replaced by the FSB, for domestic intelligence, and the SVU, for foreign intelligence.

I hope that you enjoyed *The President's Dossier*.